A SEA SOUGHT IN SONG

I0641267

Creative Texts Publishers products are available at special discounts for bulk purchase for sale promotions, premiums, fund-raising, and educational needs. For details, write Creative Texts Publishers, PO Box 50, Barto, PA 19504, or visit www.creativetexts.com

A SEA SOUGHT IN SONG – THE HEIR AND THE HERALD BOOK 1
by AUSTIN GUNDERSON
Published by Creative Texts Publishers
PO Box 50
Barto, PA 19504
www.creativetexts.com

Copyright 2022 by AUSTIN GUNDERSON
All rights reserved

Cover photos used by license.
Design copyright 2022 Creative Texts Publishers, LLC

This book or parts thereof may not be reproduced in any form, stored in a retrieval system, or transmitted in any form by any means—electronic, mechanical, photocopy, recording, or otherwise—without prior written permission of the publisher, except as provided by United States of America copyright law.

The following is a work of fiction. Any resemblance to actual names, persons, businesses, and incidents is strictly coincidental. Locations are used only in the general sense and do not represent the real place in actuality.

ISBN: 978-1-64738-070-0

A SEA SOUGHT IN SONG

BY AUSTIN GUNDERSON

CREATIVE TEXTS PUBLISHERS

Barto, PA

To Kay
whom I dare not use as a muse
lest I write a Mary Sue

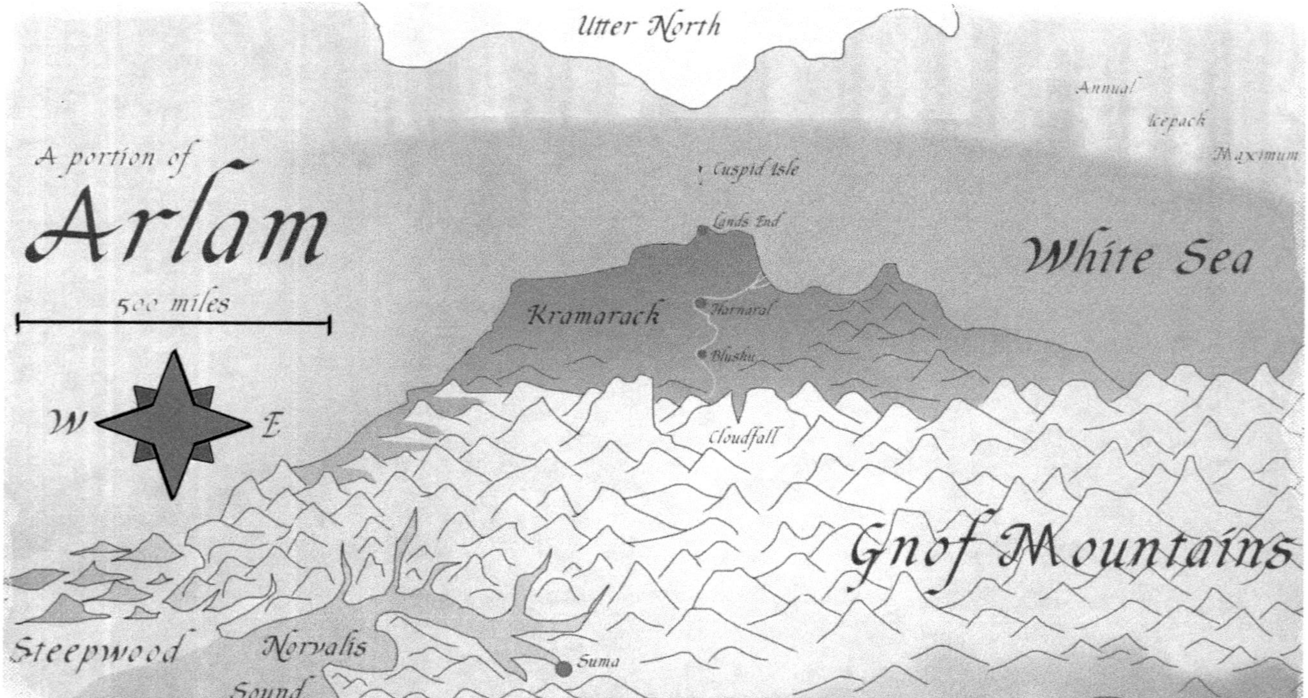

A portion of

Arlam

Utter North

White Sea

Annual kepack Maximum

Gnof Mountains

Gaspid Isle

Land's End

Murmarol

Blasты

Kramorack

Cloudfall

Steepwood

Norvalis Sound

Suma

Map of Arlam

500 miles

N
W   E
S

Seed of glory sown in sorrow,
Take as father, give as son;
Alien, with faithless marrow,
Seize a mandate seen by none.

Seed of glory born of dying,
South for judgement goeth I;
In the din of nomads sighing,
None thy birthright can deny.

Seed of glory charged to wither,
Fiercely come to fall by strife;
For a ransom approach hither,
Crush thy foe, relinquish life.

Seed of glory burst asunder,
Water Arlam with thy tears;
In a sky enmeshed by wonder,
Face the essence of our fears.

Seed of glory raised in power,
Sing in worship, sing for joy;
In thy body unite nature,
Bridge the gap and woe destroy.

TABLE OF CONTENTS

Prologue
LIGHTS
A few weeks ago, or an age

Miles had never been so afraid of his own reflection.

He could see terror in the eyes staring back at him from that sheet of placid glass. Their sockets were chinks in an otherwise formidable display. With the leather cuirass and greaves strapped over his dungarees, the bulky pack on his back, the machete and Colt .45 hung at his waist, and the M1 rifle slung over one shoulder, Miles appeared ready for anything. And he *was* ready, dammit! He hadn't slogged through hell in the Ardennes to stand here quailing like some untried boy at the threat of death.

But one look into his own eyes and all that confidence dissolved. He'd stormed machine-gun nests and danced with giant panzers, but this was different, and he knew it. And now he couldn't pretend otherwise. *Of all the forms this hatchway could've taken, why'd it have to be a mirror?*

Tok tok tok. The cane's tapping echoed in the chamber as a second figure approached from behind—stooped and slight of frame, his silver hair shaded strangely by the ceiling's blood-red light. Gnarled fingers gripped Miles' arm, and a pair of sightless eyes joined his in the reflection.

"Do not be afraid." Henry's voice was deep—a rumble more easily felt than heard. Doubtless others would've found it reassuring, but to Miles in that moment it was salt rubbed in a wound.

He swallowed, cleared his throat. "I'm fine."

Henry closed blind eyes. "It's normal, you know. The only reason I didn't piss myself the first time I went through was because my bladder was already empty. Don't ask me why." He chuckled as he patted Miles' shoulder. *Patted.*

Miles turned, wrenching his eyes away from their disturbing self-appraisal. "What happens if I don't end up in Arlam?"

"We went over this, Miles."

"Tell me again."

Henry sighed. "The crystal is inextricably linked to its counterpart on the other side. There is no possibility of transferral interference. It's basic rhomic physics. I can't tell you what kind of situation you'll find when you emerge, but I *can* guarantee you *will* emerge."

"Can I toss something through first?"

Henry arched a brow. "You won't be able to see where it goes."

"Yeah, but at least I'll know it *did* go. I'll know the other mirror ain't lying flat on its face or something."

"Very well," said Henry, spreading his hands. "Choose your projectile."

Miles considered briefly, then pulled from his pocket one of the gold coins entrusted to him by Henry for this mission. It was octagonal, embossed on one side with an image of a throne formed of living trees, and on the opposite with the profile of a much younger Henry wearing a high-peaked crown. Miles pinched it between thumb and forefinger, wagging his wrist to judge the weight.

"A goodwill offering," he muttered. Abruptly he cocked his arm and flung the coin directly at the mirror.

It struck the surface and vanished. Neither crack nor ripple remained.

A pit seemed to open in Miles' stomach. His throat tightened. *Why'd I do that? Why'd I have to draw this out? I should've just jumped straight in.*

"Are you reassured?" asked Henry.

With a strangled gulp, Miles got his throat working again. "Not really," he managed.

"It's okay, son," said the old man in a soft voice. "There's no way to make this easy. Come, let me bless you." He laid aside his cane, turning Miles to face him fully and placing a hand on either shoulder. Miles bowed his head.

"Father," rasped Henry, "hear my plea. This man journeys into darkness, terrible darkness, but to you darkness is as light! There is no void free of your presence, no abyss beyond your sight. If I make my bed in hell, behold—you are there." At this Henry's voice trembled, and Miles glanced up. The old man was *weeping*. "Go with Miles, I pray. Bear him up when all else falls. Light his path though he walk through endless night."

"Amen," said Miles after a moment of silence. Though the words had been arcane, he now felt strangely buoyed. Henry released his grip, retrieved his cane, and nodded, backing away.

This is it; the moment of truth.

Of course, the source of Miles' terror hadn't departed. It was still right there, waiting. He could almost *feel* the mirror behind him. It infused the air with tension like an electromagnetic device. Was it … *pulling* him? The hairs on his neck stood erect, and from somewhere deep within welled a primal shriek of prudence.

Don't look!

With a sudden leap Miles hurled himself backward. His body arched like a pole-vaulter's. He glimpsed Henry's mouth falling open, his hand reaching out ...

And then all bled to ice and dread. The chamber collapsed into a rectangular pane and shot away into infinite blackness. Forces howled and dark shapes hurtled past. Miles was falling uncontrollably, but also expanding, distorting, breaking apart. He couldn't *see*. His very being lost cohesion. Eldritch doors opened on unfathomable voids. His soul. Where was his *soul?*

And then a pressure. Mounting, swelling. Forcing him back together. Constricting him to a point. Had he a mouth, his scream would've ruptured his mind.

And then *crack!* he was through. A great disk, shining like a moon, shrank before him. Beyond it spread a hemisphere of stars. The cold wind roaring in his ears felt hot after Oblivion. And then a thought struck him like a boulder in the back.

I'm still falling!

He cried out, twisting in midair. Wind blasted his face. Yes, this was reality: he had a face again, and limbs, and a soul. He flailed about, connecting with nothing. Lights whirled madly in the night. Many were dim and distant, some bright and near, and they streaked in his vision until they seemed a web. A snow-globe spinning as he tumbled through freefall.

A deafening croak-scream erupted close at hand. *An animal!* Miles yelled incoherently, scrabbling for a weapon. His rifle was gone. His hand closed instead upon his pistol and he yanked it from its holster, spreading limbs to stabilize his descent so he could draw a bead on something, anything. The whirling lights relaxed, assuming their places once again. They shone most brightly beneath him, whence came the wind.

And then a vast swath of them simply vanished and sprang back. A great dark shape stooped out of the night sky, occluding the stars. Miles screamed and clenched the trigger. The muzzle-flash from his .45 illuminated a wall of iridescent scales.

Something closed upon his legs: a vise. The shock of sudden deceleration, though mitigated by an immense *strength*, snapped his body like a whip. His pistol went flying.

And then he was rising, borne aloft in rhythmic bursts by a creature pumping its wings.

Twisting about, Miles saw clearly for the first time what it was that lay beneath him. From horizon to horizon spread a city like an ember-bed. Where its burning lights gave way to starry heaven Miles could not tell.

The beast that hauled him emitted another howl. It was answered by a multitude of like voices, and Miles clapped his hands to his ears as overlapping overtones built a harmony of horror. The river of scales above him surged aside for an instant, and he caught a glimpse of the moon-like disk from which he'd fallen. Twin curves of starlessness spread from it like legs. *An arch! The mirror's been suspended from an enormous arch!* Wedges of darkness rose and fell along its length, flapping against the celestial glimmer. *Monsters everywhere. The damn span's a rookery.*

Miles squirmed, but he'd lost all feeling in his legs. *Gotta get away. Better a swift death than a slow feeding to some infernal brood.*

A harsh foreign utterance vibrated from his bones: *"Next time, Arlam itself will break your fall."*

With a lunge and rush of leathery wings, the beast somersaulted in air. Its vise-grip vanished, and Miles hurtled skyward. The moon-disk grew, its reflective surface encompassing an ever-widening angle on the shining city below.

Miles hit the mirror and flew apart into nothingness.

And then he burst from a counterpart mirror in a tiny concrete room and struck the opposite wall, falling in a heap at an old man's feet. The old man yelped.

Almost worth it just for that.

"Wha … what happened? Miles, are you alright?"
Henry pawed at his emissary, more distraught
than Miles had ever seen him.

Surprisingly, Miles *was* alright. Bruised and bloody, but not disabled. His greaves had been gouged, his pants shredded below the knee, and the flesh of his legs flayed raw, but the red light exaggerated those wounds. The throbbing in his skull was nothing a few aspirin wouldn't fix. It took him a few minutes to regain his feet, but regain them he did. Henry helped him hobble over to one of the crates stacked against the wall. A thousand apologies jostled on the frantic codger's tongue.

Miles raised a hand to forestall further groveling. "Is there another way in?"

"I don– ... a what? Another way?"

"That mirror opens upon emptiness. A mile-high drop, maybe more. I was cast back to inform you of this fact. Now, *is there another way?*"

"Th-that's impossible. I sent Harold in on Thursday."

Fear and confusion transfixed Henry's face. So intense was this reaction that Miles, holding the other's blind gaze, found himself irradiated with grief as tangible as heat from a furnace. Henry looked down, limiting his emissary's exposure.

That's the face of a man rejected by his own kingdom, realized Miles with a start. *A truly bitter pill to swallow.*

"Henry," he said more gently, "please tell me. I need to know."

"There is another way," the old man whispered. "A secret way. A backdoor, as it were."

"Good." Miles could no longer suppress the eagerness in his voice. His mind's eye gleamed with the reflected lights of an alien realm. "Take me to it. I'm going back."

Part One
KREDAK

Overture
TO FACE THE NIGHT

38 Sillinen, 779

"We live in strange times, milady," said Rikard. "Who can know what the future may bring?"

Ilina turned from her red-cloaked host to gaze south across the vastness of the highlands. Past her feet the hill wall plummeted into broad Tarn Vale, a trough which, beyond its namesake river, mounted steadily higher and farther in soft knolls and swells toward a great upsurge of land fluttering russet with windswept heather. Autumn had come and the red hills flared in fiery bloom, filling her vision. Looming above their gentle crests, far beyond the southern borders of Kramarak, white peaks clustered like a crown. The air was so crisp and clear it almost hurt to breathe.

Perhaps that would be her excuse.

A wedge of bright red snapped into her peripheral vision, then fell back. Reluctantly tearing her eyes from the heights, Ilina returned them to the figure of Rikard Harnish, heir of the highlord.

He stood like a knight overlooking the field of battle: arms crossed, head held high, long cloak billowing out to the side like a wayward banner. Immovable he was—feet planted firmly apart; sharp gaze fixed on the far distance. The same distance, Ilina realized with mild surprise, into which she had been so inconsiderately staring. *He's haughty*, she mused, *in love with his own not-inconsiderable majesty.* But then his eyes flicked back to meet hers and their liveliness—their sheer *playfulness*—brought her breath up short. *No, it's not the wind's doing*, was her sudden thought. She shuddered.

"Change is like a mast spider," she said, more to herself than to him. "Most count themselves fortunate to die without seeing one, but some men there are who risk their lives and fortunes, even their souls, to lure one from the depths."

"And some men see one whether they ask to or not." Rikard relaxed, jettisoning his air of solemnity to prop himself against a pillar wrapped with carvings. A surge of wind tousled his shock of flaxen hair into a jaunty tuft.

As fickle as the sea, thought Ilina, *but is he as constant?* "And few of those live to tell the tale," she said aloud.

1

"Yes, but those who do have become unlike other men, it is said. They speak little. They ... *see* further. Some who were wild seem tamed, and some who'd grown tired of life take interest in living once more. They are different. They have–"

"Changed." She whispered the word and felt his keen eyes flick toward her as though they'd been tugged by the wind. Strands of auburn hair snaked across her eyes—tickling her creased brow and high cheekbones, twisting down her dainty nose, thin lips, and strong chin. She raised a hand to brush them back. Though only twenty-two, Ilina had learned by bitter experience to anticipate that moment in every conversation when her interlocutor, taken aback by gravity, would politely disengage. *Others cannot be like Father; it isn't fair to judge them for it. We Lightkeepers must keep our own company.*

Nevertheless, Rikard had outlasted her expectations. He kept refusing to back down or look away, and he advanced observations at odds with her own, and seemed to find her frostiness refreshing. So it was partly out of curiosity that she'd continued to accept his invitations and attend his courtly functions. How long could he last? How much could he take?

The feeling of his examination didn't pass. After a moment, she looked up to meet his gaze.

"And is that so terrifying?" he asked, shrugging himself away from the pillar. "Should we really flee such change? Barely a year has gone by without ill tidings from the south, and already we lapse into dispassion. Some days I feel as though I wake from a slumber I have no memory of entering, and perceive apathy all around me, rising by increment like an unseen flood. I fear many of my countrymen have already been whelmed. They float along, carried to and fro by a fitful current. I do not wish to join them."

"Beware what you *do* wish," said Ilina, turning again to face the hills. "The gods have ways of turning the tiny droplets for which we thirst into gales that rage and destroy. I fear not a fitful current, but one that sweeps everything I've ever known toward the edge of a cliff."

Rikard closed the small gap between them and leaned close, trying to read his guest's expression, then reached out to lift her chin with his fingertip. She flinched, but allowed him to guide her face up toward his. Her eyes were a plea: *just let me go ... just let me be ...*

"You really *are* afraid!" he marveled, dropping his hand. "Is the future that bleak to you?"

"I fear I know only the half of it, my lord."

"But the other half need not be bleak. The Imperium has not found us. The Tunnoltans are not here. Speak plainly, Lady. What is it you fear?"

2

A SEA SOUGHT IN SONG

"Do you not feel it? A great change comes." She fell silent a moment. With how much would she trust him? He had proven courteous, yes, but that was no great feat. To *understand* her—to be taken into her confidence—and yet remain solicitous was perhaps beyond the capacity of any man reared on the mainland. How could he comprehend her chill, he of clear skies and bright hills? How could he grasp her dread? This city, though rude by comparison with those depicted in her histories, seemed distant, detached—perched at a comfortable remove from all that yet lived and moved apart from the leave of well-mannered man. Not at all like her home in the throes of the sea.

The same histories that had transported her throughout the length and breadth of Arlam also told of a time when the name of Lightkeeper had been held in even greater esteem than that of Harnish. Not for haughty splendor or deeds of war, but for a quiet vigil kept unbroken. For who would remain to await the Truant King if not the heirs of the herald he'd left behind? It was said the sky itself had dimmed when his ship, like a setting sun, had threaded the rim of the world. It was said his return would banish woe.

But that had been centuries ago. Long enough for those who kept his light to surge in the popular imagination from stewardship to priesthood, before ebbing to the fringes of respectability. Now men would pass a Lightkeeper in the street without bothering to doff their caps. Now the future of Ilina's house might well rest on her ability to secure an advantageous union.

But what's my house to me? Naught but a hollow shell, echo chamber of an empty ocean.

Aware that the sails of her reverie hung slack, she cleared her throat and spoke. "Perhaps it is easier to sense such things when one lives in solitude. Perhaps there is less distraction, less pressure to drown out the chill voices of the silence."

"And perhaps," said Rikard, a quick smile masking his evident alarm, "the solitude itself becomes a haunting presence—a thing inescapable, pitiless, and cold. A thing that sucks warmth from the bones and joy from the heart." He leaned in, placing a gentle hand on her shoulder. "A thing that, for all its silent strength, is banished easily by a leaping fire and the laughter of friends."

For an instant Ilina stared at him with hunted eyes. Her lips parted, and it seemed to her as though she might let something slip—indeed, lurid babble nearly leapt from her tongue—but the mood passed. She sighed and grinned shyly. "Perhaps you are right."

"Good," he said. "Let's go in. By now the long hearth should be blazing brightly."

"If you can find more than heather stems to feed it."

"No," he replied slowly. "No, for you we will light winter wood." A strain tinged his voice. The timber blight that afflicted Kramarack was a sore spot on his mind.

But not sore enough. "Then half the cure is accomplished."

A silence. "Ilina, I assure you: we're all friends here."

"Not even you can presume so much," she sniffed.

"Would you insult my house?" bristled Rikard. "Do you know something I don't?"

Ilina's eyes fled to the cold crags on the high horizon. She let that coldness fill her mind. "I know it is easy for men to feign friendship with those from whom they wish to benefit."

Rikard was silent. Ilina clenched her jaw, stifling her urge to turn and smile and say it was alright, that she hadn't meant it, that she took it back, that it was all a joke in poor taste, and wouldn't he take her again to Bald Tor to watch the starshower tonight? She refused to break beneath the guilt. She had to do this. She had to know. She felt him withdraw from her side like a thorn withdrawn from flesh. Despite herself, she cringed.

"Ever since you arrived here you've been morose," he said, voice low. "I've done everything in my power to ensure you a pleasant stay, but you keep casting my kindness back in my face. One might almost think you suspect me of some plot against you, but it is not *I* who need this match!" He practically spat those last words, then spun and strode to the edge of the stone portico, cloak streaming from the breadth of his hunched shoulders.

At last, she sighed. It had required all her patience to flush Rikard's ego from its den of deference. Now his true colors were flying in the breeze for all to see.

Yet even in this small victory, Ilina felt defeated. Rikard's seeming perfection had unsettled her, yes, but only because she'd recognized it as a mask. Now disappointment swelled in her breast. *I must have been ready to deny my doubt.* Had his spell truly been that strong? Had she truly wanted to believe?

And what now? Was she willing to lose his courtship along with his esteem? No, she had no alternatives. She couldn't drive him off. She had never really wanted *that*. She just needed to know for certain if he loved her. *And what if he does?* her thought demanded. *If he does love you, and you convince him you aren't interested, he'll leave! What then?*

4

A SEA SOUGHT IN SONG

She clenched her wolrum-tooth brooch and turned toward Rikard. Her thought had failed to venture beyond this point. She had assumed his eventual reaction would satisfy her either one way or the other, but now she felt even less certain than before. What could she say? *Harlith send me a true wind. Blow me to the right.*

Rikard straightened. Shaded his eyes. Ilina sidled over to follow his gaze. A rider was moving down from the hills—a black speck passing through red heather with reckless speed. Ilina shot a sideways glance at Rikard, whose vision had narrowed to exclude all but the distant figure. His mouth formed a thin line.

As she turned again toward the south a sudden gust smote her—colder far than before, slicing right through her fur-lined mantle and leather riding-dress, tearing a gasp from her throat as she clutched her teal cloak tight about her shoulders and lowered her head against the blast. She stood, forcing herself to weather the wind—rooted in place like one of the pillars yet shuddering uncontrollably.

"You'll excuse me, milady," said Rikard. "I have business to attend." He swept his cloak aside and strode from the porch, preceded by a red banner flapping past his upraised arm.

Ilina was shocked. She hadn't expected such an unequivocal dismissal. Rikard's mask, once lowered, had been brusquely cast aside. All pretense had vanished like chaff in the wind. And the wind seemed so much colder now ... so cold ... She closed her eyes. The work of her lungs suddenly demanded all her thought. After a struggle she turned aside to suck in a breath. *Stupid, stupid girl—where will you go now? To whom will you crawl? Is there no prospect you cannot throw away? Now he hates you. And all because you are so proud.*

A faraway sparkle caught Ilina's eye: the rider was crossing Tarn Ford in the vale below, the spray churned up by its mount a spectacle no less foreboding to her mind than the glow of a strange lantern bobbing down a hill-road in the dead of night. Was this because Rikard had left her when the rider appeared, or was there something about the black speck itself that inspired fear? Perhaps Rikard hadn't seen the rider at all. Perhaps she, unsettled that he'd responded in kind to her provocation, was spooking at shadows. *You will go to him,* she told herself. *You will apologize for your hostility. You will choke back your pride and honor Father's wish.*

Yet even as Ilina reached this decision her thought shifted fully to the mounted figure ascending the skirts of Harn Hill. He—for the rider was male: his white beard licked past his shoulders in two long tongues—broke from the hill's shade just as he rounded a switchback and suddenly his clothes were black no longer but silver like salmon scales, and like a salmon he flashed once before plunging back into shadow. Dust curled in the sunlight where an instant before his cloak had spread like a vast wing. Something about the sight sent a shudder up Ilina's spine.

She turned away as the rider passed out of sight beneath the great hill wall. A strange yet implacable urge to meet the silver man squeezed her heart. Even in that moment it felt ridiculous. *I need to inform myself of Rikard's dealings*, was what she told herself, *especially those from which he excludes me*. With this resolved, Ilina headed for the door through which he had departed. The wind wrapped her cloak about her from behind.

Before she had measured a half-dozen paces, a smaller door to her left creaked ajar against the wind, then flipped open to bang against the stone wall. Out stumbled Rhinya—hair fluttering across her face, cheeks bright from exertion in the cold. "Milady, milady!" cried the servant girl as she slumped against the wall, held upright seemingly by the force of the wind alone. "Come! Come and see! Forkbeard is here! Forkbeard has arrived!"

Ilina turned toward the girl and her cloak slid from her back to whip up into coursing air. Its brooch dug into her neck and she clutched at the pin to unlatch it, pricking her throat as it sprang free. She snatched the garment back down, pinning it in the crook of her bare arm and covering the remaining distance at a trot. The wind's howling seemed nearly intelligible now—a deeply unsettling sound.

"What's happening?" she shouted.

"Forkbeard!" The girl's face was all aglow. "He just rode in through the under-gate. Follow me and you'll see him!" She paused to draw breath, then waited for a response. *Like the cat that exults to offer a rat to its master.*

Ilina started, blinking. *Whence came such a morbid thought?* She nodded, and Rhinya pulled her through the door.

Silence but for breathing enveloped them with the slamming of the door as though they'd plunged beneath pounding surf. Without another word, Rhinya caught hold of Ilina's sleeve and tugged her down the half-lit hallway. Ilina, curious beyond caring, allowed herself to be led. But the girl's excitement only fueled her strange sense of foreboding.

She'd not seen Rhinya this emotional since the night the girl, in tears, had pounded on her bedroom door and begged her to kill the spider that had

A SEA SOUGHT IN SONG

crept into the servants' wardrobe. The other servant girls, Ilina later determined, had made concord to resist Rhinya's pleas in an apparent effort to fortify her maturity. But Ilina, seeing only a child in tears, had immediately snatched up a shoe and gone probing through the closet on hands and knees to the petrification of the gaggle of older girls whom she'd neglected to release from their frozen states of obeisance.

After that night, Rhinya had looked at Ilina with something akin to awe; the girl had known at the time what it meant to ask a dignitary of such repute to crawl around among her sweat-soiled slips searching for spiders, and yet she'd asked anyway. Ilina respected that. It meant Rhinya was either uncommonly brave or uncommonly fearful, and, either way, that she was interesting.

But now, in Rhinya's tow after being sought out a second time, Ilina knew it was bravery, and not merely fear, that propelled the girl's audacity. This awareness did nothing to ease her own trepidation.

The doorway at the end of the hall opened onto a narrow, pillared porch overlooking a broad courtyard. Ilina's free hand shot up to shade her eyes. The sun hovered just above the peaked rooftops of Harnaral, its golden rays slicing through the dust churned up by a quickly-swelling crowd. A babble of voices—confused yet jubilant—rose with the thickening haze.

People of all kinds were running toward the center of the square. There, a squat stone gatehouse guarded the entrance to the tunnel that led from the hillside road below. Men, women, and children streamed out of the streets that radiated from the square, shouting in passing to those who peered from windows, grinning and jostling and fighting the wind. Handcarts stacked high with wooden crates or sacks of grain slouched forward on their handlebars—forgotten, ignored. Every banner on every gable streamed in the air as though Harn Hill itself were some great misshapen ship and the highlands were high seas. Ilina squinted toward the crowd's epicenter and thought she caught a faint flash of silver before Rhinya tugged her down the porch steps and into the hubbub.

As Rhinya wove expertly through the press of bodies—dodging stray limbs and squeezing through the smallest of gaps as soon as they appeared—a voice rose above the tumult. It seemed to echo faintly inside Ilina's head, as though she'd entered an empty room and left the clamoring crowd outside.

"Where is Highlord Hansel?" it boomed. "Where is the lord of this place? Move! Move, please! Make way!"

Rhinya dropped suddenly to the ground, ducking between a man's legs. Ilina, distracted by the booming voice, thumped into the man's broad back, instantly losing her connection with Rhinya. "I'm sorry!" she gasped, straightening as the man turned and the crowd pressed them together.

It was Rikard.

His eyebrows leapt so comically that Ilina would've laughed aloud had she not been mortified. His mouth dropped open and Ilina, not waiting to hear what came out, placed both hands on his chest and shoved off into the throng. But then she was through the throng and stumbling backward into an open space and sprawling on the ground. A hand fell on her shoulder. She looked up.

Forkbeard.

His smile seemed to well up from somewhere deep within. It emerged slowly, like a deer from the forest—spreading from his mouth to his cheeks to the golden irises of his bright, bright eyes. Eyes that might've held a thousand deadly secrets or a thousand priceless jokes. Eyes so hard they seemed to dissect her soul, yet so lively as to teeter on the brink of laughter. Ilina sat for what seemed an eternity, held captive by those kindly, terrifying eyes.

But then they blinked and the light and noise and dust came crashing back in on her and she felt herself hauled upright by strong hands and set on her own two feet and she was herself again, still gazing up at a face haggard yet regal. Forkbeard loomed over her, the white of his flowing forked beard blending with the silver of his long robes and cloak. He held her shoulders as though she were a mere girl.

"Your Reverence," said Rikard as he elbowed his way into the people-free pocket, "allow me to introduce the Lady Ilina–"

"Lightkeeper," finished the old man. "Daughter of Orlim Lightkeeper the son of Glennal Lightkeeper the son through many fathers of Kredak Lightbringer, Herald of the King. It is a pleasure to make your acquaintance." He inclined his head.

Rikard, for once, was at a loss for words. Ilina just stared at the old man, stupefied. "How ... how do you know me, sir?"

"I do not *know* you, not yet. But I make it my business to know a great many things." His eyes seemed to dim slightly. "Your father was a good man, if unduly stubborn."

At this Ilina stiffened. A memory unbidden impressed her senses. A figure, face averted, black against a sea whose roar failed to whelm dire words. *'This is the hour of doom.'*

A SEA SOUGHT IN SONG

Ilina's mouth worked soundlessly, but Forkbeard just bowed again and turned to Rikard. "Come, lead the way. I must speak with Lord Hansel at once."

"Wait!" Ilina blurted. "How do you know him? My father?"

As Rikard marched off toward the hall, Forkbeard glanced back and pierced her with his eyes. His half-smile faded into the wrinkles of his bony face. "You cannot now envision him apart from the light he kept, but it was not always thus. He once was as you are now. A fledgling tern before the wind." He squinted. "Here, let me get that for you," he murmured, reaching out and jabbing Ilina's throat with his forefinger.

Her hands jerked up in shocked reaction, but not before his fingertip withdrew, bloodied. He licked it, then slowly frowned and turned, striding away. Ilina pawed at her throat but her hands came away clean.

Only then did she notice the stillness of the air.

"It's unconscionable!" The Lady Lightkeeper spun on the ball of her foot and stalked back across the small yet elegantly furnished room. Rhinya's head swiveled to track with the pacing of her honored charge. The girl sat in a chair at the foot of the bed, her hands in her lap—as demure as curiosity allowed. The Lady had grabbed her and towed her all the way back to the guest chambers as soon as Forkbeard left the square. Rhinya was bursting with excitement inside, and would've had more difficulty repressing it had she not known the Lightkeeper wanted answers as badly as she. No pleading or convincing seemed necessary to inspire official action of some kind. She had only to wait.

"How can he just walk away from me after saying something like that? The whole city seems to know of him, yet no one bothers to inform me a visit is expected from a friend of Father's. And Rikard! Rikard walks away from me to meet with him, saying nothing! Who does he think I am, a servant to be dismissed at will?"

The Lightkeeper paused her pacing, glancing at Rhinya with what could only be sheepishness. "No offense intended, of course," she amended, then spun back to face the far wall. "But I am unused to such treatment. I cannot help assuming your lord desires to keep something from my knowledge."

Rhinya sat silently. The younger Lord Harnish had always seemed to her impressive and intimidating from a distance, but she'd never served him—not even at table—and had never learned aught about him that would've contradicted the Lady's accusation. She thought of the secrets she knew—that Melinda sequestered sweetcakes in her mattress, that Miliah liked Rel the stableboy—and imagined the Lord Harnish whispering with Forkbeard in some dark corner, perhaps disclosing his interest in Lady Lightkeeper. *No, that can't be it*, she thought, shaking her head slightly. *Everyone already knows he's courting the Lady.* Well, everyone, seemingly, but the Lady herself.

"No," the Lady said. She ceased pacing and faced the wall. "No, if he wants me, he must talk to me. This cannot continue. Rhinya," she said, turning, "you are relieved of duties until dinner. Enjoy the sunshine."

Rhinya sighed and slumped. "Thank you, milady," she mumbled. She had been dismissed. Lady Lightkeeper didn't need her help to uncover the big secret. This day had become boring once again.

Ilina strode across the cobbled courtyard, her steps stiff and determined, her jaw set. Now that things had come to a head, she no longer felt confident taking such a risk. What if Rikard *did* call off his unilateral courtship in response to her impertinence? He was her last best hope to fulfill her father's assignment. She knew she should feel honored to be pursued at all, even if the faded favor of her family name was all that attracted such pursuit. If Rikard called off the chase, Ilina would have to settle for an unlearned man were she to meet the deadline.

She shuddered at the thought. And yet … it was worse by far to withhold knowledge than to lack it. Any man who excluded her would become a husband she would regret having chosen. She swallowed and quickened her pace.

The Great Hall of Harn loomed before her, its raised foundation and massive stone columns seeming to draw themselves up against her intrusion. As she ascended into the portico's shadow, Ilina kept her eyes on the double doors flanked by two guards in full heraldic regalia. She extended an arm to shove open the right-hand door.

A gloved hand closed on her wrist. She glanced up at the guard in shock. Stark white heraldry—Stone and Sword and Hand—blazed from the red field of his breastplate. *Symbols only*, thought Ilina, but the sword-hilt jutting from behind the spaulder of his left shoulder was real enough. His eyes glinted through slits entwined by bronze creatures on the elaborate mask of his steel helm. He released her wrist the instant their eyes connected, yet stepped between her and the door, joined by his counterpart from the left.

"What is the meaning of this?" Ilina demanded. "Do you not know who I am?"

The first guard dropped his gaze. "Yes, milady." He didn't sound happy.

"Then step aside and let me pass, and I shall forgive your indiscretion."

The first guard shifted his eyes to some indefinite point over her shoulder. He said nothing. Ilina crossed her arms. After a moment, his counterpart spoke up, voice slightly louder than necessary. "Our apologies, Lady Lightkeeper, but our orders state that none are to enter the Great Hall at this time."

"At this time?" she said. "And when, pray tell, will *this time* be concluded?"

"When we receive different orders."

Ilina exhaled in a sharp burst. "And am *I* to be constrained by these orders?"

The first guard cleared his throat. "Apologies, milady, but we cannot make exceptions. I'm sure you won't have long to wait."

"What are your names?"

The first guard opened his mouth, but nothing came out. Guard Two took over. "My name's Takla, and he's Brigord," he said, elbowing the other man. "We are soldiers of Kramarack, our blood runs in the hills, and we guard the doors of Highlord Hansel Harnish himself. No foreign authority can supersede our orders. Good evening to you, Lady Lightkeeper."

Ilina turned from one to the other, then stepped slowly back. "Of course," she said, voice flat. "Good evening, gentlemen." With that, she spun on her heel and stormed back down the steps.

###

As soon as Rhinya saw the Lightkeeper turn from the doors, she realized how important it was that she'd tailed her all the way to Great Hall. The Lady left the place as forcefully as she'd approached—head down, dress swinging and swishing about her legs. She still hadn't noticed her shadow.

That's because you're still hiding, dummy! With a backward glance, Rhinya leapt from her vantage by the pillar and dashed after the departing figure. "Milady, milady!"

The Lady neither slowed nor turned. "I thought I told you to enjoy your evening, Rhinya."

AUSTIN GUNDERSON

That brought Rhinya up as though she'd hit a stone wall. *When did she see me? When I turned the corner at the bakery? Did she know I was behind her this whole time?* A second later, however, she was jogging along at the Lady's side like a dog before dinner. "Yes you did, and I *have* been enjoying myself—but you need me now, milady!"

The Lady left space for Rhinya to continue, then sighed and took the bait. "Why do I need you, Rhinya?"

"Oh, you need me for many things, milady: you need me to clean your room and scrub your clothes and serve you at table and braid your hair and fetch you the best books and guide you to the observatory unseen and–"

"Alright, alright," said the Lady, rolling her eyes. "I need you. But why do I need you *right now?*"

Rhinya smiled to herself, though she still couldn't fathom why Lady Lightkeeper always had to be goaded so before she admitted her dependance on assistance. According to Headmistress Lara, Rhinya's noble charge was practically helpless on her own. "You need to get into Great Hall," she beamed. "I can show you a back way!"

And now it was the Lady's turn to stop abruptly in her tracks.

"How can you see anything in here?" asked Ilina. Her head throbbed from its sudden acquaintance with a stone lintel—a meeting which had left her preoccupied by the relative nature of height. She was not accustomed to being tall. But Rhinya tugged her forward and so she stooped, almost on hands and knees, and crouched through yet another bottleneck of rock. At least the floor was level. "Do you come here often?"

"Lots," answered Rhinya. "Sometimes, when I'm following–" She caught herself and fell silent.

Interesting, thought Ilina. *So others visit these tunnels, too.* The entrance they had used had been hidden at the bottom of a storage stairwell. Rhinya had stuck her hand into a niche in the rock, then pushed open a gap barely wide enough to squeeze through. Since then they had crouched and crawled up a circuitous route of lefthand turnings.

The tunnels were all low and constricted—seemingly designed for use by children, or maybe dogs. Ilina almost laughed at the mental image of a vast subterranean kennel, but her humor evaporated at the next blind turn as she realized it might still be in use as such, perhaps for animals too dangerous

12

to keep above ground. History books notwithstanding, she still knew precious little of the Harns or of their Hill.

Or of my own blood, it would seem.

She scowled reflexively at the thought of Forkbeard's condescension, thankful the darkness hid her face. His words had roused a rage she couldn't help but recognize as incommensurate. *Am I reacting this way because I lack insight, or because* he *possesses it?* Or perhaps there was another reason. Perhaps she hated the insight itself. *Am I truly unable to envision my father apart from his sacred role?*

But that doubt was a mere knot in the cord of her thought. The real provocation had been left implied. And from it she shrank, for it affronted her faith. *'He once was as you are now.'*

Does that mean Father didn't have to become what he is? Could he have chosen differently?

Can I?

The rogue memory returned, sucking her down like a riptide, dragging her back to a time when she'd been no older than Rhinya.

She remembered shivering in the Pavilion of Winds—that pillar-ringed, dome-roofed platform atop vertiginous Kredak Tower. Behind her the great crystal beacon, though dormant in evening golds, splashed the rotunda's interior with refracted light. Before her stretched the sea, glittering like a sheet of steel beneath heaven's pitch-black pall. The gulls whose incessant din formed the aural backdrop of her life had withdrawn before the storm, hunkering in hidden roosts, and in the comparative quiet the wind exulted like an old dread newly roused.

And at the edge of that expanse, on the very brink, there sat a man. She had feared it would be so.

"Father," she said in a voice submerged by the roar.

She edged toward his hunched shape. It had been one of his bad days. Particularly bad. She'd been looking for him these past three hours, and though she'd known where she'd eventually find him as surely as she knew down to the minute when the storm would strike the shore, she'd delayed this discovery until she had no option left. *Just once. Just once I'd like to be wrong.*

"Father, it's time to come down," she cooed. "We can watch Harlith frolic from inside."

He stirred, tilted his head. An eye glinted at her before fastening again on the deep. "Hello 'Lina. Can you feel it? He's close. Out there. Coming. Oh, he's coming. Perhaps tonight, under cover of storm."

"Yes Father," she said despairingly.

Orlim sighed. "You shouldn't lie to me just because you think I'll like what I hear, Puffin. I know you don't feel it. If you did, you'd have shown up before now."

"I'm sorry, Father." And she was.

Still he didn't move. So Ilina sank to the sun-warmed stone and scooted forward, toward oblivion's lip. As the howling void inched closer, a kind of vertigo took her. Not the gut-twisting panic described by those few mainlanders she'd invited to this place over the years, but something more vicarious—a creeping cognizance that the bonds which held her to this kind and steady man were as insubstantial as seaweed. A fit of enthusiasm, a robust gust, and worlds would lie between them. Ilina slipped her legs over the edge to dangle beside her father's. An ocean of air set her blue dress all aflutter. *Harlith spare us. Pass us by.*

"If I'm here I'll see him sooner," muttered Orlim. "A trifle after all these centuries, perhaps, but of some worth nonetheless, at least to me. I am the Lightkeeper. I should espy him from afar, not be roused in the night by a fist upon my door."

Ilina licked dry lips. "You can't live up here, Father."

Orlim was silent. His daughter fidgeted. She could smell the immanent rain. And as she watched, powerless, the sea's glimmer dimmed point by point, wave by sparkling wave. The storm front reared like a breaker intent upon the world.

"Time is short," he finally said. "You think me touched, but I tell you I have never felt so certain in all my days as watchman. The king is *near*. You understand me? I can *feel* it. It's like … like the rain, like when … when you can sense … with … in your … oh, it's no use." He slumped further, then whispered: "He *must* come soon."

A sharp sorrow washed over Ilina then, and she leaned into her father, wrapping an arm about his waist. *Why can't he be happy with what we have? Why must he always look for more?* "But think, Father! If he'll be here soon, there's no cause for me to wed." She said it lightly, like a jest that was more than jest.

A blast of wind collided with the tower, shrieking through its pillars, forcing its keepers to lean forward toward the brink. Orlim's hat-brim snapped up against his brow. He turned to his daughter, surprising her with the joy playing over his weathered face.

"Oh you pensive puffin! In the kingdom to come there will be more cause to wed than ever before! Do not be afraid. We of all people should welcome change. And he *will* come soon." Again, he scanned the sea. His eyes burned with its reflected gleams. "He can afford no further delay. For night is falling—a night in which Kredak Light will avail us nothing. Can't you see it? Can't you feel it in your veins? He will not miss his final chance. This is the hour of doom, an end to our suspense."

Ilina blanched. Swiveling, she threw her other arm around him, gripping him with all her strength as though he might cast himself into space. "Don't say that!" she screamed into his chest.

"Ilina, I …" his voice broke as he returned the embrace. "Peace, Puffin. Do not weep. We were never meant to keep this light forever. Without fulfillment, anticipation is a fruitless thing. We are envied by our fathers. Do you see? *We* are envied. We who stand *here*, on the threshold of a world made new."

Ilina raised her head and followed her father's gaze out to sea. Through her tears the horizon warped as though deluged, but then she blinked and the air cleared and she saw that they still had time left to outrun the storm. Despite herself she squinted, peering toward the world's rim where ocean and sky exchanged blows. The vault above, though endless, remained constant. Likewise the deep knew its limits. But within that hairline rift which divided the two was concentrated all potentiality, all hope, all doom.

And then a wall of rain engulfed them. The storm had arrived too soon. Father and daughter scrambled back from Harlith's maw only to be swept unceremoniously across the Pavilion of Winds and down its recessed stairwell into darkness.

Darkness.

Ilina's memory ejected her into the present. She became aware that she had been crawling for some time with no sense of her surroundings. Not that it mattered in this warren of voids. *Well, assuming Rhinya's been paying attention.* She shuddered and felt a sudden urge to break the silence. "Who else comes down–"

"*Shh!*" whispered Rhinya. "We're here."

Ilina froze. A cold breeze wafted down over her head and shoulders. Cringing lower and glancing up, she felt more than saw an empty space above the spot where she squatted.

What do you think you're doing, you fool? After this, you'll be sent home for certain.

Closing her eyes in the dark, Ilina drew in a deep breath of cool air. *Then so be it. Rikard must decide what he can tolerate, but I cannot marry an untrustworthy man simply to carry on a custom. I am not so tightly moored to Father's fate.* She stood, whacking her head on stone.

Rhinya gasped. Ilina bit her lip and bent forward, letting the pain flood her, then dissipate. When she could think straight again she felt for the stairs ahead, where the ceiling gradually slanted upward.

And why should *he earn your trust when you scuttle around in the shadows like some enemy spy?*

Ilina paused on the step. Her conscience—if it *was* her conscience—took advantage of this momentary hesitation to loose a barrage of accusations. *How would you feel if you invited him to Kredak Light and he spent his time there prying open the sarcophagus to read your mother's death-song? Would that differ from what you're doing now? With no knowledge of you apart from reputation, he has showered you with favors. Does it matter the reason? You will marry him. You know you will. And after that? Will you snuff out what glimmer of affection he has for you just to prove yourself correct? Will you condemn yourself to the life you fear just so you can say you knew it would be so? Will* you?

Ilina reeled, and nearly fell backward upon Rhinya who stood immediately behind, but then she clenched her jaw, cleared her mind of doubt, and advanced up the narrow stair. She would not so easily abandon any project once begun. She had to know what Rikard hid from her.

The steps were steep and uneven and required Ilina's full concentration. But she, accustomed as she was to cliffside maneuvering in pursuit of cormorant eggs, had to climb for only a couple of minutes before she smacked her head against the iron ring that dangled from a rusted grate above. She stifled a whimper, unwilling to break the silence. *Absolute silence.*

Wait ... that isn't right. She turned. No Rhinya.

"Rhinya!" she hissed into the blackness below. No answer.

Ilina's head throbbed no longer, but her skin had begun to prickle. She stared unblinking down the stairs. It seemed darker there, somehow. As she watched, that blackness deepened, as though its luminance continued to ebb beyond the threshold of visibility. Had she not lost her fear of the dark while still a little girl? Why then had mere breathing become suddenly an impossible task?

Where was Rhinya?

Stop cringing like a child and go find out! She probably slipped and hit her head—Harlith knows you've done so more than is good for you.

A SEA SOUGHT IN SONG

Ilina descended a step—thin muscles twitching from tautness, hand trailing along the wall to maintain her balance. The absolute silence was almost tangible. Absence had become a kind of presence, a thing that was *there*—impossible to ignore yet dreadful to assess. A kind of nausea washed over her and she almost lost her footing. She had the distinct sensation of being both blind and naked in a brightly lit room with only a heath tiger for company.

Exposed, yet oblivious.

Stop it! You're frightening yourself! Now get down there and find that girl!

She took another step. Heightened senses detected minutiae unnoticed on the way in. Like that sickening stench. That was new. Perhaps this whole tunnel complex was nothing more than a sewer, and that grate at the top of the stairs the drain from a latrine. She jerked her hand off the wall.

"Rhinya?" she hissed. "Where are you?"

The scrape of her boot on the stone screeched in her ears like the cry of some small and helpless animal. Darkness enveloped her, a crushing oblivion like that which wrapped islands' roots far beneath the heaving northern sea. Blood pounded in her ears. She couldn't breathe.

But she heard breathing.

For a long moment Ilina stood absolutely still, her body immobilized, her mind riveted by sheer, raw horror. The sound that gripped her was unlike any breathing she'd ever heard before, yet was unmistakable as such: the soft, hollow suck of inhalation alternated with a thin rasp that seemed to go on for far too long. But Ilina *felt* the sounds more than she heard them. They pulsed up from the stone to rattle within her chest as though the strange breath was *hers*. But that couldn't be; she wasn't breathing at all. And the sounds came at a cadence far too slow for any human to maintain, because no human had lungs that vast.

And, with that realization, blind panic crashed in upon Ilina's mind and she screamed, flinging herself back up the stairs and catching her heel on an uneven step and scraping her forearms to break the fall, scrambling forward on all fours and assaulting the ceiling's iron grate. It held, rusted in place. She wailed incoherently, shaking it, slamming herself into it again and again and again until it gave with a crunch and then she was up and through and in an undefined black space. She threw out her arms and stumbled into several hard objects and knocked some of them over before she found a door. It was locked. Ilina lowered her shoulder and charged and bounced back like a sealskin ball. She kicked it. No effect.

17

AUSTIN GUNDERSON

Dead, dead, dead! I'm dead. It has me now.

Ilina whirled and screamed to drown out the breathing that doubtless had entered the room by now—whether in defiance or despair or out of a childish instinct that what cannot be sensed cannot exist, she neither knew nor cared. She lunged away from the door, tripping over one of the objects she'd dislodged from its shelf. It was large and heavy and she heaved it into her arms and hurled it toward the door. *Crack!* Light burst in. Ilina dove through the splintered aperture and landed in Highlord Hansel's personal study.

She rolled, cracking her head on the edge of a writing desk and dousing her hair with black from an ornate inkwell. Lurching to her feet, she squinted in the sudden natural brightness that streamed from a small window. The door. The door was there. She bowled it open in her haste, striking the face of Rikard Harnish and knocking him to the floor. Two more men were hurrying up behind him: Forkbeard and the Highord Hansel himself.

Ilina paused in the open doorway to look back. Months later, after waking tangled in sweat-soaked sheets, she would regret this decision.

For just then the chamber's closet door burst outward, and the thing which emerged seemed altogether too horrifying to exist in the waking world.

First there was the mouth. It was round like that of a hagfish and situated at the front of an arrow-shaped head, black as pitch, that sported no discernible eyes. Sinuous limbs, strangely-jointed, radiated out from behind the head to grip the doorframe with slender pads that sprouted three hooked claws each. Two limbs were twice as long as the others, and these groped like antennae until they seized on the edge of a table, whereupon the whole creature lunged violently forward, using its shorter limbs to launch itself out of the closet before snapping them tightly against its sides as it slid out in coil after writhing coil, splintering table legs and sending a cascade of papers sliding across the floorboards.

All this transpired in an instant. When Ilina turned away, a nightmare image seared in her mind's eye, Rikard was just scrambling to his feet. The woman before him bore scant resemblance to the haughty aristocrat whose scorn he'd borne earlier that day. With her clothes torn and soiled, her arms and legs slick with blood, her hair matted with both red and black, her face whiter than Cloudfall Pass in the month of Whrenen, and her eyes as wild as those of an old Jaar seer, she resembled more a specter than a real person.

"Ilina, what's happened? How did you get–"

Ilina slammed the door on the still-emerging creature, then shoved Rikard backward. *"Run!"*

A SEA SOUGHT IN SONG

Rikard's face was a picture of bewilderment. He threw up his forearms to block a second shove. Just then, something crashed in the room behind and an aggressive squeal like that of a stuck pig punctured the words forming on his lips. His mouth snapped shut and his eyes went wide. Catching Ilina by the shoulders, he threw her behind him and snatched a hand-and-a-half sword off the wall.

For they were in the Great Hall of Harn, realized Ilina with that shrinking fraction of her mind still capable of detached thought. Swords lined the walls as high as the stone vaults arching overhead in great sweeping curves and, here and there, letting in the last crimson rays of a nearly burnt-out sun that fled before the advent of western darkness.

"*Hold the door!*" boomed Forkbeard's voice. "If it gains the hall we shall have trouble bringing it to bay. Give no ground!"

The bellowed commands focused Ilina's attention once more. She turned to see the old man and the lords of Kramarack—father and son, side by side—clustered before the door. Highlord Hansel gripped a thick-hafted pike, bracing its butt end against the floor with his back foot. Rikard clutched his sword with both hands, feet planted apart, knees bent. But Forkbeard held no weapon. He stood tall in his silver robes, empty hands extended to either side—palms up, thumbs and fourth fingers forming twin circles. As Ilina watched, it seemed to her that what little light remained in the hall concentrated itself around his figure until all else grew dark as a night without stars.

With a jarring crash a half-insectile, half-serpentine form burst through the wall to their left. Swords and wood splinters spun through the air and clattered against the floor as the beast launched itself directly at Forkbeard— maw gaping, limbs splayed as though for an embrace. Ilina would've screamed if she hadn't choked while drawing breath.

The old man barely had time to react, but react he did. He turned, bringing up his right hand and snapping his wrists around so his palms faced forward. There was a flash of light and a deafening boom and then everything went dark. Even the candle flames vanished. From the far wall came a heavy thud and clatter, then a gurgling growl that rose to an atonal keening.

Suddenly, a human voice pierced the sounds of alien fury with the unlikeliest of expressions: a song. It began in a soft quaver yet quickly grew deep and sure. It was the voice of Highlord Hansel Harnish, and this is what it sang:

"The sun went down behind Harn's Hill

19

AUSTIN GUNDERSON

When there he made his stand.
How bright his eyes, how clean his blade
How small his mighty band!
The sky was black, his blade was red
The Hill had drunk its fill,
When Harn at last sank to his knees
And everything fell still.

The hills are dry, the heather thirsts,
The stars glint in the sky.
The world waits with bated breath
To hear Harn's battle cry.
For men like Harn shall yet arise
In time of dire need.
To face the night yet see no dawn
Doth sow a mighty seed."

Lord Harnish ended his song with a loud shout, joined by his son. And Ilina woke from her stupor of fear.

The guards! she thought. *Why have they not come?*

In an instant she was running, guided by memories from earlier visits. A stool cracked against her shins and she cried out, eliciting a deep belching bark from the blackness that was the hall's far end. Shouts and thuds and squeals and other sounds of violence rang out. Flashes of light illuminated her route in a kind of inverse blinking: uniform blindness punctuated by sight. Ilina whimpered, hobbling forward more carefully now, yet more urgently. How could those men fight something they couldn't even see?

Sounds of dull pounding—fists and sword-hilts upon thick wood and iron—brought her up before she hit the doors, which apparently were locked from the inside. Finding a great ring, she heaved with all her might, but to no avail. She groped along the riveted surface and felt a bulky protrusion: the crossbar. Was there only the one? Ilina jumped, flinging her hand overhead. It brushed the upper crossbar bracket. Empty.

But how was she to move even one crossbar, a task that normally required at least two guardsmen? Ilina crouched beneath the massive plank, straining to raise it on her shoulder. It didn't even budge. She bent her knees and back and heaved, screaming in frustration and pain. No movement. Nothing. She was only a woman, after all, and shared no blood with Harn Bright-Eyes. She was helpless, useless, pointless. She sank down before the

A SEA SOUGHT IN SONG

doors—arms crossed over her face, sobbing. Those men would die—*Rikard* would die as surely as poor Rhinya—and she could do nothing but wait for death to take her too.

Is this what you meant, Father, when you told me doom would come? The king has not returned. How can you still hope? Are you mad, after all? Perhaps we're all mad. Perhaps madness is all that resists the inevitable end of the world.

Ilina curled in a spasm of fear, but then a new thought stilled her. *And since the end is inescapable, perhaps all that matters is how I face it. Perhaps Rikard is right. Perhaps redemption comes not from afar, but from within.*

And with that Ilina rose, forsaking the impassible doors. Finding a broadsword, she wrenched it from the wall. Something within her had changed, and she didn't know whether or not she approved. But she wouldn't live to know, now would she? She was about to die. And, by Harlith's breath, she would not die cowering in a corner!

"My name is Ilina Lightkeeper," she began in a whisper, "daughter of Orlim Lightkeeper the son of Glennal Lightkeeper the son through many fathers of Kredak Lightbringer, *Herald of the King!*" Her voice rose to a shout as she slashed aside an invisible stool. She reeled a little, overbalanced by the blade's weight. "I stand against you, cruel fate! I need no lost god's aid! You may steal my life, but not my soul! I defy you! Come take me!" She lashed out with the sword, spinning in a blind circle, laughing, intoxicated by sudden fatalism. "Come, spiderworm, I await you!"

At that moment, a bright bluish light burst at the far end of the hall. A grotesque tableau burned itself into Ilina's retinas, then vanished as a thunderclap rattled the swords lining the walls like scale mail. Lord Hansel, too, had procured a blade; his pike now sprouted from the monster's mouth like a toothpick. On the far side crouched Rikard, sword-arm swept back as though he'd been thrown. But Forkbeard stood before the yawning maw with arms upraised—a black silhouette against that burgeoning brightness which pulsed between his palms. A piercing squeal rent the air, and a great crash, and then all was still.

Is it dead?

Oblivion had closed in again—a blackout of the senses. Ilina's sword instantly became the lifeline of her nerve: she gripped it with both hands as though she might at any moment slip away to fall forever. Her mouth opened, then shut, silent. If Rikard yet lived, he would find her. But if she were the only one left, there would be no point in inviting any more attention. She was shaking. It was all she could do to keep the sword aloft. She felt crushed by the darkness as though it had substance and weight.

Something thumped and clattered away down the hall. Ilina started. The thudding from beyond the doors, though still faint, had grown more rhythmic: the guards must have found a ram. From the place she'd last glimpsed Rikard, however, not a sound came. Ilina was shaking so badly she could barely stand upright. And then she surprised herself.

She stepped forward.

And why should I not? If I can discard prudence in the face of despair, then why not now, when a glimmer of hope has returned?

But that logic, sound as it was, rang hollow in her mind. She challenged the darkness not to validate an abstraction but to find a man. One man in particular.

"Rikard," she breathed.

She cracked her shin on a wooden protrusion and dropped her sword with a metallic clatter. The darkness gaped silently around her. With a gasp she fell to her hands and knees, groping for the weapon. The blade's edge sliced into the little finger of her right hand as she swept it over the floor. Biting her sleeve to mute a cry of pain, Ilina hefted the weapon in her left hand and rose unsteadily.

She spat out her sleeve. "Rikard!" she hissed.

As if in reply, something moved against the far wall. Ilina heard it clearly.

"*Who's there?*" she squeaked. "Rikard, is it you? Where are you?"

A low groan. A human sound.

Ilina edged forward, sword raised and quivering. *What if I impale him?* She stopped and, after a mental struggle, lowered the blade. "Where are you?" she whimpered.

"Here." The voice came from the ground at her feet. She jumped, but managed to hang on to her weapon this time.

"*Rikard?*"

"Ilina. What of my father? Where is he?"

She dropped to her knees, laying aside the sword. Her fingers brushed his face, then found a cold bulk on his chest, abrasive to the touch, like sharkskin. She recoiled instinctively. The lifeless monster had him pinned.

"My father," he said. "Find him!"

Without reply, Ilina lifted her sword and rammed it into the hulking corpse beside Rikard's head. The skin gave, but refused to break. She leaned on the hilt.

A SEA SOUGHT IN SONG

"Ilina, I'm fine! Find my father! *Go!*"

With a yell, Ilina threw her weight against the sword and it punctured the leathery hide and drove through the soft tissue beneath like a needle through cloth. She fell forward upon the creature's turgid bulk. Pus and slime bubbled up from the cut and Ilina planted her hands in the mess to thrust herself upright. A debilitating stench flooded her nose and mouth and mind.

"By the Stone, don't bother with me!" cursed Rikard. Then the monster's discharge reached his face and the only sounds were his spluttering gags and a thick, rubbery rending as Ilina sawed the carcass open. She worked up and around, stepping over Rikard's head where it protruded from beneath the mass. When her blade reached the other side, a wedge of skin flopped out— spilling nameless organs across the floor and smothering Rikard's cry of revulsion. Then he was gone—buried.

Ilina plunged her arms into the slime. The incision *must* have relieved some of the pressure pinning him to the floor. *There!* Her fingers struck his face and she worked them down along his neck to close on his shirt. She pulled, but the floor was slick now and her feet flew out from under her and she sprawled on her back, gasping and gagging.

Rage filled her. She might be incapable of lifting a wooden beam, but she'd sooner die than let Rikard drown in viscera. She planted her feet against the creature's body, filled her fists with his shirt, coiled herself, then slowly straightened—dragging him headfirst into the air. A scream exploded from her throat as Rikard breached the slime and sucked in breath. They lay side-by-side, gasping.

Then Rikard rolled over, wrapped his arms about her, and kissed her on the mouth.

Ilina froze, shocked and disoriented. But an instant later her mind, unable to process this sudden reversal, abdicated to emotion. She melted.

A flash of light and there stood Forkbeard, his robes freshly red like flowering heather, his boney features spectral by the glow of an eerie orb glimmering through cupped fingers. His eyes—before so sparkling, so bright—sank into his skull, twin voids cast from beneath. Below him, the next Highlord of Kramarack and the Lady Ilina, Heir of the Herald, had yet to pause for breath. Rikard was the first to disengage, remembering his father. Ilina clung to him as he rose.

Forkbeard lifted his orb. And all across the floor, shadows and gleams vied over the scattered remains of Highlord Hansel Harnish, son of Hans Harnish the son of Horah Harnish the son through many fathers of Harn Bright-Eyes, Father of the Hills.

"The hills will bloom tomorrow," said the wizard, and Ilina quailed to hear the deadness in his voice. "He will need you then, Lightkeeper. Do not fly."

Ilina raised her head and straightened, intertwining her fingers with those of Rikard's slack right hand.

Rikard's knees buckled. With a crash, they struck the floor.

And far, far away—as though Harn's Great Hall had become an endless tunnel fleeing the outside world, an immeasurable shaft in the mine of sorrows, a bottomless pit whose nadir stank of death—the massive doors at last flew open.

Chapter One
RIM OF THE WORLD

18 Halanen, 781

All the world is chaos. White sea and black sky vie for dominance. Billows of saltspray writhe between heaving deep and raging heaven. No offering may calm the elements' wrath. A thousand feet down where light is unknown the waters may be as still and cold as Oblivion, but not here. Here, upon the violent rim of the world, surf booms and winds howl like drunken monsters dredged from below.

This is my home.

My name is Ilina Lightkeeper, daughter of Orlim Lightkeeper the son of Glennal Lightkeeper the son through many fathers of Kredak Lightbringer, Herald of the King. Kredak it was who raised this tower from the black rock that rears out of the sea like a breaching wolrum. Faded volumes in the Maritime Library say Kredak named his tower *Anticipation Light*. None now remember that name. Well, none save for me. But the namer—he has attained an honor unsought. Kredak Tower, men call this place. A diminution.

It was here I was born on a summer's night nearly twenty-four years ago, and here I shall die when Orlom strikes the key of my name an eighth and final time.

I begin this diary with a sense of regret. All my life I have examined the journals of the great, eager to discern their thoughts and interpret their insights. Nonetheless, the notion of keeping a journal myself always presented to me a pointless prospect. My life seemed far too ordinary to justify a record of its tedium. Who would think to open such a book, let alone to finish it? The world would not care, and all effort on my part would have been wasted. At least, this is what I told myself.

No longer.

"Life," Father says, "is like the froth of the sea—it appears in a moment of tumult, rides the crests and troughs of fortune, bursts upon the shore of death, and is gone forever." It would seem the foam of my life is about to mount a roller, if not a breaker. Even as I write I pray Orlom to strike a consonant key. And I *am* writing, for I wish now to have a record of life's tediums, lest I forget them.

In a week I shall be married.

Well, not actually married, but formal betrothal is just as bad. My life as I know it shall be over. And the more I dwell upon it, the more I see how much I love my current life. Change frightens me.

Ironic, is it not? I live on a black rock surrounded by ceaseless change. Waves lash Cuspid Isle night and day, imperceptibly blasting its granite to fine sand. Storm fronts sweep south, batter the broken shore, and vanish over the horizon. Thunderheads clear, reform, and converge once more. Both water and sky are in constant motion, especially on days such as this.

But ceaseless change is predictable change. Witness it long enough and it becomes monotonous. What terrifies me—what drives me to pen this diary in the vain hope I may somehow capture normality and sequester it safely away—is the unknown. I do not expect it. I cannot prepare for it. I may not survive it.

Aei. I'm morose today. I begin a diary to escape my fears and I've filled the first two pages with nothing else. Perhaps this wasn't such a good idea.

But now, having begun this endeavor, I am duty-bound to continue. I hereby leave the dank vaults of pessimistic foresight to climb the lofty stairs of present contentment.

I sit in Seascape Study. The sealskin couch is firm and smooth to my touch. I snuggle into its right corner, as always. When I look up, the Window of the North eclipses my vision. The glass portal looms above me—a vast oval, crisscrossed by thin bands of iron wrought like spiderwebs. When I cross my eyes and stare at them long enough, I perceive the outline of a man amidst their twisted net. A crown is on his head. Spreading rays emanate from his upraised hand. He is Harlith, god of the arctic gale. And I watch him frolic through his splintered image.

Each day when my work is done I retire here, book in hand, to marvel at the glorious wrath of nature from an unapproachable vantage. If I am weary I lay the book aside, kick off my stockings, and curl up beneath a sealskin blanket like a vixen in her den.

Night comes swiftly when the sky is leaden. My wolrum-oil lamp sputters, then flares. Shadows cast by its light dance along the ceiling's stone vaults. The Window of the North glowers a faint blue-gray, the breakers and stormclouds glimpsed through its glass melding into an indistinct amalgam of ominous yet impotent gloom.

A SEA SOUGHT IN SONG

Just listen to me. I sound like a naturalist dissecting a specimen—detached, impassive. I can't stand it any longer. Avoiding my fears won't make them disappear. So here they are.

I am an only child. More than that, I am the only child of a Lightkeeper. I am Father's sole heir. As such, I have responsibilities. Kredak Light must never, never go out—but only a descendant of the Lightbringer himself may keep it burning. It knows my touch, my voice. At sundown I summon it, and by dawn it has departed. Thus it has been for centuries, and thus unchanged it must remain lest the Truant King return in vain and on the senseless rocks be slain.

And now it falls to me to make provision for the next generation. I must marry.

For years I have lived in denial. In my foolishness I thought I could escape, that the rules might have somehow evolved when it came my turn to wed, but I cannot flee the inevitable. Now procrastination has exacerbated my dilemma. And the admission of guilt does nothing to assuage regret.

When I was small, I promised Father I would choose a man by my twenty-fourth birthday. He expects me to keep my word. I want desperately to keep my word. But I was naive then. I thought every marriage chord harmonious. And why not? Had my mother survived my birth she might have disabused me of my credulity, but it is natural for a child to idealize that which remains unobserved.

Now I know better. When I travel to town I search the old men's faces and all I find is dull indolence. Light enters their eyes only upon sight of a public house. The young men light up upon sight of me, of course, but not with the light of love, or even of proud courtesy. They are like beasts that live only to gratify their base impulses. My soul would atrophy were I to marry such a man.

Rikard, at least, suffers not from such flaws.

Oh, I am frightened—undone by the unknown. In truth, he is my only option. And yet my heart misgives me. Do I know him? Even now, after all this time, do I truly know him? And if not, then what prevents me from acquiring knowledge? Am I so dull, that I cannot discern the intents of his heart? Courtesy, discipline, courage—the very qualities he so carefully substantiates are become the source of my suspicion! Is there no pleasing me? What kind of woman am I?

Ever since that night in Harnaral, I have felt afraid. There is something amiss in the world, some cancerous rot that festers and swells and gets everywhere. From the south waft rumors of horror. The gods seem distant.

AUSTIN GUNDERSON

Rikard is far away. Even Father has withdrawn since his sudden illness. It was good of all those people to come and see him, but now they are gone and he has lapsed into unsettling silence. I dare not leave the Isle. It is difficult, even now, to imagine the world as it was, as it ought to be. In truth, change has already come. In truth, it will only get worse.

I glance at the clock that stands against the wall. It strikes the first of ten chimes as I turn away. A lifetime of monotony instills in the mind an instinctual clock which needs no winding.

As the familiar pealing reverberates through wood and stone and flesh and bone, I am shocked to find myself shuddering. It is as though each chime is the footfall of some plodding monster—an aural personification of irresistible fate. The monster stalks me. I cannot escape it, not even in my own home.

I am calm now. It is good to record my thoughts, if only to refute them. This is not the Hill of Harn, nor fate some inexorable force. Fear itself is the true monster. Change, though traumatic, need not be tragic. In a week's time the Petition of Troth shall arrive via priest from Land's End, and I shall keep my promise. I *shall* wed Rikard. Now, however, I must close you, diary mine.

It is time to light the Beacon.

Chapter Two
THE STRANGER

arlin pulled on his oar as if all the unclean spirits of Hoc roiled in *Seaskater*'s wake. Sweat poured down his brow, freezing in twisted jrivulets. His breath steamed out like a wolrum's salty blast. His parka's hairy pall didn't hide him from the gale's fury. Its mane lay plastered against his skin. He wished he could pull it on backwards, shield his face from the driving sleet and screaming gusts, sink into warm, enticing blindness.

Six days. Six days with the wind at their back. They should've sighted land by now. Any land. But what did he expect when the sun died and the sea leapt up to kiss the clouds?

A shadow stalked the deck.

Jarlin cringed despite himself. His eyes flicked to the side, dilating in fear. The stranger swept past as Jarlin heaved on his oar. High mukluks, tightly-woven furs, and that horrific weapon strapped to his broad back. Jarlin shuddered. He almost believed the others when they whispered that Harlith himself had materialized in human form to lead them to their deaths. Almost.

A plume of water exploded from the darkness astern to swallow the stranger whole. Jarlin ducked as the white torrent rushed forward through the rowers' benches. When he looked up again the man was stooping beside old Jol at the tiller, gesturing vigorously, pointing at the sky. Jarlin strained to catch any words over the howling wind, but in vain. Jol shook his head and the stranger faced the prow. Jarlin averted his eyes. There was something incredibly disturbing about the man's beardless visage—almost as though he were both man and woman. Almost.

Morbid curiosity overcame revulsion. Jarlin leaned back, his spine straining, his oar quivering as it gouged an eddy-pocked arc through the surging current, and studied the stranger from the dark vantage of his hood.

What madness would impel a man to shave off his own beard? Jarlin shivered: he could think of no respectable reason to take a knife to one's own face, but the stranger had done so every morning since he stormed into camp and commandeered this ship. It was a grave humiliation to have been bested by such a man, but fortunately that smooth jaw was his sole effeminacy. He stood tall—well over six feet, Jarlin judged. At least a head taller than any of them. And he was strong. Djor knew that now, poor soul. Yes, he was very strong, and quick. Too quick for Jaral or even Larlij. Too strong and quick for any of them. Even for all of them at once.

And so they rowed. They rowed even as a lunatic tempest harried little *Seaskater* without mercy, as voracious winds split her sail before it could be lowered, as a great black storm front reared its ugly anvil-crown far to the north. The black anvil was above them now. Mountainous waves loomed out of the night. The horizon pitched and rolled as *Seaskater* crawled up heaving slopes and slid deep into abyssal troughs. And still they rowed.

Cobweb lightning fractured the sky as *Seaskater* crested a sea-hill. For an instant the stranger stood silhouetted against a fisherman's net of white light, his strong chin and slouching hat-brim distinctive in relief. Then the thunderclap detonated overhead and everything went black.

When Jarlin's eyes readjusted, the stranger was gone. A sudden chill slithered down his spine. He glanced around. No one else seemed to have noticed. They hadn't had time; it had happened so fast. Something here was unnatural. How could a man just vanish? Had he gone overboard?

Jarlin opened his mouth to warn the others—to give the order to ship oars, ready the buoys, and man the gunwales—but the shout died in his throat. What if the others were right? What if this formidable stranger was the gale god himself, caught up into the heavens on thunderbolt shrouds? Jarlin shuddered and raised his eyes to the obsidian sky.

And then he saw him.

The stranger clung to the crosstrees, twenty feet in the air. His arms coiled about madomu-hair rope while his feet sought purchase in the rigging. Even as Jarlin cursed in recognition, *Seaskater* swooped into a choppy basin between waves. The mast whipped around like the tail of a happy dog. As the stranger scrambled for a toehold his boots slipped on the rain-swollen lattice and his legs were flung violently into space.

Jarlin opened his mouth a second time. Nothing came out. *Seaskater* groaned as she mounted a huge wall of black water. The mast lurched drunkenly. Jarlin just stared, mouth agape, as the stranger dangled out over a churning abyss, fighting for life with his nails.

As soon as he was lost, he was safe. His arms flexed and his body rose. His knees came up and then extended as he twined his legs among the ropes. He lunged upward, hugged the mast like a vise, shook his head to clear his eyes, and peered into the wrack. Lashing rain obscured his image.

Jarlin squeezed his eyes shut against the rain and stinging seaspray, rubbing his face upon his forearm. Who was this man who faced death with

A SEA SOUGHT IN SONG

such cavalier indifference? Whence did he come? Why was he here? Where was he going?

Perhaps taking so many lives cheapened one's own. Perhaps, in order to kill his own kind, a man had to give up pieces of his soul. Perhaps such loss lessened his weight, made him quicker, deadlier in a fight. Jarlin wouldn't have known. But he remembered the morning this stranger had materialized from out of the northern plain.

It had been a cold day without wind. Low on the horizon a pale sun flickered through a mackerel sky. Week-old snow carpeted the tundra. All was silent, all was still. A bleached tableau vacant of blemish. Vacant of life.

Jarlin was hunting—he and two others: Djor and Jaral. They were to his right, advancing through the drifts. He was the left flank. Every few minutes Djor's head would bob into view, then vanish again. Jarlin's spear was a dart of deadly air in his ready right hand. He loved her delicate balance, was well acquainted with all her aerodynamic peculiarities. His glance ran down the channel that spiraled her slender shaft. She thirsted for blood. He would quench her thirst this day. The white elk waited.

A strange premonition pricked Jarlin's senses and he glanced back up. His hackles rose.

A lone figure was approaching across the snow.

Jarlin's mind whirled. No Jaar this. Their clan had moved north for the spring migrations, but no one else from the village would have wandered this far afield, and no other clans had camped even remotely near this region. No one in all the world should have been farther north than Jarlin's hunting party.

No one but this solitary stranger.

Djor and Jaral would have seen him by now and hidden themselves. Jarlin, snapping out of his apprehensive reverie, dropped into a snowbank and wormed his way forward, his white bear-hide parka melding seamlessly into the monochrome backdrop. The stranger drew near, his strides eating distance, his heavy pack bobbing rhythmically, his long brown coat trailing in the snow.

Suddenly a shrill cry rang out as a white shape exploded from a snowbank ahead and to the right. Djor, unbeknownst to his companions, had crept far ahead. Too far. Jarlin swore and then howled his war cry as he leapt from concealment. Curse that Djor. The young fool wanted a kill. He would yet be the death of them all. Jarlin charged forward, closing the gap.

35

But it was too late. Djor whooped and hurled his spear at the stranger from five bodylengths. The kill was assured. An infant could have made the shot. Jarlin cringed.

The stranger neatly dodged the missile, sidestepping as it whistled past his shoulder. Jarlin could have sworn it tore his cloak in flight.

Djor paused only an instant. His ivory knife streaked from its sheath, slashing outward in a wide arc. The stranger took two steps, twirled a slender club over his shoulder, and knocked the knife away. One more step and the club connected with Djor's skull. The crunch was sickening.

Jarlin screamed. He couldn't believe this was happening. It shouldn't have happened. But it had happened, was happening, and now the stranger had to die. Jarlin's mukluks drove through the waist-deep sea of snow. Plumes of white powder billowed in his wake. As he careened forward time seemed to slow. His limbs felt languid. An invisible force seemed to press him back.

Jaral moved faster. Either that or he had been ahead to begin with. Jarlin never found out. For now, the other man entered his peripheral vision from the right flank, running like the wind, spear arm cocked. The stranger saw him too. In one swift movement he twirled his club a second time, pressed its broad end into the crook of his shoulder, and glanced down its length. A sound like a splitting ice floe burst in Jarlin's ears. A red cloud erupted from Jaral's back. He lurched, staggered forward, and collapsed in the snow, disappearing from sight.

Shouts jolted Jarlin back to the present world. His shipmates had stopped rowing. They were glancing this way and that, rising from their benches, yelling that the stranger was gone. Jarlin raised a hand to clear his eyes and felt tears amid the seawater. He could tell the difference. With a sigh of grief and fatigue he lurched to his feet to point out the stranger's perch.

At that moment the stranger dropped out of the black sky, landing with a thump in the midst of the rowers' huddle. Grizzled sailors shrieked like little girls. Jarlin had to choke back a bitter laugh.

The stranger paid them no heed. He stumbled to his feet and shoved his way to the bow. He leapt onto the peak, spun back, and gestured excitedly, pointing past the figurehead, shouting something urgent in his unintelligible tongue. The Jaar rowers crowded forward, frightened yet curious. Jarlin leaned over the gunwale and peered into the maw of the storm.

Far ahead a pinprick light pierced the roiling night.

Chapter Three
SILENT CHIMES

The vision began as it always did: with a wave of heat. Not the dry, directional heat of a fire or furnace, but the heavy, enveloping heat of an atmosphere drunk on sun—a heat such as she had never felt but in these dreams. No, not even in the marshes of the Tarn at midsummer. Not even in the throes of shame.

After the heat came the light. A glare that left her half-blind through squeezed eyelids. She opened them; she had to, if only to avoid wasting this moment. She only wished the burning would dissipate sooner, that her view would swiftly clear.

Third came the fear.

It was the courtyard; it was always the courtyard. The kaleidoscope of sunspots faded before a smooth expanse of stone running away to the edges of sight. Directly down upon it she gazed, as though she were a bird. Sometimes it was empty—as blankly gray as rain. Sometimes it was mottled with dark shapes. Cohorts and regiments.

Tonight, it was black.

Hundreds of thousands of men. Marching, marching. Wheeling and converging and reforming. Rippling like an ocean of ants. The effect was hypnotic.

Horrifying.

And then suddenly it was more. Her awareness, till this point diffuse, *sharpened* against her will. A dark mote beneath her, at a distance too great to guess, became the extent of her senses. She found herself riveted as her eyes focused and focused and *focused*. The mote resolved. It was a formation. No, a figure. No, a face. It looked up. At her.

It was void of features.

The shock of this connection jarred her. It was *too close*. She could almost make out her own reflection in the blank faceplate staring up at her. And then light caught it and exploded. Pain lanced her eyes. She cried out, recoiling. Her fingers lifted from a cool surface.

The vision ended as it always did: with a crash of coldness. Ilina Lightkeeper stumbled back from the blazing Beacon, breathing hard.

###

AUSTIN GUNDERSON

It wasn't always like this. On most nights the Beacon kindled without incident. It was the honor and burden of her blood to rouse the lighthouse with a touch. But sometimes, in the eyeblink pause between contact and withdrawal, her consciousness would jump ... *elsewhere*. Always the same place. The place she feared she could find on only the oldest maps that extended farthest south.

These visions had occurred at more frequent intervals of late. And this one had been particularly bad. She'd never made ... *eye-contact* ... before. Ilina shuddered, clutching herself, shaking her head. Trying feebly to clear her thoughts. *What just happened? Did ... did he* see *me?*

Breathe, 'Lina. Tunnolt is a lifetime's journey away. It is an alien realm you see. They cannot reach you here.

As she turned from the Beacon—her ritual discharged, her covenant renewed for one more night, one more futile iteration of an unending chain— she saw her slender shadow cross the southernmost pillar and stopped as though she'd struck a wall.

Pillars ringed the Pavilion of Winds. Beyond them all was black. Like shining trees, they stood, illumined by the Beacon in their midst. The Pavilion's namesake screamed and swooped, slashing with insatiable savagery, slinging Ilina's cloak aside until its fringes stretched like pinions, but she stood stock-still and silent, staring at the play of light before her face. For the light of the Beacon was cool and constant and her shadow as steady as the stone it overlaid. In all this wrack and chaos, the sight of that immobile shape—her shape, etched in black upon a column of light—was a strange thing, a chill vision in its own right, and she wondered at the terror of it. *For is this not what you wish? To stand firm though all else flee away? To resist the pull of the tide? To be the anchor, the rock, the unwavering light in the storm?*

This is the purpose for which you were born.

But that answer just wasn't enough anymore, and she knew it. Not for the first time, she allowed her mind to slide toward speculation. Toward heresy.

For whom was she waiting, all alone and unacknowledged, the tattered end of a threadbare strand, last of her kind in all the land? For whom was she expending her life? Was it for the fishing vessels long since harbor-bound? They had no need of her guidance; none ventured this far from shore. She could count on one hand the times Kredak Light had saved storm-blinded ships over the course of the past century. Indebted mariners never failed to make a pilgrimage of praise.

Was her vigil, then, for mighty Harlith, he who raged and thrashed all round? That answer was even less plausible: no god had need of her ceaseless fealty, her anticipation of visitation. Harlith could reveal himself whenever he chose, and all he'd chosen to show her was wrath. Had she not begged him for intercession with tears? And had he not ignored her? At times he really did seem less like a god than an impersonal force, as the Broanoshi priests would have it.

What then? Was she truly waiting on an ancient monarch whose body had never been found? The Lightkeeper Catechism leapt up in affirmation. But the answers she'd memorized as a child seemed enervated by experience, and it was a kind of self-estrangement to choose between the two.

Well, she had made her choice. And though the world humored her, behind her back it thought her mad. And sometimes she wondered as well.

How does Father do it? How does he believe? He would tell Ilina of their ancestor Kredak—how the man had gained renown in service to High King Henred the Explorer, and how he'd accompanied his sovereign to the farthest reaches of Arlam, doubling the scope of the map until at last, when they reached this desolate place, the King instructed Kredak to stay behind and await his return. Plausible enough, but the tale was so bound up with theology that Ilina had never been sure where Harlith ended and Henred began. And only a deity *could* come back now, after so many silent centuries.

And even if he did, it would be too late for her.

No. She shook herself and snatched at her cloak, quaking in the bitter cold. Her shadow wavered. *No, there is still time. I will not desert my post—not until the final moment. I am the rock that weathers the wind and the waves. I will remain though all else flee away. I will be faithful. I will be true. I will resist all change.*

I am the Lightkeeper.

With a final haunted glance at her shadow on the stone, Ilina staggered down the tower's steps and left the Beacon behind.

She paused a moment in the chilly corridor. The darkness seemed to drift and swirl beyond the glow of her lamp. From farther still a dull roar throbbed. Blindly she peered through the open door of Seascape Study, cupping the lamp's flame with her left hand to stifle its shortsighted vanity. Her eyes, still infected by light, saw nothing. She craned forward, brows knit. It was like leaning into a void.

"Strange," she whispered. The word was barely audible. She knelt on the flagstones, set the lamp down by the doorway, and pulled a small red book from under her arm. Its cloth cover was crumbling. Placing it reverently beside the lamp, she rose, faced the void again, and stepped from her pool of sight.

Instantly her senses failed. Well, just her vision, really. It was shameful how helpless she became when bereft of her eyes. She stood still, waiting for them to adjust, breaking into a cold sweat when they didn't. Something was wrong. This darkness was too deep, too thick. The Beacon should have relieved it.

She groped her way forward, arms extended, until she touched an edge of the great stone hearth. Slowly she rounded the edifice, the fingers of her left hand running along its swells. The stones were cold and slightly damp: it had been far too long since fire had dried them.

At last, she put the hearth behind her. The Window of the North arched high overhead. Rain pelted furiously against the glass. A faint blue light diffused itself through the thousand rivulets struggling over the window's wrought-iron mesh, lending tinted outline to half-shapes of furniture. Outside, churning waves glinted in the Beacon's radiance.

A tremulous exhalation betrayed Ilina's relief. This was better by far. But never before had she seen the sky so dark during daytime. The sun wouldn't set for another hour, yet she could barely perceive the hand before her face. And here she stood in perfect calm, sheltered from the elements. What of mariners foolish enough to brave such a storm? What if some poor soul *was* out there, somewhere, running adrift before ravening winds? Sudden pity smote her heart.

"Harlith be merciful," she breathed. "Play with thy vassals, use them for thy sport, yet spare them in the end. O be thou not cruel, be not angry with the helpless, but, as thy breath bears the sweet rains from lands beyond the north, bear up those who dare traverse thy trackless plains. Deliver them from certain death. Harlith be merciful."

Her recitation finished; Ilina turned to go. A blink of pure white arrested her focus and she spun back, retinas seared by the brief visual memory. The sky seemed even darker than before. Would the gale god restrain his fury? She waited a breathless moment. From far across the heaving deep his growl of menace rumbled.

A SEA SOUGHT IN SONG

Ilina moved to the window, tugging her shawl tightly about her shoulders. Dim luminance flickered over her upturned face. She leaned forward, jawline jutting from a cascade of auburn hair, until her breath clouded on the glass. She lifted a fringe of her shawl to clear it away.

In that instant, far out at sea, streaks of light split the sky like rain.

For a long time, Ilina stood before the window, gazing out at a sky which seemed to be splitting apart at the seams—stretching and groaning as the brilliant white light of heaven bled through each fleeting fissure. She smiled at her metaphor, but it was a tense smile. Harlith's play was violent enough to make her worry.

Of course, there were those who praised his storms as a necessary defense against the rising of Noghli, Dark Lord of the Deep, but to Ilina that had always seemed a poor rationale. Was it not the wind which whipped the waves, rather than the reverse? Would not the sea lie placid without Harlith's provocation? And what would transpire were he to grow truly enraged? The wind, unlike the waves, was not constrained by immobile bounds. Of course, there were stories—legends of chaos and terror, of the sea overspilling its borders—but those were from so long ago …

So, Ilina stood and watched the storm, her internal clock forgotten, its silent chimes ignored.

The cormorants on Horwell Face will be laying soon … Oh, I hope this wanton display doesn't delay them … If only I could talk to Harlith … really talk to him … calm him, make him care, the monster … But he can't care. No one cares. Why should they? I'm just one woman … Oh, but an omelet would be so delicious … It would require the last of the onion, though … If only the blight hadn't come … Why'd I have to drag Rikard through the hothouse, anyway? He brought it in with him, I know he did … Just another indiscretion for which I'll have to pay … I'll need more flour than I thought I would … and mutton, and cream, and oil, and wool, and … and a decent gown. As long as I'm going to go through with this whole thing I might as well do it right …

Just look at this, though. It's so beautiful … Beauty born of anger … How can it be …?

It was late by the time she stirred. The lightning show was over. Harlith's passions were spent. Heaven and Arlam were both still intact and the rainless wind sighed gusts of relief. It was time for bed.

41

AUSTIN GUNDERSON

She turned to go. In the corridor her lamp was burning low. Tucking the book under her arm once more and shutting the heavy door, she moved down the hallway, holding the light aloft.

Halfway up the stairs to her room she paused mid-stride, jerking her head up. *"Aei!"* she blurted. "Father! How could I forget you?"

Instantly she spun, descending the steps in a flurry of footwork. What was *wrong* with her? She *always* looked in on Father before retiring for the night. He would be so worried! Her dying light bobbed crazily as she flung it around for balance. The cavernous masonry blushed a soft gray as its joints and minute surface aberrations were plucked abruptly from the black, before being released just as abruptly into nothingness as Ilina hurried on.

She had reached the arterial corridor and was trotting around its lengthy circuit when she heard the noise. Her breath, already coming in light pants, caught in her throat. Something was pounding, thumping, hammering with a frantic will.

Something outside the front door.

Chapter Four
SUBZERO MUNCHKIN LAND

When the massive door at last eased open, Hugh Conrad was just about ready to break it down himself. His leg hurt like hell and he could feel—or, rather, couldn't feel—hypothermia's slow, painless embrace. The storm might've passed, but beneath the walls of this citadel the night was as black as a pit.

Exhausted from hauling eighty pounds' worth of gear and a hundred-twenty pounds' worth of man through surf which had no good excuse not to have frozen solid, over fields of rock as jagged as a shark's maw, and up black bluffs coated with a particularly lubricant variety of algae, Hugh was in no mood to wait. He struck the door with the heel of his bloodied fist one last time and turned around to glare at the starless sky. The wind howled like a living thing—a thing in pain. He knew how it must feel.

He turned back, gritting his teeth, and there she was.

Hugh flinched: he hadn't heard the door unfasten. But now it was ever so slightly ajar, and the timid glow of an oil lamp illuminated a wide-eyed young woman whose ruddy hair framed a pale, anxious face. Hugh stepped back involuntarily. He hadn't expected *this*.

The girl opened her mouth as if to speak, then said nothing. Hugh began shivering again and hugged himself tightly. With a shock he realized he was staring. "Um," he sputtered, "c-c-can we come in? We've b-been out here qu-qu-quite a while now …"

The girl found her voice. "*Mol sehin rin?*" With eyes riveted on Hugh's pain-pinched face, she inched the door back and gestured hesitantly toward the blackness inside.

Hugh groaned. "Does no one in this g-g-godforsaken world speak English? Yes, we would like to come in, *please!*"

The girl jumped at his outburst, but didn't shut the door. She seemed instead to realize that, what with her being inside and him being outside, the advantage was all hers. Straightening to her full height, which wasn't all that high, she shouldered back the door and held up the lamp. Her eyes flicked to either side before fastening once more on Hugh. She looked him up and down, then touched her chin to her chest. "*Rin*," she said, looking up and flashing a wary smile. "*Hi wheim Cul Kredakt grath, hat whein Harlithers rhau larlunle, larinle!*" She beckoned him inside.

"Great," Hugh grunted. "Finally." He stooped to lift the unconscious body he'd laid out behind him on the steps. The girl shrieked, dropped her lamp, and leapt back, slamming the door.

Hugh stood slowly, letting the body's dead weight flop back down against the flagstones. His blank stare wandered aimlessly before returning to the iron-ribbed door set well back within the huge stone arch. His voice crawled from bloodless lips. "U-u-un ... b-be ... lievable."

On the threshold, the girl's abandoned lamp winked out.

Ilina stumbled back from the door and stood perfectly still, arms rigid at her sides. Her flaring eyes tried to focus in the darkness, but to no avail. Her chest rose and fell rapidly. Her breath, invisible, clouded in the frigid air. Who was this man? Whence had he sprung? What did he want?

Come on, you fool, prime the light! You can't just stand here—do something! But what could she do? Where could she go? If she'd had a plan for nocturnal hospitality, it was now forgotten. She rarely received guests, and never without notice, especially not at night. Ships avoided this place, and the Beacon *prevented* shipwrecks.

She glanced right and left without any particular purpose, swept the hair back from her forehead, and retreated a few more steps, eyes fixed upon a door she couldn't see. The vestibule's inner door bumped into her from behind, and she spun to flee back through it.

You idiot! What do you think you're doing? That man could be hurt! How can you shut the door? How can you keep him out? How can you ...? Ilina shook her head violently. She couldn't let him in—not before she knew who he was. And whence came that body. From the darkness behind came the sharp echoing crack of renewed blows upon the door she had deserted.

Think! This is what you feared, is it not? The onslaught. It's because you were seen! You peered to closely, and now they've come for you!

Ilina caught a doorjamb and swung to a stop. *No, 'Lina. You can think better than that. This is just one man driven to you by the storm. He cannot penetrate the door. And when the Tunnoltans come, they won't need to knock.* She deliberately slowed her breathing, slumping against the doorjamb.

Even so ... Even so, there was no telling what manner of evil even one man might do. Unarmed, she couldn't afford to grant him entrance. Not now that Father was ... indisposed. She needed a defense, a weapon. *But what, but what?* She had *planned* for this eventuality, hadn't she? Yes. She had

A SEA SOUGHT IN SONG

known what she would do. *Why can't you remember? Think!* She pounded her fist against the wall at her back and was answered by further thumps upon the front door.

The crossbow! Yes, the one in Father's room. He keeps it there, in that chest of his. Her memory restored, Ilina shoved off the doorjamb and leapt up the stone staircase beyond. She pelted down a hallway and past an engraved door with a brass lock, bursting into her own bedroom two doors down. Her shutters stood wide open to the moonlight. Yanking open the bottom drawer of an ornate cabinet, she slipped her hand beneath a stack of folded linen, snatching up a large key. Then it was back to the brass-locked door.

But just as she was about to twist the key in the lock, her fingers froze. A whimper, nearly inaudible, escaped her lips. *What am I doing? How can I enter here? It's disrespectful. He's not ...* An acute pain occluded her eyes. Her hand drew back.

After a terrified pause she exhaled at last in a long, haggard shudder that bled her of vitality. Her eyes went out of focus. *Just make it quick. He'll understand.* She turned the key.

###

Hugh grunted as his hatchet glanced off an iron rib, scattering sparks into a suddenly paler darkness. The wind was coursing—a cold dry wind, still flowing from the north—but it wasn't nearly as strong here as at higher altitudes. The storm pall—once immense, impenetrable—was dissolving in tatters, swept away beyond a peak rising like a squat steeple to the south. A crescent moon lurked behind sliding black strata—now glimmering faintly, now gleaming like a scythe. Farther up and to the left a second silver arc, far larger than the first, sliced briefly through a dense cloudbank, leering from a tilted angle before the darkness swallowed it once more.

Hugh turned back to the task at hand, his movements sluggish and stiff. *What a nightmare this is,* he thought. *Everyone here's half my height, but their doors are giant, blast-resistant bulwarks.*

Someone had expended great pains to ensure this industrial-grade ingress would be an almighty pain to anyone trying to survive a night in subzero munchkin land. It had taken all his strength just to accrue a small mound of splinters. The oak was as hard as stone and probably even watertight, although the door burrowed deep in the lee of the tower—away from rain and blossoming surf. Hugh kept swinging but his hopes of warmth were

45

dying out. Any fire he managed to start wouldn't last more than a few minutes.

But maybe a few minutes would be all he'd have use for. Any moment now the Damsel of Distress would reappear, undoubtedly accompanied by yet another horde of spear-happy savages, and then a fire would be irrelevant either one way or the other. *Maybe they'll spare this poor sap, though.* He glanced at his unconscious companion, then staggered over and prodded him with the toe of his boot. The body didn't move.

Hugh squatted down, jamming two fingers against the man's left carotid; the man was still warm to the touch. "Huh," muttered Hugh as he straightened. "The g-g-guy doesn't even need a f-fire. Must be c-c-covered in b-blubber. F-f-figures."

At least the activity had kept Hugh's blood from coagulating. He crouched over his little tinder-pile, shielding it from the wind, and fished a canister out of the pack which lay beside him on the porch. His fingers were numb and clumsy and it took him a while just to unscrew the lid. When he finally got it open he tried to empty the contents into his palm, but he was shaking so violently he spilled all twenty matches into the tinder.

"Damn!" he spat under his breath—then: "Oh, w-well." Plucking a match off the flagstone, he struck it against the canister. It burst to life at once. Hugh grinned and eased it into his tinder, cupping it with his hands, blowing ever so slightly, maneuvering the dry splinters in precisely-fluctuating formations. For a fleeting instant the flame withered, but then it caught and spread and the other matches flashed one after another and the sweet, golden, liquid fire exploded, engulfing the splinter-heap, and Hugh could feel the heat of its burning. He leapt up, laughing, and charged the oaken door. The hatchet-edge bit deeply and he wrenched it out as wood-chips spun past his head.

Back he rushed to the little fire. In his absence it had shrunk to embers, but now he arranged new wood around the glowing splinters, cupping and cradling and blowing hard so the curling strips flared anew and licked the larger chunks with their shivering energy. Black splotches grew on smooth oak and then there was new flame and thin tendrils of smoke spiraled into Hugh's face before the wind blasted them away. He cackled like a boy who'd filled his kid brother's toy truck with nitro and dropped it down a dry well. The obstacle to warmth had become its source. *No way am I gonna freeze to death tonight.*

"*Lai!* Lai!"

A SEA SOUGHT IN SONG

Startled by the ringing yell, Hugh jumped and spun, instinctively scrambling back from his nascent fire to melt into the darkness. His right hand jerked toward the rifle-butt protruding over his shoulder, but he caught himself and forced his hand back down.

His eyes raked the hulking stone fortress that loomed above him on three sides. A penumbra of light arced above its gables, the mist-refracted radiance of the high beacon now blocked from view. The shout had come from up there … somewhere … but the moons were once more occluded, the recessed windows lost in shadow. He could see nothing.

A shrill scream rent the sighing night. "Aei! *Whem haut seh, seh taek? Whet met seh lo teht oams ta?* Whet?"

Hugh crouched in darkness at the foot of the broad porch steps. The voice echoed between the citadel's spreading wings, ricocheting from wall to wall, converging from everywhere at once. The girl's voice. In vain he scanned for movement, for something. But what light there was waned fast. Mournfully he watched as his little fire, now exposed to the wind, vanished in a spurt of smoke. His eyebrows sagged. Nothing for it but to try again.

"Look, just calm down, alright?" he shouted. "I'm r-r-right here. Sorry about your d-door, Miss, but it's kinda cold out here, you know? N-n-now would you please just let us in?"

The wind whistled mournfully. No answer rang from above. Hugh waited, still and silent, until his falling core temperature impelled him to stir. He advanced back up the steps. One moon slipped from behind its black veil, casting thin white light over the blank stone faces pocked with paned eyes in sunken sockets. The girl leaned from none of them. No movement caught Hugh's eye. Nothing. He bared his teeth in a private grimace.

A grinding sound crawled from the door and a glowing vertical seam split its black outline. Hugh stared, one eyebrow cocked, as the portal opened. There she was, the same as before. Except now, in addition to a fresh lamp, she carried a huge winch crossbow. Hugh took a step back, spreading his hands.

"*Resh ut.*" Her voice was clear, if a little loud—the words bitten off sharply. Hugh froze in place. *Just a few more minutes of this*, he thought, *and I really* will *freeze in place.*

The girl seemed to be about to speak again, but then shut her mouth and shook her head. Cautiously, she glided from doorway to porch—her eyes and the bolt of her bow never wavering from Hugh's half-amused, half-alarmed face, her movements graceful and deliberate. *And very slow*, he saw. *That thing's heavy, and she doesn't want to show it.* But there was no need for show: a twitch of her finger would be all it'd take to nullify his relative strength. She paused a moment to glance sideways at the defaced door and when her eyes snapped back to Hugh's they burned with a rage so pure it took his breath.

She reached the unconscious Eskimo—Hugh realized as if for the first time that he didn't know the man's name—and knelt down to place a hand upon his brow before checking his pulse just as Hugh had done. The crossbow never wavered from its target.

Hugh ignored it. He stood watching the girl, instinctual shock giving way to fascination and a dull sense of unease. She obviously belonged to a culture thoroughly distinct from that of the arctic mariners he'd been bullying for the past week. For one thing, nomadic hunter-gatherers had neither the means nor the motive to construct a fortress of this magnitude. For another, the girl seemed accustomed to the small luxuries afforded by an affluent society. Her face was clean, her hair brushed, her clothes pressed. And she carried herself with that unmistakable air of taut authority endemic to royal courts the world over. He'd not expected to meet her like.

You're in over your head, man. You don't know what *to expect. For all* you *know,* all *the women in Arlam look this good.* With a start he wiped the goofy grin from his face. *Must be the hypothermia.* He was shaking so badly it was getting difficult for him to hold his head up straight.

The girl stood. Hugh noted the unconscious fluidity of her movement. He also noted the ivory embroidering with which her jade-green, calf-length dress was trimmed—especially about the collar, from which radiated interlacing knots of thread to spiral over her breasts and spill down her full-length sleeves. He couldn't remember what her back looked like; he'd have to pay better attention. She wore thick stockings and flat shoes without laces. Her auburn hair fell past her shoulders, framing a face as fair as the moons.

Hugh looked into her eyes and thought her beautiful—the most beautiful girl he'd met since Reykjavik. *And that was a long time ago. Far, far too long.*

She stared back for a long moment. Abruptly, as though she'd made a decision, she sighed, lowered the crossbow, and jerked her head toward the prone body. Then she turned and strode back inside, leaving the door open behind her.

Hugh hesitated—his numb mind encumbered by a contemplation of her dress-back—then sprang into belated action. Shouldering the body, he staggered across the porch and over the threshold.

A SEA SOUGHT IN SONG

As Hugh vanished inside, the doorway's square of light narrowed to a glowing vertical seam, then snapped out. High in the hurrying sky the dwarf moon slowly interposed itself between its larger companion and the island rearing from the sea far below. The surf's boom and the wind's howl died away into uneasy silence. Concentric crescents shone over shadow-swathed Arlam: an unblinking eye sunk in the sable heavens.

As Hugh dropped the door's crossbar into place, the girl stopped and turned. She stood framed by a long stone corridor—crossbow lowered; lamp raised to dust the walls with a grainy sheen. The blackness beyond her was bordered by a second set of double doors. She sidestepped and craned her neck—looking past Hugh to appraise the door he'd shut—then backed into the room beyond, beckoning him with a jerk of her head.

Hugh hefted the unconscious man onto his shoulders and lurched toward the lamplight ahead. *Damn, this place is secure.* Entering the second door, he hurried past an intersecting corridor—*anything could be hiding down there*—and emerged through a third doorway into a vast chamber made even more spacious by shadow. Its ceiling, if it had one, was lost in darkness far above. A narrow stair spiraled up the cylindrical wall. About twenty feet up there hung a fluted ivory chandelier, its great splay suspended by cables anchored to the wall like spokes. A central cable, thick as a hawser, vanished in its ascent toward an invisible zenith.

The air wasn't noticeably warmer in here than it'd been outside. Hugh's breath emerged as a cloud. He held it, allowing his vision to clear. There was something odd about that chandelier. *What the hell ...?*

The senseless Eskimo slipped from his back to the polished stone floor with an echoing thud. Hugh stood, hands hanging limply, mouth agape. There were tusks radiating from the central ring of candle-basins. Impossibly massive they seemed. Some diverged or merged, some swept up in thirty-foot curves, some were scalloped or dimpled or pleated, some were branched like ... *like coral fronds ... or antlers* ... A chill slithered down Hugh's spine.

On the floor directly beneath this trophy-crown there was a circular table broad enough to seat at least fifty people along its circumference. *But King Arthur's asleep and Camelot's deserted, with only a girl left to guard the gate.* By the time Hugh's gaze at last returned to said girl, she'd lit two of the candles scattered about the tabletop in ceramic stands. The chamber brightened. Ivory flushed overhead and bizarre shadows swayed upon the walls. The girl turned, fixed Hugh with a disapproving stare, and then pulled out a straight-backed chair.

Ah, hospitality. Does this come with a home-cooked meal? Hugh smiled, then frowned. *I suppose I should have the Eskimo seen to first.* He gestured back toward the body on the floor.

"*Lesh!*" The girl's sharp command rang in the hollow hall. She struck the chair-back with the heel of her hand. Hugh blinked, then shrugged. *Fine—he's your problem now.* He moved forward, shucking off his haversack, and flopped into the chair as the girl backed away and circled around him toward the body.

"So is this your p-p-place, or are you just the night shift?" he asked, tapping a finger on the tabletop and cocking an ear at the resultant echoes. The girl, busy feeling the Eskimo's brow, didn't respond.

"Hey, Miss! I'm a stranger here. You mind t-t-telling me where we are? Is this ... uh, is this ..." Hugh looked at the chandelier, dredging his mind for the word. "Kra ... uh, Kram ..."

The girl looked up, her glare sharp. Hugh noticed and raised his eyebrows. "Oh, so you *d-do* know that name? Is that w-where we are? Kramarak?"

The girl, apparently satisfied with her cursory examination, rose to her feet and strode from the room without a backward glance. Hugh rolled his eyes. "Women," he muttered. Then: "Hey, you got any f-f-food in this place?"

###

When Ilina returned with bread and cheese, the man was sound asleep. In silence she stared at him for several minutes. At his brown, calf-length coat, torn and tattered and stained with algae. At his black boots crisscrossed with strings. At the scabbards strapped to his back—one sprouting a kind of sculpted wedge, the other suspiciously empty. At his brown hat, dimpled on top and circled by a narrow brim. She considered his visage: clean-shaven, weather-beaten, marred on the left by a broad scar that swept from cheekbone to chin. It was a man's face: ineffectively inscrutable. Inscrutable because it shed emotion like a tern's plumage shed water. Ineffective because such barriers would never fool her again.

A SEA SOUGHT IN SONG

Even had she known his language, Ilina doubted she could've learned more from him than he'd already conveyed. He was brash, powerful, and blissfully ignorant. Granted, mere ignorance didn't constitute a fault—but this sort of man had no regard for anything that existed outside his own head. *And that's why he's dangerous. He won't care a whit about me, but he'll certainly figure out how I can serve him. Like the Old Enemy in the south distributing gifts to bind others to his will.* How'd the song go, again? As a child she'd heard it sung.

> *A helm for hapless Helmut lent,*
> *So he shan't see what's coming.*
> *A cuirass to fay Filmin sent;*
> *'Twill be his heart's undoing.*
> *A vambrace as a Virgrad grant*
> *Shall seize his arm for keeping.*
> *All gifts from Omri's coffer spent*
> *Return to him a-reaping.*

She shuddered, snapping out of her reverie, and circled the table slowly—not assuming for an instant the man wasn't feigning sleep to lure her within reach. *But now you're just being foolish. He's far bigger than you—you took the greatest risk when you let him in the door.* Setting the food on the table, she shrugged out of the crossbow's shoulder-sling and moved across the room to the towering hearth.

Abruptly she glanced back; the man hadn't moved.

A large iron basket beside the hearth held firewood neatly stacked. Kneeling, she set the crossbow aside and began arranging lengths of kindling one at a time on the cold hearth-floor. Then she took flint and steel and struck flame. She rose, crossed swiftly to the poor prostrate Jaar, bent to gather the scruff of his parka in her fists, and strained to drag him toward the hearth. The thin strips of ivory woven into his clothing screeched as they slid along polished stone.

Upon reaching the hearth Ilina collapsed beside the Jaar, exhaling heavily. She leaned back—propping herself up with her arms, basking in the warmth. She smiled.

And then she knew the man was close at hand.

For an instant she just sat there, paralyzed, heart hammering like a gull cracking open a clam. Then she remembered the crossbow and lunged for it without conscious intent. The Jaar proved an obstacle. A small cry slipped from her lips as she sprawled over the body, but then she was up again, scrambling away, snatching the weapon, spinning to face the threat.

The man just squatted there, watching her, his face inscrutable. *As if it could be otherwise.*

Ilina's heart rate gradually subsided. Her breathing slowed. But even so, she couldn't bring herself to move. She crouched absolutely still on the slowly warming stone—one leg doubled beneath her, the other flung out to the side. Terror glazed her eyes and beat upon her brain.

Eventually the man spread his empty hands, smiled gently, and looked away, into the fire. He sat back, crossed his legs, and didn't glance at her again.

Ilina's shock gave way to sudden weakness. Her hands shook and the crossbow wavered. *What do I do, what do I do? Harlith help me! Clear my mind!* The man sat motionless, his profile bright against surrounding shadow. Ilina's mind screamed that this dispassion was merely a ruse to dull her senses, that no man revealed his true intent, that she could not for one instant afford to lower her guard.

And yet ... the solitude. It really is *a cold, pitiless presence in this place.*

With a start, Ilina realized she wanted company. The desire smote her heavily. Repressed loneliness spurted suddenly from a pinhole in the mental dike she'd built against emotion. For a full minute she struggled wordlessly. *He may kill me! Is it worth the risk?*

In answer, the crossbow sagged to the floor and the dike began to crumble. A longing for companionship, pitiful and desperate, flooded her soul. She didn't need much; just a look, a word. *I shall not fear. I must risk. I must face change, else I am undone.*

Ilina woke from the panic. She folded her legs, smoothed her dress, and turned toward the fire again, drawing a deep breath. "I'm sorry," she murmured. "I'm not much of a hostess, am I? Forgive me." She glanced at him sheepishly, catching his eyes. He smiled again.

"*Tehin sehim ut mol lo gurt,*" he said. "*Tehin yir lundrinte.*"

The corners of her mouth edged upward. The man's speech was gibberish—a language she'd never before heard—but his voice didn't seem hostile. She relaxed. *Introductions, then.*

"I would ask you for your name, and your purpose in coming," she said, shivering a little from the temperature transition, "and for *his* name and the story of his troubles," she nodded toward the Jaar, "but I do not recognize your tongue. Harlith must have driven you far. I'm Ilina, by the way. Ilina Lightkeeper."

A SEA SOUGHT IN SONG

The man gave her a blank look and shrugged.

"Ilina," she said, touching her chest. "Ilina. My name is Ilina."

The man leaned toward her, cocking an eyebrow. *"Elena ...?"*

"No. Ilina," she enunciated, emphasizing the long vowel. "Ih-*lee*-na."

He sat back and smirked. *"Elena. Tehr keem Hugh yir. Hugh,"* he said, touching the brim of his hat. *"Tehr keem Hugh yir."*

Ilina smiled. "Hoo," she repeated. It was an odd name, but there was no accounting for foreign taste. "It is good to make your acquaintance, Hoo, even if you did deface the door of my ..." she stopped speaking to stare at Hoo, who looked as though he'd just swallowed a buoy fly. His eyes and mouth scrunched and his brows slanted askew as staccato exhalations puffed from his nostrils. Unnerved, Ilina didn't know whether to back away or peer closer. He seemed to be laughing. After a moment he regained control. He looked across at her, eyebrows raised.

"Hugh," he inflected the word like a plea. *"Tehr keem Hugh yir. Hugh."*

"Yes," Ilina nodded in agreement. "Your name is Hoo." *Be gracious, 'Lina—he may be slow of mind.*

Hoo gave a deep sigh and adopted an incredibly patient expression. His gaze wandered back to the crackling fire, then swung toward her as she half-rose to lean over the Jaar's body between them. Ilina froze.

Hoo proffered his right hand and she jerked back, flicking a glare from his hand to his face and back again. *What's this? A warning? Did I frighten him?*

Seemingly caught off guard by her unease, Hoo pulled back and spread his hands in a calming gesture. Ilina relaxed. After a moment she determined to try again. She leaned forward—lowering her head and watching Hoo from under her eyebrows' dark commas. A spasm of alarm crossed his face.

Ilina rolled her eyes. *Barbarians. No manners at all.* Swallowing, she reached hesitantly for Hoo's left shoulder. Her fingers curled around its tight knot of muscle and she knew he could feel her tremble. *Better be quick.* His right hand was rising to remove her grip.

Ilina yanked Hoo's forehead down against her own—*crack!* She released him and slumped back, breathless as though from exertion. Hoo blinked, rubbing his temple, then smiled and began to chuckle through his nose. The chuckle spread to his throat.

"There," grinned Ilina. "Now you know how to say hello." She'd tugged with more force than she intended, and now her head throbbed. Hoo had a brow like a rock.

AUSTIN GUNDERSON

The two strangers shared a look in silence, amused and intrigued yet wary still, silhouetted against crackling flame.

And, with a sudden yell, the Jaar sat up between them. His cry cut off as Hoo punched him in the face.

Chapter Five
FREEDOM

22 November, 1951

Light spilled from the half-open doorway, leaking around Hugh's imposing silhouette to wash over the sloping hillside short of a low stone wall. With a sigh Hugh propped his weight against the doorjamb, fishing a cigarette from his shirt-pocket. The flash of his lighter did nothing to dispel the dark.

He remembered how that low wall had looked the last time he'd been here: abloom in dusty green ivy, speckled crimson with honeysuckle bugles like a besieged battlement in disarray. Now only lichens, gray and white, lent color to the weathered stones and their chafing woody veins. But that was during the day, when the bleak autumn sun burned halfheartedly in a sky groggy with haze. At night, in darkness, the wall seemed the boundary of some half-perceived oblivion.

Crockery clattered in the kitchen. Hugh started at a particularly loud clink, then smiled a thin little smile. Joan must've discovered another incongruity in father's collection today. She'd been driven nearly mad already, the poor woman—cataloging artifacts coveted by museums the world over yet, in this house, accorded value based on function alone. The smile broadened as Hugh thought of his father swigging milk from the royal goblet of Tuhemetet while perusing the ham radio over breakfast.

It had been five months now since that night when, in the mud-strewn lobby of a two-bit Bangalore hotel, as a weak bulb flickered behind a calico shade and the monsoon thundered in the street, Hugh had picked up the phone and felt his life capsize. The voice on the other end, tinny though it was, had wrenched him back to childhood. His father was alive.

Twenty-four years of silence had seemed final, and more than final—long enough for the pain to flare and wane, for the fallout to touch down and dissipate. Only those willing to accept it had survived. But time didn't heal wounds so much as it anesthetized them. Upon hearing that eerily-recognizable voice over the phone, Hugh's emotional morphine had run out. The following morning he'd bailed on Smith and hopped a plane. He had so many questions. *Where'd you go? Why'd you leave? Was it something I said, something I did? What about Mother? Did you really hate us that much?*

Five months later, his questions remained unanswered.

Hugh's thin smile shriveled. In agreeing to meet with his father on the other man's terms, he'd implicitly accepted a charade. Everything about this situation was surreal. Returning from India, he'd found his old man ensconced in the family estate as though no time had passed since his disappearance. The lawns were trimmed, the rooms clean, and the man himself attended by a brisk, middle-aged woman who spoke with an odd accent and seemed vaguely Asian. Was she a servant, a friend, a mistress? The relationship was unclear. But as out-of-place as Joan appeared, she didn't defy feasibility. It was Hugh's father who broke that spell.

Henry Conrad's face had aged without decay. It wasn't *old* so much as *used*, like an iron mask left out to endure the beating of sun and wind and rain. His body, though still strong, was stooped. His eyes, though still fierce, were blind.

Hugh's demand for an explanation had been waved off with an all-too-familiar evasiveness. Funny, how time's opiate had gentled Hugh's memories: he'd nearly forgotten how infuriatingly cryptic the old man could be. But the gentling process *had* accentuated Henry's good features, and, after a quarter-century, the old irritants now seemed less important than ever. The past wasn't worth the sacrifice of the present.

So to avert the kind of explosion with which his late mother would've reacted to the runaround, Hugh had decided to play along. Henry had, so he claimed, turned some kind of corner in his life—gotten out of some kind of trouble—and now he wished to get reacquainted with his son. Fine. Hugh would visit him between jobs, and make small talk, and help out around the house, and even show up for Thanksgiving dinner.

But sooner or later the old man would have to come clean.

A cold wind was coming through the birch copse away across the hill. Hugh could hear the leaves shifting, thousands of them, until the sound of their unease swelled in his mind to a hissing scream. His gaze refocused, sliding up from the lawn of scattered light, up over the rumpled wall, out into a void of pure night. A chill crawled down his spine.

Something wasn't right.

Hugh tensed, shoving away from the doorjamb, letting his cigarette stub fall dead upon the stones. He took three steps from the threshold to the grass below, eyes fixed on some indefinite point, then stopped. His thin shadow stretched over the lawn, melding with the greater darkness at the shoulders as though decapitated. The nacre inlay of the switchblade in his pants' pocket felt cold to his closing fingers. Anxiety like this was childish, he told himself. *There's no one out there. Just empty fields for miles and miles ...*

Hugh walked across the lawn to the wall. His knees were bent, his steps slow. A fear had been growing in the pit of his stomach since he'd touched down in LaGuardia the day before. There was so much here he didn't understand, and ignorance was a deadly condition. He didn't know what he didn't know. Twenty-four years was more than enough time for anyone to accrue an entire constellation of enemies—and for a man like Henry Conrad, such an accrual was almost assured. And there was nothing quite like a voracious enemy to drive a man back into the presumed security of a former life.

Hugh strained to descry the shape of the darkness. His father may have thought to sequester the past, but Hugh knew better. The past had a way of recurring no matter how deeply it'd been buried. Hadn't he himself just experienced this? Whatever it was that his father had fled, Hugh couldn't afford to presume it was dead. He had to know what he was dealing with here. He had to know the truth.

Something moved beyond the wall. Hugh sensed rather than saw it and froze in place. The light was behind him, his instinct shouted. It would give him away. He had to escape its path.

And suddenly the light was gone, occluded. "Where are you, Hugh?" asked a voice as deep and warm as an English horn.

"I ... I'm ..." he couldn't feel the something anymore. "I'm here, Father."

"Why are you sneaking around in the dark?"

"Oh, um ... I thought I saw something."

Henry Conrad hobbled down the steps to the lawn, the *tok tok tok* of his cane upon the stone a feeble yet strangely comforting sound. He stopped in the middle of the lawn, cocked an ear, and stood a moment in silence, neither smiling nor frowning. At last he shook his head, extending a gnarled hand toward Hugh. "Come inside," he said. "Here there is nothing to fear."

Hugh glanced once more over his shoulder, then took his father's hand. "I don't suppose you've saved me any cranberry tart?" he asked.

Warm amber light enveloped Hugh as he stepped back through the kitchen door. Joan—forearms white with soap froth—glanced up absently from the sink. A swath of gray hair splashed across her creased forehead. Noticing the crease and feeling unsettlingly useless after his bout of paranoia, Hugh moved over to dry the plates and bowls stacked on the dish rack. Joan smiled.

Henry stood facing the rectangle of blackness which was the doorway, then nudged it closed with his cane and slid the bolt home. He turned and beckoned with a hand. "Leave the suds, you two. Joan, where's that pie I've been smelling all day?"

"Cooling in the shed, Mr. Conrad. I'll only be a minute." Wiping her arms on her green apron, she brushed past the two men, shoving open the bolt and vanishing outside.

Hugh's fear returned in a rush and he almost leapt after the little woman, almost tried to stop her, but, catching a glimpse of Henry's face, stifled the impulse. Hugh's hand clenched the counter's edge, then slowly relaxed. He turned aside to lean over the sink toward the curtained kitchen window, eyes narrowing as though they could pierce the ivory-hued cloth and the sightless gloom which thickened beyond. He had to shake this skittishness.

They stood a moment in silence, father and son, and, as they stood, the short space between them morphed into an echoing void. At last Hugh— sickened by this and every impasse—turned back toward the door, opening his mouth to say something forgettable. Words failed to emerge.

Henry Conrad looked very, very old—like a man struggling just to remain alive. His hands shook as they clutched his cane. Before him, the half-open door was a portal to nothing. "Hugh," he whispered, eyes fixed outside, "I ... need your help."

Hugh's mouth was still open. It would neither shut nor speak. Whether reality itself had shifted or his eyes had just been opened to its true nature, he couldn't tell. He tried halfheartedly to swallow a premonition which screamed that something very important was happening, that the status quo was about to slide irreversibly toward the unknown. In his gut he knew this was the moment for which he'd waited so many bitter years. The moment of truth. Now that revelation was imminent, however, he felt timid and unsure—frightened by this sudden weakness in the strongest man he knew.

Henry turned blind eyes upon his son. "I have things I need to tell you ... things I should have told you ..." his voice broke. "I fear I have made a terrible mistake."

"Wha ... what are you talking about?" Hugh found himself adopting his father's whisper as though each swirling knot in the oak-paneled cabinets was a pricked ear, as though the cloudy sink water teemed with bubbly eyes. It seemed as though the dark doorway was sucking brightness from the room.

As Henry opened his mouth to speak, a figure materialized over the threshold. Hugh jumped, but it was only Joan, a pie balanced on each upturned palm. She shot Hugh a concerned look and brushed past the two men into the dining room.

Henry's mouth worked silently, as though his words—now that they'd formed in his mind—had to be restrained from escaping. Finally, he looked down and shook his head. "Later," he mouthed as he turned away to follow Joan. Hugh cursed under his breath, quickly shutting the kitchen door.

###

Tall candles flickered fitfully in ornate stands upon the dining table. Shadows pulsated along the walls, imbuing the ceremonial masks hung there with the illusion of shallow-breathing life. Henry sat hunched in his chair, absorbed with some trinket he'd pulled from a pocket of his knit sweater. It glinted dully through the chinks of his caressing fingers.

Hugh acknowledged Joan's proffered pie slice with an upward twitch of his lips, then lapsed back into a half-scowl. Henry had seemed strangely haunted since Hugh's arrival late last night, but this new edginess was contagious, exacerbating Hugh's own fragile mood. He gouged out a forkful of pie and lifted it to his mouth.

Henry's chair squealed against the floorboards as he lurched upright. "Let us pray," he said. The glinting trinket had vanished whence it came.

Hugh frowned. "We already said grace, remember?"

Father turned on son with a look of such wild desperation that Henry nearly dropped his fork. Across the table Joan half-rose, then sat back warily, her plate still empty. Hugh couldn't believe he was having difficulty holding the stare of a blind man. His eyes narrowed as he perceived the depth of pain in his father's milky orbs.

"*I* need to pray," rasped Henry at last. Hugh said nothing. His fork slowly descended to clink against his plate.

"Father," said Henry, shutting his eyes out of habit, "… Father."

Henry's pause lengthened until it seemed to Hugh that whole minutes had elapsed. He glanced over at Joan, who fidgeted with bowed head. Their eyes met over her glasses' rims and her gaze instantly flicked back down into her lap.

AUSTIN GUNDERSON

"Help us." The plea was barely audible, but it jerked Hugh's attention back toward his father, whose knobby chin was pressed against his chest. "We need you," he breathed. "I ... I need you. I am blind ... blind ... *blind*. Show me the way, Father. Please ..." Hugh had to strain to hear. "Please show me the way."

"Amen," finished Hugh when Henry failed to continue. He took a bite of pie and a swallow of port. Never mind if he couldn't seem to taste anything: he'd eat outside in the dark before he'd let this cryptic melodrama ruin his Thanksgiving dessert. Why solicit pity if you weren't willing to explain your troubles? Hugh snapped up another forkful of tasteless pie. His brows slid together. Joan slid a pie slice onto her plate, glanced from father to son, then followed Hugh's example. Henry remained standing; his eyes still squeezed shut. After a moment he sank back into his seat.

It was Joan who broke the silence. "Do you ... can I get you anything, Mr. Conrad?"

Henry forced a smile. "No ... no thank you, Joan. The pie is delicious." Hugh regarded his father's untouched plate and hiked a furrowed brow. Joan looked like she might leap up and flee at any moment. *Not that I'd blame her*, Hugh grimaced. With no small effort he dispelled some of his facial tension, even managing to conjure up that thin smile again. He would not be controlled by his father's eccentricity.

"So, Joan," Hugh began, "any luck yet with that fellow from Syracuse ... what was his name ...?"

"William died last month," she said expressionlessly.

He cringed. "Oh ... I ... I'm sorry to hear that ..."

"No matter." Joan shook her head as though to dislodge the memory. "Wasn't right for me, anyway. Too quiet." She lobbed a glance of pained affection at Henry, then set her fork down and fixed Hugh with a hard stare. "Which reminds me: you still haven't told us about this *job* you've been at since your last visit."

Hugh shrugged. "A dig in Bhutan with a man named Smith," he mumbled around a mouthful. "I'd rather not talk about it." *You're not the only ones who can be infuriatingly cryptic, you know.*

"Well, can you at least tell us if you found whatever it was you were looking for?"

A moment of silence. "No ... no luck."

A short exhalation of breath. "Well then, what was it that you didn't find?"

60

A SEA SOUGHT IN SONG

Hugh lifted his glass and peered into its ruby depths backlit by candle flame. His sham smile grew wistful. "Oh, nothing of importance ..."

Across the table, Henry had stopped chewing.

Joan rolled her eyes. "Well, then why did you—"

An explosion of sound cut her off mid-sentence—a thunderclap shriek-buzz that jolted Hugh out of his seat with knees bent and fists brandished. A thrill of adrenaline burst in his chest. For a brief instant, everything froze in detached focus. His chair clattered against the wall. A bloody pool of port was staining the tablecloth's embroidered heraldry beside his toppled glass. His heart labored, then sped. Time flooded back in to overtake him.

The alarm continued to screech twice per second without losing strength. Henry leapt to his feet, his face ashen. Joan froze, then popped from her chair like a cork from a bottle and scuttled out the door to the stairwell.

"Follow me." The sudden strength in Henry's voice belied his expression. He turned and strode from the room.

Hugh caught him at the back door. "Father, what is this? What's happening?"

Henry flung the door aside, nearly clipping Hugh in the face, as Joan rushed up behind. "It's too late, my son," he shouted, sounding almost relieved. "I've waited too long to tell you. Now you'll have to see." He vanished into the darkness.

Hugh caught Joan's elbow as she followed Henry outside. "What's going on?" he hissed, then, noticing the holster she was cinching about her waist beneath a long overcoat: "And wha ... what's ...?" With a hunted glance she shook him off and hurried out into the night.

"Damn," he spat. With a quick glance around the room, he slammed the door behind him.

Henry led them across the lawn, through the sheep gate in the old stone wall, and down the sloping hillside. The birch copse whispered fitfully on their left. Dry grasses neglected by the sheep whisked about their calves as they slipped through the field. Aside from the glimmering lights of a few scattered homesteads in the valley below, the darkness was complete. No moon warmed the unbroken pall of clouds. Henry flung each stride forward, nearly breaking into a run several times: a blind guide leading his people into blindness. The house alarm dwindled behind them until the only sounds were the seething wind and Henry counting steps under his breath.

Abruptly he halted and spread his arms, nearly poleaxing Joan. She recoiled and toppled back into the tall grass as Henry moved toward his left, swinging his outstretched arms. Hugh, trotting to catch up, tripped over Joan as she rose.

Henry interrupted his son's muffled curses: "Get up, get up! Look for the post."

Hugh tried to help Joan to her feet, but was swatted away. "What post?" he growled.

"The post—the wooden post! It's painted to look like a tree snag. Find it!"

The urgency in Henry's voice stifled Hugh's laughter at the absurdity of the situation. He peered into the blackness of the forest's fringe, craning his neck, straining to make out a stake camouflaged against just such an eventuality. Soon he was beating the brush like his father.

"Over here!" called Joan from higher up the slope. When they reached her she plunged into the trees beside a slanting stripe of shadow slightly taller than Hugh himself. Henry gasped with relief as he slid his hands along its knobby surface. "Must've gone farther than I thought," he muttered half-apologetically, then vanished.

The trail was little more than a deer-track winding through the wood. Hugh could see nothing. He crashed though the undergrowth, stumbling over jutting rocks and blundering into low-swept tree limbs. "Your pathfinding skills don't exactly inspire confidence!" he shouted.

No answer. Hugh paused. The murmur of brittle birch-leaves swelled around him. Somewhere, deep in the forest, a tree was groaning against the wind. "Father?"

"Follow the light ..." Henry's voice drifted back.

"What light? There is no li–" but even as he spoke, he saw a flickering pinprick of crimson and launched himself toward it, disregarding the trail. Dead branches crackled beneath his boots and live ones smacked against his upraised forearms. As he bludgeoned his way deeper into the wood's intricate tangles the red eye slowed its blinking until it burned steadily, spraying the surrounding trees with a thick carmine glow. Wind-harried leaves swirled through the rays radiating between vertical black streaks.

The red light was affixed atop a squat gray bunker in a small clearing. Concrete steps descended to a recessed doorway that yawned like an open tomb. Hugh took three steps down, then stumbled, pressing himself against the wall. He flinched at the hiss and zing of ordinance and tasted again the stench of spattered gore. For a full minute he crouched there in the quiet darkness, choking back his own bile. *Weakling!* he cursed. *It's a memory—it's done and gone. Get over it! Move on!* He smacked the concrete with the heel of his hand.

"Hugh?" his father's voice echoed from below. "Are you there, Hugh?" A metallic squeal; a flare of golden light.

"I'm here," he said. "What is this place?"

"Hurry, son. Please hurry."

Hugh lurched upright and plunged through the doorway. A spiral staircase dropped into the earth. He clattered down its steel steps toward the dim light far beneath his feet. Round and round and round he ran as though the shaft would never end. The source of light glimmered between the stair's spokes, dancing just out of unobstructed sight.

Finally, after what Hugh guessed was at least ten stories' worth of stairwell, his boots struck the concrete floor with a ringing *thunk*. A short, arched passage led to a blank wall illumined by the light of a lantern set to one side.

Henry and Joan flanked a giant hatch, through whose round central window filtered a bloody luminance. With their distended shadows curving across the ceiling arch above, the two looked like Joseph and Mary stooping over a red-haloed Baby Jesus in some bizarre nativity scene. Joan cocked her Colt .38, gripping it with both hands and adopting a shooting stance, tossing her head to clear her eyes of stray bangs. Her overcoat swept down from her shoulders in trapezoidal silhouette. Henry turned at his son's approach and hobbled away from the hatch.

"Hugh," he said, laying a hand on his arm, "you must listen to me carefully. No matter what comes through that door, know that it shouldn't harm you."

"Shouldn't harm me ... *shouldn't?* The hell's *that* supposed to mean?"

Henry clenched a fistful of Hugh's sleeve, pulling him down until their faces were inches apart. "What I mean is ... is ... is that it has no authority over you. It has no *business* harming you. That would be ... wrong."

"Wrong ...? Of *course* it'd be wrong! Father, this is *madness!* What's going on here?" Hugh made to remove his father's hand, but Henry tightened his grip, wrenching Hugh to his knees.

"I am sorry, Hugh," he said thickly. "It is my fault you do not understand. I have deprived you of the truth in the hope that you would be spared the pain I have suffered. I have been a fool. You've always deserved better than this. Forgive me," his voice quavered. "Please forgive me."

AUSTIN GUNDERSON

"Forgive *what?*" Hugh felt anger tightening his gut—anger he'd made a point to swallow long ago. His voice boomed in the concrete vault. "You think I didn't know you've been keeping secrets all this time? You think you can just disappear for twenty-four years and no one will notice? You think *Mother* didn't notice? If she were here, you think *she'd* forgive you? You've told me *nothing!*"

Henry stiffened at mention of his dead wife. His face, already pale, seemed to drain of all life. "I told you, Hugh," he croaked, "I can't tell you. You have to see for yourself."

Abruptly releasing Hugh's sleeve, Henry moved to the hatch. He felt for the depressurization wheel, drew a deep breath, and bent his back to crank it loose. Joan stepped back and leveled her weapon.

"Wait!" said Hugh. "Where's *my* gun?"

"Like I said," grunted Henry, "nothing here should harm you."

As his father leaned on the squealing wheel, Hugh finally registered the depth of insanity to which they'd all plummeted in the space of half an hour. A numbness cleared from his mind. His blind father was opening a locked portal in a secret bunker buried beneath thousands of tons of rock and concrete. Something here was wrong. Very, very wrong. He had to put a stop to it.

But even as Hugh scrambled to his feet the room resounded with an explosive *click*. The massive round door swung slowly inward, releasing dull red light which seemed to sap color rather than lend it. Joan dodged through the widening doorway—a brief black profile subsumed in ruddy haze. Henry followed.

Hugh hesitated the merest of instants.

A scream echoed from the red-lit chamber—a short, sharp cry like that of a swooping raptor. Joan.

Without another thought Hugh leapt through the hatch.

The room was small and square. Its bare concrete gleamed with the light of a single tinted lantern set into the ceiling. On the right hand and on the left hung two great mirrors: the former edged with scrimshawed ivory, the latter with spiraling gold. Beneath this golden mirror, Henry and Joan crouched over a crumpled object. A step closer and Hugh saw that the object was a body. A human body, barely. *Like the bodies at Buchenwald* ... Hugh's bile came rushing back. He had to turn away just to breathe.

Henry looked up. The furrows of his face had become rivulets for tears. His fingers brushed the body's bald scalp and sunken cheeks and cradled the sagging chin. "Why?" he wept. "Why, God?" Turning back to the heap of

A SEA SOUGHT IN SONG

skin-draped bones, Henry pleaded in a whisper pathetic for its hope. "Miles … Come back to me, Miles …"

Hugh's head snapped back around. His eyes went wide. "*Miles …?*"

No. No, it couldn't be. There was no resemblance. This man was old—old and broken. His left arm had been severed from his body at the shoulder. Not even a stump remained. Chains dangled from iron bands on his wrist and waist. Scars crisscrossed his bleach-white skin. Jutting bones deformed his shape. Hugh had seen Miles Cornwall just last year—at that function in London. He'd thumped the man's left arm in greeting. The war had aged Hugh's former comrade only one decade, not five. This *couldn't* be Miles.

Hugh's head was spinning. He struggled to move, then settled for simply standing up straight. His father had kept this man underground? Without food, without water? Without—Hugh glanced at the soiled loincloth—without clothing? For how long? Why? And who *was* this, anyway? Despite Hugh's denials, the man's face was growing disturbingly familiar. Rationalization was draining away before a desperate, droning desire: *this must be a dream … a nightmare … it can't be real …*

Sobs wrenched the slump of Henry's shoulders. "Miles … what have I done to you, Miles …?"

And then Hugh saw it at last. The face of his friend—drained of life, buried beneath the scars.

Something shifted in Hugh's psyche at this recognition—something tectonic. A discordant resonance pulsed, as it were, from bell towers in every hamlet of his mind, blending in the air as his interior landscape shuddered. The clangor rose in his ears like that of the breeze which foreruns a storm. Anger, pure and unqualified, geysered from his heart and surged through his arteries and spread up his capillaries like the ripples of an incoming tide felt deep within an estuary. And then, just as his fingers started twitching from the sound of it, a vast hush fell.

"Did you do this?"

Henry raised his eyes at his son's iron monotone. He opened his mouth, slowly, to reply—then choked; he could say nothing.

But it didn't matter. Hugh heard in his father's ravaged silence an answer which transcended conscious expression: a wave of grief so visceral it nearly forced him back a step. He would never ask again.

"Who *did* do this?"

Henry's mouth worked soundlessly. Hugh—strangely detached, strangely objective—observed to himself how this one evening had robbed his father of more words than had the whole of his preceding life. As he waited, allowing pity to wedge itself beside the wrath that steeped his being, Hugh noticed, as though for the first time, the presence of Joan. She had risen from her crouch—backing against the wall and gripping her weapon with white knuckles, her lips a bloodless line. From side to side flicked her eyes, bouncing between the chamber's ends … between its *mirrors* …

Hugh glanced up to meet his own gaze burning out of a golden frame. Just over his shoulder loomed the ivory-rimmed glass in dim reflection. Hugh whirled. From the far side of the chamber his eyes burned back just as brightly. His surroundings seemed to fall away and suddenly he stood alone, transfixed by infinite replication. A man in a mirror in a mirror in a mirror in a mirror …

And then it seemed to Hugh as though his narrowing eyes glimpsed something just beyond the farthest visible iteration of his image, just past that threshold of perception where all the world constricts to the black infinitesimal and imagination wrings license from oblivion—where what seems to be a final reflection at the end of infinity isn't so much another mirror as it is a doorway, a portal, a passage through the vanishing point. The world seemed to shift ever so slightly and Hugh shot out a hand to steady himself and his eyes twitched, losing the something. He strained, but the vision was gone.

"What …" he hissed, turning, eyes tinged with unaccountable fear, "*what* did this?"

Henry's mouth still gaped, but, before his voice could rally itself, the scarred skeleton draped over his arms lurched up in violent convulsion—flailing, grasping, clawing the air. Long and broken nails raked Henry's cheeks; red streaks now alternated with salty ones. Henry, instead of pulling away, pinned Miles' arm to his side, hugging him close as he thrashed. Miles' eyes were squeezed shut but their lids bulged and squirmed with frantic movement from beneath. His head snapped back and his mouth opened.

"*Omri* …"

Henry stiffened and Hugh shuddered at the guttural croak which echoed in the concrete room and seemed to fill the mind the way the putrid fumes of a dead animal crumpled at the roadside fill the nostrils. Joan edged back along the wall as her pistol swung slowly in their direction.

"*What* did you say …?" Henry's voice was barely audible.

Miles raised his head, locking his shut eyes on Henry's blind stare. His lips twitched upward. Hugh's skin crawled. "*He* now rules the land," Miles rasped. "He rules, and you are welcome not. If you send even one more spy, it will mean war."

A SEA SOUGHT IN SONG

Hugh looked at his father and watched in shock as the man's expression relaxed into a sneer. Henry, his horror replaced by simple contempt, reared back and slapped Miles full in the face. It was as though he'd cut a puppeteer's string. Miles sagged back limply. His eyes snapped open.

"Where am I?" he asked in a voice quiet and weary.

"You're back," replied Henry.

"What's more American than apple pie?" Miles posed the query like an accusation.

Henry hesitated. "What?"

"The truth! Quick!"

"I'd … uh, I'd have to say …"

Hugh, brows knotted with incredulity, blurted his own opinion: "Making out with Rita Hayworth by the light of fireworks on the Fourth."

Miles turned, face lighting up like a Roman candle. "Hugh!" he gasped, "You're here! How …? But then I *am* back." With a long shuddering sigh Miles closed his eyes and leaned back into Henry's cradling arm, a smile of release—sweet, pure release—spreading outward from his lips. "I'm back," he murmured. "I'm back, I'm back, I'm back."

"Great," said Hugh. "Where the hell were you?"

Miles' smile evaporated. His eyes slid out of focus. "Hell," he replied matter-of-factly.

Hugh blinked, but, before he could follow the question up, Henry shifted his weight and lifted Miles in his arms. "No more talk," he said. "You need food and sleep. Joan!"

"Mr. Conrad."

"Get bandages and blankets from the storeroom and take them to my study. And heat water. And bring the sword."

She vanished through the hatch.

"Hugh …" Henry's voice strained for strength while the echoing walls mocked his effort. His mouth shut, then opened again. He struggled visibly, but something in his voice box kept catching his breath. Hugh interrupted.

"I've got him," he said. Gently, he lifted his friend from his father's arms. Miles weighed less than a Rottweiler. "C'mon, let's go." Out from the concrete tomb Hugh stepped. The light warmed from red to gold.

###

They were passing through the birch wood by the time Henry found his voice. Hugh had been clenching his jaw with impatience all the way up the

67

spiral staircase, grinding his teeth tighter with each clanging step. He wanted to grab his father by the shirt-front and shake him till the answers spilled forth like dust from a beaten suit: where this fallout shelter had sprung from, why his friend—seemingly unconscious now, slung over his shoulder—looked like Death itself, how come Joan was in on it all, and what he could do to shake this irrational sense of absolute dread. Over all these mysteries hung the source of Hugh's bitterness—the void, the gap between father and son, the question Hugh *knew* his father had at last been ready to answer earlier that evening: where he'd vanished to for twenty-four long years. So when Henry cleared his throat over the breathing of the trees, his son thought himself more than ready for what was about to come next.

He wasn't.

"I'm older than I look, Hugh."

Hugh snorted. "You're not nearly as old as you look."

"You speak foolishly," snapped Henry. "Pray do not interrupt me again, unless it be with a worthy thought. Though," his voice dropped, "I am at fault for your ignorance. In all I say now I ask your forgiveness for a neglect and deception which shames me, son. Shame is what fetters my tongue—not a reluctance to reveal the truth. I wish it were not so. But God gives me the strength to overcome shame. I will overcome it. It is the least I can do, if only for your sake.

"You don't know who you are, Hugh. You don't know who you are, for you don't know who I am. And I'm trying now to tell you and cannot find the words."

Abruptly, Henry stopped. Hugh, leading the way for his blind father, took several more paces before he realized his feet now crunched the loam alone. He turned. Henry stood half-lost in shadow, portions of his face and body blending with the surrounding darkness. Wind hissed swiftly through the forest's corridors—cold, cutting wind. Miles whimpered; his head twitched against Hugh's back.

"I am a king," said Henry.

"A king! A king of what?"

"Of nothing in this world."

Hugh, shuddering from a sudden cold sweat, almost laughed aloud in cynical relief. "Father, if this is about the Kingdom of God, I don't know how many times I have to tell–"

"*No!* I am *not* talking about God's Kingdom. In that realm there is only one Lord. No, the place of which I speak is unknown to you, but it is a place nevertheless as corporeal, as carnal, as any you have ever seen. A place of extremes—of both dream and nightmare. A land vast beyond imagining, ancient beyond reckoning, harsh beyond foreboding, beautiful beyond describing.

"It is the land I ruled for seventy years. A land which needed me in its darkest hour and gave itself up to me in exchange for its life. The land which by right of inheritance belongs to my only son and heir."

Hugh stared in horror. His father was mad.

"A land," continued Henry, his whisper nearly lost in the wind, "usurped by an enemy far more powerful than ever I had feared."

Hugh had never been one to bottle up his thoughts. "You're mad," he said.

Henry's blind eyes gleamed strangely in the moonlight. "Am I?" he asked. "Am I indeed? Perhaps I am. But then sanity itself has become a tool of the Enemy—a comforting ignorance, a serene complacency, a gateway to blind oblivion. Perhaps God has chosen the mad things of the world to confound the things which are sane. Who in their right mind would choose to believe reality when given a safe alternative? No, I am not sane—not as the world reckons sanity. But I am trustworthy."

"Trustworthy?" hissed Hugh. "Why should I trust you? You *left*."

Henry was silent a long moment. The wind quavered quietly. "You should trust me because you have no other choice," he said at last.

"No other choice?" Hugh actually laughed. "Yeah, in your dreams. In case you hadn't noticed, I'm an adult now, Father. You no longer control my life."

"And neither do you! I'm sorry, son, but, whether or not you like it or even acknowledge it, your life is part of a much larger story. Events have been set in motion which will sweep you away unless you lift up your head and open your eyes. Fires have been kindled which only you can put out."

"Uh-huh. And who kindled the fires, Father?"

"I ... I'm not sure. At this point, my only answer would seem an impossibility. There's something at work here I do not understand, Hugh. Something terrible has happened. Hugh," he said, slowly shaking his head, "I need you. Please help me. I ... I'm scared. Scared, Hugh. Scared of what might happen."

Hugh stared, his mind a boiling cauldron of confusion, pity, rage, and revulsion. After a pause in which even the wind held its breath, he spoke softly, deliberately: "Here's what's going to happen. I'm going to walk back to the house now. I'm going to make sure my friend isn't about to die. Then I'm going to ask you a series of very specific questions. You will answer me clearly, without riddles, without ambiguity. Then, when I have heard your answers, I will get in my car and leave. You will not try to stop me. Do you understand?"

Quietly: "Please, Hugh–"

"*Do* you understand?"

Very quietly: "Yes."

"Good." He turned, vanishing into the night.

###

Miles lay asleep on the couch in Henry's study. They'd bandaged the fresh cuts on his bare feet and covered him with a blanket, but he hadn't returned to lucidity for any of it. His breath rattled softly in and out, in and out—a vaguely unsettling accompaniment to the hearth's brittle crackling. Henry, Hugh, and Joan sat in three wingback armchairs, watching from across the room as the blanket slowly rose and fell. Hugh couldn't help observing the fingers of Joan's right hand as they compulsively tapped the pistol in her lap.

Dusky red light flushed Henry's face. He gazed unblinkingly into flame.

"It was the summer of '26. It had been three months and thirteen days since I'd seen her. Your mother," he appended in response to Hugh's unseen look. "Three months, thirteen days. And you were still so small when I left … I lifted my arm and you just hung from it like a squirrel … you wouldn't let me go. You wouldn't let me go."

A long pause. Hugh stared at Henry, unsure what to expect or how to respond. He didn't want to upset his father's unprecedented vulnerability.

"Our Slavey guide would go no farther," said Henry. "Yamoria, that was his name. 'Den of Spirits.' That's all he would say to explain his reluctance. I knew then that we were close." His voice dropped. In spite of himself, Hugh leaned forward.

"The Slavey are an ancient people," the blind man whispered. "It is said their ancestors fought with the Tungusic nomads against the mighty Xiongnu Empire. Perhaps the thing was given them as a gift for their valor. Perhaps they carried it seven thousand miles to a new continent where their descendants lost all knowledge of its nature beside the fear it had always inspired. Or perhaps it had always been there. Perhaps it rose from the earth when man fell in Eden.

"We found a cave by the lake. It smelled of must and … something else. A spice. Cinnamon. Didn't think much of it at the time.

70

A SEA SOUGHT IN SONG

"Set into a niche in the rock was a mirror. Uncracked. Unstained. So clear it seemed less like glass than a hole punched in the fabric of space. I stood a long time, mesmerized by the very sight. I felt drawn to it, summoned by my own reflection. The frame was ivory. You saw it in the vault."

After a moment, Hugh realized the statement was a question. "Yes, I saw it," he said.

"And what did you see?"

"Uh … there were figures carved into it … dragons, mythological creatures. That kind of thing."

"No!" The syllable leapt with startling force. "Not mythological."

"Of course, they were—"

"*That night*," interrupted Henry, "after we made camp, I returned to the cave alone. I had to see it again, to face once more that faint flicker of alien movement in a thing which by rights should have shown me only the world I knew. Enchanted, I was. Mad with curiosity. Nothing could have stopped me."

Henry sighed and closed his eyes. "I reached out to touch my reflection and my hand went straight through the glass."

Hugh blinked. "You mean you broke it?"

"No, Hugh. My hand vanished as though I'd thrust it into a barrel of water."

Henry's words hung in the warming air.

"What did you do?" This story had begun to worm its way beneath Hugh's skin. He shook himself slightly to settle his hackles. *You can't be scared*, he mused, *unless you believe him. But what could be more frightening than that?*

A smile, brief and bitter, cracked Henry's lips. "I wasn't given much choice. When the grizzly appeared at the mouth of the cave, sniffing and snorting, shutting out the moonlight, there was only one place I *could* go."

"In." Hugh's whisper broke a stillness. He lifted his eyes from the heart of the fire to his father's face. Its lines were stretched in a grin, faint yet fierce. And, in that moment, Hugh knew that he believed.

"I … I cannot describe it," the old man murmured. "It feels like falling into an ocean with an anchor tied to your ankles … like drowning … with knowledge that the muck thousands of feet below has already closed over your soul … like death … like oblivion. I will not bore you with attempts to convey the sensation in words. It felt like a lifetime, though it couldn't have lasted more than an instant. But …" and here Henry's blind gaze swung at Hugh like a maul, "when the shock had passed, I floated beneath a clear blue

AUSTIN GUNDERSON

sky as wind ruffled the treetops and the sweet scents of spring suffused my head and the songbirds poured their voices into the morning air." His eyelids slid shut. "God in heaven, they were so many. Their symphony swept me away."

"What are you saying, Father?"

"The mirror you saw is a portal to another world. One which I entered twenty-five years ago as you would understand it. Last year I returned to this world through a similar portal, which you also glimpsed in the vault."

"What do you mean, 'as I would understand it'?"

"What I mean is that time is relative. While you aged twenty-four years, I aged seventy-one. Hugh," he leaned forward, mouth tight, eyes wide, "I spent a lifetime in Arlam."

Hugh barked a laugh. "That'd make you over a hundred and ten!"

"Like I said: older than I look."

Hugh's eyes went hard. Something tapped at the back of his brain. Something close at hand was different. Something important had changed. "What happened to Miles?"

The old man cringed. "I do not know."

"What do you mean, you don't know?" Hugh had to restrain himself from shouting now. "It was *you* who sent him there, wasn't it? *You* who showed him the way. *You* who led him into your secret bunker to lose himself in time and space! *You!*"

"I do not deny it."

"Then how can you be ignorant? You are responsible!"

Henry opened his mouth, then shut it. His blind eyes swam. As Hugh rose to loom over his father in anger, he identified the cause of his unease: Miles had ceased to breathe. Too late this awareness! For no sooner had the mental connection been made than Hugh's peripheral senses caught Joan's sharp inhalation, the white blur of her arm as it jerked the pistol from her lap. Hugh spun, then stepped back, stunned.

Miles had sat up. But this was not the strong man Hugh once had known, nor even the broken man he'd met just tonight. This was something different. Its eyes bulged wide and white—rolled all the way back into its head. Its lips had peeled back into a hellish sneer. Its bony fingers slowly kneaded the blanket. Every sinew in its body stood out with the force of maximum exertion.

The sight was frightening. But far worse was the sudden *closeness* of the room—a feeling of humidity, of claustrophobia, and a crawling of the skin

72

A SEA SOUGHT IN SONG

like that elicited by an unknown observer who steps abruptly from a shadow close at hand. Something … *else* had joined them.

"Mr. Conrad …" Joan's voice quavered as she backed toward the crackling hearth.

The blood drained from Henry's face. He rose, backlit by flame. "Miles …?"

The Thing that had been Miles gaped its maw in a guttural laugh. "You fool! Did I not warn you I would come? Did you not know there is no escape? I am *here*." At this last word the Thing's voice dropped three octaves. It stood upon the couch, the blanket sliding off its body and crumpling to the floor.

"*Joan! Sword!*" Henry screamed the words.

Many things then happened at once. Joan bent to pull a scabbarded sword from the floor behind her chair and flung it at Henry, who somehow snatched it from the air. The Thing that had been Miles coiled itself like a panther and leapt from the couch, colliding with Joan as the sword left her hand. *Crack!* went the .38, punching a harmless hole in the ceiling as the Thing's fist spun Joan's forehead into the mantlepiece. The gun landed in the fire. Again and again and again the Thing lashed out in the space of an instant, ripping Joan's coat, gouging flesh from her face, batting her out of its way. Henry staggered back, flinging the scabbard off his blade.

Adrenaline exploded in Hugh as though it were the shock wave from an atom bomb he'd watched bleach some distant horizon. In a rush of fear and rage he regained motor control and charged the Thing, tackling it, carrying it with him over an armchair and into the wall. But then the Thing was atop him somehow, and his trachea collapsed, and he was weightless, and a table's edge drove into his back, and the world slipped sideways as he gaped for air.

Joan rose to her hands and knees and clawed in the fire for her weapon. And the Thing took her by the nape of the neck as though she were a kitten. She mewed in wordless horror. In plunged the Thing's fist. On withdrawal, it trailed entrails. Joan's body collapsed aside into the hearth, scattering coals.

"*Omri!*" bellowed the old man. He faced the Thing across the flames which caught on Joan's hair and clothes, the sinews of his forearms rippling as he clutched the sword like a flagstaff before his face. He seemed to grow, somehow. His brows swooped low over white orbs which caught the red light like marbles of polished stone. "You are not welcome here." His voice rumbled out like the growl of distant thunder—a faint yet inexorable threat. "Return whence you came. In the name of the Christ I rebuke you."

AUSTIN GUNDERSON

The Thing's head snapped to the side as though it had been slapped. When it raised its eyes again, a mad clown's grin crawled over features already hideously stretched. "Always weak," it rasped. "Always crying out for help. You are *alone*, Conrad. No help is coming." With a sudden gesture it splayed its fingers. The fire leapt up, then vanished as though all oxygen had been sucked from the room. Bloody coals glowed faintly. Hugh, who had been straining to recapture his wind, gulped smoke and choked.

"Wrong you are." Henry's voice was surprisingly calm. "Were I alone I would be dead by now. But neither my life nor my death alters the fact that *you are unwelcome here!*"

As he shouted these last words, from which the Thing recoiled, Henry stepped over Joan's body and rammed his sword forward. A white light exploded in Hugh's dilated irises. Whether it came from the Thing itself or from the sword that impaled it he could not tell. But as darkness flooded back in its wake, the sweat on Hugh's skin grew chill as it did when he rested on a snowbound ridge and the heat of exertion evaporated into space. The stifling presence was gone.

For a long moment the only sounds were Hugh's frantic inhalations and the sizzling of Joan's hair where it smoldered and curled.

Henry moaned and sank to his knees in a swirl of ash. He felt his way to Joan, cradled her head in his lap. Hugh, lungs functioning again at last, sensed his father's silent sobs without hearing a sound, so great was the grief which poured from the old man to wash the smoke-choked study. Moving slowly, as if trapped in some nightmare he despaired of escaping before a distant dawn, Hugh stumbled to the desk drawer. He struck a match and kindled the wick of a kerosene lamp.

The light flickered over a gristly tableau. Overturned furniture lay scattered about Joan's disemboweled corpse and Miles' skeletal form, from which protruded the sword as though from a block of stone. Blood was everywhere. Between the two bodies knelt Henry, head bowed as though to avoid a judgmental gaze his blindness would never allow him to meet. Hugh felt lightheaded. He reached for the table's edge to steady himself, then stumbled toward the hearth.

The sword, he now realized, was beautiful. The blade, hilt, handle, and pommel seemed to meld together as though fashioned from a single lump of metal. Strange characters danced down the fuller. He leaned forward to inspect it, curled his fingers over the pommel's odd concavity. Tears stained the steel's dull darkness, inching their way down the blade.

"H-H-Hugh?"

A SEA SOUGHT IN SONG

Hugh started, barely catching himself from toppling backward. Henry turned. It was Miles again: eyes bright and clear, face full of peace and pain. Hugh tried to smile but his mouth twisted itself into a knot as he fought to suppress sobs like those which wracked his father. "I'm here, Miles," he managed.

Miles' eyes slid into focus. For the first time, it seemed, he noticed the sword. He fixed Hugh's eyes with his own. "You ..." he gasped. "You must take it. Here," he clasped the blade in his bare hands where it jutted from his belly and pushed upward, slicing his own palms open. "Take it. It's for you."

Hugh's chin worked. Blinking desperately, he eased Miles' hands apart. *If the sword leaves the wound ...* "No, no, not for me. You keep it a little while."

"No!" The man's eyes went wide. "Take it! *You* have to do it, now! We're all waiting!"

Hugh glanced at his father, whose face was indecipherable. Back to Miles. "What are you–"

"Take it, take it, take it, it's you! I see it in your eyes! You *must* take it!"

"Alright, alright." His hand folded around the pommel, but the blade stayed buried in flesh. "I've got it."

Miles closed his eyes and smiled a long, slow smile. "What's more American than apple pie?" His voice was fading like an echo down a hollow, winding chasm. He chuckled and his stomach spurted blood. "That's why I wouldn't trust them. They never knew the answer ... not in all those years ..."

Hugh stared at his friend in wonder and grief and dread, watching helplessly as Miles' life drained away through chinks in the fabric of space and time, leaning closer and closer and closer to catch his climactic word.

Miles' eyes snapped open. "Freedom," he breathed.

Chapter Six
THE BEACON

19 Halanen, 781

Hugh woke to the shrill crying of seabirds. He lay on his stomach, limbs tangled in woolen bedsheets, face smashing a sealskin pillow, nearly smothered by soft warmth. He stiffened, dredging memory for context. Nothing came. Nothing except three days and nights of sleepless terror on a ferocious arctic sea. Oh, and a black knife-edge of rock that'd exploded through the hull of his ship and flung all but two survivors to their deaths. And a beautiful woman with a crossbow and crosser attitude.

But this was all too fantastic; it must have been a dream. He must still be in his father's house. In a minute he'd have to stumble into the kitchen to wolf down some eggs. It was a long drive to Boston, and Smith wasn't the patient type.

Oh ... wait ...

Light clear and pale flooded Hugh's eyes as he sat bolt upright. If his dream had been real, if it had all actually happened—he slumped, shrinking into himself—then the horrors upon which it was predicated were real as well. He'd have to fall back asleep if he wanted to shut this nightmare out, and that would be no escape. Hugh raised his head, brows stormy, and flexed his arms to launch himself from bed.

The road to Boston had never seemed longer.

The mattress on which he'd apparently thrashed all night softened an alcove set into the stone wall of the small chamber. A faded wooden desk, its edges etched with intertwining strands of seaweed, sat against the opposite wall next to a shut door. A padlocked sea-chest crouched below an embrasured window. One latticed windowpane stood slightly ajar. Hugh flung it open, inhaling the pungent reek of sea life belched up by an angry ocean and left to suffocate on unforgiving rock. The window faced the north, faced the sea: a square portal of blue framed by shadowed stone.

Hugh twitched his head up, tossing back a deep breath, then exhaled slowly. He ran his fingers through his shock of blond hair, combing it back from his brow as he surveyed the fresh aftermath of chaos. His mood festered despite the keen air and light. He could see no sign of the ship—no plank, no spar, no sailcloth, nothing. Nature was a swift purifier. *If only it'd work that way for me ...*

He sighed in frustration and glanced down to find his equipment missing. His gun, his pack, his coat—last night he'd dropped them there at the foot of his bed. Now they were gone. He stood a moment in bewilderment and then spun again, spitting air and smacking the stone lintel with the heel of his hand. How could he have been so stupid? She'd taken them during the night! While he slept, oblivious! He lashed out again, then stood, nursing the throb in his hand, breathing heavily.

Enough! He'd been careless, that was all. He'd let his guard down just long enough to conk out in a strange tower. *How many more times do you have to get burned by a pretty face before you learn your lesson?* But mere anger wouldn't return his belongings now. He needed a plan.

The door was locked. It would've surprised him if it hadn't been. He eased his weight against it and felt no movement: it'd take some doing to break it down, and the noise would alert anyone standing guard. That left him two options. Either wait here for his captor to reappear—assuming the woman *was* his captor and not just some maid who'd stayed up late to wash crockery and had since remanded him to the care of an authority even less accommodating than she—or else ...

The narrow window had been sunk deeply into the tower's stone exterior, and thus afforded him access past its panes. Hugh clambered up and crouched on the sill. Here in the shadowed embrasure the air was perfectly still. He inched his way down the slant until the walls widened beyond the spread of his arms. It hadn't entered his mind last night to appraise the tower's stonework for scalability, and now he fumed at this oversight. Some kind of thin gray algae lubricated the incline. The actual side of the tower eluded his view.

Lowering himself to his belly, Hugh wriggled forward to the edge. The tower's face fell away, smooth and dark, for at least ten stories before melding with a mass of solid rock that pitched upward slightly before plunging into the spray. Vertigo assailed Hugh, but he fought it down.

Submarine flotsam glistened at the tower's foot: kelp bladders and crustacean carcasses and the remnants of things more vague. White gulls seethed in flocks or dropped one by one toward a flapping, struggling melee below. The cold wind muffled their shrieks. Beyond the gulls, beyond the sheer rocks and booming surf and far above the choppy sea, the pink blush of dawn had nearly bled from the sky's cirri.

A SEA SOUGHT IN SONG

The fall was too great; he'd never survive intact. Hugh cursed and leaned out a little farther. There had to be something else ... another way ... *There!* About ten feet below him, a small patch of wall seemed extra dark. Easing forward till his shoulders projected beyond the edge of the sill and his spreadeagled limbs strove with gravity along its slick surface, Hugh saw it clearly: another embrasure, directly beneath him.

Within ten minutes he'd scrambled back inside, filleted his blankets with the jackknife from his pocket, and knotted them end-to-end into a twenty-foot cord. He then wound this around his fist, placed his pillow against the wall beside the window, pulled the left windowpane open against his pillow, and quietly struck out its glass. After shaking off the shards, he tied one end of his cord to the now-empty window frame and climbed back onto the sill, casting the rest of the rolled-up cord out into space. He wasn't at all certain the wooden frame would support his weight, but with a shake of his head the thought was banished. He'd made his decision. No use carping about it now.

Hugh undid his belt so he could loop the cord around it once at his front. Though this meant he'd have to wrestle with the knots at regular intervals, it would take some of the strain off his arms and help him control his descent. He backed to the edge, pulling the cord through his belt with one hand while the other kept the slack clear of his feet. Now he stood at the precipice. Now was the moment of truth. He took a deep breath, tugged on the lifeline, and dropped over the side.

Ilina landed in a maelstrom of beating wings and snaking necks. She swung her oar with both hands and the black shapes floundered back, bawling and posturing. The din reminded her less of a screaming match than of a belching contest she had once, to her great discomfort, witnessed in the common room of a wayside inn she had thought reputable. But at least no one there had belched at *her*. Here, she was the center of attention.

This ledge alone held at least fifty nests, and their glossy guardians were all eyeing her now, dodging and swaying like fighters looking for an opening. The sunlight glinted off their sleek, jet plumage and the thrashing spread of their wings filled Ilina's vision like funereal laundry hung up to dry in a windstorm. She fought the urge to shrink down and clamp her hands over her ears—to vanish into the crowd until the riot ceased. A single thought kept her strong.

Silly girl—they're just a bunch of birds!

AUSTIN GUNDERSON

Wielding her oar, she waded in among the flock to a cacophony of protest. Cormorants might just be birds, but that didn't stop them from standing at over half her height and flinging their serpentine necks about wildly in an effort to dig their bills into her flesh. Experience indicated they were best appreciated at oar's-length.

The routine was simple: pluck one egg from each nest, wrap it in a wad of cloth, stow it safely in the satchel, and escape to the next ledge in one piece. Easier said than done, but ever since that first wild rush when, as a wide-eyed girl of five, she'd clung for dear life to her father's neck when he plunged into the flapping fray, egging had become one of the highlights of her year—a kind of breathless dance taken up with hostile partners.

Swooping into a gap opened by her spinning oar, Ilina snatched up a sky-blue egg while bringing the paddle back around with her other hand to topple a cormorant into its neighbor's nest. She pinched a scrap of cloth from her sash, swathing the egg one-handed. It vanished into her bulging leather bag. She dodged back and forth—stamping through the thick white crust of droppings that slimed the rock, cramming eggs into her bag and swatting away recalcitrant birds—then scrambled over a clutch of boulders and dropped onto a narrow track that cut across the cliffside.

The roar of the breakers below swelled in her mind as the croaking and flapping subsided. Birds innumerable hung suspended in the middle air between her and the surf like fish in an ocean clear as crystal, deep as heaven—white gulls and black cormorants and mottled ospreys stalking the skies. From a distance they appeared motionless, but all around her they rose and fell on the waves of the wind, adjusting their wings with slight twitches as ceaseless as those of Jaar sailors balanced upon mastheads.

Always they face the wind, Ilina mused. *Wind is change, and they ride the change as though riding a horse yet remain themselves unmoved. What can outlast them? Though this island sinks its root into the heart of the world, it will eventually crumble away. Perhaps the supple outlast the strong. The birds have no root, yet they defy the storms.*

And yet ... and yet they nest among the rocks.

She sighed, a small sound drowned in the rushing and booming. There was meaning here—she just knew it. The birds knew something she did not. But she would learn. Of that she was even more certain. For if she failed to learn ... *Aei, best to avoid such thoughts.*

She had been away too long already; she knew that, and yet she stood as though transfixed and let the stark beauty of the seascape flood her senses.

A SEA SOUGHT IN SONG

The storm last night had been terrible, but now the sky, the very air was so fresh, so clean …

She shuddered. What an efficient god she served.

The sun was halfway to its zenith by the time she stirred. The men from the sea would be up by now, and wanting to eat no doubt, and it would take her at least another hour to reascend Horwell Face and hike back home without breaking her fragile takings. She turned to go.

But just then something caught the corner of her eye and held fast, snapping her head around after it. A glint, a gleam, a flash of something that reflected the sun. It wasn't the waves—it didn't bob or sway—and its brilliance seemed only to grow. Ilina raised a hand to shield her eyes from the glare. It—whatever it was—came from the rocks at the base of the great cliff. *But nothing in nature is so refulgent.* Abruptly its light dimmed and then went out, but Ilina continued to stare as she slowly unslung her satchel. For just beyond the rocks, out among the flashing waves, a dark, half-submerged mass was nosing the shore. A listless interloper. A shipwreck.

The castaways came from here.

The spiral staircase curled away in silence. The cold stone walls would easily conduct the slightest sounds, scattering them into little sonic shotgun blasts ricocheting away into darkness, but now there were no such sounds. No shouts of alarm, no warning footfalls. Not even the soft rasp of grit under Hugh's own boots, for the floor had been swept clean. Ready for inspection.

Hugh grinned. The inspector had arrived.

He glanced back into the small room whose single shuttered window he'd staved in from outside. It resembled the interior of a beehive: hundreds and hundreds of rolled-up scrolls packed the wooden honeycombs covering the walls. This library was near capacity. Only a few rows near the ceiling contained vacant hexagonal slots. Hugh had checked.

He'd pulled out a few of the scrolls, too, and unrolled them on the squeaky-clean stone floor, but the letters that crowded their parchment in tight little lines of script were utterly unknown to him. He'd pulled out a few more at random. One had been scribed in what was clearly a different, yet equally strange, alphabet. This discovery had given Hugh pause. *Multiple written languages. An island could contain one. But two … two requires a continent.* He'd sat a moment in thought, then returned the scrolls to their pigeonholes.

AUSTIN GUNDERSON

Now the cold spiral beckoned. But should he hang a right and ascend, or turn left to plunge downward? *The tower's top is a terminus. If I start there, I'll leave nothing unexplored behind me.* The right it was, then.

He passed a locked door that presumably led to his cell. And then an endless procession of likewise-locked doors fell past him as he climbed. *This isn't solving my problem at all.* With each new latch he vainly jiggled, Hugh became more and more on edge.

At last the stairwell ended in a brief landing and an arched door wrought with clever stonework. Illumination streamed from a circular skylight which was paned, so it seemed, with pure crystal. Sinuous creatures and ribbons of unintelligible script twisted up the stone on either side of the door to meet overhead and it was there, at the apex of the arch, that the shaft from the ceiling fell full, and Hugh was forced to shade his eyes against a dazzling outburst of prism-shattered light, reflected by the graven image of a man.

His robes were sleek, his crown tall, and his sword long. He held it point down to his left, while, with his right hand raised high and his fingers splayed in a gesture of authority, he filled the heavens with radiating lines of light, or power … *or something.* Diminutive figures clustered in a semicircle under his feet, as though he were floating in air.

Hugh approached slowly, eyes fixed on the static icon, sensing despite himself the lingering aura of some long-departed force. As he reached up with his fingertips to brush the feet of the king, it seemed to Hugh that for an instant the world ran in reverse—that radiance burst from the stone figure's right hand to stream upwards out the skylight.

Hugh jerked back his arm as though from a hot coal. He stared a moment longer with slitted eyes to make sure the impression had been imagination, then turned the door's handle and ducked though the archway.

Stone steps continued to curve up before him, but no ceiling topped this final flight. As Hugh ascended, the walls dropped away on either hand to reveal a broad and level platform vaulted by a high dome of stone supported around its circumference by eight smooth pillars. Between these pillars, eight archways opened without parapet upon a world of empty air.

But all these peripheral details Hugh noticed only later, for, from the moment his head first cleared the level of the floor, his attention was suddenly and completely riveted upon a single object. Indeed, he could think of little else for some time after his halting steps had at last closed the distance between himself and the focus of his awe. His pupils dilated despite the light. His breath came shallow and quick. *Get a hold of yourself, Conrad. This can't be real. Think, dammit, think!*

82

A SEA SOUGHT IN SONG

But he couldn't think. For in the center of the stone platform stood a diamond the size of a Sherman tank.

###

The sea's breath hung thickly in the air, churned and renewed by each new wave that exploded over the rocks to vanish down a labyrinth of sharp-edged crevices or slip calmly into variegated tidal pools. Ilina, her tunic and trousers beaded with mist, picked her way across a haphazard landscape that seemed barren from a distance but, upon closer examination, teemed with life. Though she stepped lightly, the crunching of barnacles jarred the soles of her boots with each and every footfall. She couldn't hear this crunching, of course. The noise of the breakers had risen to an unremitting thunder which drowned out even thought.

Ilina leapt over a crevasse to teeter atop a boulder, dropping to hands and knees to recover her balance. She swept damp strands of hair from her eyes. This vantage commanded a wide view of the rocky shore. Horwell Face rose like a chalk-white wall to the left, blocking out the eastern sky, while ahead the boulder-strewn talus at its base snaked around a promontory to vanish in a haze of salt spray. The wind had subsided but little since last night, and the vast ocean clawed at Cuspid Isle with implacable ferocity.

It was from this battleground between land and sea that the gleam of light had caught her eye. The shipwreck was close now; it had to be. She'd let it hold her eye as she descended the great pale cliff that now loomed above. Not for an instant had she lost its place. But all that concentration had come to naught as soon as she reached sea level. For everything had seemed so much different from above—so finite, so two-dimensional. This chaotic jumble of mussel-crusted rocks bore little resemblance to the landscape she'd surveyed from on high.

Where are you, interloper?

A small, dispassionate part of her mind recognized the foolishness of this self-appointed quest. She had pressing duties and responsibilities—*guests lodging in the tower at this very moment, by all the Deeps!*—but her will had been captured by an urge stronger than mere duty: a strange, insistent feeling she knew well but would never pretend to understand. It was the sensation that traversed her spine before the onset of a storm, the premonition that called her to the bluffs in time to watch a starfall, the *awareness* which denied her peace in the darkest hours of the night. It was how she knew this costly diversion was far more important than a morning spent paying courtesy to propriety.

It was a feeling that grew only stronger as the tide ebbed and the sun ascended its great compass, transforming the boulder-banked tidepools into mirrors of quivering light. Ilina raised a hand to shield her eyes from the blinding sheen.

And then she saw it. Shining no longer, the thing was now a rent in her sight: a shaft of black untouched by the glare. It protruded obliquely from a crevice between boulders only a little distance from the sea's curling lip.

Ilina dropped from her perch and approached the object. A sudden hesitancy had overcome her—the same instinct which whispered *caution* in the presence of a beached wolrum, though, if such heavy creatures could surge back up from the abyss of death, she had yet to see it. Or perhaps it wasn't fear that slowed her movements so much as a surreal reverence, the sense that a great weight of history had settled upon this place and hour, that the untold future would hinge upon her actions of the next few minutes. Whatever the case, Ilina found herself reluctant to rush forward. She moved in slow motion as though ascending the steps of an altar.

The black object was a sword. It stood upright in the rocks as though thrust there by some negligent hand. Its hilt bore no insignia apparent to the eye, and seemed fashioned from the same slab of metal as the blade itself. The tip of its pommel had been hollowed out, as though for a gemstone now missing. Ilina felt this should mean something to her, that its significance should be apparent, and her inability to identify the source of this sensation rankled. But what disturbed her was the weapon's size. Its crossbar alone exceeded the length of her forearm. This was a giant's sword, and beside it she felt very small indeed.

Raising her eyes seaward as though the weapon's owner might at any moment emerge from the depths, she beheld a carcass proportionally vast. But here was no monster straining to prison the final glint of guttering life within a house of flesh: the wave-washed shelf that now opened below her was strewn with wreckage of a less organic sort, remains of the death throes of a beast of wood and tar. Here a spar jutted from the surf, there a broken plank or a great curved rib—and in the center of all, flapping in tatters from a tilted mast, a sail as blue as a twilit western sky. A ship of the Jaar, foundered on her isle.

This was indeed Hoo's ship. *And that sword ...* She turned back and the black shaft seemed to fill her vision. *That sword must belong to him, too.*

A SEA SOUGHT IN SONG

###

Hugh Conrad had never been particularly enamored of riches themselves, only of what they could do. The home of his childhood had been furnished in abundance with those small luxuries incidental to upper-class America, estimable to the average citizen, and palatial to most other corners of the inhabited globe. Indeed, until he joined the army, he'd harbored scant notion of his own privilege. The war had acquainted him experientially with the fact that not all men had private boats and planes at their disposal. But far from fostering conceit or condescension, this new awareness had been, in Hugh, rolled up into that careless liberality which is the singular prerogative of those born into wealth. He was more than happy to give anyone a lift on his boat; all one had to do was ask. The solicitor didn't even have to be an attractive young woman.

The irony of Hugh's occupation—"treasure hunter"—provided him no end of amusement. He had no need of treasure, though he *did* enjoy the hunting. Whatever the motives that drove him to track down priceless relics—whether simple habit, the thrill of the chase, or an escape from the persistent shadow of a long-vanished father—the acquisition of riches had never been among them.

It was thus with no little surprise that Hugh found himself gazing gape-mouthed at a treasure beyond even the fevered imaginations of those who longed for such things. In the face of such a fortune, even his abundance seemed like poverty. Surely a diamond of such colossal proportions would be worth more than the collective gems of planet Earth were they to be heaped up in one place. And yet here it sat—unwatched, unguarded, and exposed on all sides to the raging elements. *But how would one steal it? The thing must weigh a hundred tons. I'd need a mobile crane ... and a haul truck ... and a cargo ship in a deep-water port ...* It didn't occur to Hugh for some time to consider how such a thing had ended up atop a stone tower in the first place.

Hugh circled the giant gem as he would've circled a cornered tiger: slowly. This was something so far beyond his ken that he'd actually perceived it as such before anything crazy had happened. He was learning. This time, he wouldn't be caught off guard. But as his eyes flicked to and fro across the intricately-faceted surface—the fevered work of a hundred gemcutters or the sole magnum opus of the lifetime of a genius—he thrilled to a fleeting yet distinct impression: he poised upon a threshold. There was more here than met his eye.

AUSTIN GUNDERSON

He couldn't explain it; this diamond, as huge as it was, felt ... *tight.* There was a tension about it, like that of a balloon ready to burst. As though it held more empty space than the sky itself. He shuddered. *No no no, not again, not now ... aren't women supposed to be the ones who get all the premonitions?* But even as Hugh berated himself, things which had lain hidden from his sight began to lose their shyness. The hairs on his neck roused themselves as the gem began to glow.

At first it might have been nothing—a faint shift of refraction, a freak spasm of his nervous mind—but then came a moment when the change was beyond doubt. An inner light stirred in the cloudy depths. Hugh tensed, suddenly overcome with terror, intuitively aware of a power—a *presence*— close at hand. To his shame, he wanted nothing more in that moment than to dive for the stairs and slink away into the bowels of the tower beneath. But to this urge his limbs refused to respond. He stood rooted in place as the air around him seemed to dim, as his vision contracted until the still-bright stone seemed to fill the world.

Wild sensations crashed against him like waves upon the shore. His perception seemed to expand. Behind him, to the north, lay nothing: an endless sweep of pristine desolation, wracked by fits of howling rage or lost in preternatural silences. Before him, to the south, the world teemed. A vast weight of life perfused his mind unbidden.

Beasts of forest and mountain and marsh and plain—bears in their thickets and owls in their snags—and creatures unfamiliar—and people— innumerable people speaking and working and loving and building—raising cities over the crumbling bones of the ancients—jostling in marketplaces and hammering on anvils and crying from mastheads and whispering in bedrooms and crowding around fires small and large—from the sputtering clump of brush in the cot of the poorest shepherd, to the roaring blaze on the greatest hearth in the highest tower in the land, the heat of life leaps forth.

For an instant it was as though the souls of millions welled up within Hugh's own like a cloud of fireflies in a midsummer's twilight, darting and sparking and dancing just beyond reach. Unthinking, he reached out to them. His fingers brushed the gem and the world turned white.

White drained to black. Hugh stood in a vast courtyard. Fires circled him, rippling columns of red which rose from stone bowls. It was deepest night.
So, he has sent you. How ... disappointing.

A SEA SOUGHT IN SONG

The voice crawled up Hugh's brain stem and he cried aloud, crashing to his knees, clawing at his own head. It was *inside* him.

A low chuckle seemed to split his skull. *Not terribly prepared, are you?*

In response, Hugh writhed upon the stones. His own thoughts had shattered like the shards of a glass let slip by nerveless fingers. It was all he could do to contain this new voice within the bounds of his brain.

What did he tell you, Boy? That you were someone special? That the world was yours? That nothing here would harm you?

The laugh which followed was a molten brand jiggling in his sinuses. His back arched as he screamed in silence.

Oh Conrad! You insult me, Old Man! And I was ready! I was finally ready to face you! But it seems I must face boredom instead.

The voice had receded somewhat from his consciousness. Its focus had shifted. Just enough … barely … for Hugh to open his eyes.

The source of the voice was not hard to identify. A figure stood between two great gouts of flame, taller than any man Hugh had ever seen, cased all in gleaming armor without chink, robed with thick radiance that only deepened the encroaching black. The lofty helm stared at him blankly—its single horizontal slit the sole aperture in that articulated exoskeleton. Hugh clenched his teeth as pain came flooding back. The gleaming man raised a finger and Hugh's mind flew apart once more and he spasmed like a fish in a boat bottom.

You are pathetic. Unworthy of my time. Only one thing there is which would have granted you power against me, and you failed to bring it. And so Henred Conrad has added this evil to the endless record of his sins—that he willingly relinquished his only son to face the judgement which by right is his. The mountainous figure curled its fist and an irresistible force somersaulted Hugh backward onto his head. His vision exploded into splinters of black and red. He couldn't draw breath to fuel his screams. The figure raised its fist.

And then a great weight collided with Hugh out of nowhere and he spun away into darkness.

Ilina extricated herself from Hoo's flailing, clutching limbs, shuddering as she scrambled to her feet and faced the quickly-cooling Beacon. That terrifying foreign darkness yet tinged the pulsing glow. Alone and at a loss, she raised her hands palm-outward toward the light—a weirdly vulnerable gesture for such a place and time. *Oh gods, how long was he here ... what has he done ... what can he do? What should I do? Gods help me ...* Without conscious intent, she began mouthing the Prayer of the Desperate.

Across the face of the world a chill wind was blowing. Strands of loose hair slipped from Ilina's braids to slide over her face. And still the dark light swirled deep in the Beacon's bowels. Her hands trembled—thin shadows silhouetted by boiling afterglow. At last she became aware of the movement of her lips. She licked them and began again verbally, though her words would have been audible only to one standing a lover's distance from her face.

> *"I come bearing no gift,*
> *I come lighting no fire;*
> *All is sand that you sift:*
> *You know I am no liar.*
>
> *I have something to plead,*
> *But no toll for my time;*
> *You must pardon my need,*
> *Else my pride be a crime.*
>
> *Raise your gates, O havens afar,*
> *And open the ways of the sea;*
> *Lift the seal of ruthless fate,*
> *So your favor may find me."*

She paused and then, raising her voice, spoke a single clear command.

"Shut the window."

Instantly the light went out, sucked back into itself like the tendrils of a prodded anemone. A subtle tension, until now unnoticed, evaporated from the air.

Ilina slumped against a pillar. She propped her head back and closed her eyes.

When they opened, it was upon Hoo's penetrating stare. His mask had fallen away and his face filled with conflict. She held his eyes, searching them, knowing this moment would not last. She saw fear in that gaze, and pain, yes, and a rage which took her breath, but over all else there loomed an unwavering steadiness which held sway like a drover wrestling a willful bullock. His control was not a mask; it was his center. But he was out of his depth. *But he lit the Beacon ... and turned it black ...*

"Who are you?" she whispered.

Hugh stood, swaying slightly. He felt violated—pierced by a scrutiny far more painful than that chronic anonymity which had come to epitomize all torment in his life. But his neck wasn't broken. His limbs weren't bruised. Besides a dull ache in his temple, he felt no pain at all. No foreign voice echoed in his bones. *Was it all a dream, then? Or am I just going crazy?*

No, it wasn't just him. Something was wrong here: something about the light. *Why is the sun in my eyes? It'd risen above the lip of the ceiling, last thing I remember.* Now it was shining under the opposite side of the dome. *But it couldn't have been more than a half-hour since I got up here ...*

Swirling like loose papers in a gale of uncertainty, Hugh's thoughts broke to chase a hundred futile threads of surmise which all converged on the woman standing before him. *Elena, that's her name.* She who'd sung the stone to sleep. *She just saved my life, didn't she?*

Her eyes caught and held him. They were as wide as mirrors, reflective of the newly cloud-rimmed sky, and glazed with a stark, quailing awe which chilled him more sharply than any wind. As he watched, she seemed to shrink into herself until the quiet power evident in her bearing only a moment before had been swallowed up by dread.

That she should so effortlessly shut down that demented diamond only to cower before his face came as a double shock to Hugh. "What is it?" he asked, fighting to level his voice. "Elena, what's wrong?"

"Hat seh yir, ut?" she murmured. *"Ca om Molrinkal oam yir. Aei rhomel, met thom fit yir? Ca ame whul yir teht gurlorschich?"* Without lowering her gaze she hesitantly slid one booted foot behind the other and bent at the knees in a gesture Hugh couldn't help identifying as a curtsey—a baffling formality which only exacerbated his unease.

He spread his hands in confusion and advanced a step. "Elena, what's going on? What just happened to me?"

The girl stiffened and Hugh stopped moving. The blood had drained from her face. *What did I do?* Though he hadn't a clue what had frightened her, it was plain to him that any attempt to control the situation would only make matters worse. She was jumpy, that was for sure.

AUSTIN GUNDERSON

He let out a slow breath and tried to remain motionless as color returned to her cheeks. *But is that just another trick of the light?* He couldn't tell what was real anymore. *How long did that lovely little dream last, anyway? Did I fall asleep standing up?*

With an abruptness that made him flinch, Elena whipped around and strode to the head of the stairs. She bent to lift something from the stones, her movements stiff, her limbs ungainly. Like an innocent forced before a firing-squad without hearing the charges against her.

The object she raised was long and dark. The sword. She had the sword. *How'd she get the sword?*

With halting steps, she returned, swaying a little, then sank to her knees, bowed her head, laid the blade across upturned palms, and offered it up to Hugh. A swirl of wind caught at her hair, splashing it russet where it fluttered in the sun. The sword, though held in the same beam of light, remained dark as a night without stars. The only sounds were the soft rush of wind through the pillars and the cry of a soaring osprey.

It took a concerted effort for Hugh to pick his jaw up off the floor.

Chapter Seven
PREVARICATION

Ilina descended the spiral stair of Kredak Tower as though in a dream. Not that she felt perfused by some ethereal sweetness or calm like the poets meant whenever they wrote of dreams—*that* she had not known since girlhood. Indeed, she sometimes wondered whether poetry's sole function was to splash fantastical paint over the primal disquiet lurking just beyond the sluice of sleep. Surely no one actually *wished* to enter that place.

For Ilina Lightkeeper, wakefulness was a reprieve from dreaming. Had the waking world comprised her greatest ordeal, how simple her life would've been! For though she herself remained pinned in place after shutting her eyes, other things—things furtive and cruel and strange—were then at liberty to pay her visitation. What small measure of power she held over her own body was then forfeit to forces beyond her influence or understanding. That was how she felt now, as she slowly descended the stair.

His coming had caught her unprepared. She who had considered herself watchful, she who had thought herself wise! Her whole life she had imagined this day. Ever since her father dandled her upon his knee and sang softly of faithful Kredak and his great Anticipation, ever since her young eyes had first extricated the gale god from his web in the Window of the North, ever since she had perched on Father's shoulder to search empty horizons for the bright golden sails of *Worldswalker*, ever since then she had waited. And yet, in the end, even Ilina Lightkeeper, last of the Vigilant, guardian of the Beacon, daughter through many fathers of the Herald of the King, even she had shut the door in his face.

Shut? Nay—slammed! I slammed my door in his face.

A booted foot struck the step behind her and tension seized the tendons of her neck. With effort, she stifled the urge to break into a run. *Slowly, softly.* She must not insult this man with her fear.

But why do I fear him so? He has done me no harm. Is the fault mine? If he truly *was* the one whose coming her father had never seemed to doubt, shouldn't she be ecstatic? Shouldn't she laugh and dance and sing the *Rhonolarinlesh* and present the gifts as Father had taught her? Shouldn't she signal Land's End and summon a ship? Oh gods … shouldn't she say her farewells and prepare to part from the only home she'd ever known? She shuddered as duties long-disregarded swamped her memory.

AUSTIN GUNDERSON

So that's it, she thought. *The change he brings proves no less terrifying than that necessitated by his absence.* But no—there had to be more. A familiar fear would not suffice to explain this present dread. She was ill with it. Like a precious apple carried from beyond Cloudfall and sold for a day's wage only to disclose a core of rot, her most sacred hope was turning to sludge in her mouth. What was *wrong* with her? Yet even as she flinched from the question, she thought of a better one.

What was wrong with *him?*

Her hand trembled and the flame danced in her little oil lamp, but she fixed her eyes on the corresponding wash of light as it backed the darkness around the spiral's central pillar, and she plodded on. She would not glance over her shoulder. She would not indulge her fright.

And frightened she was, for he made scant sense. The Awaited One would not be unfamiliar with the Old Tunnoltan tongue, nor would the god of the arctic gale be overcome by his own storm. There was an ignorance about Hoo, a transparent ineptitude with the rudiments of culture, that disturbed Ilina. Not because he seemed strange to her, but because *she* seemed strange to *him.* That she should be unknown to her own god was not a thought she wished to entertain.

But it had become clear to her that the man now following her into darkness would know nothing she didn't teach him.

A more terrifying thought her mind could not have conjured, but one had been foisted on her nonetheless. For this man, this stranger walking mere paces behind, had turned the Beacon black. The darkness had retreated before her strongest incantation, but just barely. What this signified she did not know. That this was the uncertainty which now sat in the pit of her stomach like a knotted rag, fetid and heavy—of that she was certain.

Had she erred to relinquish the sword? In that moment it had seemed so right, somehow—obvious, even inevitable. But the sensation had passed. Now she wondered what in all the worlds had compelled her to simply give up such a powerful object—for she sensed its power even from a distance like she sensed the heat of her lamp. *Was it out of guilt over my initial unfriendliness?* No—her action had arisen from a deeper urge, one to which she could not now honestly object. For the sword was Hoo's possession. That at least was clear. Ilina could not in good conscience have kept it from him, even had she known with certainty that he was not the Awaited.

But I have no such certainty. Upon returning from the cliffs, before discovering Hoo's escape, Ilina had finally determined why the sword had been tickling her brain. With stomach knotting in apprehension, she had once

A SEA SOUGHT IN SONG

again invaded her father's disused room, and once again unfastened the hasps of his old sea-chest. Propping the sword up against the iron-ribbed wood, she'd withdrawn an oblong object bound in oilskin, and reverently unwrapped it until just its tip was showing: an emerald bulb that capped a thick black rod. Careful not to touch the gem, she'd held it up to the strange concavity in the pommel of Hoo's black sword. Closer and closer and closer she'd held it, until finally it clicked into place.

It fit perfectly.

Granted, this meant little. The bulb was convex, the pommel concave— of course they'd correspond. The ancient Scepter of Kredak was not some key fitted to a singular lock. But still … they *looked* the same. The same curves, the same silky blackness. Held together, sword and scepter became virtually indistinguishable. *If this is a hoax, it's an awfully well-informed one.*

But there have been pretenders before. And accurate descriptions of Kredak's famous scepter are not impossible to obtain. Surely a blade could have been forged in imitation. Surely, I should withhold judgement.

Ilina trembled and slowed, shooting out her left hand to steady herself, for the stairwell suddenly seemed to pitch forward like a chute into the black. *Great Orlom, let it not be him,* she prayed—then paused for a instant, shocked by her own wish.

Send someone else. This man frightens me.

Hugh caught himself just in time to avoid bumping into Elena from behind. A moment later she'd resumed her descent, having riveted his attention on her shapely behind. But even that couldn't hold his focus for long. He found it difficult to walk, let alone think, yet his mind was running on overdrive.

Who am I?

The gleaming figure in his vision had known him. It had recognized him instantly. And now this girl who'd stolen his stuff had found and returned his sword.

What do you mean, 'your sword'? It's no more yours than the boat you smashed on this godforsaken rock. You brought it to honor the wish of a dying man—nothing more.

Hugh clenched his jaw, nearly stumbling as the memory—still fresh and raw like a bleeding wound—soaked his senses anew. His knuckles whitened around the sword's hilt at his side, and he twitched its naked tip back up to keep it from scraping the stone steps behind. *What is it about this damned blade that compels people to thrust it into my hands? It's weird.*

Had it not been for his father's irritating insistence and his own sentimentality, Hugh never would've brought the thing. It wasn't a weapon he would've chosen to carry. For one thing, it was far too huge to wield with any finesse. Even were he experienced with swords—which he wasn't—killing a man with this slab of steel would be like smashing a fly with an armchair: exorbitant effort needlessly expended in pursuit of an end achievable by much simpler means. For another thing, the Westley Richards .577 double rifle he'd laid at the foot of his bed last night was like an armchair that broke the sound barrier at the twitch of a trigger. No contest.

Unfortunately, *that* particular weapon had been requisitioned by Elena, She Who Sings to Stones, the girl whose flickering lamp drew him ever deeper into the bowls of this echoing fortress. He only hoped she wouldn't decide to indulge any primitive curiosity and wind up with a dislocated shoulder before he managed to reacquire his Boom Stick.

And he needed to reacquire it soon. He couldn't afford to linger here. Time was slipping away.

A metallic clink interrupted his thoughts. Elena had paused on a landing just ahead and was fiddling with the lock of an iron-rimmed door. She straightened and shoved and, as the door squeaked inward, the glow of her lamp slipped through to illumine a figure seated cross-legged in the center of an empty room. The figure raised its head. Its beard bristled like an irate animal, and its silence was a scathing slap.

It was that little Eskimo Hugh had dragged from the wreckage of the boat.

Ilina held Jarlin's gaze, careful to squelch in herself even the tiniest flicker of regret at having treated him with such negligence. His kind, she reminded herself, deserved far worse. Besides, this incarceration would eventually enter the canon of Jaar legend—passed down from generation to generation until the unwilling houseguest grew into a conquering god—if Harlith saw fit to return this man safely to his snowbound village.

So Ilina held his unblinking gaze for five more minutes to establish her prestige. Behind her in the stairwell, Hoo sighed and slouched against the wall like a peasant. That Ilina didn't cringe in embarrassment was a testament to her control. Only when she began to fear that her eyeballs might shrivel did she finally blink and speak.

"*What has brought you to the Isle of Dead Talk?*"

She allowed herself a slight smile in response to his quick blink of surprise. It was always gratifying to witness a Jaar grapple with the fact that a foreigner could speak his tongue. To his credit, Jarlin seemed to be taking this revelation in stride—no doubt because he had yet to realize that Ilina was even now perusing the tale of his life's deeds as scripted with ivory strips in the fabric of his parka. After many moments he spoke, but his voice carried none of the animosity for which she had been bracing. Instead it was flat, resigned.

"*I came here at the will of a tall stranger who spits stones through men's bodies. His hunt is in the lands of dirt, and the might of my clan was not enough to keep him from commandeering our ship.*"

Ilina felt a chill at his words. She very deliberately did not turn to look at the man who stood behind her in the dark of the stairwell, the man to whom she'd entrusted that fearsome sword, the man who, to judge by his newfound stillness, seemed to be taking an interest in this conversation.

"*What does this man hunt in the lands of dirt?*" she asked.

Jarlin shrugged and said nothing.

"*Whence did he come to your ship?*"

"*He is a stranger, as I have already told you.*"

Ilina bristled. "*You forget yourself, Jarlin son of Harjim son of Lanic. Do not think to evade my thought. You did not survive the hungry sea and the demons of Hoc to prevaricate before me like a puffin that can't decide whether it wants to dive or fly. Now answer my question.*"

To her acute annoyance, Jarlin merely smiled. "*You are clever to have seen my story. But it may disappoint you to learn I am not as credulous as you were perhaps expecting. For one thing, I am protected from your spells by an amulet you cannot see, Lady of Dead Talk.*" He inclined his head ever so slightly. "*For another thing, I see the stranger of whom we speak standing behind you this very moment. If you must know his origin, why not ask him?*"

Ilina cursed inwardly. Jarlin's parka had said nothing about his being a chieftain of his clan, yet no other explanation would suffice to account for this placid impertinence. He'd spent nearly eighteen hours in solitary confinement without exhibiting noticeable discomfiture. The strip of smoked meat lying untouched by his knee bespoke his obstinacy. Further attempts at intimidation would only diminish whatever respect she still commanded in this man. It was time to switch tactics.

"*I do not speak his language,*" she admitted after a pause. "*Hence my need to ask you.*"

Jarlin started. For the first time since Ilina had stepped foot in his cell, fear sprang into his dark eyes. "*Not even you?*" he blurted. "*But you ...*" He trailed off, recomposed himself. "*It is said,*" he continued in a steadier tone, "*that the Lady of Dead Talk knows every tongue under heaven.*" He fixed Ilina with an almost accusatory stare, as though daring her to dispute such a widely accepted truth.

Ilina, for her part, had to fight to keep her face free of astonishment. It seemed that among the Jaar, tales grew in the telling even faster than she'd assumed. "*Nevertheless,*" she said, breaking her own rule against prevarication, "*I cannot communicate with him. Even you must understand the implications of this, and how important it is that I discover his business.*"

Jarlin studied her face in silence. Then his gaze slipped to the side, to where Hoo loomed in the shadows. "*He came out of Utter North, where no man dwells,*" whispered Jarlin at last. "*When first I met him eight days past, his eyes saw only the south. And each dawn since that day has found him nearer his aim. For your own sake, Lady of Dead Talk, do not hinder him. He knows not the meaning of mercy.*"

"*What do you mean? Speak plainly.*"

Jarlin's eyes hardened—twin flecks of obsidian glinting back the lamplight. "*Fourteen of my brothers lie in ice because they opposed the will of that man. Make not their mistake.*"

Ilina said nothing, hoping her face remained equally taciturn. Her grasp of this situation—feeble from the beginning—was swiftly slipping. Could the Jaar be believed? Why would he fabricate a story that attributed weakness to his people? Nothing north of the Gnofs was as unbending as a Jaar defending his superiority. As the old saying went, 'To daunt a Jaar, visit a bar.' But what besides an ethnic susceptibility to alcohol could account for the fact that a Jaar whaling ship had apparently become the personal ferry for a culturally-ignorant, out-of-place stranger? And why would Jarlin pull an oar for Hoo only to denounce him from this cell? His tale of slaughter was surely a fabrication. But what had prompted it? Was it resentment over the loss of the ship, the death of a fellow crewman? But what sailer could resent such a captain? Hoo had personally borne Jarlin's unconscious body from the lashing surf to the door of Kredak Tower. And hadn't Hoo treated Ilina herself with respect, though she'd threatened him with a crossbow, confiscated his strange weapons, and locked him in his room? The more she considered, the less she understood.

A SEA SOUGHT IN SONG

"*Arise, Jarlin,*" she said aloud. "*Eat my meat without shame. Whatever darkness haunts your steps, your coming here was not without purpose. The Lady of Dead Talk has spoken.*"

###

Elena turned, brushing past Hugh without a sideways glance, leaving the cell door open behind her. Hugh, annoyed by his ignorance of what had transpired, was gratified to glimpse the little Eskimo's look of astonishment before the girl and her lamp vanished around the curve of the stairwell. *Yeah, you and me both, pal.*

The Room of the Round Table—still devoid of knights—appeared much as it had last night. Elena briskly circled the vast wooden disk, touching her lamp to sixteen candles and spacing their multiplied points of light at equidistant intervals around the table's edge. Watching in abstraction, Hugh wondered if she really *was* just a maid, an indentured caretaker of this estate, and if the absent knights were due for dinner. He hefted the sword to his shoulder. *And what if you've just been volunteered into their ranks, huh?*

For the very first time, it occurred to Hugh that, by accepting this weapon from Elena's hands, he may have tacitly agreed to any number of attendant obligations. The blade seemed to grow heavier as he contemplated an array of delightful possibilities for cross-cultural entrapment. His carefully-blank expression soured. *You need to secure* her *cooperation, not give her your own free of charge, dammit!*

Elena startled him out of this train of thought with a directional jerk of her finger. He followed her silently out the doorway through which he'd entered last night, took an immediate right down a dark cross-corridor, and, after a couple more turnings, stood before a recessed wooden door upon which had been graven a familiar figure. Elena set down her lamp in order to fish out a key for the overlarge lock, and Hugh once again stood face-to-face with that kingly idol who oversaw admittance to the tower's top floor.

Lit from beneath, the Man with the Radiant Hand acquired an almost malevolent intensity. The wood of the door was wan and worn with age, and a hair's-breadth crack had split the idol's cheek. Its left cheek. Hugh lifted a finger to trace his own scar from eye to jaw.

He only flinched a little.

The lock clicked and the door swung inward, releasing a dazzling burst of light. Hugh stepped back, raising his free hand to shield his eyes; after the dimly-lit gloom of the tower's interior, actual sunlight was blinding. Elena swept up her now-redundant lamp and plunged into the brightness. Hugh took only a few tentative steps before his constricting pupils regained sight and he stopped to gape stupidly.

The space in which he stood—he couldn't really call it a *room*; perhaps *atrium* was a better word—was vast and airy, at least three stories tall. The opposite wall seemed made of glass: a massive window spread from floor to ceiling. Its radiance, bisected in the foreground by a single column of stone, suffused his face with warmth. On either hand, the atrium ran on into the shadow of vertiginous shelves—row upon row of partitions receding from sight. Bookshelves, that's what they were. For as Hugh turned, he saw that the wall behind him held nothing but faded tomes as far and high as his eyes could resolve them. He swayed backward, staggered by this unexpected weight of scholarship.

"Rin, Hoo!" Elena's muffled call jerked Hugh's mind back into focus. He caught his balance and directed his feet toward her voice, threading a pattern of waist-high wooden cubes that crowded the floor before the window, their sides bristling with drawer-knobs and their tabletops strewn with parchments and inkwells and unrolled scrolls darkened by intricate maps of sea and land and sky.

The stone column grew, its splayed foundation assuming the form of a huge, four-sided fireplace. Lofty bookshelves marched past as he advanced: chalk-lined tree-rows in a managed forest of knowledge. He squinted against the glow of dust motes which hung suspended in air like submarine sediment. Elena vanished up one of the shadowed aisles and he hung a right to catch up.

When Hugh reached her, she'd grabbed a wheeled ladder and was towing it along a sunken iron rail which ran the full length of the stack. Metal joints squealed intermittently and pulley-strung ropes quivered on either side of the ladder's uprights. Hugh's eyes followed its steps all the way up to the top of the stack nearly ten yards overhead, where the ladder's bracketing beams curled over the lip of the highest shelf mere feet below the ceiling. The books didn't seem to get any smaller the higher they'd been shelved. *Man, I'd hate to be the librarian on call.*

He blinked. *Oh, so that's why she wanted me here. Figures.*

But when Elena finally arrived at the column of shelves she sought, she didn't even shoot Hugh a glance before toeing the ladder's steel prong onto a notch in the track and, with a quick steadying breath, scrambling up the rungs. Hugh tilted his head appraisingly as she ascended. *Too bad she had to go and change out of last night's dress ...*

A SEA SOUGHT IN SONG

Elena stopped halfway up to hook one leg through a rung and lean out over the side. The ladder creaked alarmingly and Hugh, prompted by some instantly-resented instinct, snapped out a supporting hand. He converted the reflex action into a plausible stretch and yawn, but needn't have bothered: Elena, heedless of the ladder's complaints from her perch fifteen feet above, was hauling heartily on one of the pulley-ropes.

A kind of cage descended slowly from on high to settle around her. From its top there sprouted an articulated metal arm that carried a trough. This she swung around to abut one of the honeycombed shelves in front of her, spinning a hand-crank to telescope the trough out toward the opposite stack.

Leaning forward, she drew forth a scroll from one of the stack's apertures. It was huge, and long, and just kept coming and coming. As she eased it into the trough's cradle, the cage sagged. But its ropes—taut as iron bars—held it level. Hand-over-hand, Elena lowered the whole contraption to the floor.

At an imperious gesture from the girl, Hugh stepped forward to heft the back end of the scroll. He grunted: it was even heavier than it looked. Elena hugged the scroll's front end to her hip with both arms, straining to keep her back straight. Together, they began staggering back the way they'd come. The girl was tenacious—he had to give her that.

This scroll was more of a rug, really. Hugh's lips quirked as he tried to imagine the number of tightly-rolled bodies a library like this might be able to stockpile. *Hell, you could fit more than one in this scroll alone.* He tightened his grip, only to feel his fingers sinking into the parchment. The thing was coming apart! He glanced down in alarm to see a layer of fur springing erect along the edge of his arm.

His own hackles rose in response. *Calm down, you idiot—of course this is a pelt. All parchments start out that way.* But no one had bothered to shave it before the drying. *And the thing's over twenty feet long. It can't possibly be a single hide. There has to be stitching.* But, stare as he might, Hugh couldn't see it. No clever little hems, no neat undulations of thread.

A cold sweat spread from his spine. His fingers slipped, ploughing up long-plastered hair, and he nearly dropped his end. Elena cast him a tight-lipped glare over her shoulder, but he paid her no heed. *What monster could have provided a hide of this size? And what hunter could have taken it? Should I be on the lookout for mammoths?*

They returned at last to the great circular table. Hugh propped his sword against its edge, nudging a candle aside with his elbow, and then he and Elena heaved the scroll up onto the wooden plane. He knelt to finger the

AUSTIN GUNDERSON

parchment's furred fringe as the girl, exhausted beyond pride, slumped against the table's edge to catch her breath.

But before Hugh could do more than admire the density of the dead creature's coat, Elena had recovered her composure and sprung lightly onto the tabletop. She shoved one end of the scroll one way, then nudged its other end the other way, then began kicking at it, unrolling it, spreading it open and centering it until it filled all the space within her candle-ring. The hide was heavy enough that it required no weights to lie flat.

Finished, she hopped down and stood before Hugh. They were so close she had to crane her neck just to meet his gaze. She seemed suddenly small, vulnerable. As he searched her eyes his questions came rushing in all at once and his mind choked with fury at the futility of speech, that unyielding division between them. *What am I doing here?*

Hugh felt desperation then. He sensed he'd struck a logjam in the river of time, and decided he'd have to leave this place by nightfall. He couldn't afford to linger in limbo. *This girl won't help me. She doesn't know who I am, and can't give me anything I need.* He steeled himself to act—to seize her and lock her away and tear this tower apart in search of the tools she'd stolen. Somewhere in his heart, a shutter slapped shut. But it rattled.

"*Rin,*" said the girl gently as she brushed past Hugh's tensed arm. And that single word was like a breeze that banged the shutter open again, for Hugh understood what it meant, what it *must* mean, and he turned slowly and followed Elena as she mounted the stone steps which whorled the walls of the room and sliced into the ceiling and spiraled up the tapering tower to the diamond far, far above.

They passed the ivory chandelier suspended in air. Its branches seemed even stranger when viewed from this angle. The flames below lit the skeletal web like some wakeful underworld. Having already traversed this stairway twice, Hugh wondered to see the change wrought by mere candlelight.

Higher and higher they climbed, until the stair was forced to gouge its path along the overhanging inner face of the domed ceiling as it converged upon its capstone, and there was nowhere left to go except straight up the stem of the tower.

But here they stopped. The table's disk spread seemingly just beyond their feet—a vast tracery of gold and black. For the chandelier now hung directly beneath them, and its silhouette, like the flood from an overturned inkwell, painted strange seas upon the map. For it was clear now to Hugh that the huge scroll *was* a map, or a piece of one, and that it had been for his sake that the girl had unfurled this figurative face of an alien world.

A SEA SOUGHT IN SONG

Elena proffered a thin spyglass. Wordlessly Hugh took it, raised it, focused it on one of the larger splotches of gold. She was talking again, insistently this time—asking some kind of question, making some kind of gesture. He ignored her. His hand and eye and mind had frozen in place and, for all he knew or cared, the universe might've been doing cartwheels round the circlet of his lens.

Kralalahad, City of Swallows, Sieve of the Ever-Stooping Sky. Those were the words. They'd been inscribed in black ink on the surface of the parchment. And Hugh could read them clearly, because they were printed in plain ol' English.

Chapter Eight
DEAD TALK

*Y*ou speak English. With the words came awareness. Hugh mouthed them, squinting with riveted eye at the map below. Other names, other places there were—other cities and kingdoms and lands spreading to the circumference, each labeled with the same bold, flowing script. The massive parchment was dark with letters. He couldn't believe it. It didn't make sense.

"You speak English." The words were an indictment. Hugh whirled on the girl, who shrank back, terrified. She'd duped him, led him on! She'd understood every word he uttered since arriving! Why would she conceal her comprehension? What possible reason could she have for deceiving him so? His knuckles whitened on the spyglass.

"You speak English." The words were a plea. Elena lay curled into a ball against the curve of the stairwell, shielding her head with her arms. Her whole body quivered. Slowly, Hugh lowered his hands to his sides. All he'd done was raise them. *Please, please speak English. I have so much to ask you. So much to learn. And I'd rather learn it from no one else, not even on Earth.*

"Speak to me, please." After a deep breath, he dampened the force in his voice. "Elena. Please." She peered over her forearm. "Please, Elena. Please speak to me."

Her voice struggled to sound strong. *"Whem ham tehm ta, Rhim? Whet ham tehm seht rhauhu mah? Laktai teht, fik whem lish teht oms larinleshes nal Cul Kredak met connak."*

Hugh snarled and smacked the wall, then gritted his teeth at Elena's flinch. "This isn't a game, girl. Lives are at stake here. Hell, the souls of the *dead* may hang in the balance. If you can understand what I'm saying, give me a sign. I don't have *time* for games."

Slowly, with visible effort, Elena unfolded from her crouch and rose to face Hugh until her chin drew level with his chest. At her sides she clenched small fists. *"Teh haum ut whein seht yir, cu whalnal seht rin,"* she said, the words crawling singly from her lips as though they straggled after a long journey, *"ane ut fi lo omet Lihm Anahammah fik hir hamsil culs yisleh oam lammah. Ut fi!"*

Hugh glared right back at her. What *else* could he do? If she *did* understand his words, a career in cinema would be a cinch for her. She exhibited no tells he could detect—no stifled flickers of recognition or infinitesimal hesitations to indicate this was all some elaborate act.

And what if it is? You can't do a damn thing about it, that's what. What, will you force her to talk despite her reticence? What would that *entail?* Hugh shuddered at the speculation. He had no desire to listen to anything he could force her to say.

"Damn it," he hissed, "I *want* to believe you."

Elena said nothing. She, too, seemed at a loss. *And if that's the case ...* A sudden insight flashed behind Hugh's eyes like a strobe, blinding in its simplicity. Its afterimage was still smoldering as he descended the steps three at a time.

Ilina was panting by the time her shoulder struck the library door, banging it open. She cringed in sympathy at the cracking sound. *That's a first.* Would any of her forebears have dared fling this work of art against its stone frame like a shirt beaten in the wash? *Perhaps so. Perhaps that would explain the split in Harlith's cheek.*

She now regretted admitting Hoo to her home. *What in all the Deeps was I thinking? He's a foreigner!* Without a reliable means of communication, she was at the mercy of his infantile comprehension. Even a map was subject to misunderstanding. *I have to regain control. I cannot allow him to twitch my strings to his tune.*

But even as she had this thought, her eyes adjusted to the glare and registered Hoo himself, stooping over a low table in the midst of Seascape Study, slashing at a precious parchment with a big black brush.

Ilina screamed.

Hoo barely had time to turn before she was on him—flailing, striking, scrabbling to slap away his tools of vandalism. But he snatched her arms from the air nonetheless, effortlessly swinging her around and slamming her onto the tabletop. In a single gasp she found herself flat on her back, pinioned. Hoo's arms bulged through his shirt.

Ilina felt herself begin to shrink, to crumple beneath a torrent of darkness, but then the sudden rage drained from Hoo's eyes like an ebbing tide and his grip on her wrists relaxed. Her breast rose and fell as she sucked in a shuddering breath. The blackness drew back from her vision and she, rather than dwelling on the departing terror, focused a withering glare at the man who now leaned over her prone body. She struggled to no avail. *Lost god or no, I will bite the lips from your face if you try to kiss me, you benighted carrier of calamity.*

Hoo's eyes widened in what could only be mockery at her outrage, but then narrowed again as an impish grin seeped across his face. Down came his brow with a sudden thunk against hers. She froze. *What will he do, what does he want?* But he merely looked at her with laughing eyes, waiting, it seemed, for a reaction. *So. He fancies himself a jester. How ... amusing.*

Ilina wrung out her rags of sentiment, squeezing into her lips the hint of a reciprocal smile. *I cannot trust you, Hoo, but I'm afraid I must appreciate you. Few in this world are capable of ingratiating themselves to me. You are bold indeed to try.* She twisted in his grip to appraise the damage he'd done.

And there, scrawled in big black letters, lay a message. It stood out against the faded text of a parchment Hoo had yanked seemingly at random from a nearby stack. And Ilina could read it. *He wrote it, and I can read it.*

In wonder and terror her eyes flicked back up to Hoo's deceptively genial face looming above, but she couldn't wrest them from the message for long. She breathed it in, the smell of it, the biting reek of wet ink that linked the disparate kindreds of Man.

"Where are my things?" it said in the Script of Secrets, the writing of the Book and Map, the language known, perhaps, only by the Old Couriers in the faraway south, and by one last surviving Lightkeeper clinging to the northern rim of the known world. Had some resurgence of scholarship eluded her notice? *How can it be?*

She searched Hoo's face. "You restrain me still," she murmured. "Release me, sir, that I may answer your query."

And then a hand from nowhere gripped Hoo's shoulder and a pale knife flashed toward his throat.

A rove beetle scampered along the strip of flesh, tasting as it touched. Jarlin could hear it in the dark. At least three insects in this cell had stirred in response to the presence of meat, though this beetle was the only one he'd glimpsed while the Lady of Dead Talk attempted her interrogation. Behind their faint chitters and through millions of tons of stone rolled the sonorous heartbeat of the sea. But it was to sounds neither delicate nor vast that Jarlin hearkened now, but to the quick step of the Witch and the plodding tread of the Stranger as they retreated down the stairwell.

Nineteen, twenty, twenty-one ... When the big man took his twenty-fourth step, Jarlin's crossed legs stiffened and straightened, lifting him silently upright. The rove beetle, startled, skittered away to the wall.

Like a breath of air Jarlin spiraled down the tower.

He stood now in a doorway that emptied upon a deep, deep cave. Below him, tiny lights sprang into being one by one, forming a circuit. There stood the Stranger on the fringes of radiance, watching the Witch as she pressed flame to wick. They seemed so remote.

Strange that she should trust him with a sword if she knows nothing about him. And stranger still that he should bear a blade instead of that terrible pipe with which he spilled so much of the People's blood. The Witch withheld the whole truth, yes, but what was it she elided?

Could it be that she *did* know this stranger—that he was, in fact, in her employ—yet she had found herself unprepared for his arrival? Perhaps they usually conversed through a translator—someone now absent from this castle. Perhaps the Stranger had learned something which the Witch sought to pry from his mind. Perhaps he had set out from this place as a member of a larger party, and now she wished to know the fate of his former companions. *If that's the nature of her query, I can provide a plausible explanation.*

Jarlin closed his eyes. The death-screams returned to him then—faint yet near, thin yet piercing. The last cries of his kinfolk as flying stones ripped the souls from their bodies. A wave of helpless rage crashed into him. He shuddered, struggling to remain upright beneath its torrent. *Why did the Lady of Dead Talk let me go? Surely, she recognized how I feel. Surely the hate shone in my eyes, no matter how thickly I veiled my thoughts. Surely, she foresaw my intent. Surely ...*

And then Jarlin's eyes snapped open, for he saw how he had answered his own question.

The faraway figures vanished through a doorway and Jarlin padded in pursuit down the circuitous stair. Shrieks out of the past ricocheted off the insides of his skull. Something about all this stone seemed to funnel and magnify the illusory sounds. *Pain fades swiftly on the cloud-coated plains, but here ... in a place like this, sorrows could echo forever.*

Jarlin paused in the open doorway. Behind him, candle flames guttered in a silent breeze that swept out of the darkened passage. He bent to slip his

A SEA SOUGHT IN SONG

wolrum-bone dagger from its sheath in his right mukluk. Its razor-fine edge remained muted, slipping through light as easily as it incised flesh.

And then images burst in his mind to accompany the bodiless cries. He saw again the Stranger's mad snarl and heard the deafening roar of his pipe as Jaar warriors fell like stampeding madomul before his hailstorm of death. He gaped as the smooth-cheeked giant disarmed Larlij the Laughing in close-quarters combat, slitting the champion's throat with the blade of his own storied spear. And then he saw himself, prostrate and quaking not from fear but from relief as the Stranger lowered his pipe and lifted his eyes to the water's edge and to the ship moored there.

Jarlin staggered back up from the cold stone floor. He would cover his skin with the feathers of the tern; he would let the shame slide from him like water. *But how can I surprise a sorcerer? How can I succeed where all my clan has failed?*

Jarlin stood before the carven door. Light spilled from its arch. He passed the idol embossed on its wooden surface, noting the smooth face and making a circle with his thumb and fourth finger to ward off evil. His amulet in the Cave of the Rock felt worlds away.

And then all he could do for a time was stare. The library surpassed his most fanciful imaginings. *This is the center of her power. This is where the dead talk.*

At last Jarlin forced himself to stir. The foreigners were returning. He ducked behind a low desk and peered between its legs. The Stranger's big boots clumped after the Witch's hard-sole moccasins, his stride languid relative to her short quick steps. They moved slowly, keeping a constant distance from each other. *Bearing something long and heavy.* Jarlin glimpsed it as they negotiated the door, but couldn't make out what it was.

Are you helping me, Witch? wondered Jarlin as he crept back down a curving passage, careful to stay just beyond the Stranger's backward glance. *Are you risking everything to give me the opportunity I need? Will you turn your magics against this man if I strike suddenly from cover? Will our combined strength be enough?*

If it was her goal to distract the Stranger, the Lady of Dead Talk had certainly woven her spell. She was up on the great table now, dancing between the candles, unfurling what looked to be the mainsail of a ship. The Stranger stood stock still in silhouette, his back to the passage where Jarlin crouched in shadow, his great sword propped against the table's edge five paces from his hand. *He is unarmed, oblivious. You will never get a better chance than this.*

AUSTIN GUNDERSON

The Witch finished her dance and glanced up and Jarlin could've sworn her eyes met his. Then she hopped off the table and approached her guest to stand before him. They were close enough to touch. All the Stranger's attention was focused on the woman. *Now, now! This is the moment!* But Jarlin didn't—couldn't—move. *How can I stab a man in the back? Would he do the same to me?*

And then the Witch brushed past the Stranger and walked off, leading him back to the spiral stairway. *No, no! What are you doing? I can't attack him from below!*

Cursing himself for timidity, Jarlin edged forward to the corridor's corner. Past it there was no concealment. The floor before him lay brightly lit and fully exposed to the eyes of those above. He himself had enjoyed the advantage afforded by that stairway only half an hour earlier. There was nothing he could do now. He would have to bide his time.

But he didn't have to bide it for long.

Jarlin had barely noticed the clatter before it swelled to a crescendo of footfalls. He drew back, shrinking against the wall as the Stranger burst out of the great room and barreled pell-mell past him down the black passage. The thumping receded. A door slammed. And Jarlin lay shuddering like a hare backed into a dead-end burrow.

Rise, you lout. He didn't even see you, yet you grovel. How shall it be when he looks you in the eye? Get up and face him like Jaral did. Get up and justify your manhood torc. Get up!

Jarlin had barely gathered himself before swift steps heralded the approach of the Witch. He sucked in a breath and rose, turning to face her as she swept up. He knew by her flinch that she'd seen him, but then her eyes snapped forward once more and she quickened her pace and was gone.

Jarlin stood dumbfounded. *What is it you want of me? What am I supposed to do, follow you like a dog?*

Since he couldn't conjure a better plan, that's exactly what Jarlin did. Except he moved more like an arctic fox than a dog—padding soundlessly through the vast warren of rock, weaving desperate death-spells in the air before his face with a dagger born of death, shadowing the slim young woman who, he realized with horror, had effortlessly assumed an inexplicable power over his actions. *Spirits of air bear me up. I have entered the den of the dead yet wish to join them not.*

A shrill cry pierced his prayer. The Witch had jettisoned her composure. Jarlin started; the passage ahead was suddenly vacant. But light streamed from a familiar doorway. He peered inside.

A SEA SOUGHT IN SONG

The Stranger lay upon the struggling Witch, pinning her to a tabletop.

Jarlin dithered between fear and rage. His limbs spasmed, then stopped. *I have to! I can't!* The Stranger head-butted the woman and Jarlin took a step forward. He was nearly inside the room. *This is your moment! You must act before he takes her! If not now, when?*

He gnashed his teeth and clenched his fists. *I can't! I wish to live. Even now my fear outweighs my shame. Is that not the greater evil?* Yet not even this admission could help him. He was still just standing there, shaking.

He watched as the Witch glanced away from her tormentor, saw the strength in her eyes as they sought the doorway where he stood, felt her resolve from afar as she turned back to face her fate. Though the lone witness to her plight stood as static as the wooden sculpture in the door, still she scorned surrender. Her lips moved in her own tongue—the tongue she didn't know he knew—and Jarlin craned to hear. "Release me, sir," she said.

And then suddenly Jarlin couldn't take it anymore.

He charged forward and grabbed the Stranger's shoulder, yanking him up off the Witch and arcing the knife around his neck to slit it open on the backstroke. But the Stranger dropped his chin to his chest and drove an elbow backward into Jarlin's armpit and the backstroke floundered, grazing the Stranger's jaw, glancing off his collarbone.

Then the giant twirled an arm around Jarlin's own arm and a viselike grip closed on Jarlin's wrist and he felt himself twisting, falling, robbed of his balance, as the Stranger rose. *The knife, the knife, mustn't lose the knife ...!* But the knife sprang from his fingers, clattering to the floor, and the giant kicked it away. A fist drove into Jarlin's kidney and he sagged. But the Stranger's fresh blood had spattered on Jarlin's face, and this unlooked-for proof of the enemy's mortality—more than any rage or shame—gave Jarlin the strength to lash back hard.

He stamped on the Stranger's shin as the man's huge hands levered his arm over his head. The giant's grunt of pain and a momentary release of pressure was all the opportunity Jarlin needed to break free and tumble forward and convert his fall into a roll that put a table between himself and his adversary. He sprang back up, recovered knife in hand, and was immediately struck in the face by a flying scroll. The next moment the Stranger had skirted the buffer table and was pummeling him with another parchment-wrapped rod. Somewhere behind them the Witch was shrieking.

The rain of blows was overwhelming; Jarlin knew he must end this fight soon or die. He dropped his guard and dodged forward to get inside the other's reach but a backhanded stroke of the scroll clipped his temple and he crumpled at the giant's feet.

###

Hugh lifted his boot—a hammer hovering over the neck of this feral brute. *Yet another face to inhabit my nightmares. But it can't be avoided, now.* His own face twisted in revulsion as he sucked in a preparatory breath and glanced away.

And there stood Elena, eyes wide and lips bloodless, holding up an ink-splashed parchment which shouted a single English word: *"Stop."*

Hugh lowered his boot to the floor and grinned. He'd finally made contact.

###

As he hauled the little Eskimo's unconscious body up the tower stairs for the second time in twenty-four hours, Hugh Conrad contemplated the relative merits of communication.

Eloquence had never been his forte. *'Don't just* say *something,'* Professor McDougall had scolded after handing back an umpteenth C-grade paper. *'I've taught this class for twenty years. You can't say anything I haven't heard a hundred times before. Say it in a non-obvious way. Come at it sideways. Sneak up on it. Sing it. Use your imagination!'* But pretty words were mere embellishments. The core thing was information and its transmission—the sharing of thought. If the core was vacuous, its embellishments would snap under pressure as easily as the brittle twigs of a shrub without root. It was the core that mattered. It was the core that would last.

In the real world, no man cared about eloquence unless he could first convey meaning. Without a shared core, different nations might as well be different species. So Hugh had sought to expand his core, and each new language he'd learned had seemed to pull together the fragmented human race a little more solidly.

But since his arrival in this frigid wasteland a week and a half ago, he'd been alone. Oh, isolation wasn't a new experience for Hugh—but its ache had always been dulled by the knowledge that all he'd have to do to be heard and understood once more would be to cross an ocean or descend a mountain or break free from a cell.

A SEA SOUGHT IN SONG

The mirror had severed him from that assurance.

Now he was alone without hope of connection. His speech consisted of either self-directed complaints or functional gibberish which at least seemed to convince others he wasn't some kind of demon. His questions went unanswered; his thoughts loitered, unshared. In the time since that damn snowbank had coughed up those angry Eskimos, he'd met dozens of people and been forced to kill most of them because their only means of communication had been knives and spears and arrows. He'd hated it. He just wanted to talk.

And now he could.

Elena jumped back as the listless body slid from Hugh's shoulder to flop upon the floor. Hugh straightened with a grunt.

The strip of dried meat that'd lain in this cell since last night lay crawling with beetles. Elena picked it up and shook it, stamping on the insects where they fell, then draped it carefully over the prone man's throat. With a summary glance at the bare accommodations and a brisk nod to Hugh, she left the room and bolted the door behind them. She bent to lift her lamp from the landing.

Hugh held up his parchment: *"Why did you let him out?"*

Elena cringed, but whether from guilt at her own recklessness or from ire at his continued desecration of her precious paper, Hugh couldn't tell. She snatched the sheet from his left hand and grabbed the pen from his right. Back in the library, he'd stuffed a stoppered inkwell in his pocket. Now he set it beside her as she knelt upon the floor.

Elena glared at the document laid before her, then carefully inscribed her retort: *"My tower is not a prison."* She rose with dignity, shoved the message into Hugh's arms, and stalked off down the stairwell, taking the light with her.

"So, this *is* your tower," Hugh said aloud. "Well then, why'd you lock him back *in?*" But Elena didn't bother to respond.

They sat facing one another in Seascape Study. Failing light from beyond the world warmed all colors yet left the room's air chill. The Window of the North glinted rose-golden along its spiderweb of seams that shattered the sun's rays into strange patterns on the walls and stacks. The waves outside were shallow, and their ridges sparkled. The sky—cloudless, naked—

AUSTIN GUNDERSON

blushed a pale red. *I, too, feel exposed,* thought Ilina. *Now that he can understand me, what will he make me say?*

She shook her head to dislodge the alarm. She was mistress here. Only an authority greater than hers could contest her power, and what cause had she to fear such displacement? *Power is not authority, power is not authority,* she chanted silently to herself. *But neither is authority power,* mocked a harsh voice in her head.

Oh gods, I stand on a brink. Harlith sleep not. Rouse yourself from slumber! The calm sea seemed suddenly deserted—a vast gulf of nothingness upon which Cuspid Isle drifted like a rudderless ship. Her grip tightened on the arms of her chair.

Upon the knee-height cabinet between their chairs were stacked fresh sheets of blank parchment—*thank the gods I ordered a new sheaf last month!*—along with duel pens and inkwells. Hoo had already ruined one historical document—a record of spice shipments from the port of Tlingsti in the year 84 A.H., if she'd correctly deciphered the fragments left to peek from under his scribblings. She'd sooner drink from the brine pit in the cellar than allow him to ruin another such page.

Hoo began their exchange as soon as he'd flopped into his chair. Adjusting the bandage he'd wrapped under an arm and over a shoulder to cover Jarlin's cut, he grabbed a parchment and writing board and bent to his work.

While out gathering the blank sheets, Ilina had decided it was wisdom to defer to Hoo's initiative in their conversation. The man was agitated, impatient—that much was clear. *And why shouldn't he be? You ignored your sacred duty and willfully exposed a guest to peril. The fact that he's still alive to question your motives bespeaks a life cut shard by shard from the unyielding ice of mistrust. When you justify the suspicions of such a man, is it any wonder Harlith withholds his breath? Pray now, 'Lina, as you've never begged before!* Ilina's lips moved soundlessly as Hoo's pen scratched away.

The scratching ceased. Ilina opened her eyes, then squinted. Hoo apparently expected a lengthy dialogue; his writing shrank against the upper-left corner of the sheet. *"My name is Hugh,"* it began, *"not Who. Get it right. Who is a question, and Hugh is the answer. I come from a faraway land. I am on a journey. You have taken items that belong to me. I need these items. Give them back."*

Ilina took a breath and a parchment. This Hugh had lost none of his momentum. Guilt-wracked or no, she would *not* sell answers cheaply. *Yet how should I answer his salvo?* She felt her body grow stiff under Hugh's intent gaze as she translated her thoughts into an ancient code she'd never before heard spoken. It took her far too long to adjust for grammar. *"Thy possessions are safe. Yet I shall return them not unless thou shouldst delimit to me their function."*

Hugh grimaced, put pen to parchment, and paused. *"Bring them,"* he finally wrote.

Though Ilina's face remained blank, solidified like an apple left uncovered to the frost, her agitation slipped out through grammatical miscues. *"They purpose and operation necessary thou first describe. If must, thou pictures draw."*

Ilina jumped at Hugh's sharp laugh. The strange man slapped his knee and leaned back in his seat, chuckling. His eyes were bright but not hard. Ilina just stared. She had expected anger.

He hunched forward again, still snickering, and turned his sheet of parchment lengthwise. Then he began to sketch. What quickly took shape was an image of the strange pipelike object Ilina had examined and then delicately returned to its scabbard during the night. Arrows terminating in terse captions began radiating from the device on the page. Ilina tilted her head to decipher the labels as they appeared. The unobstructed end of the thing's coupled tubes was a *"mouth that spits lead,"* the reflex angle a third of the way up contained *"chambers of sudden fire,"* and the triangular end was intended to prevent the weapon from *"flying backward when it attacks,"* a claim that could not have made less sense.

Ilina leaned forward to write upside-down along the top edge of Hugh's sheet. *"What is its end?"*

Hugh glanced up, his face a question. He pointed at each end of the device he'd sketched and raised an eyebrow.

She rephrased. *"What is its purpose?"*

An instant's hesitation. *"To kill from a distance."*

Ilina nodded and sat back, gesturing for him to continue. She concealed the tremor in her fingers by spreading them upon the arms of her chair. Jarlin's tale of horror didn't seem so fanciful anymore.

The sun sank in the east, casting its rays skyward like a man who throws up his hands at the revelation that a wearisome task must be replicated the following day. A few wisps of cloud shone fiercely in upper heaven. Stragglers from last night's storm, they'd been plucked from the rose backdrop like a covey of young ptarmigans clipped by lamplight while hurrying across a hill-road at night.

AUSTIN GUNDERSON

Hugh was studying her. She knew this because his pen had yet to resume its scratching, and because she could feel his gaze. Her skin prickled—a surprisingly pleasant sensation. *Pleasant? He's a killer! He killed fourteen men!* But if that incident was anything like the scene which had played out in this very room an hour ago, she could hardly blame him. And besides, his scrutiny didn't pierce her like Rikard's. It was intent, yes, but gentler, warmer. Like a diffuse heat that comprehended her as a whole woman without any need for dissection. And so it was that she found herself smiling a small smile when she at last turned to meet his eye. He quirked his mouth and started another sketch.

It was the hand compass he'd stowed in a small pocket of his pack. She'd spent half an hour marveling at its cunning construction. *"This thing is known to me,"* she wrote, then immediately wondered whether it would've been wiser to wait for Hugh's description. Now she had no means of verifying his veracity. *Fool girl. Flattered by friendly eyes, you cast away all caution. If he leads you into a snare, the fault will be your own.*

The next image was of a bent rod stoppered with glass. Ilina recalled the device to her mind. Its shell had been cast from a strange lightweight metal which lacked timbre when flicked. She knew it was hollow, but had feared to open it lest she release some kind of poison. According to Hugh's caption, it was a tool for creating light without fire. *Interesting. The rhomic craft must have advanced considerably in the past few years to produce a lumaan this compact. Could be a prototype. Likely undergoing field trials.*

Which meant that this man might be nothing more than some wayward scientist separated from his party by a blizzard and harried by the Jaar. But that theory failed to account for the sword. It shed no light on that strange swirling blackness in the heart of Kredak's Beacon. And it couldn't begin to explain the fact that she was communicating with a total stranger in a language that'd been dead for half a millennium. *Stop grasping for alternatives. Straighten your spine and face what is.* Ilina's chin ticked up.

Hugh finished his sketch and brandished it for review. His parchment had run out of room. He watched Ilina's eyes flick over its surface for a moment, then flipped it around and wrote, *"Now return my things."* The heat of his stare was pleasant no longer, but scorching. It defied contravention.

Ilina nodded. She had exhausted the tactics of delay. Without rising from her seat, she stretched out a foot to nudge one of the small doors on the side of the cabinet. At this application of pressure, the door sprang open. She gestured to Hugh with an uplifted palm, then pointedly looked away toward

A SEA SOUGHT IN SONG

the high window and the colors which deepened beyond its myriad panes. *Orlom preserve me, for I have relinquished my leverage.*

Hugh carefully drew his rifle, haversack, and sword-scabbard from the cupboard. They appeared unmolested, but he knew better. *So. First things first.*

He broke open the rife and inspected its chambers. Satisfied the weapon hadn't been tampered with, he tugged loose his pack's straps, upended its contents onto the seat of his chair, and knelt to examine them.

His compass pointed straight out the window in the direction from which he'd come. Since his arrival here, he'd been assuming that direction was north. *And if it isn't north, God help you.* He grimaced, toggling his flashlight's switch, then grinned to see Elena twitch in response to the flash of light; she'd been watching him from the corner of her eye.

He hefted his hatchet with one hand, then wrenched at its head to make sure it hadn't been loosened. He unrolled his wool blanket to find it free of holes. His mess kit was clean and his canteen empty. His aluminum ammo box was sealed still. He popped its lid to sift through its meagre contents: five ration bars, an empty matches canister, and twenty-four .577 rounds—all that remained of his most precious commodity.

It'd have to be enough.

Hugh crammed it all back into place and looked up at Elena, who was sitting very still. He inked his pen and smoothed his sheet of parchment, then hesitated before bringing the two together. *"Thank you. May I ask you some questions?"*

"Thou mayest."

"Where am I?"

Elena frowned as if considering. She raised her pen, then did nothing but glare at her page for a full minute. *"In Seascape Study of Anticipation Light on Cuspid Isle in the White Sea,"* she wrote at last, *"But those names may hold naught but a shadow of their true meaning in thy tongue. Never before have I had cause for a translation such as this. I fear I am unequal to the task."*

"How far away is the land of Kramarack?"

Elena's eyes locked on Hugh's. Her irises, he was startled to realize, were a deep, dark blue—as deep and dark as the troughs of an ocean roiled by a pitiless north wind. In the sunset-light from the window they gleamed

115

almost purple. They were eyes that mirrored the twilit sky; drinking knowledge like the heavens drank light, hoarding it close against the onset of night. Hugh felt himself leaning, straining, holding his breath as if by so doing he might plumb the depths of these twin pools that had drowned so much of this strange new world. But then she dropped her eyes to her parchment and Hugh was left blinking in the fast-fading light of day.

"Approximately twenty leagues south," she wrote, *"over sea and under sky."*

Hugh remembered hearing that a league was about three miles. *Sixty miles of ocean, then. And the boat nothing but driftwood now. Damn it all, anyhow. "How can I get there?"* he asked.

The girl pierced him with another thirsty glance that left him unaccountably breathless. *"In five days time, the ferry shall arrive from Land's End. If thou shouldst abstain from belligerence in the intervening time, thou mayest take passage thereon. No vessel moors here on Cuspid Isle,"* she added with a glint in her eye, *"so do not think to abscond with one."* Hugh cursed silently at this unwelcome answer to his unasked query, while attempting to assume a suitably insulted expression. Elena rolled her twilit eyes.

Now that his immediate questions were out of the way, Hugh moved on to more tenuous ones. *"Have you heard of a man named Daniel Forsythe?"* Elena squinted, then shook her head. *"What about a man named Miles Cornwall?"* Another shake. *"Or a man named Henry Conrad?"*

This time the shake was slower in coming. A strange look, like mingled fear and hope and disbelief, washed over her face and then vanished—a sand-etched word erased by the tide.

Hugh perked up. It seemed she knew *something*, but wasn't confident in that knowledge. She just needed the right piece to complete her mental puzzle. *"What about a man named Omri?"* he pressed in a sudden burst of enthusiasm.

Her reaction was not what he'd hoped. The instant that name appeared on the page, the door of her face slammed shut as though kicked. She stood and strode toward the window but then froze mid-step and swayed slightly as though she'd just gotten off a merry-go-round. Her hands balled into fists at her sides.

Hugh watched, uneasy, as she extended a stiff arm to steady herself against a tabletop. Her delicate fingers slowly clenched and unclenched. Then she spread them flat upon the table, pivoted around its edge, and returned to her seat.

A SEA SOUGHT IN SONG

"No further answers shall I grant thee," she wrote swiftly. *"Now thou must answer mine. Who art thou? Whence comest thou? What seekest thou? Wherefore dost thou voyage from the north? Answer me."* She put down her pen, flipped the parchment around, and glared at him. All light had faded from her eyes.

"Jeez," blurted Hugh. "Who I am, where I come from, where I'm going? You want the meaning of life, too?" He quirked his eyebrows and delivered his very best lopsided grin to absolutely no effect. Some strong emotion had chilled her. *Either she hates Omri or fears him. I must know which.*

Hugh rubbed his face absently and stared at the parchment. Now that he had his equipment back, he *could* just get up and be on his merry way. But if what the girl had written about a lack of local vessels was true, then he'd come all this way just to get relegated to square one. And if she was indeed his only ticket off this rock, he couldn't afford to anger her any further.

Hugh sighed. Elena's forthrightness in answering his questions probably counted for something, too. His eyes refocused on the stiff yellow page spread before him—an empty dinner plate he was expected to fill with the contents of his mouth. *Where to begin ...?*

At the beginning, I guess.

"I come from the land of New York," wrote Hugh. *"It's very far away. You've probably never heard of it. But don't be alarmed,"* he added, glancing up at her. *"It's a land of mortals just like this land. A week ago, I learned that a friend of mine was in danger far to the south of here. I set out to rescue him. On the way I was attacked by a tribe of nomads, including the man you're housing upstairs. I took their boat, and some of them insisted on going with me so they could reclaim it once I reached Kramarack. But then we were shipwrecked here. Myself and the man upstairs are the only survivors."*

Elena was already scratching away at a reply by the time Hugh flipped his parchment around. *"The man who would have slain thee claimed to have met thee eight days hence. If thine account is true,"* and here she pierced him with a look both hard and hungry, *"thou translocated thyself from New York to the village of nomads in a matter of days. This would place New York in Utter North and make every Jaar a liar who claims he belongs to the hardiest of peoples."*

She stopped and waited—her gaze as intent as that of an osprey, her whole body as taut as that osprey's talons upon their seizure of some squirming prey. It was a question. She had posed a question. *Now you have to answer her question. Why'd you give her a specific detail? Damn that little Eskimo and his big mouth!*

117

AUSTIN GUNDERSON

"No," he wrote. *"New York isn't in Utter North."*

At this the tight line of Elena's lips, much to Hugh's disquiet, curved up. *"And yet thou wouldst have me believe thou didst embark upon this journey from a land like unto mine. Thine own words gainsay thee. Now tell me truly, Stranger Hugh, whence comest thou? I adjure thee by the Beacon of Light: withhold no truth from my sight."*

Her effortless perception was bad enough; her smugness was unbearable. Hugh rolled his eyes and groaned. Elena just sat back, crossed her arms, and waited. The tension seemed to have departed her limbs. Did she think she'd scored some kind of *point* off him or something?

Hugh snorted, then sighed. *Oh, what the hell—just tell her the truth. What's she gonna do? You've got your gun back, after all.* He put pen to parchment.

"I traveled to Utter North through a door in space. New York isn't part of your world."

Ilina reeled. The penstrokes on the page before her gaped like rents in the fabric of reality. She had thought to catch this man in a fabrication, tearing away his mask to reveal an impudent impostor. Instead she had disclosed the object of her fear. He was not a god. He had made that assertion mere minutes before. And yet he came from another world. He was a blight, a stray, a vagrant spirit of unknown aim. He couldn't be the One whose coming Kredak Light had been shaped to anticipate. *Could he?*

It struck Ilina then like a breaker surging through sharp rocks: the terrible import of the decision she faced. In this moment was imprisoned the purpose of her birth, and that of every Lightkeeper before her through the ages. Though she might slip past this moment and go on living and achieve great things—marrying a man who deserved her respect and preserving her line for generations to come, gathering the collective knowledge of Arlam under a single roof and digesting every last word of it until she swelled with understanding, cataloging the stars of heaven and stripping them of their secrets until she perceived the hour of her own death inscribed in twinkling light—it would all be in vain if she failed to correctly identify this man. This was her sole task as Lightkeeper—all else was ancillary.

Ilina shuddered in terror. She had thought herself ready. She had thought herself worthy.

A SEA SOUGHT IN SONG

Hugh's huge hand descended on her shoulder, startling her from her daze. *"Elena ... Elena,"* he repeated softly, comfortingly, as though soothing a jittery horse. He squatted on his haunches beside her seat, his eyes concerned to the point of condescension.

"It's *Ilina,*" she snapped absently, "not *Elena,* you dunce. Ilina. Get it right."

This outburst elicited another eyebrow raising on Hugh's part. He seemed fond of that particular facial gesture. She fixed him with a blank stare until he hauled down the brow and pronounced her name correctly. *Small triumphs. Eyes back on the path before your feet, 'Lina. Place each step with care and you'll reach the clifftop sooner than you think.*

"Where didst thou learn the Script of Secrets?" she wrote.

This gave the Stranger pause while he reclaimed his seat across the table. *"You mean English? What we're writing in now? Learned it as a kid. I speak it, too."* He declaimed some gibberish with mock solemnity, then grinned. *"What about you?"*

Ilina was beginning to feel lightheaded. *"I studied it for many years from ancient texts."*

"What do you mean, 'ancient'?" he asked, his solemnity grown suddenly real. *"Don't you people use English today?"*

Ilina narrowed her eyes. Was the man out of his mind? *"I am the only one within a thousand leagues capable of recognizing a single letter of this script."*

As she watched Hugh's face turn white at this apparent revelation, Ilina found herself reminded of a certain shipwright in Land's End to whom she had inadvertently divulged the spherical nature of Arlam. Had she been a Broanoshi priest or even a scholar from Harnaral, the man would've chuckled politely as though it were all a joke and then guffawed over her idiocy with his pals at the pub later that night. But she was more than a mere priest or scholar: she was a Lightkeeper—*the* Lightkeeper—and most Kram still revered the guardians of Kredak Tower. The man had looked straight into her eyes and believed her, and his affability had flown asunder like so much chaff in the wind.

In vain she'd labored to repair the damage inflicted on his psyche. Though his hyperventilation slowed somewhat after repeated reassurances that no, he wouldn't plummet into space were he to venture too far down the planet's curvature, and no, there was neither cable to cut nor pedestal to upset had one a mind to bring the whole globe crashing down out of heaven, she doubted the man would ever fully recover from the shock of such a shift in perspective. That's why science had to be kept secret from the masses.

And that's why it disturbed her to see Hugh's face turn paler than that of the poor shipwright.

"Then why did you show me the map?" he asked. He was reaching now, grasping at spiderwebs. *"Why did you assume I could read it?"*

"I assumed nothing. I merely provided thee with an occasion to identify thine origin and destination. Everyone knows the world when they see it. I wished to be of service in the event thou required guidance."

Hugh put his head in his hands. At a loss, Ilina just stared. She could think of nothing she'd communicated that he shouldn't have already known.

Eventually Hugh lifted his eyes. Darkness was flowing freely across the face of the heavens outside, and his expression was difficult to read in the swiftly failing light. To keep the night at bay she had only to fetch an oil lamp from a table across the room, yet she remained still. Something warned her not to break the mood of this moment.

Hugh reached into his pack and withdrew an oblong object bent at one end. Ilina had just enough presence of mind to fling a forearm over her eyes before blinding light burst silently over the table as though emitted by a miniature Beacon. She lowered her arm, squinting. Hugh was holding his lumaan-device aloft with one hand and writing intently with the other. Now she just felt silly. She glanced across at the nearest unlit lamp, then lowered her gaze to her lap.

Hugh spoke something terse in the language he called English, drawing Ilina's eye. He'd posed a question on his parchment: *"How long ago did Henry Conrad leave?"*

After a minute or two, Ilina realized that her mouth was hanging ajar. She swallowed with difficulty. Why would anyone ask such a thing? *"How comest thou to know that name, but not the answer to thy question?"* You speak as if you hail from the past.

Hugh's brows crashed down. With a flick of his wrist, he underlined the first three words of his question.

"If scholarly consensus is accorded credence," she shut her eyes, struggling to sustain a placid exterior, *"the years since then are seven hundred and ten. Wherefore dost thou inquire?"*

Silence suffused Seascape Study. Hugh sat motionless, as though unwilling to acknowledge the exchange that had just transpired. And all the while the darkness deepened outside, and the Beacon remained unlit.

A SEA SOUGHT IN SONG

"Why do I ask?" repeated Hugh aloud as, shoulders hunched, he stared at nothing. "I ask 'cause I crawled here through a crack in time. Father came back five months ago. Dan left a week before I did. What's a week out of five months? One twentieth? What's a twentieth of seven hundred? Thirty-five? It's been thirty-five years since Dan got here? He's probably dead by now. I'm too late. My father's kingdom is ancient history."

Ilina cocked her head, sweetness and suspicion skirmishing over her face.

"I ask because I know the man," he wrote. *"I am his son."*

Beyond the Window of the North, high on the bluffs overlooking Horwell Face, sedges slouched toward the south and sighed suggestively to the ever-seeking wind. Several of the stiff stalks, having been shortened in passing by a keen blade clumsily carried, bowed not so low. *A sword. A sword borne from the seashore.* The wind coursed on.

Beyond tiny Cuspid Isle, over fathomless deeps and featureless plains, the ocean's black breast rose and fell in fitful slumber. A sudden gust ruffled the wave-ridges white, whipping salt-spray into the saturnine sky, but no one was present to sense the sting. Even seabirds, long since scattered to the shelter of distant cliffs, couldn't scent the tang of sword-severed sedge. The wind coursed on.

Beyond the heaving deep, above the ceaseless surf which slammed against Land's End, by the weather side of a battered boathouse on the dockyard outskirts, stood an old man hooded and cloaked, whose hood fell back as he raised his face and spread his arms. His white beard split down the middle and flew to the sides like a second pair of arms as the wind bore down upon him, and swirled around him, and flooded past him up the slope. Eyes fast shut, he drank it in like burning incense. And still the wind coursed on. The world spread before it.

Chapter Nine
CRACKS

T he week passed swiftly. Spring had come to Cuspid Isle; spring, with all its lavish excess and wild pageantry. Black-capped terns screamed and struck at anything essaying approach, white-plumed cormorants squawked and swayed to the drunken rhythms of an unheard song, smooth-shell crabs scuttled steadfastly through the stones, and bright bearberries peeped from calf-high cover, their red eyes dewy at dawn. The burgeoning din ran unabated for more than three-quarters of the sun's daily circuit. Night was an ebb tide. Nature's hollow spaces were filling out, its scarcity being engulfed.

There was so much that needed doing, and so little time to tend to it before the long darkness came surging back. There were herbs to harvest, vegetables to cultivate, medicines to mix, and storm damage to repair. Broad cracks had appeared roughly a hundred feet up the east face of Kredak Tower during autumn's opening squalls, and Ilina had weathered the intervening months by evacuating the compromised chambers of furniture and coating their interior walls with layer upon layer of lime mortar. But now that Harlith had made his bed in the depths, it was high time to knock up a new batch of putty to reinforce the tower face itself. The gods only knew what manner of buffeting would have to be borne if next winter proved worse than this last. Yes, spring lacked busyness like the sea lacked salt.

And on top of it all, there was the man.

At first his presence was petrifying. She'd feared she would misidentify him, feared his displeasure, feared the changes presaged by his arrival. But when he'd failed to share or even comprehend her concerns, her perspective had started to shift. If he was indeed an existential threat, he at least remained unselfconscious. Now she exchanged words with him easily. Their written conversations had proven quite tolerable, really, once he'd accepted the fact that he was stuck here until the week ran out. If she concentrated intently enough to actually clear her mind, she could almost imagine Hugh as a normal human being instead of the incarnate heir of an ancient usurped deity.

Almost.

For Hugh *was* the Awaited One. That, however unlikely, was Ilina's conclusion.

AUSTIN GUNDERSON

The facts had left her without alternative. For though Hugh had emerged from the northern wastes, he wasn't in league with the Jaar; indeed, as his erstwhile captive had so violently demonstrated, he'd incurred their enmity. He could read the Script of Secrets and, were he to be believed, actually *speak* it as well. He possessed magical tools of incredible power, and bore a blade that—at least superficially—resembled the Lost Sword of Ascension. The Beacon responded to him strangely. But more than all of this, he claimed descent from Henred Conrad, ancient High King of all Arlam.

He was the son of the King, he said: not the King himself. And this assertion made all the difference, because it was in its light that his petty ineptitudes became supporting evidence. It made sense that a recent arrival wouldn't know how to behave. Alternately, if his faux pas were attributable to idiocy ... well, Ilina refused to credit the notion that an obtuse barbarian who didn't know the difference between a headtap and a footstamp was capable of pulling off the greatest hoax in history.

It wasn't as though no one had ever tried to fool a Lightkeeper before. Riebald the Impostor had attempted it in 645 and ended up eyeless, and then Thantonis had sailed south with a host of Jaar only forty years later, and everyone knew what had become of *him*. And on both occasions there had been *signs* of the deception—details that refused to fit, indications that not all was right. Try as she might, Ilina sensed no such signs in Hugh.

The first test of her resolve came only minutes after Hugh's declaration of pedigree, when she realized that, for the first time in her life, she had failed to light the Beacon before sundown. Initially horrified, she consoled herself by reasoning that the Awaited One's arrival effectively nullified the need for Anticipation Light. She even fantasized that her sudden forgetfulness was the result not of mere distraction, but of prophetic fulfillment. It had to be a sign.

But the implications of this outlook proved too frightful to entertain; within the hour she was convinced that, unless Kredak Light shone like it had every night since the dawn of the era, hundreds of mariners would be dashed to death in darkness. Never mind the fact that no ships came within ten leagues of Cuspid Isle by night—the glow which swelled at her touch in the heart of that great crystal calmed her own heart like a song softly sung. She moved her fingers over its brightness and told herself that things could still be the same even though everything had changed.

Ilina had relayed none of these trepidations to her father. In fact, she hadn't visited him even once since the night of Hugh's arrival, when his frantic filleting of the front door had interrupted that very errand. That she

124

should prove so remiss was a weight upon her spirit, a burden of guilt which hung lower each sundown as she, on her way to bed, passed the stairs descending to her father's chamber and kept her eyes fixed firmly ahead.

The causes of this neglect—likely and otherwise—became fodder for endless debate in the committee of her mind, with the prevailing interpretation being that a simple fear of disapproval was preventing her from revealing either Hugh's presence in the Tower or her decision to Declare him. But if she feared to present that decision for the judgement of her own father, how could she possibly think to take it before the world?

She was training tomatoes in the kitchen hothouse—bunching their stalks between the oil-blackened fingers of one hand while reaching for a spool of twine with the other—when it first occurred to her that activities interrupted by Hugh tended to remain interrupted. Snatching the twine with greater force than she'd intended, she looked up to find her fist clenching snapped stalks. *This cannot continue*, she decided, opening her palm and letting the green stems fall.

That night she descended the stairs to her father's chamber and gave him a full report, outlining her plan. To her relief, he voiced no opposition.

Meanwhile, Hugh occupied his time verifying as many of Ilina's statements as he possibly could. After what she'd said about his father, he needed to *know* whether she was a trustworthy source, to be certain he wasn't being had for a second time in a row.

Hugh had known when he'd taken that Bhutanese job that it was a bad idea to leave his father alone. The man had only recently materialized from a quarter century spent God-knew-where, only to take up residence in the Conrad family estate Hugh had abandoned when his mother went and drowned herself in the well out back. The old place had been half-derelict after decades of disuse. Hugh hated it, but hadn't been able to bring himself to sell it. Perhaps this nightmare might've been avoided if he had.

Regardless, Smith's pitch had been persuasive, and Hugh had been eager to reestablish distance between himself and his old man. And Henry's weirdly-solicitous girlfriend seemed more than capable of attending to his needs. So Hugh had returned to India.

He should've listened to his fears.

For no sooner had he left than it appeared his father had begun recruiting his known associates for a mad scheme to retake a parallel universe. Dan

AUSTIN GUNDERSON

Forsythe lived just down the road, but Hugh didn't know how his old man could've gotten ahold of Miles after all those years away. Maybe Hugh had left an address book lying around. Regardless, an offer had been made, and the fools had jumped at it. And now Miles Cornwall was dead, and Daniel Forsythe missing in action. All in the space of two weeks. *Or seven hundred years.*

If Ilina penned the truth, chances were that Dan was just as dead as Miles, and Hugh's rescue mission futile. He hoped his hostess was given to exaggeration.

The second day of his island confinement was spent climbing the squat peak he'd glimpsed by moonlight the night of his arrival. Its lower slopes bristled with thickets of salmonberry and stunted alder. Mosquitoes swarmed him as he shoved his way through the green tangle, their collective whine nearly drowning out the gurgling of a stream lost somewhere in the brush. At first Hugh settled for periodically pummeling the bloodsuckers as they queued up on the back of his neck, but less than a mile later he'd begun windmilling his arms. He was about to break into a run when an incline of talus rose out of the shrubs ahead.

He bounded up lichen-crusted boulders, hauled himself over a knob of bare rock, and emerged into a steep meadow dappled with wildflowers. Here the frantic mosquito-screech gave way to the complacent drone of bumblebees lurching from blossom to blossom. Some of the flowers looked familiar to Hugh, while others, particularly a species whose concentric petals alternated between purple and blue, had to be alien.

The wind rose—overwhelming the bee-drone, buffeting the meadow-slope, washing it with a whiff of sea-smell—and Hugh stood transfixed as every single flower, whether red or blue or purple, paled to purest white. It was as though a great wave had crested the rocks ringing Cuspid Isle and shattered upon the hillside. An instant later the meadow was varicolored once more.

Hugh remained motionless for some time afterward, skin prickling to the wind's pulsation, gaze held by the ebb and flow of hue. When he resumed his ascent, it was with slower steps.

The view from the summit revealed no secret boats moored in concealed marinas. Cuspid Isle bulged like a teardrop toward the south, rising till it buckled into crisply-margined cliffs. An uninhabited upthrust of black and green in the midst of a restive gray plain. In the distance he could just make out a second, smaller island shrouded in haze.

126

A SEA SOUGHT IN SONG

Below him to the north rose Ilina's black spire, its massive crystal topper glittering in the light. But even more glaring was the tower's lack of apparent function. The northernmost tip of this isle was also its lowest point, yet it was there the tower stood, facing away from civilization. Hugh estimated its height at over three hundred feet—a wonder of engineering, especially in this remote place. Why? Why build something this huge in the middle of nowhere? Had the architect expected a mass migration that never materialized?

On the third day of the Awaited One's stay, Ilina found him wandering in the library shortly after dawn, pulling out and leafing through books seemingly at random before returning them to their slots. After successfully restraining herself from another bout of violence, she informed him in no uncertain terms that if he desired to read a book, he would have to ask her to fetch it for him. She braced herself for a deluge of requests, but needn't have bothered.

"Anything in English" was perhaps the strictest parameter he could have stipulated. It was met by only a single title. One which happened to be tucked beneath her arm at that very moment. Hugh's eyebrows rose when she reluctantly proffered it.

They rose even higher when he gingerly lifted the red cloth cover. *"Where did you get this?"* he wrote. *"Do you have any more like it?"*

"It was brought here by Tunnoltan monks about five centuries past," she wrote. *"It is a secondhand copy of the Book of Blood, a great fable from the era of the High King. It is said there are naught but three such transcripts in the whole of Arlam. Treat it as thou wouldst a newborn child."*

She turned on her heel and then hesitated, struck by the inadequacy of her exhortation. Spinning to face him again, she snatched back the writing paper. *"In the event that thou art inexperienced with newborn children,"* she added, *"I entreat you to take care."*

With that, she stalked away.

Prior to Hugh's arrival, the upcoming ferry run had been a routine event. Ilina had planned to greet the local priest when he disembarked the boat, sign Rikard's Petition of Troth, make small talk over tea and scones, and then wave as the man departed. She couldn't leave the Light unattended, after all—not with Father laid up like he was. But now all that had changed. Now she had to accompany the Awaited One and Declare him to the Kram. Now she had to be on that ferry when it set off for the south.

Ilina hadn't been ready. A single-minded liturgy, a lifetime of expectation, and still Hugh had caught her off guard. Since then, her head hadn't stopped spinning. There were so many loose ends to tie up before she left for the mainland. New ones occurred to her by the minute. They dangled before her mind's eye, swinging with each step: an entire season's worth of chores.

If she was right about Hugh, if he truly *was* the rightful king, then the next few days might comprise her sole remaining opportunity to discharge her custodial duties. She would not have it said of her that she'd left Kredak Tower in disrepair. She was the Lightkeeper, and, by Harlith's breath, she would keep the Light.

Ilina began to run.

Six hours later, Hugh had yet to discover any dissimilarities between Ilina's battered red book and the Holy Bible. Not that he was terribly familiar with *that* text—his mother hadn't managed to drag him to church since he'd left home, and the manner of her death hadn't really motivated him to seek solace in *her* beliefs—but he did recognize a few passages, and couldn't find anything that seemed totally out of place.

Even the flyleaf illustrations felt unexceptional: crosshatched renditions of the Good Shepherd, crook in hand, and the Lord Triumphant, hand raised in power as trumpet-wielding angels formed ranks within the clouds. *A familiar motif: everybody loves idols who shoot light out of their digits.* Hugh flipped back from one image to the other, admiring their ordinariness. These must have been meticulously reproduced.

The story itself began with the creation of the world—of Earth, not of this place—and went on to follow Abraham and Moses and King David, who sure spent a lot of time bellyaching in the Psalms. Most of the books of prophecy seemed to have been written by schizophrenics, but Hugh remembered them sounding that weird back on Earth. Jesus still taught in parables and the people still turned against him and put him to death, and he still came back anyway to keep annoying them till the end of time.

Hugh's father must have had a Bible on his person when he landed here. After he became High King—Hugh still couldn't even wrap his mind around that concept—the book would've been the sole available work of literature

A SEA SOUGHT IN SONG

in the native language of the ruler of Arlam, so it made sense for it to have attracted scholarly interest. This copy was typed, not scribed, so the Tunnoltan monks must have had a printing press at their disposal, with type pieces set in English, no less. Which begged a question: why the rarity? *Guess the Bible never caught on in Arlam.* Hugh snickered softly. Now there was an idea he *could* imagine.

But at least this explained why Ilina kept addressing him with "thees" and "thous."

Hugh's fourth day on the island was occupied by an examination of the Great Hairy Parchment, which had been left out on King Arthur's Table following the altercation with the Eskimo in the library. Not only was the thing immense, it was also one of the densest maps Hugh had ever seen. Place-names in hairsbreadth script jostled each other over regions which from a distance appeared blank, intruding between even the individual letters of more prominent designations. No spaces were left empty save the seas.

But Hugh couldn't see those spaces anyway, at least not from the stairtop alcove that afforded him a bird's-eye view—to which vantage he'd retired after it become tedious to orbit the table's edge while squinting at fine print. From above, the seas were blacked out by the intricately-crafted chandelier.

Or were they? For the sake of certainty, he sketched the silhouettes formed by the chandelier's frond-antlers and checked them against what he could make out of the map's coastlines from floor-level. No discrepancies were apparent. He marveled at the engineering behind such a precise alignment.

On the morning of the fifth day, a storm arose in the north. It spread swiftly over the sky, black on blue, like an oil slick from a sinking ship. Hugh could smell it coming even in the sea-humid air. He leaned on his windowsill, inhaling deeply.

Behind him, a flurry of steps and the squeal of his half-open door announced Ilina's arrival. Hugh turned to find her clad in grubby tunic and trousers, hair tied back, eyes frantic. Wordlessly she flopped against the doorjamb, winded, chest heaving most distractingly. After a moment she shoved herself upright, gestured for Hugh to follow, and took off down the stairs. He snatched his coat from the bed and plunged after.

Hugh was surprised. Since she'd chewed him out in the library two days ago, Ilina had seemed content to let him fend for himself. He'd been able with limited success to engage her in conversation over food, but her responses had been consistently guarded, and she had the annoying habit of rising from a clean plate while he was still partway through some attempt to compose an inescapable question. The sheet of parchment he kept folded in his pocket was littered with sentence fragments.

But those were from mealtimes; the rest of the time he saw none of the girl, exempting brief glimpses snagged in passing as she beelined between far-flung tasks. Thus far she'd rebuffed his every offer to help with whatever it was that occupied her so heavily. Which meant that Hugh, having been banned from interacting with the imprisoned Eskimo, was forced to provide for his own entertainment.

For some reason the girl seemed to approve of his fascination with the hairy map and—to a lesser extent—with the library itself. Her intimate familiarity with the latter's contents had Hugh hunting in vain for some kind of Dewey Decimal labeling system. Whatever the organizational template in use here, it sure wasn't alphabetical—Hugh didn't even need to know the language to figure *that* much out.

Had the girl actually read every single book in this place? Whenever he'd mentioned the various manuscript titles buried in dense longhand in the margins of his father's Bible, Ilina had actually risen from her plate to fetch each and every one of them, plus others whose scrawled references he wouldn't discover until later. The margin-notes weren't hers, though she obviously knew them by heart. They seemed to be a running linguistic commentary kept by … whom? His father? Some ancient monkish scholar? There was no attribution.

Whoever it was had left him a lexicon. Word equivalencies, pronunciation guides, grammatical notes—it was all here, scribbled around and between the already-tight lines of text. Someone had begun translating the Bible. This explained how Ilina could read and write in English, yet fail to recognize the language when it was spoken aloud. Fascinated despite himself, Hugh had gradually given up on his attempts to draw the Mystery Maiden out of her shell: the book was more communicative.

But now, apparently, Ilina needed him.

She led Hugh out the front doors and around the side of the citadel until they stood at the base of the tower where it abutted the surf. A thick rope ladder hugged the stonework, hanging the entire distance from the tower's top to the rock beneath. Its upright ropes had been weighted with stones where they met the ground. Hugh craned his neck in astonishment. *How long does it take her to coil that thing when she's done with it?*

As she'd done in the library, Ilina swung easily onto a low rung. The ropes, stiff with knots, barely even sagged under her weight. Without bothering to ask for Hugh's pocket-parchment, Ilina jabbed a finger at his chest, then pointed to a pair of ropes dangling beside the ladder, one of which was tied to a heavy, barrel-ribbed bucket brimming with creamy paste. She made a fist-over-fist hauling gesture, then scrambled up the ladder like a sailor up shrouds.

Hugh squinted. He couldn't make it out clearly at this distance, but it appeared the two ropes were actually a single rope that ran through a pulley leaning out over the tower's top edge. *The paste must be mortar she's using to reinforce the stonework. But with that storm coming in ...* Hugh glanced northward in alarm.

A shout from above refocused his attention. He positioned himself beneath the pulley and began hauling down lengths of rope. The bucket rose. It was less heavy than he'd feared, but still no cinch to lift. It scraped against the tower wall as it ascended, raining down a stream of grit which sparkled in the sun.

Hugh grunted, dragging the rope down with his whole body and stomping on its slack before lunging up for a higher handhold. Coils began sprawling beneath him, untended. He'd finally caught the girl's sense of urgency. *Why must she do this now? Will the mortar even have time to harden before the rainstorm hits?*

Hugh looked up. The girl had stopped climbing, but the bucket wasn't even halfway to her level. He cursed and redoubled his efforts. She was high enough now that a stiff breeze could've flicked her off the wall.

When the mortar-bucket finally drew even with Ilina, Hugh was drenched with sweat and panting for breath. The wind was still light, but even so it cooled him quickly. Away to the north, the black cloud-slick continued to spread. But now a pillar of shadow beneath it was heaving into view. With a sickening lurch of the stomach, Hugh realized the shape he'd been watching coalesce wasn't the cloud's base, but its crest—the sky-wide anvil of the most massive cumulonimbus he'd ever seen.

A glob of mortar struck his shoulder. High above, Ilina was digging into the bucket with a long-handled spoon and slopping putty against the tower. That this was a rush job was obvious from the quantity of spillage splattering the rocks and burdening the brim of Hugh's fedora. He gritted his teeth, shook his head vigorously, and tried to snatch glimpses of Ilina's progress without getting hit in the eyes. Every so often she'd shout and wave at him, and he'd let out a few feet of line so she could move to a lower section of stonework. The ground around him was growing white as blackness swallowed the sky to the north.

AUSTIN GUNDERSON

A soft whoosh was the gust's only warning. It flipped up the brim of Hugh's fedora, scooted the ladder-weights along the base of the tower, and swept up his coat from where he'd shucked it, flopping it against the stones. A thump and a cry sounded above, and Hugh braced for a cascade of mortar putty, but none came: the wind had plastered a streak of it all the way down the tower. Ilina made to grab the reeling bucket but suddenly jerked back to clutch the ladder as a second gust sent everything swinging anew.

Ilina finally snagged the bucket and began furiously flinging mortar at the tower wall and slapping it into place with the flat of her spoon. She waved frantically and Hugh lowered the bucket a few more feet. The wind's rushing was now a continual sound. A blast of spume completed the whitening of the tower's foot. Hugh shook himself free and glanced back. The swiftly darkening sea was scored by an endless queue of boiling white lines, their crests sheared by the wind. The vast black anvil filled heaven. Its burgeoning column of cloud, lit strobe-like from within, blotted out the north. Light was dimming fast.

"Hey, hurry it up!" Hugh shouted. He doubted the girl could hear him over the wind, but she should be past needing his encouragement anyway. Why was this job so important to her? The tower seemed sturdy enough to him; couldn't she just wait till this damn hurricane blew over? "*C'mon!*" he bellowed over the rising rumble. "No to-do list is worth this! Let's get outta here!"

Ilina kept slopping.

Hugh fumed for a moment, then brightened. What was it about this girl that managed to convince him she was actually in charge of anything? With a grim grin, he began lowering the bucket hand-over-hand. An indignant shriek punctured the storm's tumult. Hugh's grin twisted into a grimace. How violent would Her Ladyship's protest be *this* time? He rolled his eyes, then spun in response to a sudden, rising hiss.

The rain struck. A solid wall of frigid sleet collided with Hugh's face, slamming him against the tower. His hands snapped open without his consent and the rope shot away, its coils whipping into the air as the torrent pressed its advantage to smother and pound. The roar of the storm was absolute. Hugh gasped and choked on water. He could neither hear nor see.

But he knew that somewhere above him there plummeted an eighty-pound bucket.

Hugh curled his arms over his head and dove forward, cutting himself on the slick rock and sliding over an unseen lip to tumble down an incline. Behind him, the bucket's crash leapt above the din.

A SEA SOUGHT IN SONG

Ilina. Would she be next?

Hugh opened his eyes. He lay on the last shelf of bare stone above a churning maelstrom of surf. He scrambled to his feet, then staggered as a huge wave ruptured on the rock beneath him and exploded high overhead with concussive force. He turned, buried beneath whiteness, flinging saltwater from his eyes, and squinted into the blackened sky.

There she was.

###

Ilina clung to the ladder with the grip of a vise, her arms and temple bloody where they'd been beaten against the wall. The ropes groaned and skittered along the stonework. Untethered she was: a banner loosed upon the breeze. A bauble caught in Harlith's hair—ignored, incidental. Just a bubble of froth upon the waves of the sea.

"You don't care, do you?" she screamed into the storm. "I'm just a pawn, to be moved and forgotten! My whole life I wait, and who do you send? A man who doesn't even know who I am! If it's selfish of me to care, than I wish you were selfish, too! You *don't* care—how can you? You can't even *feel!*"

As Ilina raged at the heavens, something in her heart seemed to burst, as though staved in by the wind itself. Bitter tears coursed over her face, mixing salt from her body with water from the sky. She shook more than could be accounted for by the worrying of the wind.

Ever since that nightmare in the Hall of Harn, the gods had seemed to retreat from Ilina's awareness. Perhaps that was because she was actually looking for them—truly *looking*—for the first time in her life. Perhaps the placid certainty of her youth had been nothing more than childish delusion. Had her father ever doubted as she did now? Had her father ever really *believed?* Perhaps he'd just imitated so many in the Broanoshi priesthood in teaching what he thought *should be* instead of what he knew for a fact to be true. But was there any way to tell the difference? Shouldn't she be able to ask?

"Well, shouldn't I?" she croaked. "Aren't you the one with the answers? Who am I, O Mighty Harlith, Master of the Arctic Gale?"

She quaked at her own insolence, yet whitened her knuckles further and forged ahead, gasping against inhaled water and the tower's sustained bludgeoning. "Who am *I* to gainsay you? Who am *I* to rebel? But how can I obey when *you* remain silent? And how can I pledge to you what you've never sought? My heart is cold to you, my god." Her voice choked off with a sob. "Awaken it, if you can.

"Awaken me."

The tower rushed up and plunged her into darkness.

###

Hugh had only ten more feet left to climb when the wind cracked the ladder like a whip against the wall and Ilina lost her grip. She caromed off the stones and fell facing the sky, limbs limp, unflailing. She would pass him in a second.

Hugh flung himself bodily away from the tower, twining his legs in the ropes by instinct and hoping against hope they would hold. Out stretched his arms as he and Ilina swiftly converged.

The impact wrenched his spine. His fingers slipped helplessly over her body, then closed on an ankle. He squeezed with all the strength he possessed, not knowing whether he was airborne as well.

And his fingers held.

But Ilina kept right on falling, and her weight dragged him down. The back of his head collided with the tower, but he didn't let go. He held on, hanging upside down and backwards, facing the maw of the storm.

"Tehr rhom?" the groggy words slipped through to Hugh as the wind took a breath. *"Seh thomish yir?"* Ilina, chin pressed to chest, was gazing up at him. She did not scream. She did not struggle. A strange light coruscated her eyes.

Lightning fractured the sky above, spreading like a vast spiderweb beyond Hugh's feet—the distant river system of an inverted world. The thunderclap nearly shook him free of the ladder. A bolt as broad as the tower itself leapt from its peak to slice skyward and vanish. Its burning afterimage bisected Hugh's vision as he inhaled the acrid scent of fresh ozone. He couldn't figure out why he hadn't been fried.

"Ilina!" he shouted, snapping her out of her reverie. "Hey! Grab the ladder! We have to get down!" Ilina's eyes, loosed from Hugh's, began darting this way and that. Fear took hold. She flung out her arms, flailing for support. Her ankle twisted in his grasp.

"Ilina!" Hugh barked, and she grew still. Then, slowly, she reached behind her back and located the ladder, clutching one of its ropes with both hands. Her gaze found Hugh's again and she nodded firmly, then flashed a

A SEA SOUGHT IN SONG

grin so bright and unexpected that Hugh released her ankle as much from surprise as from intention.

With a precise twist, the girl flipped herself neatly upright. The ladder jerked in response, but her feet snagged rungs from midair. Then she climbed up beside Hugh and helped him disentangle his legs and right himself. In moments, they were both putting distance between themselves and the raging sky.

Darkness swathed Cuspid Isle long before nightfall. The chill halls of Kredak's citadel echoed to the surf's mad flailing. Hugh wandered aimlessly for a time, wet hair and clothes dripping on the stone. A strangely spirited Ilina had retired to her chambers to change out of her sopping outfit as soon as he'd got her safely past the front door, but something had kept Hugh from following her example. An unsettling premonition had lodged in his brain—inscrutable, yet strangely insistent. He could feel it taunting him, whispering that things weren't quite right. And so Hugh paced the halls in garments still thoroughly soaked. Eventually he found himself in Seascape Study, surrounded by a library lost in shadow.

The great window arched before him like a submarine porthole. Water streamed over its surface in an almost uninterrupted sheet. What he could vaguely discern of the world outside was all heaving black hills and towering explosions of white. He groped in the blue-tinged darkness for somewhere to sit and stumbled upon a broad stone lip seemingly designed for that purpose. It was a hearth. He sat, solitary spectator to the ravages of nature's wrath.

The flue behind Hugh gradually leached the remaining warmth from his body, moaning deeply as it mouth-breathed. He shivered and shoved his hands under his armpits, but made no move to leave. *The girl, that's what it is*, he thought. *It's the way she looks at me. Like I'm some kind of god. She's been weird like that ever since she found me touching the gem, but back then it was an expression of uncertain respect, of fear. That's what made it bearable. But now ...*

Now it's different, somehow.

Hugh was suddenly aware of Ilina's presence in the room. She stood beside the fireplace, gazing out the window. She'd let down her hair, donned a sleek dress which fell to her calves, and draped a fur mantle about her shoulders. After a moment spent drinking in the sight of her, Hugh cleared his throat. She started, then recovered almost instantly and sat a few feet to his right. For a long while they neither spoke nor moved, unless it was to shiver.

Eventually Hugh had had enough of freezing. "Hey, do you have any wood for this thing?" he asked, turning to face her and jerking his thumb toward the fireplace. She raised her brows quizzically. "Wood, you know?" he sketched logs with his hands and pointed again at the hearth, making an upward flickering motion with his fingers. "You know, for fire? For heat? You got any of that stuff lying around here? 'Cause now might be a good time to break it out, you know?"

Ilina's eyes glinted in the dim light. She slowly nodded, then broke into a smile, genuine and full. She rose, gesturing for Hugh to follow, and lead him out of the library, through Round Table Room, where she set flame to the wick of a hand-lamp and snatched up a blank parchment, and down a stairway which vanished beneath the floor by the wall. The locked door off the first landing had stopped Hugh from discovering what lay beyond during his initial exploration—but Ilina had the key, of course, which she now produced from around her neck.

Hugh's skin prickled as he crossed the threshold. This was more than a mere storage room—in fact, he couldn't see firewood stacked anywhere. They entered an octagonal chamber, counterpart to that windy pavilion perched three hundred feet above. The glow of Ilina's lamp shaded smooth swells of stone. A broad arch in the center of each wall emptied upon blackness. Sinuous bodies squeezed the arches' edges in sculptural relief. The air was static and cold. So cold. Hugh caught his teeth chattering and clamped his jaw shut to silence the sound.

Ilina extended her lamp through an archway, lighting up a floor-to-ceiling wall of split logs arranged with the precision of a jigsaw puzzle. Hugh's brows shot up. If this room extended farther back than the six feet currently visible, then it contained an immense reservoir of fuel—easily enough to last several winters. He moved to extract an armful, but Ilina's touch on his arm brought him up short. Gooseflesh broke out over his body. He told himself it was because of the cold.

A line had formed between the girl's brows. She dropped her hand and looked away, fiddling with parchment and pen. At last she unstoppered her ink-bottle and expressed a thought: *"There is someone thou shouldst meet."* Leaving the parchment in his hands, she vanished through the opposite archway.

A SEA SOUGHT IN SONG

Hugh's whole body went as taut as a recoil spring. He'd dropped into a half-crouch before he even realized he was afraid. *There's someone down here she wants me to meet? Someone I haven't met already?* Something was very, very wrong. But Ilina had taken the only light, and so he had to keep pace. He cursed silently, then slipped after her receding silhouette.

The room she'd entered was more of a hall, its length indeterminate. The polished floor gleamed faintly beneath Hugh's boots and rang with his steps. Octagonal pillars supported the ceiling, alternating with alcoves that withdrew from the walls on either hand. Some of these housed large stone chests with intricately sculpted lids. The cold was almost painful now, and his breath hung in the lamplight like a nascent fog. Ilina had stopped at one of the recesses ahead and to the left.

She took a step forward and knelt before a box of stone, resting one hand on the lid. She bowed her head.

And suddenly Hugh understood.

"If it please you, Father," said Ilina, "I have brought him. He doesn't yet know you, and I couldn't bear to make the Declaration without having at least performed introductions."

She cocked her head at Hugh, who had warily approached. He seemed on edge. "I pray you approve him," she continued softly, "and that he warrants your blessing. I understand him not, Father, and not merely because he is male. I have known him only five days. His customs are strange. His language is archaic. He is ignorant of much he should know. But in the time of his stay here, I ..."

She trailed off. How could she say it? It was difficult enough for her to identify her own thoughts, let alone express them cogently. *That's because they're emotions, not thoughts,* snarled her implacable logic. With a grimace, she waited for the spasm of self-incrimination to pass.

"What I mean to say is this: I favor him." There. She had said it. "He is brash and bold, yes, and dangerous." She paused to consider Hugh, who at this moment looked distinctly uncomfortable. "But only when necessary," she concluded in a whisper. "And not to me. If it please you, Father, share your thoughts on Hugh Conrad, Claimant to the Withered Throne."

Finished with her appeal, Ilina leaned forward and pressed her ear to the sarcophagus. Orlim Lightkeeper had never been a loquacious man, but sometimes, in desperate love and breathless quiet, his bereaved daughter could still hear him speak. She *had* to. But Orlim had been speaking less and less often of late. Either that, or her attentiveness had waned. The knuckles of her right hand whitened where they gripped the stone. She squeezed her eyes shut, swallowing heavily.

Hugh fidgeted. Ilina scowled at his discourtesy, but her irritation evaporated almost instantly. *Silly girl—introductions go both ways.* She bowed and rose, retrieving her parchment from Hugh.

"*Hugh Conrad,*" she wrote, "*prithee allow me to introduce my father, Orlim Lightkeeper, who hath waited his whole life to meet thee.*"

Hugh looked stricken.

This is weird, decried Hugh's mind. *Her father's lying here in a crypt and she talks about him like he's alive. Is this some form of denial? And she thinks he's been* waiting *for me? Is she* trying *to unnerve me? If so, she may have succeeded.*

But he let her take his hand and guide it to the sarcophagus. The stone was smooth and cold—like ice against his skin. A prone figure had been graven deeply into the lid, a man with short beard, strong cheekbones, and sagely brow. Hugh could see the resemblance.

He glanced sideways at Ilina, and the plaintive sincerity in her eyes cut short his cynicism. *She really believes*, he realized. *She isn't faking. She's letting me in, showing me what's close to her heart.*

He knelt beside her. She pressed her ear to the stone once more, and, after a moment's hesitation, Hugh followed her example. Their noses were mere inches apart. The fog of their breath commingled in the frigid air. Ilina had closed her eyes, and Hugh studied her as though she were a sculpture, a work of inert art left to decorate a tomb.

Eventually, after he'd begun to grow genuinely concerned about hypothermia, her eyes opened, troubled. She nodded at him absently, then bowed to the sarcophagus and rose.

Hugh rose without bowing. He'd heard nothing, of course. It was just a dead body in a box of stone. He didn't believe in spirits that lingered after death. He wasn't even sure he believed in spirits, period. Unless they came from a bottle. He shivered. *What I'd give for a stiff drink right about now ...*

###

A SEA SOUGHT IN SONG

Hugh warmed up quickly by lugging wood. That night, bright fire lit the Window of the North for the first time in far too long. Cackling and popping, it flung shades across Seascape Study and cudgeled back the darkness. Before it sat a man and woman in eloquent silence—their faces turned to the stirring shadows, their backs to the fluttering flame.

Chapter Ten
THE FACE OF THE DEEP

The sixth and final dawn arrived under cloak of fog. Ilina crossed the threshold of Kredak Tower and stepped into fallen cloud, a world wreathed by white. Chill droplets beaded in her hair and dripped from her bangs. The throb of the sea was hushed; the wind had bated its breath. All was still. Ilina ran her fingers over the door's freshly-chipped surface, marveling at the mark Hugh had already made upon her life, wondering when she'd get the chance to enter this door again.

Despite the lack of visibility, the walk to the landing didn't take long. Ilina had delayed until the last minute. Horvold was nothing if not punctual, and he always docked the ferry in a sheltered cove just west of Cuspid Cape. It was there that a rocky decline, carpeted in sedge, sloped toward the water's edge before plunging beyond sight. A stubby stone quay jutted from the shore, waiting.

Ilina could just barely make out its far end through the mist.

Beside her stood Hugh the Claimant, his left hand gripping an elbow of Jarlin the Chieftain, whose hands were bound behind his back. Though Ilina trusted the Jaar with her own life, she harbored no illusion about his intentions toward her otherworldly guest, and had approved Hugh's precautionary measure. Jarlin's eyes had flashed when Ilina urged him apologetically to submit to such an indignity, but now his face was painstakingly blank, his gaze absorbed by the toes of his mukluks. He carried food for the group in a satchel slung slantwise over one shoulder.

Once they made port at Land's End, two days' hard walk eastward along the White Road would take Jarlin to Tejilim where, among the dry-docks and salt-separation troughs, lived a small community of Jaar emigrants. Ilina smiled a tight little smile. Jarlin would hate it there. The Kramish Jaar were relatively liberal—some of the men even shaved their beards!—but they *did* maintain contact with their kin in Utter North. She would write on Jarlin's behalf to Sanja Nerelish, who represented Tejilim District at the Council of Kram in her late husband's stead. If Jarlin's fortune improved, he might be able to rejoin his clan in only a few months' time.

If only Ilina could say the same.

She glanced at Hugh, allowed her eyes to trail down his brow, his cheek, his jaw, his arm. His right hand hefted the valise containing the Book of

AUSTIN GUNDERSON

Blood that fascinated him so, Ilina's garments of office, her ceremonial crest, and a black rod wrapped in oilskin. Hugh knew not what he bore; he had accepted the locked case on his way out the door without inquiring after its contents. And that was as it should be.

As for Ilina herself, her arms were occupied with a long bundle tightly rolled. A great banner, its emblem timid still. Very soon it would unfurl its face to the world. The Declaration ceremony would require each of these sacred items, and more. Ilina prayed they would be enough. For the Withered Throne was still far away—less so in distance than in time. Many clever minds would have to accept her conclusion before a decision could be reached and criers dispatched to every hamlet and high hill under heaven.

Her face clouded. It should not be thus. Yet such was the bitter aftertaste of the strife within her house. The disunity. The defection. Her father had borne this weight his whole life—and so had she, ever since he'd fallen ill. A shadow of desperation it was: the certain knowledge that there remained no one else, that even the smallest lapse in duty would void the strivings of countless forebears. Her margin for error was too thin by far.

Had the world been set to rights, her Declaration as Lightkeeper would be law as surely as an edict from the lips of any sovereign in Arlam. More so. But the world was as ill as her father and piety a thing of the past. She was the last of her line, culmination of centuries' worth of anticipatory attrition. Fraying tassel of a threadbare tapestry, rubbed raw by the wall of ages.

So debased was the name of Lightkeeper that Ilina actually found herself bargaining with suitors! Rikard, though a decent enough man all told, would never have dared to propose a prenuptial contract had he lived before the rise of Thantonis, before schism and treason had shaken Kredak Tower to its root and forever fractured her family's power. Now the Broanoshi strayed from the gods, teaching the people damnable heresies about *forces* and *fates*. Now she was forced to work with the Lords of Kramarack—to *cooperate* with them—simply to survive. None feared her displeasure. None took her at her word.

And she doubted even Kredak himself would've had an easy time convincing *anyone* of *Hugh's* bonafides.

Ilina shook her head, flinging condensation. *The future will never improve for your fretting, 'Lina. You cannot escape the change. Cease your flight. Turn and face it. To face it is to triumph. Redemption comes from within.* She lifted her chin, pulled in a slow breath. She was just an ordinary woman with a job to do. The fact that her mission was sacred had no bearing on her capability. She would either succeed, or fail. But, whatever the outcome, she would not quail, would not turn away. It was in the doing that duty was discharged. In the attempt that honor was attained.

Ilina stepped out onto the quay, shivering despite her traveling garb: woolen dress of deep blue, leggings and mantle tinted frost-white, and flowing green cloak thrown over all, clasped at her left shoulder with a silver brooch. The soles of her boots struck the storm-scoured flagstones in silence. With no grit underfoot to furnish friction, she twice slipped and had to flail and twist to keep from falling. She peered through the mist as it swirled over the stone outthrust, then glanced up to where a faintly brighter region betrayed the sun's position. A sudden chill wracked her body.

The ferry was late.

Hugh shifted his weight from foot to foot. Why had Ilina insisted they troop out here so early? She knew how to tell time—indeed, a clock stood in the corner of every sizable room of her citadel—but he was pretty sure they'd been standing in front of this deserted dock for upwards of forty minutes now.

With a sigh he rolled his shoulders and cracked his neck. The little Eskimo twitched, glancing up at Hugh from a corner of his eye. Hugh smiled. That one had seemed altogether too calm this whole time, like a monk lost in meditation. It was good to know the stoicism was all for show. It made Hugh feel better about the mantric screech rising from the basement of his mind. The one telling him he was too late, too late, too late.

Though he'd finally found a reason to doubt Ilina's sense of timing, it hadn't improved his mood. Even if her historical estimations were off, eons had to have elapsed here since his father's exit. Enough time for copies of the old man's Bible to start crumbling like antiques. He'd asked to keep the book, and Ilina had assured him she'd stow it safely for the trip. It was like she didn't even trust him to keep his own pack dry. *What a paranoid. The shipwreck wasn't my fault!*

But Hugh was feeling a paranoia all his own, a nervousness that went beyond concern for Daniel Forsythe. It was more like what he'd experienced on the night of Miles' return, just before his father's madness had congealed into an alien world and swallowed him whole. Like the apprehension he'd felt as he approached the giant diamond. *Am I developing some kind of prescience? Every time I get this feeling, something weird happens. And I'm really feeling it now ...*

An ache twinged Hugh's bladder, and now it was his turn to cringe. *But I can't relieve it; I gotta keep tabs on this delinquent.* He glanced at the Eskimo, whose eyes flicked up again, though his body neither moved nor tensed.

Aw hell, what could he do? thought Hugh. *Nothing, that's what. It's me he hates, not the girl. And he won't be able to get the jump on me again.*

He released the other man's arm and set down Ilina's handbag. Turning to her as she returned from the dock, he poked his own chest, then circled a finger out toward where the shore vanished in the fog, and then back down to point at his own feet. She nodded in understanding.

Jarlin watched the stranger go. He watched as the black sword and magic club bobbed on either side of the man's rucksack, as the long coat swung about his shins. He watched as the mist took him without offering up so much as a ripple to mark the ingress.

Jarlin didn't smile to see the stranger go. And he kept his eyes fixed on that unbroken whiteness for many minutes afterward.

Hugh meandered along the shoreline, crunching shells underfoot and skirting boulders that loomed out of the mist. He kept one ear open for the ferry's approach, but he might as well have been enclosed in a padded room for all the sound that reached his ears. The cries of seabirds far above were but faint echoes, the slosh of the waves to his right no more than a muffled murmur. Fog-formed droplets slipped down his oilskin coat. Cupping his hands over his mouth, he warmed them with his breath.

He knew the girl was planning some kind of detour once they reached the mainland. No doubt she'd try to launch an inquest into his claim of royal parentage, a claim for which he was still kicking himself vigorously. *You knew that name held power here. No matter what else he's become—no matter what else he's done—Father was never a liar. At least not with words. You knew his name would bring you notice. And yet you just had to blurt it out. And ever since then she's given you that look of leery reverence.* Hugh grimaced.

A SEA SOUGHT IN SONG

This worry might prove groundless, of course. Perhaps Ilina's interest in him was purely academic. Perhaps she just wanted him to write a history book: 'On the Planet of the High King, or What It's Like to Not Know You're Royalty.' Hugh snorted. Unlikely. But, whatever her intentions, whether or not she envisioned his role in her roadshow as voluntary or compulsory didn't much matter to him.

He had to keep moving. There was no time to loiter, regardless of who wished it. Lives were at stake far to the south, beyond kingdoms and continents too immense to imagine. His road ran through hostile nations whose customs were exotic and whose languages were strange …

Hugh stopped walking. Languages. What was it Ilina had said? *I am the only one within a thousand leagues capable of recognizing a single letter of this script.*

Yeah, that was it. *Damn.*

He needed her as a translator. This altered things. It wouldn't be enough to just slip away when her back was turned; now she'd have to accompany him, willing or not. There was no way he'd ever find Dan in a timely fashion without the ability to communicate. But would it be any less difficult to make the journey with a haughty young woman as baggage—and potentially antagonistic baggage at that? Hugh shook his head. At least if she was with him, he wouldn't have to worry about whether she was spreading rumors behind his back.

Speaking of which, it was high time for him to rejoin the others. But not before relieving his bladder. Putting a knob of rock between himself and the direction from which he'd come, he worked his way down to the water's edge and unbuttoned his fly. Relaxing, he looked up.

And there, materializing from the mist only fifty feet ahead, drifted a silent ship.

The distant shout was muffled yet unmistakable. The grinding crunch that followed was even less ambiguous. Ilina nearly dropped her banner at the sound, then propped it atop her abandoned valise before darting forward to squint against the mist.

Nothing but glistening black rocks and swirling white fog met her gaze. Hugh's voice burrowed back toward her, raised in unintelligible incredulity: *"Lai? Lai! Arhimu nah? Whe yir seh?"* Something had startled him.

And it wasn't either of *them.*

AUSTIN GUNDERSON

Ilina glanced back at Jarlin, who'd dropped into a crouch, eyes wide and darting. Motioning him to follow, she took off down the shore.

###

The boat, now wedged among the rocks, listed and groaned with each new pulse of the tide. With his rifle-butt buried in his shoulder, Hugh swept the empty deck again from his perch atop a nearby boulder. Nothing moved onboard. Of the crew there was no sign. The boat itself seemed in decent condition, though. No storm damage was apparent beyond a rent which traversed the single square sail—red as blood—from top to bottom. The scar gaped at Hugh; a cat's-eye portal to the unknown.

A clatter of stones announced Ilina's arrival. Hugh spared her a quick glance before returning his focus to the vessel. Her gasp recalled his attention. To his surprise she scrambled up beside him, dug in his coat pocket for the writing tools he kept there, and scribbled out a message: *"This is the ferry. Something is amiss."*

"You said it, sister," he muttered. Behind them, the little Eskimo stumbled out of the fog, then froze upon meeting Hugh's glare. Hugh broke his rifle open and jammed it under one arm, then took the parchment from Ilina. *"Wait here,"* he wrote.

Snapping his rifle up, he dropped from the boulder, and, with a leap and a grunt, swung himself single-handed over the ferry's prow and onto its deck. He stalked amidships and vanished down the hatch.

###

The ferry continued to sway and grate like some hulking wooden frog. Ilina brought her hand to her mouth, bit down upon a knuckle. She should've stopped him, should've called him back. Not that he would've come, but at least then she wouldn't have felt so helplessly complicit.

Everything about this situation was wrong. Horvold would never abandon his ferry over a mere rent in the sail. He loved this ship like his own daughter, had piloted her for half a lifetime. She was his pride and joy, not to mention his livelihood, not to mention his duty. No, whatever had caused that tear had also made off with the pilot. And while such a feat might not have proven difficult had Horvold been the ship's sole occupant, his crew was comprised of men half his age and twice his weight. Something terrible had done this.

146

A SEA SOUGHT IN SONG

Ilina glanced at Jarlin for some measure of reassurance—some small indifference to allay her paranoia—but the Jaar had turned his back upon the boat. His gaze was fixed instead on the rocky slope behind them which rose toward Kredak Tower. He cocked an ear as though listening. A breeze had picked up and the mists were writhing. A chill slid down her spine.

Just then the ferry lurched and something crunched into the rocks only a few feet away. Ilina yelped and whipped around only to face an annoyingly amused Hugh.

She shut her eyes, heart hammering with stymied adrenalin, and when she opened them again he was shaking his head. The ferry was empty. *But then what ... and where ...?*

She surprised herself then by reaching out and gripping his arm, neglecting to mask her emotions. *Things here are beyond my control, Conrad. I cannot protect you. Will you protect us? Can you protect us?* Hugh squeezed her shoulder, met her eyes, and for once they were on exactly the same page. Talking without words.

Then Jarlin screamed.

Farther up the slope, the mist had dissipated somewhat. A hole was opening in its pall. Beyond that hole loomed the vast black bole of Kredak Tower, its pavilioned crown still buried in cloud. Ahead, the little Eskimo had fallen upon his face as though kowtowing to an idol.

Hugh froze, eyes raking the scene, uncomprehending. Overwhelmed by an inexplicable sense of immanent horror.

For a long moment all was still. Then the tower sprouted legs.

They scissored slowly away from the walls at an impossible height, monstrous black struts undoubling again and again into his line of sight until the tower itself seemed to have split apart like some lightning-lashed fir. They spread like the shanks of a wolf spider that'd drawn itself up for concealment. Apparitions of waking nightmare unreal in their enormity. A noise like grinding millstones filtered down through the fog.

"Harlith tehlet grath," choked Ilina. Her face was ashen.

The enormity, still hidden behind the tower, lifted one of its legs. Higher and higher it rose as the angle of its skyward-pointing knee-joint widened. When its single-pronged claw was at least thirty feet off the ground, it split at the shin into two jointed sublegs, each of which terminated in a talon half the thickness of that which they'd formed when aligned. The new talons hung idly in midair, then came stabbing down into rock which shuddered and cracked beneath incalculable weight. The monster lurched into view—a living tower of darkness, the trunk to countless branching spines.

And Hugh sprang into motion. He flung Ilina behind him, leapt from their boulder, and hit the ground running. Tossing his rifle from right hand to left, he stooped down and yanked the Eskimo to his feet by the scruff of his parka, propelling him forward in a scramble for higher ground. "Board the boat, Ilina!" he bellowed. "Find a pole and cast off! Get the hell outta here!"

The rocks trembled as the monster took another step and emerged fully from behind Kredak Tower. Its legs were all splitting now, bifurcating at their joints like so many fire-blackened tongs. A putrid stench smashed into Hugh as he ran.

Ahead of them the slope leveled off into a sedge-haired knoll before rising and tapering toward the citadel. Hugh pulled up, releasing the Eskimo to stumble to a slack-jawed stop, and then whipped a knife from his boot and sawed through the other's bonds.

The Eskimo looked up at Hugh, sharp confusion slicing his stupor. Hugh shrugged and tossed him the knife. Then he turned, planting his feet and raising his rifle.

In the time it'd taken them to reach the knoll, the monster had closed half the intervening distance. Hugh could see now that in form it was like unto a spider—a sixteen-sublegged spider that stood fully a hundred and fifty feet tall. *Vitals, vitals, look for the vitals.* The thing was plated in an exoskeleton that appeared a thousand years old, knobbed and pitted with glistening growths and trailing seaweed like some submarine mountain raised to life. Articulated spines—whether arms or mandibles or antennae, Hugh couldn't tell—flailed slowly over the stalking legs. *Gotta find the vitals. Oh God, where's the vitals?*

There. High atop the central trunk, above the waving spines, glittered a cluster of sunken bulbs that could only be eyes. Maybe.

Hugh sighted along his Westley Richards .577 double rifle, a weapon designed with a charging bull elephant in mind. His finger tightened on the trigger.

###

The deafening double boom, though stifled by the fog, was followed by a screech of such depth and volume that it felled Ilina like an arrow to the

A SEA SOUGHT IN SONG

head. A thousand bull elk in autumnal chorus could not have achieved a noise so rattling, so piercing, so incapacitating. The mast spider was keening. Ilina squirmed among the rocks—eyes clenched shut, palms pressed tight over her ears. Eventually the ringing seemed to lessen. She raised her head.

Hugh stood before the monster—firing and reloading, firing and reloading. Inaudible, ineffective. A small flame burning beneath the shadow of death. So very small. The mast spider towered above him, greater by far than the largest specimens of its kind ever recorded in the annals of man. Like a god of Oblivion it rose, like Noghli himself, older and crueler than the waste beneath the world. *He has risen. Harlith has failed! Noghli is risen from the depths and stands before me in power. I am undone.*

Ilina tried to get up but her knees buckled, struck the stones. *All is lost.* She gazed at the mountain of darkness that would soon engulf her. Felt her body relaxing, her will departing. *End my suffering swiftly, O Dark Lord of the Deep. Strike thou the note of my name. Recall me to the nothingness.*

But no; Harlith had not failed. He lived. He stood alone between her and death—ferocious, defiant. His fiery weapon lit the darkness like lightning. It rammed his shoulder with each new blast. And the Lord of the Deep recoiled.

Hugh. Harlith! Can it be they are one and the same? Can it be that he is real?

Down came a talon. Ilina's heart vaulted into her throat, choking off a scream. The whole world had fallen silent.

At the last second Hugh leapt aside. He stumbled and nearly fell, caught his balance, dodged a second talon, and sprinted for Kredak Tower. Talons rose and slammed back down as the mast spider pivoted in pursuit. *No, no, no! What are you doing, Hugh? Come back to the ferry! Let us escape!*

But even as this hope leapt in her breast Ilina knew it was illusory. From the sea this monster had come; from this monster the sea would offer them no refuge. Ilina rose on unsteady legs, took a step forward. *And where are you going, you fool? What can you possibly do to help?*

Well, that would depend on what Hugh was trying to do. *Which is what? To climb the tower?* Yes. *To climb the ladder you left dangling in the storm last night?* Of course. *To get a clean shot at the spider's head?* What else?

An idea sparked in Ilina's mind. She spun for her valise.

Jarlin stood, his right hand still outstretched, still gripping the knife where he'd snatched it from the air. *Why, Stranger? Why must you mock me*

149

so? Why must you grind salt into my wounds? And why haven't I gutted you like a beached seal where you stand?

The answer was only too obvious, only too painful. *Because you know me as a coward. You know I'd never attack you without the advantage of surprise. For six days and nights I hauled oar for you without lifting a finger in challenge. When I struck, I struck from behind. Because I knew I stood no chance. Because I knew you were the stronger. Perhaps even strong enough to ward off the beasts of Hoc.*

For the sake of such strength, I will swallow my rage.

A shadow enveloped him. Carapaced pillars swept past and drove into the stone, tearing up boulders like clods of dirt upon withdrawal. A crunching and groaning came from everywhere. Vile water sluiced over him. And then the vast shadow was past, and Jarlin stood atop the hillock watching the sum of all nightmares stalk the leaping Stranger down the headland to the tower.

Why are you running, Stranger? Do you think to escape? There is no escape from a god once it sets its eye upon you. Not even my amulet could help you now. We are all dead unless you kill the god. If you don't, it will drag our souls to Hoc and there consume them.

A spine of terror pierced his numbness. Here, he had encountered a fate worse than death. And when death becomes a preferable alternative, fear will mimic courage.

Jarlin found that he was running. Running like the wind and rain, like sleet across the steppe. Flying to aid the man who had destroyed his life.

Hugh sprinted past Ilina's front door and skirted the citadel's west wing, interposing its stonework between himself and the monster. Rising for three stories at his right hand, the ancient fortress, survivor of ten thousand storms, formed an all-too-ineffectual shield. One ambitious step would carry the spider over the gables. This was a game of Gain High Ground Or Die. Which was a game Hugh had yet to lose.

He grimaced. *There's a first time for everything.*

The tower loomed. But where was the ladder? Hugh cursed and kept sprinting. *There.* The storm had whipped it around to the east and tangled it upon itself many times. The weights on its end had served only to anchor it askew once the winds finally died.

Hugh slammed his rifle into the sheath slung over his shoulder, lunged, caught the heavy ropes, and began to climb. Reach, pull, catch, step. Again and again and again. The ladder swung and lurched. It twisted around, scraping him against the wall. It creaked and groaned. Hugh gasped for breath.

But he wasn't fast enough. He'd only ascended fifty feet when a wall of shadow filled the fringe of his right eye.

###

Jarlin climbed the leg of the god as though it were a storm-lashed spruce. Beneath him the ground was a blur. Carapace as fertile as a tidepool proffered him plenty to cling to. Mussels and barnacles sprouted from its clefts in abundance, and the Jaar was glad of his gloves. The knife thus far had found no purchase. Above him was the god's lowest joint; perhaps its shell was weaker there.

Up heaved the ground. Jarlin embraced the leg with all his might, but the shock of impact dislodged his grip and he snapped backward, falling free. *No! Not like this.* His outflung hand snagged a clutch of mussels, which tore through his glove and sliced deep into the meat of his left palm.

Howling, Jarlin hung on. His knees cracked against the god's leg as the ground once again fell away. He forced his arms to bend, forced his bloody palm to grasp a higher handhold.

He screamed. He climbed.

And at last he came to the lowest joint. To the soft tissue and iron-taut tendons that flexed beneath the armor. And, screaming, he plunged the knife as deep as it would go.

The monster spasmed, drawing its limbs together like a ship tossing oars, its bone-rattling voice as the thunder of a tempest to Jarlin's seabird cry. Up pincered the leg, crushing the Jaar in its joint. His pulverized body slipped free to splatter on the stones.

###

Breath huffed in Ilina's throat, straps bit into her hand, skirts swished about her legs, rocks jarred her feet, and, beneath it all, a basso growl shook the world. Her mind felt both empty and turgid. Her thoughts were piling up behind some kind of blockage. She knew there was danger, but it seemed so distant, so abstract. *Can't hear it.* She wasn't sure her ears were working, but her nose sure was. A stench hung in the air alongside the fog. It clung to her skin like condensation—the odor of refuse, of decay, of a thing buried in

AUSTIN GUNDERSON

Oblivion since before the High King reigned. The ground heaved and tilted as she ran.

The mast spider stood before her. Above her. Around her. *Back, back! Too far in!* She dropped into a crouch as a taloned leg swooped overhead like a falling tree. Talons were swooping all about her now—falling and rising in an apocalyptic jig. Ilina stumbled, fell, and scrambled backward on all fours. The stones cut her hands. The ground trembled. At last she managed to rise, only to trip over a mangled corpse. She gaped in horror.

Jarlin. His left mukluk was still pristine—strips of woven ivory spiraling up its length like little eels of death. The rest of him was pulp.

From above came a quick double-thud. All around Ilina, leg-trees bent as before a gale's blast. Some skidded askew. The monster reeled away from the tower.

Numb, Ilina raised her eyes in time to see a bright flash leap from a window embrasure. Hugh had twined himself in the ladder's ropes and planted his feet on the sloping sill. He snapped open his weapon, fumbling with his rucksack as the monster recovered its balance. Something fell from his hands. He grasped frantically at the air, then turned, unslinging his pack and planting it behind him, drawing a small box from within.

It's now or never. Ilina upended her valise.

Its precious contents spilled out with a clatter, and she fished through them, blind to all but the oblong oilskin object at the bottom of the heap. She snatched it up and unwound it to disclose the Scepter of Kredak. The black rod lay dully in her palm. Innocuous. Inert.

She scrambled backward until Hugh vanished behind the monster's bulk, then held the rod aloft and aimed it at the tower. It glistened darkly as she stared down its length. Through the faceted rim of the jewel that bulged at its tip, the spider's spines refracted like splintered spears. A distortion of an abomination.

From the gemstone ran an emerald runnel like a tear-streak down the rod. It pooled in a shallow little swatch beside Ilina's thumb. She shut her eyes, took three quick breaths, and pressed the swatch.

With a crack that sounded loud even in her deafened ears, Hugh's huge sword burst through the monster's body to slam pommel-first over the scepter's end. The impact threw Ilina flat on her back and knocked both rod and sword from her grasp, flipping them up and away. They separated in midair, bounced off the rocks, and careened into the fog.

###

152

A SEA SOUGHT IN SONG

Hugh spun and gaped. Something had yanked the sword right off his back. He felt behind him. Right through its sheath! *What the hell ...?* The sheath's leather was sliced all the way down its length as though some invisible hand of incredible strength had simply flicked the weapon out and tossed it away. It made no sense.

The monster. It grabbed the sword. I didn't even see it coming.

With a snarl he jammed two new cartridges into the rifle's breech. With a flick of his wrist the barrels snapped up. With a roar he shoved the stock into his shoulder and double-tapped the trigger. The monster lurched. Dark fluid, gelatinous and steaming, dribbled down its chitinous head.

Hugh stood eye-to-eye with death. He snapped open his weapon, glaring. Reached for more rounds. Bumped his fingers around the empty corners of his ammunition box. A sudden chill settled on his spine.

So that's it. I'm done. Too proud, my boasting. Too vain, my nerve. Didn't make it far, did I, Father? So much for your assurance.

"*Damn you!*" he screamed aloud, snatching his spent casings and flinging them at the thing's cluster of lightless eyes. "I am Hugh, son of King Henry Conrad, heir to the throne, rightful lord of this land! Kill me now or bow! Decide whom you serve, you pus-filled ruin!"

A moment of silence seemed to stretch forever. Then the monster toppled.

It came plunging down upon the tower, a ten-thousand-ton wrecking ball with only mortar-bonded stone to withstand its descent. Its impact was an earthquake, its embrace an upheaval. The windowsill shook, tilting beneath Hugh's feet. He grabbed for his pack and caught it, but then the sill was no longer under him and he cracked his elbows on its lip as it shot skyward to leave him thrashing in space. The rope ladder whipped past, but Hugh's hands were full. *Rifle or pack, rifle or pack?*

Hugh groaned and let the rifle go. His fingers closed on a rung and he jerked to a stop directly over the monster as the rifle glanced off its head to vanish in the cloud of dust roiling up from below. Hugh swung for a moment, then kept descending. *Wait ... wha ...?* He raised his eyes.

The mist disgorged a ceiling of stone. The tower was coming down.

Ilina felt her consciousness dislocate. It recoiled as if by instinct, throwing distance between itself and this cataclysm in order to survive such a shock intact. It observed from a great remove, helpless to intervene, as a small woman watched her ancestral home—mightiest manmade wonder of the north, bastion of hope for the civilized world—crumble into dust as it plummeted from above. The small woman wept. Her consciousness kept silence, its grief and rage too poignant to express.

She watched herself watch as her Kredak Tower fell. As a small figure dropped amid the airborne wreckage to hit the mast spider's head where it had penetrated the wall. The figure skidded and slid across the oblong shell as blocks of masonry rained from above. Over the side it went, swinging a hatchet into one of the creature's eyes, and then it was lost in the swelling pall. The tower's top third formed an acute angle with the ground as its stonework imploded below. The Pavilion of Winds flew apart like chaff. The Beacon of Hope fell free, its facets glinting even in cloud.

This isn't possible, grasped Ilina's thought. *This must be a dream. A vision of foreboding, a portent of peril to come. It cannot be that Harlith's coming would destroy my world. What is there that I haven't given up for him? Since the moment of my birth have I not been a sacrifice? Have I not abandoned all hope of freedom and love? Have I not believed in him when all others scoffed? Will he now repay my devotion by drawing this creature of Oblivion to my doorstep to bury it in the rubble of my home?*

No, this cannot be. Orlom would not allow such injustice. It must be a dream. It must.

It wasn't. The tower landed. Shattered. And Arlam trembled anew beneath Ilina's feet.

Hugh knew he was still alive not because he couldn't breathe, but because this inability worried him. *If I were dead, I don't suppose I'd care, now would I?* He tried again, yawning his mouth and tightening his chest, but nothing happened. He opened his eyes and saw only blackness.

Panic set in. *Maybe I'm dead and in hell. Maybe hell isn't fire and brimstone; maybe it's an eternity of needing to breathe and not being able to. Oh God no ...* Losing his head, Hugh struggled upright only to crack his temple against a hard, gritty slab.

Stone. Beautiful stone. I'm still alive and the world is solid. He slumped against a neighboring block, gaping gladly until his wind returned with a rasp and a lungful of rock dust. He choked and hacked to clear his throat. Beside

A SEA SOUGHT IN SONG

him, the grit was beginning to feel slick beneath his hand. *Blood. Probably lost a lot of it.* At least he could still move all his limbs.

A rumbling, a scraping, and light rent the blackness. Gray shapes sprang from nothing. Swirling powder choked the air. Hugh wrenched his legs out of a pile of rubble and crawled toward the rent, but just as he reached it the ground shifted again, cutting off the light. A slide of talus buried his arms and he scrambled back, smacking his head and slicing his shoulders against protruding stones. He'd been wrong; the world was far from solid. *This whole ruin's in motion. It's heaving like the sea. What's happening?*

It took him only a moment. *Aw, hell. The monster ain't dead yet.*

To his left burst the brightness of another rift within the rubble. Hugh ran for it in a crouch.

Ilina trembled like a twig stuck in the wind-lashed sand. She raised her hands to hide that unthinkable stripe of empty air occupied by the tower an instant earlier, but instead curled shaking fingers over her mouth and bit down hard, unable to look away, unable to pretend. *Everything I know ... everything I am ... gone.* She was lost, bereft, adrift. A bird without nest, a ship without harbor. That Beacon which had been for others a mere landmark had been for her an abode, and by its light she had seen the world. In its snuffing all else grew dark. Naught but estranged itineracy awaited her now.

As she knelt—clutching herself, wracked by sobs—Ilina gradually became aware of a new sound: the low groan of slowly shifting stone. That portion of her mind still dedicated to self-preservation raised its voice above her general lamentation, and she gave it leave to interject. *You fool, it's not over yet!* But it was over; nothing was left. *Idiot, you are left!* And what was she without Anticipation Light? *I don't know. Why don't you get up and find out?*

Ilina raised her eyes in time to see an entire swath of rubble bob down and bounce back up, spilling debris and spewing dust. *Oh, gods no ... oh Orlom, please ...* She wiped salt from her eyes, tried holding her breath between gasps. A chill beyond despair flooded the sanctum of her soul. Harlith had failed. Hugh had not survived. And she was now alone with Noghli.

"I come bearing no gift," she whimpered, flattening herself among the rocks like some small prey animal. "I come lighting no fire. All is sand that you sift. You know I ... you know ... oh, gods above and below," she hissed.

AUSTIN GUNDERSON

"*What* do you know? You have never felt what I feel. You have never known what I fear. You are mighty and aloof. Why don't you come down here and *show yourself? Coward!*" she screamed. "You watch and wait for my obeisance before deigning to get involved, but my need won't wait for your pardon! God!" she choked, hanging her head. "I know you neither know nor care, but, for the sake of your *own* honor, lift the seal and show me your favor. I am undone."

The hill of stones before her shifted with a great grinding crunch. From out of a crevice stumbled a haggard figure, his face a gray mask, his tattered garments striped by red. He looked wildly around, then ran toward her. Ilina's mouth fell open. Hugh Conrad *had* survived.

She scrambled to her feet, unsure whether to strike or embrace him, but was denied the opportunity to decide when Hugh grabbed her half-raised forearm as he dashed past, yanking her bodily down the slope and back toward the ferry. She snatched her valise in passing, hoping there was still something in it. Boulders became a blur beneath them, but Ilina's feet pinned down points of solid ground seemingly of their own accord. She kept pace with Hugh as behind them a smoking ruin thundered and shifted awake. They fled through the mist—two mortals who had dared challenge a god. Ruin rose behind them.

"Wait, wait!" cried Ilina, breaking Hugh's grasp and diving to one side, to where sword and scepter lay askew among the rocks. Before she could heft them he was at her side again, expression dark. Seeing the look in his eye, she lifted the scepter and slid her thumb over its swatch. The sword jerked up of its own accord to snap hilt-first over the emerald end. Hugh jumped back, nearly tripping over a jagged stone.

Ilina did not smile. A coldness gripped her. She turned slowly, hiding the strain of the sword's sudden weight, and held it up at Hugh point-first. His face grew hard, his eyes hot and sharp as shards fresh from the fire.

They stood thus for an instant or an hour.

Of what worth your pride? Of what value your wounded honor? In retribution for your loss, will you cast away all that remains?

No. But neither would she forget.

Ilina's thumb relaxed and the black sword clattered at Hugh's feet.

Shooting her a final penetrating glance, he bent for the blade, seized her hand, and ran.

156

A SEA SOUGHT IN SONG

The ferry hadn't moved. In the sheltered cove it clattered, listless, rocks nudging it back and forth as the rising tide pressed it to the shore. Ilina scrambled atop Hugh's boulder and he grabbed her, swinging her over the gunwale. Her dress flared in midair and she released his hand, turning nimbly, dropping to the deck in a crouch. He leapt after, boots striking the boards as Ilina let fall her valise and dashed to the sternpost.

Shrugging off his pack, he bent to wrestle an oar free from its fastenings under the port rail while risking a glance behind. Mist had poured back in with the tide, swathing Cuspid Isle in a chill shroud, concealing the absence of its architectural marvel.

Hugh swore. These oddly-knotted ropes rebuffed his prying fingers. What was the girl doing? If they didn't get this ship in the water, they were both as good as dead.

"Ilina!" he shouted, "Help me get these oars out of–"

The ferry lurched violently and Hugh pitched forward, smacking his temple against the gunwale. He sprawled on the deck, felt a rasping groan come shuddering up the hull. *Wha ...?*

He scrambled upright to gape in astonishment at the surrounding rocks, which receded swiftly to vanish in the fog. Whiteness closed in: a spectral sea suspended in midair. Hugh felt the condensation brushing his cheek and knew he was in motion. He leaned over the side to see a bow wave forming.

Looking up, he saw Ilina standing at the prow—no, it was the stern: they'd backed out of the cove—with her right hand pressed against the upward-curving wood. A sudden rush of air teased her hair.

This was incredible. The ferry was now plowing along steadily without so much as a gust of wind or the dip of an oar. The deck trembled at each swell pierced by the bow. The single square sail billowed *backward*, its cat-eye whistling in a low pitch. Was this boat attached to some larger vessel lurking in the mist? Was it being towed out with an automatic winch?

Hugh approached Ilina from behind. She spared him a glance, then continued staring out into unbroken whiteness. Water beaded on her face. Her hand was splayed upon a football-sized oval of glass embedded at chest height in the ship's massive sternpost. Something glittered at the oval's heart, though Hugh couldn't tell what.

More magic. Wonderful. Just wonderful.

They clove through the fog and it closed behind them, undisturbed. Water thudded against the keel and rushed along the hull. Creaks and groans ran through the wood. The sail's lips whistled. All else was silence.

All else was silence.

AUSTIN GUNDERSON

They were in deep water now, Hugh was certain, and getting deeper every moment. He'd seen no gradual gradations of blue during his reconnoiter to the hilltop; the seafloor would have dropped away beneath them almost as swiftly as the shore had receded from sight. The monster couldn't reach them here.

But such knowledge conferred no comfort. He turned and cocked his head and strained to hear something else. Something beyond the silence beyond the sounds of magic flight. Something like grinding millstones. Like a thousand bugling elk.

Only soft staccato sobbing reached his ears.

In the stern of the boat, staring forward, facing the inscrutable south, Ilina stood stern and straight as a mast. Her shoulders shook but her head remained high. She had not—*would* not, Hugh sensed—let it fall. He drew near again and saw the shimmer upon her cheeks, the contractions of her throat. Her grief touched him, moved him, so visceral it was. He thought he could actually feel it.

This woman had watched her home crumble before her eyes, had seen a mountain of stone inter her father's tomb beyond reach. He thought of his own father—long beyond his reach from this alien wasteland, and now freshly cut off once more. They had switched places, father and son, sundered by the mirror. He tried not to think about that too much; when he did, it hurt.

But now, gazing upon the agony displayed in Ilina's beautiful face, he became suddenly aware of his own pain as something more than a stigma best concealed. It was the common ground between them, the tenuous bridge he might cross to give and find some small measure of comfort. He reached out. Laid a hand lightly on her shoulder.

She twitched, shrugged him off. Shot him a vicious glare.

And the ocean erupted around them.

The world tilted and Ilina cried out as she slipped, losing her grip on the glass. She flung out a bracing hand but stopped short of the deck, cradled in Hugh's all-too-eager arms. With a spasm she squirmed out of his grasp. The waters were roiling and heaving. Something was rising from beneath. Something big.

It breached the surface a hundred feet ahead, just on the edge of the mist. A vast hulking darkness gleaming with froth—the chitinous crown of a god returned to his element. The cluster of its eyes was gouged, hollow. Water dark with pus sluiced from pits and seams to stream into the sea as the abomination rose.

How it had overtaken them Ilina did not know. The paths of Noghli passed beyond human ken. Not for the likes of her was such knowledge. But as the ferry—released from its rhomic connection to Land's End—drifted inexorably forward with residual momentum, a single panicked thought snagged in the tatters of her mind: she wished she knew how the Lord of the Deep had done it. She wished she understood.

But the mast spider loomed very near, now—just over the railing!—and Ilina's thought itself had become a fickle thing. She was suddenly conscious of the creature's immensity—that like an iceberg it descended far beyond her sight, that it stood now upon the very floor of the sea and eyed her as she would've eyed a beetle clinging to a twig. She raised her eyes to meet its gaze and stood eclipsed before dead recesses yawning in darkness and emptiness—ancient beyond memory, frigid beyond endurance.

A sense of vertigo wracked her and she crumpled to the deck, no steadying hands present to restrain her fall. Noghli's visage filled her vision. For lo, the cracks and slabs of his skull formed the outline of a face as dead as that of the Jaar he had crushed, as cold as a hearth bare and buried. The warmth of her body departed in a rush, siphoned off by the void behind that countenance, by the Hand of Oblivion itself. The god's gaze was unendurable. She was too small to scream. Too empty to exist.

Eight nodules sprouted from Noghli's head. A crown. From the tip of each a spiny tentacle slid. Encircled the ship above and below. Entwined about her soul.

All was lost.

###

Hugh slipped into memory as the dark waters closed over his head. No longer depthless was this deep, but shallow and choppy and sliced by ordinance. The corpses of his comrades sagged beneath the surface like bloated growths in a macabre kelp forest. Blood befouled the tide. Horrified, he panicked, struggled, clawed for air.

He broke the waves and the vision was gone. But what replaced it was worse by far.

The monster rose only yards to his right, blocking the path of the ship. Stock-still it stood, and the heaving of the sea, apparent only by contrast, broke upon it and washed over it as though it were an oil rig assailed by storm. Of its appendages he saw none. But the water here was dark and cold—dark as a wood on a moonless night, cold as the teeth of the frost. Beneath him, even now, massive limbs were undoubtedly uncoiling. Little time remained.

His hands knifed down and his body stretched out and he drove for a point just beyond the creature's crown, putting the monster between himself and the ship as water scraped like scalpels against his skin and his left hand clutched the girl's black rod in a bone-white grip.

Hugh stalled out and turned, treading water, looking up as he gasped for breath. The crown had sprouted whiplike horns. They snaked away toward the boat. He was alone now, bobbing in the open sea, minutes away from hypothermia and sundered from his only chance of survival by an apparition of nightmare. Unsmiling, he raised the rod. His arm shook so violently he could barely point the thing.

For some strange reason he felt the need to speak. "I am Hugh Conrad," he said through clenched teeth, "and I require your life." He thumbed the emerald swatch.

A black splinter flipped end-over-end past the fringe of Ilina's constricting vision, vaulting over the gunwale and plunging into the face of death. A deafening scream ignited in the air. Tentacles convulsed. One passed just over her head, severing the ferry's mast and shattering its sternpost before cannoning into the sea.

The falling sail snapped into the corner of her eye—a red wedge, strangely familiar. Spray rained upon Ilina as she lay inert and staring. She couldn't see the dead face anymore. In its stead was naught but an odd motif of scum-encrusted plates. Where had Noghli gone?

Ilina would never learn. For in that very instant, the mast spider's legs gave way and its head plummeted from sight. Its stinging scream was drowned in a boom of inrushing sea. The ferry lurched forward, spinning with those waters that reoccupied the void.

Hugh shuddered as the sword slammed hilt-first into his rod. A blinding white light leapt up and was gone. A tingle ran up his arm and into his chest—an electric surge of vigor. He stood up straighter in the water. The monster cried out and collapsed, and Hugh slid forward as the swirling depths sucked it down.

The ferry rushed up, its hull looming suddenly, and Hugh smacked into it and scraped alongside it, nearly letting go of the rod and sword. Barnacles tore at his shoulders and lacerated his scrabbling arms. The hull bore down like a linebacker. Hugh gripped a patch of barnacles, spread-eagling himself against the slick wood to keep from getting shoved under and mangled by the keel.

At the last instant, just before the froth overwhelmed him, he found a foothold and leapt up, grabbing an oar-lock and hauling himself aboard. He sprawled upon the deck—gasping, bleeding, cramping from the cold. The rod slipped from nerveless fingers. Its deadly extension, uncoupled, clattered against a carpet of crimson cloth.

The fog was lifting now. Splintered timbers creaked to the rhythm of the swells. No wave crashed; no seabird shrieked. In silence, in a ship small and crippled, Hugh Conrad and Ilina Lightkeeper drifted over the dark face of the deep.

Part Two
KRAMARACK

Cadenza
THEIR END IN OUR EYES

*I*f *the end of a thing is better than its beginning*, mused Silvus as he clung to the creaking hull, *then what of a thing that begins with an end?*

The Seaport of Suma didn't look as though it faced an end. Indeed, the sun had barely crested the western horizon—a bloody orb breaching the surface of the deep. Between the opposing slopes of the fjord it rose, and its shafts set the harbor alight. Seabirds squawked, sailors shouted, and savvy shopkeepers set about their soliciting almost before there were shoppers to see. And yet this place had come to the close of its time as surely as a school of herring surrounded by a seine. Silvus was here to raise the net and land the catch.

No man enjoyed a beginning that required his destruction. Resistance would be fierce.

Silvus Relisham, Commander of the Silent Host, Scourge of the Lord of the Air, relaxed his fingers. His huge mace slipped from his grasp, vanishing with a percussive splash. Prudol Fjord was about fifty feet deep this far out from the quay, more than sufficient to accommodate the largest vessels. Indeed, it was not depth that this port lacked, but breadth: galleons crowded together behind the breakwater like sheep in a shearing shed, their bare masts and spars bristling as though the inlet were a valley filled with fire-ravaged firs.

Silvus pictured his iron sphere burrowing into the silt on the bottom, the plume of its impact merging with the general murk. He flexed his fingers and leaned out over the shadowed water. A sharp silhouette regarded him from below, a hole cut in the depthless blue sky, head crowned with coral clouds. No man perceived the depth of his own softness until he encountered something hard. Pain and loss freed every man to choose the way of strength.

Only those so liberated would survive this day.

Behind him on deck, sailors scurried to attend the rigging. The fleet had received its orders late last night from a courier astride a frothing horse: make sail for Dolamin with all possible speed. The long-anticipated assault had begun. Admiral Norvald was to enter the Sapphire Sea, blockade the fortress of Noloth, and prevent the Tunnoltans from flanking the southern front at all costs. This ship—the *Rampart Errant*—had been among the latest to arrive at the rendezvous and had thus been forced to drop anchor nearly a quarter-mile from shore. Only a single row of galleons separated it from unoccupied water. It would be among the first to leave the harbor.

And among the first to die.

"Hoy, you dere!" bawled a gravelly voice. "If yer gonna loiter, ah'll tip ya o'er da side so ye can do it in da drink! Jump to! Up da shrouds wid ya!"

Silvus didn't turn. Instead, he reached inside his open-fronted sailor's vest and produced a golden rod about six inches in length and one in diameter. One end glinted a deep green, like emerald, and splayed into a flat-capped pommel. Silvus pointed this end down, away from himself. He hopped backward off the railing, planting his feet in a wide, bent-kneed stance.

"Hell's charred hands," swore the voice from behind. "Is it a thief ye are?" Bare feet thumped toward him.

Silvus shut his ash-gray eyes and inhaled deeply, curling the fingers of his right hand around the golden rod. Upon that hand he wore a glove of fitted leather which exposed his index finger to the second knuckle, and he felt the rod shudder and stiffen as it made contact with his flesh.

A wind from the sea swept over him then, plastering his loose white uniform against his body, whipping strands of lank hair free of his bandana. The tall two-decker frigate directly ahead of him, first to weigh anchor, had unfurled its sails in preparation to beat windward through the jetties and into open water. Geometric calculations tumbled through Silvus' mind. A heavy hand fell on his shoulder.

Silvus Relisham grasped the golden rod before him with both hands and swung it up with all the force he could muster. His muscles bulged as though heaving a heavy weight. Fifty feet ahead, a black streak erupted from the deck of the turning frigate, spraying wooden fragments high into the air and snapping a mizzenmast spar in flight. The hand on Silvus' shoulder went slack. Men across the water cried out in shock.

Down swung the rod in Silvus' hands, and something that moved faster than sight dove from the sky to punch a second hole through the frigate. Up again and down, and red gore joined the airborne splinters as a hapless sailor disintegrated above a hole that hadn't existed an instant before. The frigate groaned, already listing.

Shock turned to terror as the surrounding vessels took up the alarm. An attack! An attack from nowhere! Men were screaming, running, abandoning the doomed ship. They ignored their officers' shouts and leapt from its sides, falling like a human rain.

A SEA SOUGHT IN SONG

Silvus Relisham removed his left hand from the golden rod, lifted his bare right forefinger, and then turned, elbowing the dumbfounded bosun in the stomach and flipping him flat on his back with a vicious uppercut.

Silvus glanced up. Pandemonium had gripped the *Rampart*. Its crew swarmed the larboard railing, scanning in vain for the source of their peril. Its captain, as ignorant as they, paced the poop deck, bellowing orders and gesticulating wildly. Ships further down the line were on the move, turning into the wind. The logjam was breaking up. Soon these vast war machines would have room to maneuver.

Silvus couldn't allow that to happen.

He broke into a run, yanking a second glove from a vest pocket and tugging it onto his left hand. It was stiff, its palm and thumb threaded with emerald. Over the deck and up the stern steps Silvus charged. The helmsman shouted a warning and the captain spun, but Silvus curled into a forward roll, bowled the man's feet out from under him, and rose again with a fluid grace, his somersault flowing into a sprint as behind him the captain's head struck the deck with a crack.

A golden sphere the size of a crab apple had appeared in Silvus' left hand. A single emerald fleck marred its sheening surface. He kept the bare tip of his left forefinger from touching the thing as he ran. Cries of anger boiled from behind.

Silvus leapt onto the taffrail, flung the golden sphere high into the air between his ship and the next, and launched himself out into space. Falling, he ripped open the front of his white uniform shirt, exposing thick leather straps that crossed his chest diagonally from shoulders to waist and met over his sternum in a diamond-shaped iron plate. Embedded in the plate was a single golden bead, and it was to this bead that he pressed his left forefinger an instant before hitting the water.

But Silvus Relisham didn't hit the water. Instead he jerked to a stop in midair, legs swinging up as his body sagged within its cradling straps, which hung now from the golden bead, which hung from nothing. Silvus fell no longer but swooped, gradually losing altitude and picking up speed, rotating an invisible pivot suspended high overhead. His feet trailed in a wave. Then he was clear of the sea and rising, rising, rising toward the neighboring ship that now filled his field of vision.

As he swept up over the bowsprit he flung his right hand behind him, golden rod extended. Clenching his right index finger around the rod's warming surface, he released his chestplate bead. Silvus' pendular motion abruptly stalled out, but his momentum proved sufficient to carry him over the deck of the ship. Awestruck sailors gaped at him from below.

Silvus felt it then: the power, the joy. The fury. Here, in this moment, he was supreme. A god. None could touch him, none could oppose him. The little people who fled his point of impact were as far beneath him as a writhing clutch of maggots was beneath the self-important squalor of ordinary men. How *dare* they gaze upon him? None would do so and live. A wordless roar tore free of his throat. Whipping his rod-hand over his head and down before his face, he reached back with his left and circled his finger and thumb.

Silvus struck the deck in a crouch. The golden sphere darted from heaven to smack into his emerald-palmed left glove at the same instant the three-decker galleon two moorings ahead ruptured from within, a towering whitewater plume geysering skyward amidships. Silvus straightened as a deafening thunderclap staggered the surrounding sailors.

As much as he longed to lash out, to lay about him, to show these lower beings the true meaning of might, he knew his success depended on the enemy's continued confusion. No man—not even Silvus Relisham himself—could hope to obliterate an entire armada having once been identified as the source of its destruction. So instead of indulging himself and snapping the nearest man's neck, he slid one foot obliquely behind the other and spun, raising his rod directly overhead. From behind came a boom of detonation; his mace must have split the galleon's magazine on the backstroke. Heat blasted the nape of his neck as he lunged into a forward swing.

Two ships away, a barque with red sails shuddered. Silvus frowned and began chopping his rod up and down in both hands like a headless axe. The barque cracked and groaned, its anguish audible over the roar of flames and the crash of secondary explosions, and bodies flung themselves from its sides as its mainmast splintered and fell.

Its death throes were obscured as the *Rampart Errant* swung about, coming between Silvus and his prey, bloodying its jib sail in the rising sun. The galleon had flung open its gunports and was searching for something to kill. Drifting smoke channeled the sun's light into amber shafts that winked in and out among the armada's blossoming arbor of canvas.

"It's him!" screamed a voice too close for comfort. "Look at him! He's the one doing this! *He's doing it!*"

Time to pick up the pace.

Silvus dropped and spun, lashing out with a leg and knocking two nearby men to the deck. Up snapped his head and the small crowd flinched from his gaze. Good. They were learning. He took off down the deck toward the column of smoke, knocking men out of his path.

He relied on their uncertainty. For though his weapon projected the strength of his arm far beyond the reach of other men, such extension could leave him vulnerable. By touching the golden rhoma crystal of his rod, he linked it with a fleck cut from the same stone and buried within his black mace. Rhoma remembered its original form. The exposure of only a single gem-fragment to the currents pulsing through human flesh activated the latent properties of all corresponding fragments as though no intervening space existed between them.

Rhoma. The power of the void. A substance capable of opening holes in the fabric of reality, of simply eliding whatever got in the way, and thus of binding things together. There was no seal like that of a vacuum.

Found in crystalline form across the face of Arlam, rhoma of different kinds was known to exhibit a variety of properties. And, in the laboratories of the Imperial City, rhoma-cutters built devices that bypassed the ordinary laws of physics.

Golden rhoma voided gravity. When activated by contact with flesh, it allowed the invisible gravitational force to pass through its substance like water through a sieve. No longer attracted by the ground beneath, the crystal's fragments rotated freely about its center of mass—in this case, a point about a foot beyond the pommel of Silvus' golden rod. The fact that activated golden rhoma didn't fly off into space, jettisoned by a spinning planet, was how it could be deduced that Arlam had a rhomic core.

But that hypothesized connection was weaker, which allowed for so much fun.

By separating and then linking the mace and rod, Silvus was able to effectively stretch his weapon to incredible lengths without generating a commensurate increase in mass. Thus it was that, with an effort no greater than that required to swing an ordinary mace, he could send a sphere of solid iron streaking across the sky with sufficient speed to create a thunderclap and puncture the hull of a ship.

A weapon of this kind was known to the initiated as a Flail. It was an implement of intimidation reserved for special demonstrations, a tool of terror to cow the masses. But its use left him exposed to enemies inside its fixed radius.

Fortunately, Silvus Relisham possessed more than one variety of rhoma.

The crack of musket-fire burst from one side and Silvus redoubled his speed. Men in coats of bright white and dark green poured from the main hatch ahead, brandishing their projectile weapons like playacting boys in some petty display of machismo. It appeared that someone had finally called the marines.

With a flick of his wrist Silvus lobbed his golden sphere into the air between the foremast and mainmast, then froze it in space by pressing the bead on his chest as he vaulted the forecastle railing. Over the ship's waist he sailed, and the marines who caught him in their peripheral vision either dropped their muskets outright or smacked them into their comrades' faces while attempting to aim. Silvus released the bead, hit the quarterdeck at a dead run, pocketed his sphere, and extended his golden rod behind him, flat-capped pommel pointed out. His index finger slid toward that end. Toward its emerald.

Emerald rhoma voided space. And a fleck cut from this rod's crystal was buried within the iron sphere that rested on the floor of the fjord.

A grinding crunch exploded from behind and the deck quaked beneath his feet. Men screamed and died as Silvus' huge black mace shot out of the sea and straight through the ship's forecastle, shattering the knot of marines and colliding with the tip of his rod to lodge there, affixed. The impact threw Silvus to his knees, but he scrambled back up and kept running without a backward glance. He had no *time* to revel.

Men clustered in the stern ahead. Officers clad in burgundy and black, their cloaks fluttering. After what they'd just witnessed, they wouldn't stand aside without a fight.

Silvus grinned, releasing the rod's emerald pommel, and his mace thudded to the deck behind. But then his bare flesh met the rod's gold once again, reestablishing the gravitational link, and his bent right arm straightened with a jerk as the mace leapt after him, bumping and scraping over the deck. He strained, windmilling his arm, and a black orb came from the side to smash into the men twenty feet ahead like a cannonball fired from an adjacent ship.

Blood sprayed, bones snapped, broken bodies struck the starboard rail. Those men not standing in the wrecking plane either dropped where they stood or spun to larboard, flinging Silvus from their minds. They knew projectiles traveled in nice, neat, parabolic arcs. They knew the attack couldn't have originated from the strange sailor sprinting aft.

Fools. Idiots. *Animals!*

Silvus passed them in a flash—pocketing his rod, hurling his golden sphere, and leaping out over the sea. He swooped toward the next ship like a gull in flight. Like a stooping osprey. Like the pendulum of a vast clock that chimed the hour of doom.

The mizzenmast met him with a rush of rigging and a crush of canvas, and he collided with the course yard, grasping it fast before he rebounded. For an instant of time, Silvus Relisham dangled over the deck. But then he heaved himself atop the spar, clutching it with his knees, and worked his way along its length. He grasped a rope, stood unsteadily, and slung his sphere at the sky. Then he stepped off the spar.

The sails above him shrank, then grew, their tree-height poles swaying drunkenly. Wind surged in his ears. The mainmast rushed him and he caught it. Held it fast. This ship was now his. A sudden certainty smote him that, if he so wished, he could lift the vessel by its mast and spin it round his head.

Silvus frowned. No, that wasn't true. Why would he have had such a thought?

He glanced up. An alarmed face vanished behind the topmast platform just overhead. Silvus snarled and leapt vertically, seizing the futtock shrouds that stretched up at an inverted angle between the mast and the platform's underside. He hung by his arms, considering. If the man above was armed, further ascent would be suicide. Every approach left Silvus exposed.

Abruptly he let go of the shrouds with his right hand and snatched his golden rod from a trouser pocket. Pointing it straight down, he clamped it with his forefinger, linking it to the mace far below. His whole body went rigid, straining.

And then his right arm rose from his side. Though the ship rocked and his feet whorled in midair, his bulging arm rose still. His body slowly deviated from the vertical, swinging out toward his left as though to offset a great weight raised by his right hand. The shrouds creaked and the tendons of his wrists stood out like ropes themselves, and, as he brought his hands together above his head, the center of his gravity gradually reoriented itself. The rod now stood erect, pointing at the topmast platform. Silvus relaxed his right forefinger, jammed the rod back into his pocket, and grabbed the shrouds with both hands.

With a sharp crack something struck the platform from above. A splintered extrusion bulged through its underside. The ship yawed and Silvus' mace rolled right off the platform, dropping to the deck far below. Cries and curses heralded its havoc. Silvus swung his legs back and forth and caught the shrouds with his feet, then hauled himself over the platform's lip. The peeping sailor was dead, his skull crushed, his brains underfoot.

AUSTIN GUNDERSON

Sails surrounded Silvus as he stood. This wasn't the view he needed; he had no line of sight. With a curse of his own he kicked the prone body off the edge and scrambled up the topmast shrouds. Reports rang out from below as musket-balls zipped past.

Silvus surfaced from the sea of sails, sprang onto the crosstrees, and—hugging the topgallant mast with one arm and shielding his eyes with the other—scanned the battlefield. Behind him ascended a pillar of smoke. It roiled up from the gutted remains of the neighboring galleon to be disbursed by the wind through the forest of masts. Silvus leaned into that wind and it embraced him. It clasped his body and filled his mouth, savoring him with a sibilant moan. His perch lurched drunkenly to the ship's every shiver; beneath him rolled a tumult of water and wood.

But Silvus Relisham paid his peril no heed. For while most of the armada's van had obliged his expectations by sailing in circles as soon as the headland tower had signaled "*No Enemy Sighted*," a massive three-decker with sails of blue had veered off from the pack and was approaching the harbor entrance a quarter-mile away beneath spreading canvas. If it escaped unscathed, the fleet would swiftly follow.

Silvus' knuckles whitened around his golden rod.

With sudden fury he flung up an arm, whirling the rod above his head, gripping the mast as the ship groaned and swayed. A ribbon of black spiraled up to circle him a hundred feet out—an iron orb made serpentine through persistence of vision. Faster and faster spun his arm. Splinters exploded from the crosstrees, torn free by musket-toting marines who'd gained the platform below. And then the shock wave struck.

It crashed in from every side, crushing Silvus in an invisible fist. His ears nearly burst asunder. The whole ship rattled, pinioned by unending thunderclap, as though the roar of all the storms in all the world had been concentrated here. As though the world itself were ending.

Silvus bared his teeth in an inaudible scream. This storm he had made—it was angry. *He* was angry. He *was* the storm. His loose garments whipped to one side as he brought his arm around in a final circuit, lifting his forefinger an instant before the rod's pommel flashed past the distant focus of his wrath. His ears rang in sudden stillness.

A mountain of spray erupted a hundred yards beyond the escaping ship, which pitched forward through the ensuing waves, its blue sails billowing. A great boom echoed to and fro across the fjord.

Silvus lowered his head, panting, right arm extended. Crack of musket and whiz of ball had stilled. Marines swarmed the rigging no longer. Indeed,

A SEA SOUGHT IN SONG

it appeared he had the ship almost to himself; the surrounding waters teemed with struggling bodies. Silvus chuckled, clamping his forefinger around the rod once more. He straightened and brought his hand up as though slinging a sack over his shoulder.

Behind him, a quarter-mile distant, a ship moored at the quay itself crumpled and died in a spout of spume. Silvus turned then—jaw clenching, brows plummeting, eyes kindling—clasped his rod with both hands, and slashed it back and forth in a semicircle. Distant screams of wood and men mingled in a cacophony of horror. Masts teetered and fell, dragging tangled webs of rigging down into the chaos.

But now bold Blue-Sail's deferral had run out. Silvus rounded on it just as it drew abreast of the disturbed water left to dissipate after his rangefinding strike. Little did it realize the white splotch was a target. Silvus' arm arced over his head. Down it came. He leaned into the blow. And Blue-Sail exploded. Flinders twirled through the sky.

As if in echo, a thunderous cascade of concussions rocked Silvus' ship. He spun, searching, and there, emerging from behind the black column, trailing smoke like windblown hair, came the *Rampart Errant*. It held steady on a parallel tack, readying for another broadside. The shouts of its gun-crews carried faintly over the intervening waves, a distance significantly shorter than a quarter-mile, yet farther than that between the crosstrees and the seafloor. Silvus cursed violently. He should've killed that oaf of a captain when he'd had the chance. Now he'd lost the element of surprise.

"... *ire!*" The wind nearly quenched the command.

Silvus hurled his golden sphere and flung himself into space an instant before a second cannonade slammed into the ship. The mainmast, its sails deflating, toppled behind him as he fell. He slapped the golden bead on his chest and swung outward, away from the creaking, splitting, rumbling carnage. Out over open water littered with corpses and flotsam too small to bear his weight.

To cross such a gulf, two swings would be necessary.

Silvus sucked in a breath as he dropped within fifty feet of the water and began rising again. At the apex of his trajectory he released the golden chest-bead and activated the emerald vein in his left glove, raising that hand as he plummeted from the sky like a string-cut puppet. An eternity seemed to pass as the golden sphere sped toward him. Ten feet lost. Fifteen.

At last it smacked his palm and he redirected that force, cocking his arm and flinging the sphere back up in a single fluid motion. The sphere rolled off his fingertips as he sped backward toward the waves. Another eternity passed. Twenty feet left. Fifteen.

At the last possible moment Silvus clutched his chest, connecting to the sphere, and lurched laterally to skim across the swells. He looked up. The *Rampart* loomed large, but not large enough. This second swing wouldn't be enough to carry him over the deck, and he was fresh out of altitude to expend upon a third. He'd have to think of something else.

Silvus touched his rod's emerald pommel. Behind him, his black mace exploded through the hull of the ship he'd just vacated, slamming into the rod and jerking his body in flight. He accelerated briefly. With an underhand heave, he released the mace to fall between himself and the *Rampart*'s larboard rail. It disappeared beneath the surface as he neared the upper limit of his inverted arc and began to slow. Ahead, men in green and white elbowed the gun-crews aside, leveling muskets. Silvus shut his eyes.

Eight heartbeats later, his eyes snapped open. He flipped the golden rod so it pointed backward in his right fist, then released the golden bead on his chest and grabbed the rod with both hands. His arms seemed to shoot straight up as his body dropped below the level of the rod to dangle in midair. Yet still he rose, impelled by residual momentum.

Slower and slower Silvus arced forward. He stalled out directly above his mace as it slowly sank under his weight into the floor of the fjord. There he hung, a stationary target in plain view. All the marines opened fire.

But their musket-balls passed through empty air, for Silvus was already descending on the ship in an overhand arc, picking up speed as he flew. He'd vaulted his own mace on an invisible pole.

His loose vest and trousers flapped frantically as the deck rushed up to meet him. The *Rampart*'s marines scrambled backward, tracking his trajectory, leading him with their muskets. Smoke bloomed across the quarterdeck as a dozen guns discharged at once.

But Silvus wasn't there. He'd stowed his rod and extended an arm, snatching a shroud in midair and spinning away from the line of fire. He vanished behind a mast and didn't reappear.

"Find him, dammit!" bellowed a wiry sergeant. "He's right here! Don't let him escape!" The men spread out, eyes sweeping the sky.

But the black streak came from beneath, slicing obliquely through the hull and taking a man's head off his shoulders. Marines screamed and fired in vain at the orb as it circled around for another pass, oblivious to the figure who slipped from behind the capstan, drew the sergeant's own cutlass from its sheath, and slit his wiry throat with it when he turned.

A SEA SOUGHT IN SONG

The sergeant struck the deck, face plastered with a look of almost comical surprise, as Silvus slowly turned with rod outstretched, drawing fire and attention away from his advance. Two more fell to his arrogated blade before a yell from the poop deck gave him away.

Silvus dropped the cutlass and dove to the side as lead perforated the air where he'd been standing. It was the captain who had seen him; he'd heard enough of that man's caterwauling in the week it'd taken to sail up the coast that he'd have recognized the sound in his sleep. Now, at last, he would bequeath the gift of silence.

Breaking his connection to the mace, which slingshotted away and plashed into the bay, Silvus Relisham spun, sprinting for the stern. He ignored the ladder and leapt for the rail, snatching its lowest rung with both hands. Quicker than sight he planted his feet at hand-level, then stretched to grab the top rung, and then, with a spring and a twist, flipped his body over the rail to land upright before the helm, knocking the musket from the hands of the marine assigned to guard the captain. The man lashed out, but Silvus simply shifted his weight, curling his fingers around the arm that flashed harmlessly past his face. There was a sound of splitting bone and the marine followed his own fist headfirst, flailing through the air to land with a sickening crunch.

But by then Silvus was past the frozen helmsman and ducking the captain's saber-slash. The stiffened fingers of Silvus' right hand drove into the fool's solar plexus at a precisely-calibrated angle. The saber sprang from an abruptly limp grip. Flipped end-over-end. The captain's pupils dilated in terror. His mouth snapped agape like that of a fish, and like a fish's mouth emitted no sound. Silvus grabbed him by the shoulders, spun him around, and shoved the golden rod pommel-first into that yawning hole.

Then he touched the emerald.

The captain's head, displaced by Silvus' mace, burst like an overripe melon let slip from a cart. Beyond, beams and bodies sprawled in a tight tunnel of carnage that shot straight through the starboard hull. Behind, the faithless saber buried its face in the deck with a soft thunk. The helmsman, though attempting to stand perfectly still, shook like a dead leaf in the breeze.

Boots drummed upon the quarterdeck, charging the stern ladder from below. Silvus released the pommel of his rod and, gripping his gore-slathered mace with both hands, rolled it right off the poop deck. It disappeared over the edge, provoking yells as men vacated its path. Their line would recover quickly. But this petty squabble had gone on long enough; it was time to bid farewell to foolish *Rampart Errant*.

153

Silvus grabbed his rod, locking the mace at a distance of thirty feet. He raised his arms and the black orb flew from the deck to hover beside the mizzen sail exactly thirty feet above. Then he brought his arms down and across his body, making a clockwise circuit. A splash fountained up off the starboard rail. A shudder rippled the deck as the mace punched entrance and exit holes in the hull below the waterline.

The mace, suspended overhead once more, wept salt tears upon Silvus' hair as though mourning the fools who refused to accept their part in this glorious beginning. Again Silvus wheeled his arms. And again. He twirled his rod like a baton as chunks of wood and pockets of air roiled the waters on either side.

Extending his left hand, Silvus fingered his thumb's emerald vein to call the golden sphere to his palm. And then he was off—over the taffrail and across the waves before his pursuers knew they were doomed.

As it turned out, the *Rampart Errant*'s abortive attack was the most effective opposition to Silvus' rampage mounted by any vessel in Admiral Norvald's fleet. Resistance on the next eight ships in line ranged from nonexistent to severely disorganized. Unaided by even a rudimentary understanding of the enemy it faced, the navy's discipline, valor, and conventional tactics served no purpose beyond assuring its own predictability and guaranteeing its own defeat. And thus, when Silvus fell from the sky onto the fjord's southern shoreline in a crunch of pebbles half an hour later, a string of tilting derelicts sprawled in his wake—a newly-laid breakwater.

Silvus straightened. Above him loomed the stone signal-tower that marked the end of Suma's quay. Its crenellations, empty of movement, raked the western sky like a gap-toothed jawbone. Smoke ascended behind their teeth, staining the swath of azure above. Smoke not from the ships moored offshore, but from the town itself. Distant booms and thumps contended in his ears with a wind which streamed from the sea. The assault was evolving as scheduled.

Silvus jogged lightly up the stone stair, crossed the level platform of the quay, and rapped on the tower's sally port. Two quick taps, a single tap, and three quick ones again. A bolt thudded back and the iron door squealed ajar.

A SEA SOUGHT IN SONG

"Hail, Lord Commander," said a large man in the crisp blue-and-white tunic, trousers, and leather jerkin of the City Watch. "All is made ready. Do you require your armor, or will you report to the Master now?"

"The Master is aware of all that transpires," said Silvus by rote as he stepped into the torchlit chamber, shutting the door behind him. "How fares Talmica?"

"He has overrun the western wall and advanced as far east as Woodwell Street. I am afraid that resistance has been savage and sustained." As he spoke, the man beckoned two others out of the shadows. They wore watchman's uniforms and carried padded clothing.

Silvus set his rod and sphere on a nearby table, unfastened the straps of his harness, stripped out of his sailor's attire, and began pulling on the thick undergarments offered him. His mace he'd left embedded in the fjord's southern flank. It would return to him when summoned.

For now, he adopted a different guise.

"Be not afraid," replied Silvus. "A lack of ferocity would only indicate dissemblance. They fight because they see their end in our eyes." He stood, stepping into the sabatons placed before him by the squires, who began working their way up his body, bearing sections of plate armor from the iron crates stacked along one wall, fastening them to his legs with cunning straps, careful at all times to handle the armor only by its edges. The plates' surfaces shimmered strangely in the guttering light. Almost liquid they seemed.

The large man dipped his head. "As you say, my lord. Myself, I would rather the Master had come here himself and have done. Clean. Efficient. Not this piecemeal carnage."

"Yes," said Silvus, spreading his arms to the sides as the squires gingerly attached his breastplate. "Efficient. And costly. We have not come merely to destroy, Kothold, but to establish. If the end we make of our enemies is not *remembered* as such, what will keep them from reversion? It is their *will* we fight. It is their *minds* we conquer. If the Master himself came here, who among these savages would survive to sow a new spirit in their offspring? We seek not an end but a beginning, free from the baggage of might-have-beens. We are here to demonstrate once and for all that they could not have prevailed had they tried."

Kothold bowed low. "Your wisdom eclipses me, Lord."

"It is not easy, my friend. There is much of you to eclipse."

The quip, which Silvus deadpanned, dispelled the dour mood. Kothold chuckled, and the squires relaxed slightly. This was important. They couldn't afford to nurse raw nerves—not here, not now. Regardless of Silvus' glib assurances, the danger they faced was real.

Of this they were only too aware. Vastly outnumbered, embedded deep behind enemy lines, they had each of them waged their own private war with the mounting weight and pressure of this mission over the past six months. For some, it was their first operation as ghosts of the Silent Host. For others, it would be their last. But though they each confronted their own private end this day, they *would* not falter now, not on the cusp of such a grand beginning.

The squires had finished with Silvus' arms and hands and begun assembling his gorget. "Where have they massed?" he asked Kothold. "Show me their strongest point."

The burly watchman unrolled a map on the table and weighted it with candlesticks, but at that moment a messenger burst through the inner door. A woman. A stablemaid in a brown mantle, her cleft skirts swirling around her high boots as she skidded to a halt within the pool of torchlight. Her black hair shimmered. Silvus turned his head and she dropped to one knee.

"My Lord Commander," she gasped, "I beg leave to present my report."

"Speak."

"The Suman militia has broken through to the City Watch. They are rallying in the eastern square. It is rumored that Admiral Norvald has assumed command."

A slow smile spread Silvus' lips as his squires lifted the tall octagonal prism of his helm and lowered it over his head. "No wonder it was so easy," he murmured as his face vanished. "He hadn't left the beach." The helm locked in place with a soft click.

At a gesture from Kothold, the squires backed off into the shadows. A silence fell. The torchlight capered across a visage of blank planes, flitted down a body of narrow, flat panels tightly articulated, and glinted from eight gauntleted fingertips. Silvus' bared forefingers looked tiny by comparison. In the fickle light, the armor's surfaces seemed even livelier than the stablemaid's hair. Silvus held out his hand, palm up. "My sword," came his muffled voice.

A golden rod—longer than his first one—was placed upon his palm. The fingers of his right hand curled about it.

"My lord?" asked the woman, her breath recovered. "What are your orders?"

"Signal Thotta to reinforce Talmica. They are to commence heavy shelling immediately. Then lead me to the eastern square."

A SEA SOUGHT IN SONG

The woman was on her feet. "Kothold," she rapped, "get me Thotta."

Kothold passed her a thick-rimmed hand-mirror about six inches in diameter. It looked awkward in his huge fist—a delicate tool not intended for the likes of him. The woman splayed the fingertips of her right hand upon its surface, shutting her eyes and mouthing an incantation. A shudder rippled her skin and a cool light burst upon her face. She lifted her fingers but kept a thumb pressed to a corner of the mirror. She held it up and, as she did, its light flickered across her sharp features as though occluded by movement.

Silvus studied her, studied her face, studied her eyes, in whose penetrating hazel was reflected the face of a man looking out from inside the looking-glass. The reflected man covered his mouth with two fingers. The woman nodded once, then raised her left hand and made a series of swift gestures. The man repeated his opening signal and the stablemaid lifted her thumb. The cool light vanished.

She looked up. "Follow me, Lord," she said, and was gone.

It was the scarves, thought Silvus. It was the scarves that presaged this people's fall. That marked them as ripe. It was the way they spread before his feet, ribboning from motionless necks, crisscrossing cobblestones, bunching between bodies—swaths of indigo and teal, now dyed a contrasting hue as their coarse wool steeped in the red wine of death. In death, the women of Suma hailed him. They laid their necks under his feet, spreading their scarves over the street. Though they knew it not, it was he whom they had dressed to greet. And Silvus strode upon the carpet of their scarves.

A stillness had fallen over the shipyard district. Talmica's troops had been through here not a quarter-hour past. Silvus smiled. That man could be called many things, but haphazard was not one of them. He would go far if only he learned to see the ocean in the waves.

But he would have to learn quick: little time remained for advancement. The Expansion, so long in gestation, was now nearly complete. Silvus could sense it. Even now, at this moment, as he walked streets carpeted with scarves, the last of the heathen kingdoms were falling into place, finding fulfillment as pieces of a greater whole. The unbearable tension of history, after seven hundred years of inflammation, was being released in an unstoppable catharsis. Soon their long labor would be finished.

AUSTIN GUNDERSON

Yet even as he smiled, a sliver of doubt lanced Silvus' heart. He froze, feet straddling a corpse, startled by a cold whisper from nowhere. *And then what?*

The stablemaid turned, her eyes a question. *Stablemaid, ha!* Perhaps that was the problem: he'd been at this too long. Gotten in too deep. Had he forgotten his own face beneath the mask? Was that why he suddenly shied at success? The Master had still greater plans. He knew this. The battle might be drawing to a close, but the war was far from over. His kind would be needed again after Arlam was set free. He released an imprisoned breath, enjoyed a small catharsis of his own.

"It is not far now, my lord," said the woman. Her eyes had narrowed— her brows converging, her whole face sharpening even further, if that were possible. She seemed … *suspicious*. Silvus was surprised; Corporal Lirish wasn't the skittish type. Perhaps she too harbored doubts. He'd have to attend her debriefing before the Suman Task Force disbanded to move north.

"Take my sword," he said aloud, shrugging the blade off his shoulder and proffering it hilt-first, "and stage it on the roof of that building. I want to make an entrance."

Lirish's chin dipped once. She took the sword—dragging it to the timber-framed hall he'd indicated, walking it upright hand-over-hand to lean against the eaves—and then scaled the wall, swinging lightly onto the roof. She danced up the incline, skirts flying, pulling a blade twice as long as she was tall. Her black hair, wind-whipped, vanished behind a gable as Silvus turned toward the thud and throb of distant battle.

It was time to close this chapter. To begin again with an ending. He could sense it drawing near, could feel its dissonance beginning to coalesce, could nearly hear the swell of its tuning. It was close now, so close. Silvus spread his arms in welcome.

His skin prickled as he advanced up the street, the walls on either hand alive with echoes of violence, the broad space before him perfused with smoke and light.

###

Silvus Relisham, Commander of the Silent Host, Scourge of the Lord of the Air, whirled amidst the fray. Overhead, the stone towers and steeply-pitched roofs surrounding Suma's eastern square spun madly against the darkening sky. The wind had shifted northward and the black pall it bore thence threw the foreground into bright relief. Prim shutters had been slammed in haste, and broad windowsills swept of their floral displays, and the blue of their wood reflected vividly the garments of those men who roiled the square, and the red of breeze-snapped banners complemented that which fountained up from bodies cleft by a ten-foot length of steel.

There was a beauty to it, a poignancy. It throbbed in Silvus' veins. That the ends of so many petty little stories would, in their confluence, open a new era. That, though these men knew not why they died, their blood would water the soil of a land liberated under the Master's mighty hand. Silvus leaned back, relaxing into the centrifugal force, allowing his blade to counterbalance his weight.

His right forefinger lifted and the huge sword shot away, spinning through the crowd, shattering a storefront and burying itself in the back wall. Released from balance, Silvus was flung backward. But he tucked his feet over his head, batted the ground away with both hands, and landed upright, his back to the frantic press of guardsmen. In the space of a breath, they seized the offensive.

Seven musket-balls burst simultaneously from his chest.

With deliberate slowness, Silvus turned. Smoke puffed from all directions now as every soldier with a weapon scrambled to discharge and reload. And, as lead rounds began punching through Silvus from every angle, the men around him cried out and fell. The plates on his head and chest seemed to ripple like pools pocked by rain.

He raised his arm and touched the green pommel of his rod, summoning the sword. The rod jerked outward as the blade detached itself from the back wall of the shop, passing through a man's body en route to its counterpart. The two halves met with a clang that rattled the square like a giant bell.

The echos and gunshots died away into petrified silence. From elsewhere came the distant booms and thumps of a sustained cannonade. The flagstones shook with it. But here, in this moment, in Suma's eastern square, not a soul stirred. Silvus stood in their midst—a hulking, blank-faced pillar of slate, the thin slit before his eyes betraying none of his expression.

Silvus grinned wildly. He turned slowly in place, raising his ten-foot sword above his head, clenching his teeth and breathing rapidly to suppress the strain of lifting such a heavy weapon with only a single arm. An unnecessary effort: this audience required no showmanship. They had already seen him in action, they had already bought his act. The bodies of their friends, tangled in their feet, would not allow them to dismiss his power. They would believe anything now, the fools. Silvus' grin broadened until it nearly split his face beneath the expressionless helm.

AUSTIN GUNDERSON

With a sudden shout, an elderly officer shoved his way through the front row of onlookers, whipped out a rapier, stumbled forward over a mound of slain, and dove inside Silvus' reach. He came to his feet and lunged and buried his blade halfway to its hilt in Silvus' chest. It slid in effortlessly, sprouting from Silvus' back, seeming somehow elongated.

The man cocked his head in confusion. It was the same look Silvus had seen in the eyes of the gravelly bosun, the wiry sergeant, the caterwauling captain—the mien of a man wondering too late whether he'd ever really had a chance. Whether a small adjustment in thrust trajectory would've placed his blade in that hairline seam now discernable between gorget and helm instead of in this viscous breastplate. Whether he could still trust his own senses or was already wounded and dying and slipping into delirium. Whether he had full hours or mere seconds left to live. And whether countless others would die because of what he'd just done. It was the face of none other than Admiral Norvald himself, Silvus suddenly realized.

Of course it is; how could it have been otherwise? "For are you not the very heart of Suma?" whispered Silvus in the admiral's ear. "And are you not *lost?*"

The old man's face was white. "What are you?" he quavered.

"The beginning."

Without lowering his sword, Silvus reached behind the small of his back with his left hand, slipped a dagger from its sheath there, and put an end to the admiral's self-doubt. The awful spell remained unbroken, the crowd motionless as Norvald slumped against the knees of his nemesis.

Leaving his dagger planted in Norvald's face, Silvus reached up and smacked the protruding hilt of the man's rapier with the heel of his hand, punching it straight out his own backplate to clatter on the stones behind.

An echoing clatter came from the left. Then another from the right. Then dozens. Then hundreds. The Sumans had given up. Their weapons fell from nerveless hands to strike the slabs like drumsticks on a snare.

The sound of it was music. Like the prelude to a symphony. Like the overture of dawn.

Chapter Eleven
TO RECALL THE KING

25 Halanen, 781

"No, *no*," cried Hugh as he convulsed. "My father isn't evil! Don't *say* that!"

The faceless figure turned away, flicking dismissive fingers. The stone platform crumbled beneath Hugh's cheek, its chunks raining into an ocean of cloud, of roiling darkness vast as heaven, lit from beneath by crimson strobes. Hugh's stomach filled his throat and he gritted his teeth to prevent its escape. The clouds rushed him. In moments he was lost in their vaporous embrace with nothing beneath him but fear. Red flashes blinded him and he thrashed as he fell, tangling himself in mist. For the clouds were comprised not of water but of a fine fiber like cotton candy, a mesh that stuck to Hugh as he plunged deeper and deeper. It accumulated swiftly. Soon a ropy web was tearing at his face and limbs without even slowing his descent. He screamed.

And his hand found the sword.

Out of the scabbard it swept, rending the entangling web. A blast of white light, and Hugh was again falling free. Below him churned a dull red sea. A sea of blood. He twisted to look back.

Faceless followed.

The armored man plummeted headfirst, right arm extended, fingers splayed. As though driving his victim before him toward the distant sea. A roaring rose then, and Hugh's vision shook. The air had thickened. Faceless extended his left arm out beside his right. Like Superman. The roar became a scream as the two figures accelerated in midair. And Hugh flung the sword.

In defiance of gravity it leapt. Like a shell from a cannon. Like black lightning from the earth. It punctured the breastplate of the faceless man, bursting through him like a bullet through a beam. Shards exploded outward, sparkling in their own light. A thunderclap struck Hugh, punching him down into the bloody sea.

Hugh's eyes snapped open. All he saw was red. He gasped and spasmed, clawing his way up out of a … sheet?

No, a canvas. A red sail, torn and toppled. A blanket bunched up to hold in the heat.

And now he remembered why. Dammit, it was *cold!*

Hugh shivered, grabbing handfuls of the sail and tugging it closer, then froze as a low groan issued from the bunched cloth behind him.

Ilina. He exhaled.

Turning slowly, he found her curled up against the depression he'd made during the night. Her dress was stained and rumpled, her hair damp and matted, and yet such details were of no account to Hugh beside the almost painful beauty that was the curve of her neck, the delicacy of her fingers, the sharp, clean lines of her face. He sucked in a breath. After a day and a night of frigid distance, it seemed she'd finally conceded the cold shoulder competition to the elements themselves.

Too bad he didn't have time to give her the attention she deserved.

A sharp grating sound interrupted his thoughts. The hull shuddered. Hugh and Ilina had taken refuge belowdecks—wedging themselves among crates of rigging and barrels of provisions, swaddling themselves in salvaged sailcloth that didn't really counteract the cold.

There wasn't much more they *could* do; both oars had been lost during the attack, and, with the mast gone, the wind was no longer their friend. Not only that, but the magic glass object Ilina had used to propel them away from the island had apparently been destroyed when the monster smashed the sternpost. Three separate means of locomotion, all disabled in one fell swoop. The beast couldn't have been more precise if it'd tried.

A shaft of rich ruddy light fell from the open hatchway at the far end of the deck. Ilina shifted in her sleep, clutching at the covers and catching Hugh's hand instead. He started, then froze.

They'd been huddled in here for at least thirty-six hours, or whatever that translated to in indigenous units of time-measurement. It might've just been him, but Hugh could've sworn the days and nights were longer here. He was tired, groggy. At first he'd attributed it to residual disorientation from his plunge down the portal. Then, when it persisted, he'd chalked it up to sleep-deprivation. But after a week of nights spent in a soft bed in the tower, Hugh had to face the fact that this chronic exhaustion wasn't about to vanish.

How, then, could he explain the sudden surge of strength imbued by the cold touch of this sleeping girl? Slowly, carefully, he interlaced their fingers.

No further storms had overtaken them, and Hugh had begun to wonder whether that was indeed a good thing. They needed to make landfall, and make it soon. They couldn't afford this imprisoning calm. The ferry stocked enough cured meat for several days of sailing with all hands. For Hugh and Ilina, that translated to two weeks' worth of food on the outside. And they needed to reach not just land, but also civilization itself before their rations ran out.

But now even this imperative of self-preservation seemed to fall away as Ilina's fingers tightened unconsciously between Hugh's own. *If we could just stay like this ...*

The grating noise again. Ilina relaxed her grip and Hugh slipped away, stepping over her prostrate form to stumble toward the hatchway. The cold slowed him like an unseen web.

Light streamed from the hatchway at a severe angle, its radiance exploding against the nearby bulkhead, its beam glittering with dust and clouded by Hugh's condensed breath. It was in that moment, standing in the shaft of light, head upraised, that Hugh recalled another such shaft atop a once-mighty tower, and wondered again at the intangible power exuded by that graven image of the man with the shining hand. Who'd he been—a king, a god?—and why had the tower's builders revered him so? Ilina had called her tower 'Anticipation Light,' but what had it been anticipating? A colonization effort that never got rolling? The return of some exiled leader?

Whatever it'd been, the wait was over. No tower remained to anticipate anything. Hugh climbed the ladder and emerged on deck.

The sea stretched before him like a rippling sheet of aluminum, its glare nearly blinding after the darkness below. He raised a hand to shade his eyes. Though he felt no wind, the metallic waves all seemed to be coming *at* him in regimented array. The air was rich with roaring. Hugh turned.

The landmass filled his vision. Highlands drenched in sundown gold— vast, indomitable, bright against the somber sky, mounting steadily higher and farther in ridges unnumbered till distance hushed their glow beneath white peaks serrating the world's rim. Hugh swayed and stepped back, overbalanced. An immense *weight* rose before him, and it seemed to his mind's eye that the shape of Arlam shifted at this verge, as though it were the sea, not the land, that formed the perpendicular, streaming toward shore like an endless waterfall.

"Kramarack," said Ilina from behind him.

163

AUSTIN GUNDERSON

Kramarack. The Hidden Kingdom, Crown of the World, Land of Bloodstained Hills. It was here that Ilina's father had fallen ill, here that her faith had been fractured, and from here that her prospective husband haled.

House Harn, the chief among the Kramish fiefdoms and an unswerving ally in peacetime and war for as long as anyone could remember, had lately allowed its relations with the Lightkeepers to lapse. Only a union between Rikard Harnish and herself could close the diplomatic gap and secure a future for Kredak Tower. That was her mission, her duty, her destiny. It mattered not that the contracted priest had perished before he reached Cuspid Isle; a substitute would be found, Rikard would re-draw the terms of the Petition of Troth, and the marriage would proceed without interruption. It had to.

Now if only she could figure out where she was.

The distant mountains she knew by name, of course. There was Kaloth the Razor, so called because of the mile-high precipice separating its summit from its principal glacier; there was dread Gurculin the Vengeful, which no man had traversed twice. Its shoulders glowered in the shadow of Arakul the Sentinel, in whose lap lay Cloudfall Pass and the Gate of the North, sole approach to the highlands, frequented only by Habridi caravans bearing spices, sugar, seeds, and satin from beyond the Sea of Sand.

Ilina was accustomed to the craggy procession. It was as comforting to her as the trimming on a map: an impassable bound of knowledge, and beautiful to boot. But the nearby landmarks were foreign to her eyes. The hilltops formed a strange crisscross, the coastline an unfamiliar curve. They had drifted far off course.

The world was round, not flat. It was not a place of tidy boxes and fixed boundaries. Its trimming was untrustworthy. The Gnof Range was not a border, but a relatively small feature affecting universal prominence. There were lands beyond it, vast tracts; Ilina knew this better than most. But it was just as foolish to ignore the niceties of known topography as to neglect the tracts beyond the trimming. Both oversights could leave one lost.

If she had to guess, she'd say Harnaral lay to the east. A mild easterly current prevailed between Cuspid Isle and the mainland, and had probably carried them west toward the Pockmarked Cliffs. But just how far east they'd now have to travel was beyond her reckoning.

The deck shook and tilted. Rock crunched wood beneath their feet. Hugh slipped, blundering into her as he groped for the gunwale. She shoved him away and sprawled on her back. His touch roused her bile. Her fingers balled to fists. *I hate you, vandal! Begone!*

A SEA SOUGHT IN SONG

She shook her head. Unclenched her hands. No. No, that couldn't be right. What was she thinking? He had done nothing to her. Nothing. He couldn't have. It had all been a dream.

A dream.

She rose as the ferry lurched. Steadied herself as it listed. Hugh had gone below for the supplies. Good. Maybe he would find her banner as well. She seemed to have misplaced it.

Hugh's boots struck sand like iron ingots latching to a magnet. Spray from the impact leapt up to drench him. The sand was coarse underfoot, the water burning cold. He rose from his crouch and did not sink—the ground held his weight with the solidity of a sentry at attention. A proud land, this.

He turned and looked up. Ilina peered at him over the gunwale, her sharp features shining in the chiaroscuro light. He held out his arms.

She lifted one leg over the rail, then the other. And then she slid off and fell and he caught her. And she sank into his arms and fit there perfectly, and he felt the firm contours of her body and inhaled the *closeness* of her, and the gap between them had closed so suddenly that he staggered and then just stood there, silent and transfixed.

But then she shoved at his chest and he, surprised again, relaxed his grip too quickly, nearly dropping her in the drink. She landed deftly despite it all. *Idiot! She wasn't looking for a snuggle!* He adjusted the pack on his shoulder and sloshed after her up the beach. The derelict ferry slanted from the waves behind: a pilgrim returned to its motherland to die.

He caught up to Ilina, who didn't spare him a glance. She just kept walking—out of the shallows and across the sand, soaked skirt slapping against her shins, handbag bumping her hip. Hugh shrugged and kept pace, studying her from the side. Her gaze seemed weirdly distant, unfocused. The high-tide embankment approached. Beyond it rose a long steep slope clad in head-high heather.

Hugh stepped in front of her and she stopped just in time to avoid a collision. She glared up at him. He glanced around, snatched up a chunk of bone-white driftwood, and began writing in the pebbly sand.

"Where are we going?"

He passed her the wood. *"East,"* she wrote. *"To a city."*

"You know where we are?"

AUSTIN GUNDERSON

"Have I not dwelt in this realm all the days of my life?" Tossing the wood aside, she stormed up the embankment and plunged into the heather. The fact that she had evaded the question was not lost on Hugh. But he couldn't say as much as she had and so he, seeing no better option, gritted his teeth and followed her rustling route.

Dusk came swiftly. By the time the sun met the eastern horizon, Hugh and Ilina had put only two ridges behind them. The third proved taller than the first two combined, and in the failing light its ascent grew increasingly difficult. Unseen rocks and roots snagged at them with each new step, and even branches vanished in the sub-shrub shadows, their brittle latticework an ineffective yet persistent obstruction.

After the umpteenth graze to Hugh's face nearly gouged out an eye, he dug his flashlight from his pack and flicked on the beam. A girlish yelp came from the darkness ahead. Hugh grinned, then passed a studiously blank-faced Ilina, who fell in behind him. He supposed she preferred to keep his magical lightwand where she could see it.

At last they emerged onto a summit bare of brush. Hugh stowed his light. Put to this kind of use, its batteries would fail before the week was out. He dropped the pack and let his eyes readjust to the darkness as Ilina stood silently by, watching him.

A chill wind was blowing. On their way up it'd been blocked by the ridge, but now they'd stepped full into its path. It streamed from the highlands to swirl about them, playing keep-away with Ilina's cloak, then sighed as it plunged toward the sea. A crimson streak stained the eastern horizon, purple swelling above it like a bruise. One of the moons had cleared the mountains, its disk nearly topped-up with white, and it bathed the ridgetop rocks in a muted monochrome.

This night would be difficult. Hugh had crammed his pack with cured meat from the ferry, so they were set for food. Shelter, however, was at a premium. The temperature had plummeted at least ten degrees in the past hour, and probably had further to go. He had nothing with which to make fire, and the heather offered scant insulation. He'd pushed for the summit in the unlikely hope of glimpsing someone else's fire somewhere in all this vastness, but, besides the moon and vanished sun, no points of light were apparent.

166

A SEA SOUGHT IN SONG

He sighed. And then Ilina sidled up, bent to rummage in his pack, and pulled free a flint and steel. She thrust them wordlessly at Hugh, then wandered off to take a seat on a nearby stone.

Hugh gaped at the items in his palm. *She gave me a fire-starter? When? How? And why?* He turned his gape toward the girl in mingled awe and irritation; she just sat there, staring at the moon. Then, after a full minute of this, he hauled up his jaw and got to work.

The crack and thunk of Hugh's hatchet glanced off Ilina's ears as she got up to circle the hilltop. A comparably cacophonous dispute throbbed within her mind.

Strive as she might, no strong-arm tactic or blunt declaration would convince the Council of Kram that Hugh was anything more than an inept impostor. He had entered a delicate arena, though he knew it not. But she had planned for this, had anticipated it, and had gathered the regalia of his office to match the ancient sword he bore. She would have wielded those items as weapons, would have brought their full psychological force to bear upon an unprepared assembly of petty-minded Councilors. Would have shocked them from their slumber to acknowledge the immanent storm.

But those were might-have-beens. The regalia was gone—both his and hers. She knew not what had become of it. Didn't remember losing it. It was the strangest thing.

She spun and paced and grappled with the implications. Without those accouterments her way forward would be far more difficult, if not impossible. The Council would view her as it always had: as a bizarre girl clinging to the vestiges of former power. They would assume that she, desperate to bolster a precarious political position, had allowed herself to be taken in by some charlatan—or, worse, had colluded in his charade. A hostile Council was certain, a vindictive one probable. They might even move to censure her. It could be the opening for annexation sought by their progressive faction for decades. They could occupy Cuspid Isle, seize her assets. She could lose everything.

Where were the crest and banner? How could they have disappeared? She couldn't have left them behind—her father wouldn't have let her. She'd thought the crest at least was safe in her valise, but when she opened the bag she'd found only the Book of Blood in an interior oilskin pocket. Ilina mentally retraced her steps. She remembered carrying the banner from the

167

tower, remembered it with a clarity that cast what came after into shadow. She had boarded the ferry with it, hadn't she? She must have. After all, she was here now, in Kramarack. The ferry had taken them across, obviously. Had one of the crewmen stolen it? She couldn't remember. Come to think of it, she was having trouble remembering the crew at all. It must have been an uneventful trip.

Ilina shook her head, sank onto a stone. Her head hurt, and she was cold. Ever so cold. She hugged herself, tried to think back. Had she left it on the ferry when she disembarked? Images came to her, odd memories of a splintered hull slanting from the waves. The ferry had been damaged en route, hadn't it? Yes, of course—that's why they were camped on this moor instead of thawing out at a wharf-side inn. She must be tired. A good sleep would clear her mind.

Maybe then she'd be able to think her way off this shoal.

The darkness was complete by the time Hugh's fire blazed. He and Ilina sat opposite one another—she staring into the flames, he trying not to stare at her. The stacked heather crackled softly, its little spadelike leaves curling and flushing scarlet instants before combustion.

The hatchet had made swift work of several shrubs from a downslope thicket. They were so dry they'd caught fire almost instantly, and Hugh was grateful for the hilltop clearing where windblown sparks had space to whirl without igniting a wildfire. That their campfire would be visible for miles in every direction was just an added bonus. They were in friendly territory, according to Ilina, and contact with the natives was not only advisable but imperative.

The girl's face flickered red as she leaned in. She rotated her hands, clenching and stretching her fingers, evenly distributing the heat. Hugh's eyes, now acclimated to the fire, could no longer pick out the moon in the sky. Blackness yawned like a void beyond Ilina's huddled form.

It unsettled Hugh, thinking of the unseen vastness which surrounded them—hissing, shifting, rustling with the wind. And the wind was moving still. It skirled about the hill like a questing animal, nosing at their periphery. And all the while they sat upon an island of light high atop an ocean of black, lit as with a flare, brilliant and blind.

Hugh shuddered, feeling very small, glancing compulsively over his shoulder. As much as he kept telling himself they were in no danger, this exposure just felt wrong. The monster on the island had appeared without warning. How long would it be until the next unforeseen encounter?

He turned again to Ilina and saw now that she shivered. *Of course, you meathead.* While he'd kept his blood pumping by chopping and hauling heather, what had she been doing? Sitting and waiting. She looked half-frozen, even swaddled in her voluminous cloak. And suddenly Hugh had his first good idea since they'd made landfall.

He dug his bedroll from his pack, scooted around the fire to sit beside her, then lifted the blanket's woolen folds above her shoulders. Her eyes flicked to the side, slamming into his, and his face broke out in what he hoped was a disarming grin. *Don't think about how good she looks. That's not helping.*

But Hugh couldn't help it; beauty like hers couldn't—no *shouldn't*—be ignored. That'd be unnatural. Unappreciative. He hoped she knew that. She probably didn't. *Careful, man, careful.* His grin grew stale on his face.

Eventually, Ilina resumed her study of the flames, leaning back into Hugh's offering. He exhaled softly, still holding the blanket's corners.

Slowly, slowly, ever so gently and gradually, Hugh relaxed his outstretched arm. And Ilina tilted her head against his shoulder as he eased her close. And his grin was so fresh that it hurt his face.

They stayed like that until all that remained of the fire was a bed of embers stoked by the wind. Both moons now blazed from heaven, their paired light outshining the coals.

To keep his mind sharp, Hugh cast it away from present circumstance. He wondered what Dan Forsythe had thought of this place upon arrival. He grinned as he imagined the older man's joy. Ever since Hugh could remember, Dan had been enamored of the ancients' wisdom. Surely it would have seemed a fantasy to enter a world untainted by industry and populist ideology. *My father wouldn't have had much trouble recruiting Dan. Miles, on the other hand ...*

Hugh shook his head. He'd thought Miles had renounced adventuring. The man had seemed content with his dull gig in London. *But no one can know the heart of a man but the man himself, as Dan always used to say.*

Hugh wondered what Dan would say now. And whether he could still say anything at all. Or whether he spoke apart from his own will with the voice of another. A voice dark and cruel. *A guttural croak from the pit of hell ...*

Ilina shifted against Hugh, startling him out of a half-dream in which his magic sword had started scooting along the ground of its own accord, leaving a bloody trail in the dirt. He gave his head a firm shake and shot the thing a glance: it still lay beside him, dressed down in the split scabbard that he'd bound with strips of sailcloth. He patted his coat pocket: the magic rod hadn't moved. He felt Ilina follow his gaze. She was awake.

Remembering something he'd been planning to ask her, he pulled a blackened heather-stem from the remains of the fire.

"Why was your tower named Anticipation Light?" he scratched in raw charcoal on a bare flat canvas of rock.

Ilina twitched and pulled away, casting him a hostile look. He immediately regretted the question. *You never* can *leave well enough alone, can you? You never* can *be content with what you have.*

But the girl didn't rise and leave. Instead, after a stiff moment, she rubbed off Hugh's words and replied with eight of her own: *"To recall the High King until his return."*

"You mean Henry Conrad?"

She was very still. A slight nod.

Hugh swallowed. *"But he has not come, and now the tower is gone."*

Ilina turned on Hugh, and it was as though his very substance had shifted to her eyes. Her mouth dropped open in soundless horror. Shoving him away, she scrambled up and stumbled back, the blanket slipping from her shoulders to fall in a heap. Then she spun and ran. The darkness swallowed her whole.

Hugh sprang to his feet. "Ilina!" he shouted. The wind howled in reply.

###

Ilina swam in blackness. Out of the circle of light and into the night she plunged, crashing through heather, stumbling on rocks, tripping over roots, unseeing and unheeding. The brush tilted madly, shaking with each frantic footfall. *Must get away, must get away, must get away, must leave!* Her mind was screaming and she didn't know if her mouth had followed suit. Didn't care.

Oh Harlith where have you gone? What have you left me? Why are you silent and cold? Harlith's voice hadn't always been vacant—had it? Ilina clutched at shreds of memory. Of imagination. Of something, anything. Anything but the image that had reared up in her mind in response to Hugh's cruel words.

The tower is gone.

And Ilina screamed for real now, clutching at her head, her eyes. Her foot caught on something and she tumbled headlong down the slope, slamming into shrubs and glancing off boulders and tearing at her face as the terrible vision tore unimpeded through her mind. The imploding stonework. The acute angle between the tower and the rock. The Pavilion of Winds, flying apart like chaff. The Beacon of Hope, its glimmer lost in a swelling pall.

Oh gods it's real, oh gods it's real, oh gods it's real! Oh Orlom take me! Let me sink like a stone. Let me float upon your crest. Spare me from this memory!

How had she not known? How had she not seen? Until Hugh wrote his cruel words she had thought her tower stood. *What is wrong with me? What madness afflicts my mind? Why does my past hide its face?*

The pain. Oh the pain was real and so she knew the memory was real, too. Ilina sobbed into the dirt, her cries lost in the wind. For there was dirt pressing her body—wet, sticky dirt—and the wind screamed anew overhead, whipping the heather about like so many stalks of grass. The hills sloped up around her, black shadows against a faintly silver sky. She could fall no farther.

Shock had encased her body, distancing her from whatever injuries she'd sustained on her way down the slope, but her mental shock was just now burning off. Apparently she'd been in denial unawares when this destruction came upon her, but now that shield was gone. She roared and shrieked until her mouth was full of dirt.

###

Hugh leapt down the slope, dodging brush and vaulting boulders, hollering Ilina's name. The beam of his flashlight spasmed in crazy arcs as shrubs briefly burst from blackness to flash past upslope. *Surely she can hear my crashing, if not my voice,* he thought as he bowled straight through a thicket higher than his head. But he could barely hear the sound of it himself, the wind was so loud. Like a wailing presence in the air.

"Shut up!" he shouted. His chances of catching her dwindled with each passing moment. If she kept her footing and held a course only slightly divergent to his, they could be miles apart by morning. And in this undergrowth, all she had to do was fall to the ground and she'd be invisible until he planted a boot on her back.

Damn, damn, damn! *What'd I do* this *time? Insult her ancestors? Blaspheme her gods? Commit some arcane offworlder faux pas? How can I possibly know? The woman's a panic attack waiting to happen.*

And he was gonna get her back. A knob of rock passed beneath him as he vied with the wind for volume.

###

As the acuteness of grief subsided along with the physical shock, Ilina's sobs changed pitch. No longer untrammeled, her wordless pleas abandoned their ambition of altering the past and focused instead, with a quiet and ferocious intensity, on present-tense survival, breaking off partway through each breath as she struggled to retain consciousness and regain some measure of composure through constricting knots of pain.

Her movements were confined to an arena of inches. The wind corkscrewed around her, chill as the trackless deep, swooping down from encircling hills backlit by a brighter shade of black, pinning her in a lightless pit.

Except for that one light. There, beyond the whipping twigs, rounding the edge of a ridge. A little light it was, barely more than a gleam. It descended slowly—a guttering star fighting to stay alight, a strange lantern bobbing down a hill-road in the dead of night. Ilina felt a chill that had nothing to do with the wind.

She tried to rise but her strength was gone. And the wind had become a weight, a burden, a heavy hand pressing her into the loam. She moaned. Where was Hugh? Why had she run from him? What had come over her? She couldn't remember ... something he'd said? Maybe? *Perhaps I stepped away from the fire and fell. But then how then did I end up all the way out here? And where is 'here'?*

Ilina twisted as far as she could, gritting her teeth against the pain. Where was Hugh? Why had he not come for her? Had he ... A thought struck her like a blow. Had *Hugh* done this?

The distant glow had grown. She could see now that it *was* a lantern, bobbing steadily nearer, unerring in its approach. The vast emptiness of the highlands seemed suddenly *present*—a watchful encircling foe that warded off all help. Isolation was bad enough, but that was a known quantity; she had lived alone for years. Worse by far than the longing for company was company's implicit threat. Other people couldn't be trusted, least of all strangers. And here she lay—lost, and wounded, and far from home, and exposed to passersby. And in this desolate place there were no passersby, only interested parties.

A SEA SOUGHT IN SONG

She whimpered, and was surprised by the sound of it. For the wind had died away as though it'd never been. An eerie stillness settled, cupped within cradling hills. Her breathing grated in her ears and nearly drowned out the footfalls crackling upslope. A cool light washed over the heather. Ilina looked up and was blinded.

"Ilina!" bellowed Hugh as he hurtled over the moor. The wind screamed him down. Darkness was total; only the bright cone projected by his flashlight pierced the void. Having encountered no sign of the girl in his headlong descent—neither broken branch nor indented dirt—Hugh was losing hope. *But she must have marked something ... she can't have disappeared ... she was too distraught to leave a clean trail.*

The slope seemed to be leveling out ahead. Maybe it was time to cut across the ridge and double back. Hugh slammed into a boulder and paused, panting and ... and listening. The wind was gone. Just like that.

He looked up, brows colliding. Scrambled up the boulder. Swept his light over the little valley below. There was something down there, just beyond the reach of his light. He flicked it off.

It was another light. Held aloft by someone who stooped over a prone figure clad in blue and green.

Ilina.

Hugh dropped from the boulder and shoved through an obstructing thicket. Ahead, the stranger had lowered the lantern and knelt beside the girl. The light died, then leapt back up. The stranger began to glow.

Hugh was running.

I have no weapon ... where's my weapon ... need a weapon ... He'd lost his rifle. Left his sword at the summit. *Dammit, I need something! I'm out of my depth!* The light strengthened ahead, stretching the shadows, transforming intervening shrubs into gossamer tangles that thronged a dazzling sphere, bright and cold as diamond. Hugh swept them aside. And, as he crashed into the clearing, he remembered the magic rod.

The light dimmed as the stranger turned. Hugh plunged a hand into his coat pocket. A visage old and wild assessed him from beneath a broad-brimmed hat. A gnarled hand drew back—palm up, thumb and fourth finger circled. A coiled beast of incredible power, twin tongues of white rippling from its head.

AUSTIN GUNDERSON

And Hugh snarled, curling his fingers about his rod as he thrust it out to one side, and a sharp *crack* came from above as the huge sword materialized to reconnect with its extension. Far upslope, silhouetted against the moonlight, an outcrop of rock exploded. The sound of it rumbled around and around in their hill-bowl—a cascade of echoing thunder. The stranger brought his arms up, crossing them, blazing with light, and Hugh skidded to a halt, muscles bulging, sword upswept, teeth bared. He felt a power coursing through him and, though he didn't know the first thing about swords, saw his immanent strike unfold before his mind's eye as though the weapon itself knew precisely what to do. As though it required all his strength just to restrain the blade.

The two powers stood opposed for an instant or an eternity, facing off over Ilina's motionless form.

And then the stranger's eyes widened. He lowered his arms and knelt. Bowed his head to the ground. His long white beard spilled into divergent streams, spreading over the roots and leaves. His lantern was glowing again and he was dim, as though it had always been thus. Hugh blinked.

"Long have I awaited this moment." Hugh started, shooting a glance at Ilina, but it was the stranger who had spoken. The same stranger who now raised his head and peered almost sheepishly from under a broad hat-brim and bristling brows, his wrinkled face the very picture of relief.

"I will be honest," continued the old man. "I had despaired of seeing you in my lifetime. And this one," he gestured at Ilina, "has never even understood what it was that she anticipated." He reached down to press three fingers against her bloodied forehead.

Hugh lurched forward, jerking his blade back up.

"My lord," said the man, "I beg your indulgence. Her situation is delicate. I have broken the congestion, but if I do not quickly calm the storm and call her back, she may withdraw beyond my reach. Please. Let me call her." He fixed Hugh's gaze firmly. Imploringly.

Hugh didn't have a clue what to say, how to react. "You speak English?" he finally blurted.

The old man's smile welled up from somewhere deep within. It emerged slowly, like a deer from the forest—spreading from his mouth to his cheeks to the golden irises of his bright, bright eyes. Eyes that might've held a thousand evil schemes or a million miraculous cures. Eyes so hard they seemed to sift Hugh's soul, yet so lively that he felt a chuckle stirring in his belly, dispelling the adrenalin—or whatever it was—that urged him to attack first and converse later.

174

A SEA SOUGHT IN SONG

"How is it that you know you have not suddenly mastered Kramish?" asked the old man with a wink as he splayed his fingers upon Ilina's brow. "I jest, of course," he added quickly as tension returned to Hugh's shoulders. "I know many ancient tongues, but none so obscure as this which I now speak. How is my enunciation? It has been long since I have encountered an English interlocutor."

"Uh, good," said Hugh after a moment. "It's perfect, in fact." He couldn't think of anything else to say.

The old man smiled again and slid his fingers back together. He closed his eyes, sighed, then lifted his hand.

"Well, aren't you gonna call her ... or whatever?" asked Hugh.

The old man said nothing. And then Ilina groaned, rolling over. Hugh dropped his sword and knelt beside her as the stranger stood and withdrew. The girl's clothes were torn and soiled but her body didn't display any visible injuries. Hugh slipped a hand under her neck, supporting her head, holding it steady as she opened her eyes.

They were full of tears.

She lifted a hand, rested it on his arm. Her eyes swam, glistening in the lantern-light. She closed them and they spilled. Hugh felt his throat tighten. "What happened to you, girl?" he whispered. "Are you alright? Did he hurt you?"

Ilina smiled as she wept. She reached up, made a fist in Hugh's coat-collar, and pulled him gently down to bump his brow with hers. "Hugh," she said matter-of-factly. Her eyes slid shut.

"Ilina, do you know this man?" Hugh pointed at the stranger, who stood with hands folded at the edge of the clearing, face shadowed, silently watching. Ilina didn't look up.

Hugh grunted in self-chastisement, scratched his question into the soil with his free hand, then hefted her into a sitting position. She glanced from text to man, then leaned aside to trace a single word upon the bloodstained loam.

"Forkbeard."

Ilina slumped again and Hugh laid her down softly. "You," he said to the old man, rising. "Forkbeard, or whatever your name is. Thank you. For whatever you just did."

The man known as Forkbeard then did a very strange thing. Instead of acknowledging this credit, he prostrated himself before Hugh. "It is the honor of my life to serve you, my lord," he said. "As the mood of the rock moves the hand of the wind, so shall your word move me. Until the hills themselves lose heart, my service to you shall not cease."

Forkbeard looked up. "Welcome to Kramarack, Son of Conrad. I tremble to report that your kingdom is unready."

Chapter Twelve
THOSE WHO LISTEN TO STONES

Awash of wind and crackle of cloth engulfed Hugh's ears, drowning the old man's voice. The company's cloaks streamed and snapped like flags, the brown banner of Hugh's duster joining Forkbeard's flashing silver and Ilina's forest green. The heather shied from the blast, fluttering like a ruffled sea, and the company opposed this motion as one, shifting on their mounts to brace themselves against the rushing air. Their plodding steeds—short, stocky, hairy horses Ilina had referred to as *rhami*—didn't even flinch. They seemed indifferent to all but the path before them.

"What was that?" Hugh shouted.

"I said," answered Forkbeard over his shoulder, "you will need to procure a new hat when we reach Harnaral. The one you wear now reeks of *commoner*." Forkbeard's own hat had gone into his saddlebag shortly before the wind picked up, and now the bright sun glinted in his flying mane and upon the distant peaks bared like the teeth of Nidhogg's lower jaw.

Hugh set his own jaw, tugging down the brim of his battered fedora. "The hat stays," he said.

Forkbeard twisted in his saddle and cocked a comically-bushy eyebrow. Hugh stared him down—no trifling feat, considering those eyes' hypnotic intensity—and after a moment the old man shrugged, returning his gaze to the hill-road before them. It wound to and fro—switchbacking up hillsides, cutting around outcroppings of lichen-crusted stone, diving into dells where the air was still and steeped in a scent like sap and smoke. But as much as it conformed to the lay of the land, this path had been leading them unerringly southeast since they'd broken camp in the predawn glow.

After Ilina's battering the night before, Hugh hadn't expected her to be in any condition to move, let alone sit a horse, but the girl had seemed suspiciously unharmed and energetic when Forkbeard roused them after only a few hours of sleep. Whether *he* had slept at all was a matter for conjecture. The last thing Hugh remembered before flopping onto his bedroll—exhausted from jogging back up to their campsite, extinguishing their fire, and lugging all their supplies over the next hill to Forkbeard's four-horse hitch-line—was the old man sitting and smoking, silhouetted against the moons.

AUSTIN GUNDERSON

Hugh didn't know what served more to alleviate his unease with this situation: the unconcern with which perennially-paranoid Ilina treated Forkbeard's unexpected arrival, or the fact that the man's mannerisms and appearance were so stereotypically those of a wizard.

"The weirder this place gets," muttered Hugh, "the more familiar it seems."

"I beg your pardon?" said Forkbeard.

"I said you seem familiar with this area. Do you live around here?"

Forkbeard chuckled, a measure of bass notes. He'd introduced himself last night as Lhewen Mahru, but it'd been too late: the nickname etched in the dirt by Ilina had already lodged firmly in Hugh's brain. And for good reason—Lhewen's flowing whiskers were styled into twin streams that swept all the way to his knees. Except now they flapped in the wind alongside his cloak, and he flipped one over a shoulder as he spoke. "My home, when I have one, is far from here. But I have trod these paths for many years with only an occasional shepherd for company and so, when word came of your ferry's disappearance, I volunteered at once for the search."

"There's a search? But how could anyone have known we'd been attacked?"

"The Land's End ferry is never late," Forkbeard frowned. "How could it be? Of all the ships in Kramarack, it alone is equipped with a rhomic guidestone. In former times it would have made the Cuspid Isle run eight days a week. When the first night passed without the ferry's return, search parties were dispatched."

"A whatsit? Guidestone?" asked Hugh. "You mean that glass ball in the prow that Ilina was touching?" Forkbeard nodded. "But what … I mean why … oh, never mind." *I wouldn't understand your answer anyway.* "Then how did you find us so quickly? We'd only just made landfall."

"The wind led me to you."

A chill sprouted in Hugh's spine at that matter-of-fact tone. The man actually meant it. *And I'll be damned if I don't believe it, too.* Hugh swallowed and changed the subject. "So how do you know Ilina?"

Now it was Forkbeard's turn to slump. "Through no pleasant circumstance, I am afraid. It is a long and tragic tale. Suffice it to say that we have seen death together." He fell silent, and the wind followed suit.

They had entered a bowl between hills. Here and there, patches of sun-sculpted snow huddled behind boulders. Just ahead, the trail split—the right fork curving up to hug a ridgeline, the left plunging into a stream-wrought

A SEA SOUGHT IN SONG

valley. Ilina glanced her doubt at Forkbeard, and he nodded to the right. After a few minutes of climbing, they had reentered the wind's domain.

Hugh was unhappily contemplating the ways in which his status as the object of a rescue operation would disrupt his plan to fly under the radar when Forkbeard again spoke up. "No," he said slowly, "you *do* need to hear the tale. I would be remiss to withhold it. It forms a stalk in a story that will soon intertwine with your own. When we reach Harnaral," and here he turned to fix Hugh with an appraising eye, "you will find that not all are pleased by your coming. The Council of Kram lost its foresight long ago; their opposition is a given, and of little concern. Far more grievous to our cause is the dissolution of Highlord Rikard. His father's death showed us all to be fools, but his response has been one of fear and denial. And as a result our peril has only grown."

"Wait," said Hugh. "Back up. What death? Whose father?" He forced himself to pay attention. If public scrutiny was inevitable, his understanding of local political machinations could quickly become all-important to the continuation of his mission.

"On the night Ilina and I first met," said Forkbeard in a tone that forced Hugh to lean forward in his saddle, "the Highlord of Kramarack was slain in his own chambers by a giant spiderworm." The old man shot Hugh a glance. "In case you do not know, this is not a common occurrence. Not only is the creature's primary foodsource concentrated a good twenty leagues to the north, but there is also the fact that said foodsource is a variety of aquatic tuber. The giant spiderworm, terrifying though it may appear, is no predator. And yet an individual of the species managed to infiltrate the Great Hall of Harn, center of Kramish strength, and, with singleness of intent, destroy the most powerful ruler north of the Gnofs. I was there at the time. I was *there*, in the hall. And yet even I could not prevent the creature from killing Lord Hansel." Forkbeard's voice was strained.

Hugh was no longer having trouble paying attention. "That doesn't make sense. Why would it do that? Could it have been trained? Directed somehow?"

Forkbeard smiled bitterly at Hugh. "Ah, my lord. If only you had been here then. *Those* are the obvious questions, are they not? And yet Rikard Harnish, Hansel's son and heir—who was *also* there for the attack—has refused to consider them. He insists that the animal merely strayed too far from its feeding grounds and went mad with starvation. No matter that this would constitute the first such incident known to science. No matter that there exists a known threat to Kramish sovereignty with the capacity to carry out such an untraceable assassination. No matter. For Rikard Harnish, Highlord of Kramarack, has been cowed into quiescence. He is *convinced* we must give our Enemy no pretense to strike. But the Enemy has already struck!"

"What enemy?"

Forkbeard was silent a moment. When at last he answered, it was in a voice colder than the wind. "He has borne many names. At present he is known as Omri Daramal, Imperator of Tunnolt."

Hugh started. "*What* did you say?"

The bitter smile again. "Ah yes. I suspected you might have heard it. Lately he has grown less cautious. The re-adoption of that ancient title is one of many signs that an age of peace is ending."

"Wha–" Hugh checked himself, prioritized his questions. "How'd you know I'd recognize that name?"

Forkbeard gave him a flat look. "You are your father's son, are you not? Omri was his greatest foe."

Ilina hunched in the saddle. She wrenched her cloak away from the wind and wrapped it about her shoulders. Those other two were getting on her nerves. They'd been at it since before dawn, yammering away in Hugh's harsh foreign tongue with barely a word spared for her. It was bad enough that Forkbeard knew the Script of Secrets; that he could actually *speak* it was unbearable.

But speak it he could, and speak it he did. And, just like that, she'd lost her status as interpreter. Gone were her garments of office, gone the Banner of the King, and gone too her contribution to discussion. Nothing was left for her but to pretend disinterest while straining to catch even vaguely familiar syllabic constructions. Thus far she'd noticed none.

She looked down at her phlegmatic mount. 'Feather.' That was the name Forkbeard had given her to call it. Perhaps because of its hairy legs. In her ill temper she hadn't thought to talk to it or encourage it in any way. She couldn't even remember if it were a *he* or a *she*, and she wasn't about to lean out of her saddle to check.

A part of her had identified this petulance as petty resentment. The other parts of her didn't care. She had waited too long and suffered too much to be jettisoned at the final hour like some expendable courier relaying a message

A SEA SOUGHT IN SONG

to her betters. She was a Lightkeeper—the *last* Lightkeeper, by Harlith's breath—and as such was integral. She would *not* be elbowed aside!

"Forkbeard!" she called, not deigning to turn around. "What is the current topic of conversation?"

Both of them fell silent. *Forgot I was here, did you?* She repressed a grimace.

Forkbeard cleared his throat. "We have been discussing the tragic events surrounding your previous visit." A resigned sigh. "In light of the southern menace."

Ilina stiffened. She should have known he would waste no time. *Stupid girl, this is your own fault. You had Hugh's ear for an entire week and made nothing but small talk.* "And what conclusion has been reached?"

"Ilina, this is not a question of conclusions. It is a question of evidence. I have yet to present that which best supports my position, and yet Hugh's first reaction, unprompted by me, was to express doubt in the official account."

Now Ilina did turn. "And have you explained to him what will result if you're wrong?" she snarled. "Have you described what could be lost? Does he know the extent of the Power now rising? Do *you?*"

"I am certain you will compensate for my every omission."

"Then the answer is no," hissed Ilina. "And how could you? No one knows the Enemy's full nature. There are only those who insist on baiting him, and those who have the good sense to abstain."

Forkbeard was unruffled. "That is a false dichotomy. You assume our Enemy will respect our intentions. But he has already demonstrated utter disregard for our antiquated notions of neutrality, our false assurance of mutual nonaggression, and he will continue to do so again and again and *again* until we are left with no alternative but to face him in open conflict. And by that time it will be too late; he will have chosen the field. Again, we dispute not over conclusions, but evidence. If you acknowledge the evidence, then the conclusion is inevitable. If you see a heath tiger surmount your wall, you will fit an arrow to the string before it can attack your flock. We must take action before it is too late. *We* must choose the field."

"Your analogy needs work, Forkbeard. Try imagining yourself at the base of a sheer ravine. A single stone clatters at your feet. Will you shout with all your might to catalyze the incipient landslide?"

"You assume–"

"No, not even that does it justice. I have a better one. Imagine a waterfall. Imagine Torrolin Fall. You stand dwarfed before its cataract, subsumed in the roar and thunder of it, deafened to the world, and in the weight and terror and thoughtless force pouring before you you see death. A droplet strikes your cheek. Do you step forward, or shrink back?"

Forkbeard was silent. Ilina glanced at Hugh; he looked like a man trying to identify some half-remembered scent. His eyes flicked between her and the old man. His horse's ears were flicking, too—the company had splashed across an upland rill teeming with flies, some of which had apparently decided to escort them the rest of the way.

"You are truly frightened," Forkbeard murmured at last. A statement, not a question. But then he just had to ask: "Is the future that bleak to you?"

Ilina laughed bitterly.

"What is it?"

"Nothing. You just sounded like someone else for a moment."

"Ilina, think. If the enemy is as strong as you suspect, then nothing in Arlam can oppose his will. Let us assume it is as you say—that the outcome is predetermined, that hope is a form of denial. Does it matter?"

"Does what matter?"

"If all ends be one, then only means remain. You have some knowledge of Omri—more than most, I concede. Would you *willingly* submit to such as he is? Would you wait demurely for him to snuff the candle of your freedom? Or will you, despising fate, cast your freedom in his face?"

Ilina's eyes roamed the passing hills and vales. As she considered what Forkbeard had said, an age-old aphorism popped into her head, then out of her mouth: "The fish of Glassen Lake have a tendency to last; to catch one is a feat worth an angler's weight in bait. The overeager oaf puts his arm into his cast; the savvy strategist understands 'tis best to wait."

A pause. Had Forkbeard actually *huffed?* She wouldn't look. Her eyes tracked a black speck circling heaven's azure vault.

"Cute," said Forkbeard finally, "but not pertinent. If the end is inescapable, all that matters is the manner in which we face it. Those are *your* words, confided when last we saw one another. Has much changed since then?"

Ilina swallowed, then lifted her chin. "Hugh has come."

"Yes, and his coming is a sign in favor of decisive action! His appearance now—in our hour of need—is no accident. The Awaited One has a power none of us can claim. I have seen it! With him by our side we can face the Terror of the south!"

"No," Ilina whispered just above the wind. "No, don't you see? Now that he has come, we have *hope* again. The prophecies are true, and all our waiting not for naught. An end has opened to us that does not demand our deaths. I can no longer afford to scorn fate nor cast my life away. Not now that *he* is here."

"And if he should choose to fight?"

Ilina was silent. *The Awaited One wouldn't choose that. He wouldn't choose to throw lives away for the sake of his own pride.* But Hugh the man … the man she knew … In her mind she saw again a boot raised with finality over a helpless Jaar. No, she would not lie to herself. The Hugh she knew would probably choose war even without provocation. *But not if he understands the peril*, she admonished herself. *Not if I make clear to him the cost …*

"Ilina," repeated Forkbeard, serious, "what if the Awaited One chooses to fight?"

He won't; I won't let him. "He has not chosen yet," she said.

###

"What was that all about?" asked Hugh after lengthening silence made it clear the exchange had reached an impasse. The slope they now ascended seemed to stretch forever. Even the mountains hid behind it.

"Ilina objects to my strategic assessment," answered Forkbeard. "She deems our Enemy too powerful to oppose."

Hugh snorted. *If the people of Kramarack are anything like the Jaar, that's not surprising.* "And why is that?"

Forkbeard faced forward to address Ilina. *"Hugh haum mol, whul sehim tehler Gurhimin lanirhom lo utaresh haut."*

After a bit of back-and-forth with the girl, Forkbeard turned to Hugh with a sigh. "The Lady Lightkeeper says she would prefer to communicate her concerns directly and will do so when next we make camp."

Interesting, thought Hugh. *Does she distrust him as an interpreter, or is she just jockeying for prominence?* Either way, this was a perfect opportunity to play them off against each other. *But by what means, and for what end? You have to step carefully now—there's too much here you don't understand.*

Last night, Hugh had briefly described the monster attack to Forkbeard, who'd frowned and said nothing. Now Hugh wondered what the old man had been thinking. "The thing that crippled our ship, is it a common threat?" Hugh asked. "Should I expect to meet more of them?"

"The Great Mast Spider is one of the rarest life forms in all Arlam," said Forkbeard slowly. "It is nearly unknown to science. Indeed, there are many who think it a myth—a fantasy fabricated in dank tavern-corners by shipwreck survivors desperate to lend meaning to their loss. That you encountered one is astonishing. That *it* encountered *you*—that it launched an unprovoked attack on land ... that is unthinkable." Forkbeard fell silent.

Hugh shifted uncomfortably, hitching himself forward in the saddle. The trail had given up switchbacking and decided to cut straight up and over a rocky knoll. Here and there it appeared that stones had been shifted to clear a path, but footing was still treacherous and the travelers had to bend almost to their horses' manes to maintain balance. Soon they had entered a kind of cutting. Rock walls rose on either hand, and wind whistled in their faces.

"Have you had any dreams lately?" asked Forkbeard suddenly.

"What?" said Hugh. "What do you mean? What're you talking about?"

"Have you had any dreams?" he repeated. "Visions, premonitions, memories you recall for the very first time? Have you seen anything strange that was not truly there?"

Hugh stiffened, his senses burning with an aftertaste of horror—of a voice speaking in his skull, of laughter like a molten brand. He felt again the shock of being punched into a bloody sea. This line of questioning struck too close to home. *How can this man possibly know what's happening in my head? Is he in on it, somehow?*

"I take it from your silence that the answer is yes," said Forkbeard.

With effort, Hugh kept his voice neutral. "Why do you ask?"

"Why do you think the mast spider attacked?"

Hugh let his contrary streak stall for time. "I dunno—why do *you* think?"

"I think it attacked for the same reason the spiderworm did. Because it was told to."

"That's ridiculous. Who would give the order? No one even knows I'm here! Just you and Ilina and a bunch of Eskimos."

Forkbeard turned, fixing Hugh with a fierce eye. "No one?"

An image burst in Hugh's brain. A night sliced by red in rippling columns. A tall figure, blank-helmed, cased all in gleaming armor without chink. *'So, he has sent you. How ... disappointing.'*

Hugh opened his mouth, then checked himself. *Do I trust you, wizard? Do I know what you really want? Is now the best moment to speak?*

As if to spare him this decision the ravine's walls fell away, leaving the travelers on a high hilltop beneath an open sky which had warmed with the onset of evening. All around them the highlands rolled on into the golden distance, and above all loomed the hoary peaks. The wind was at rest; it

A SEA SOUGHT IN SONG

sighed through the grasses and seemed to soothe their steeds, who lifted their heads to whinny in unison. The escort of flies was gone.

But it was not the wind or the light or the view that captured the company's attention. It was not the absence of flies that obliged Forkbeard to face forward. Instead, it was the sight of the stark black obelisk slanting from the highest point of the hill like an oversized nail protruding through the backside of a beam. The eastering sun glinted from its facets until they seemed varnished with flame.

The company rode closer. The monolith was about thirty feet tall, but had once been taller; a rough stump capped its height prematurely. Hugh counted eight sides, though the jet stone was so chipped and weathered now it was difficult to be sure. Its base was lost in a knot of heather.

Forkbeard broke the silence. "This is an ancient monument," he murmured, "erected in the days of Harn. I had forgotten it stood in our path."

Hugh looked at the sun, then at the lay of the ground. Then he swung a leg over the saddle and dropped into the grass. "We camp here tonight," he announced.

Ilina had been sunk deep in thought when they reached the hilltop, and now, as Forkbeard rubbed down his horses and Hugh gathered kindling—with the timber blight, it was all kindling all the time in Kramarack these days—she again withdrew inward. It was critical that she dissuade Hugh from attempting to engage the Enemy in a contest of strength. This presented a daunting prospect: such restraint would contravene everything she saw that he'd come to believe about conflict. It would seem like madness or cowardice to one such as he, especially if Forkbeard managed to persuade him that the Enemy was the aggressor—an outcome which seemed already foregone.

Nonetheless, it was imperative. Before the week was out and if all went well, Hugh could find himself named a Knight of the Kram and granted martial authority, at the very least. Ilina's fears that her Declaration would see rejection had abated somewhat; the support of Forkbeard for Hugh's claim was no small thing. But the old man's influence was a double-edged sword. And so it fell to Ilina to be the voice of sanity.

But how? How could she convince Hugh? What could she say that would make a difference in his mind?

Despondent, Ilina began to pace. Forkbeard ignored her, and Hugh, after a few sidelong glances in her direction, concentrated on clearing their campsite. As the sun slowly sank and the light thickened, Ilina's steps were drawn toward the monolith several hundred feet upslope.

Before long she found herself at its foot. From this angle its stone flashed no longer, but seemed to absorb the light like a pool. It was old stone—older even than the menhir on Bald Tor—or else was showing its age through long neglect.

Ilina turned slowly, taking in the panorama. The coast was far behind them now, the mountains far ahead. The hills rose and fell forever like the rollers of a hazel sea. No column of smoke striated the horizon or wafted in the salt-sharp wind. This was the wild backcountry of Kramarack, trod only by shepherds and Broanoshi hermits and poets seeking a feral beauty they could never possess. Strange that such a monument should have been raised in a place so abandoned.

You're one to talk, Ilina chided herself, *you who live in a tower on the rim of the world*. She smiled. Perhaps the Kram had lived here once, then moved on when the memorial lost its meaning? She wondered what it had meant.

Ilina pushed through the encircling heather and laid a hand on the sun-warmed stone. Here at its base the monolith was crusted with lichen and twined with trailing vines. As she moved her hand over its surface she detected a shallow pattern of ridges and depressions. *An inscription.* She began scrubbing at the surface, sweeping aside the vines and crumbling the lichen until scratches scored her palms. She hopped to clear a spot above her head, then sneezed in the rain of detritus that followed. At last the writing stood out, defined in low-angle light.

"Whem fi laktai?" said Hugh at her shoulder.

Ilina only jumped a little, then blushed. What a sight she must present. She brushed fingers through her hair and sneezed again at the ensuing dust-cloud.

Hugh seemed unperturbed. He repeated his question, pointing at the engraving.

Taking a breath and refocusing her attention, Ilina realized she could read the weathered writing. It was Old Kramish, so it took her a few minutes, but in the end it was easy to render into English. Hugh pulled a parchment and pen from his coat and Ilina started transcribing.

The inscription was the Law of the Land—a famous edict generally attributed by scholars to High King Henred Conrad. To Hugh's father. Ilina's fingers trembled, spattering ink, and she began the line again.

A SEA SOUGHT IN SONG

"Hear me ye peoples of Arlam,
And heed my pronouncement this day:
Let he who makes war on his neighbor
Gain doubly the fate he would pay."

It was a cryptic statement that had been subjected to much debate in the second and third centuries. Eventually, a consensus had emerged around Torwell's reading, in which the Law was a proscription against preemptive warfare. This interpretation had been underscored over the centuries by the well-documented failures of every attempt at international conquest until the rise of the Tunnoltan Imperium. Nowadays, Torwell's philosophy was dismissed as utopian determinism and the Law, when it was discussed at all, was said to apply on the individual level. No wonder this monument had seen neglect.

But Ilina could use it.

Hugh looked thoughtful, but hadn't made to take the parchment. So Ilina added another line, with an arrow to indicate the proceeding stanza. *"Thy father said that."*

He glanced at her sharply. She held his eyes.

"What does it mean?" he asked.

"It means aggression and wisdom are divergent paths. The machinations of warfare are capricious. If they cannot be relied upon in the most ideal of circumstances, how canst thou think to outmaneuver that Enemy before which the whole world shrinks?"

Hugh blinked at her fire, then quirked an eyebrow. *"Forkbeard tells me that Omri has struck first. Are you telling me self-defense is unwise?"*

"Nay!" Ilina shot a withering glance toward the campsite. *"I am saying that if the Enemy wished it, he could overwhelm this land like a hawk subdues a vole. That he hath yet to do so should not be construed as a sign of weakness. Who knows what games he plays? Perhaps his mind is elsewhere—wouldst thou focus it upon us? Perhaps he thinks us beneath his notice—wouldst thou convince him otherwise?"*

Hugh squelched a sneer. Ilina's reasoning was nonsense. He thought of Chamberlain and Munich and the promise of 'peace in our time,' and closed his eyes. Breathed in and out. *Why does it always come to this? Why do good men trust in tyrants for their peace? Why do they scrape and plead and leave*

187

it to men like me to mop up their mess? Why must the children always pay for their fathers' irrational faith?

A thought struck him with an almost physical blow. *Earth just went through hell to learn this lesson. What if Arlam hasn't learned it yet? What if I'm standing on the brink of another world war—right here, right now? What if this is 1938 all over again?*

A moan escaped him, and he stuffed a knuckle between his teeth to stifle further outburst. *I can't do this, can't go through it again. It's too much. I can't mop up another one of your messes, Father.*

I just don't have it in me.

He looked up, belatedly aware of Ilina's all-absorbing eyes. She was so slight—so strong and fragile, so brittlely austere—and thought herself so shrewd. But of what worth was her judgement? How old was she, anyway? Where had she lived but in her tower? What did she know that hadn't been learned from books? Hugh looked into her eyes and thought he saw the innocence of appeasement, the fear of one who thought destruction came through those who refused to treat with tyrants. She knew no better; she hadn't seen what he'd seen.

"If you put your trust in Omri, he will betray you," Hugh scratched out. *"If you think he waits for provocation, you deceive yourself. He waits for opportunity. And there is no better opportunity than that provided by misplaced trust."*

Confusion clouded Ilina's eyes, swiftly replaced by something like sadness. She laid a hand lightly on his arm and gave him a look that stopped his breath. It was a look of chill pity and grief sharp as thorns. *"Thou sayest such things because thou knowest him not. Thou art excused, but not I. I know of his strength as sure as I scent a coming storm. I would not think to sue for peace with a foe that possesseth neither kindness nor honor. I wish only to live long enough to see the Awaited One's advent."*

The fear misattributed by Hugh to concern over diplomatic misstep he now saw to be of a deeper nature. It tinged Ilina's eyes and pinched her lips— an irrepressible dread of death, of loss, of ultimate failure. Her terror had lead to paralysis.

Oh God, why me? Why must it be me? Haven't I given enough? He would have to awaken an entire world. If the Omri described by his father had risen again, then he had no choice.

Dammit, yes you do! You can just keep heading south! South, straight into the jaws of this beast. And what would happen if he left this nation undefended? Would these people die in their delusion? What if he ended up needing support, and had only a bench of fearful fools at his back? Was *he* willing to leave himself undefended for the sake of expediency?

Hugh took the pen. *"And what if Omri is responsible for the destruction of Kredak Tower?"*

Ilina recoiled as if slapped. She stared at Hugh with eyes wide and lips parted in horror. Too late he remembered what had sparked the previous night's panic! Afraid she would bolt, Hugh grabbed her arm.

It was the wrong move. Ilina cried out and kicked his shin, wrenching herself from his grip and backing against the obelisk. The two of them eyed each other, poised.

And then Hugh sank to his haunches and lowered his head. It was just too much—the madness of Miles' death, the terror of the portal, the brutal battle for the Eskimos' boat, the waking nightmare that was the mast spider, the weariness borne of hunger and cold and journeying for days on end, days he could *swear* were too long even for the arctic in summer. And now *this*.

He began to snicker uncontrollably. Laugh out loud. His body shook with it, and he flopped onto his back in the dirt, uncaring. *Let her run off. Who am I to stop her? It's her world.*

Eventually Hugh opened his eyes to see Ilina looking down on him with a vague disgust. She held out the parchment above his face. *"Wherefore didst thou say that?"* it read. She let the parchment fall, then dropped the pen on Hugh's nose. He cursed and glared, but Ilina didn't flinch.

"Because it's a reasonable inference," scribbled Hugh without getting up. *"If Omri was behind the spiderworm attack, then it stands to reason that he directed the mast spider, too."* Hugh couldn't help but notice the pattern. "Jeez, what's with all the spiders?" he wondered aloud. "Is this some kind of purgatory for arachnophobes?"

Ilina, eyes on Hugh's scrawl, blanched as though she'd swallowed something fetid. *"What mast spider?"*

Hugh sat up. Something very weird was going on here. *"That's the name Forkbeard used for the monster on your island. Do you call it something else?"*

Ilina rubbed her temples. She seemed frightened. Hugh proffered the parchment and pen, but she didn't accept them. *Fine. See if I care. Pout on your own time.* He flopped back down.

###

AUSTIN GUNDERSON

"Ah, here you are!" exclaimed Forkbeard. He pushed through the heather, glancing up at the exposed inscription, then down at Hugh's sprawled form. Of those two sights, Ilina judged him more surprised by the latter.

"Come Ilina," he said. "Come Hugh—*rin, larholmai fit yir.* I have a fire going, and potatoes ready to cook. Or perhaps you would prefer to keep discussing the obsolete dictates of the ancients?" He fixed Ilina with a knowing eye.

She ignored him, hanging back as Hugh heaved himself to his feet and trailed after Forkbeard. Her head hurt and she bit back tears. Was it not enough that she had to contend with one of the most powerful men in the North over the fate of the civilized world? Was that challenge insufficient, that she should be forced to grapple with the overactive imagination of her offworld charge?

Why would he lie when he knows I know the truth? Is he trying to undercut my credibility? Is he mad? Is he trying to drive me *mad?* The world tilted, its hills rolling like real waves, and Ilina thrust a steadying hand against the monolith to ride out her vertigo. Once the ground had returned to solidity she remained propped up by the stone.

Why do his declarations affect me so? She seemed to recall a similar episode—it had been recent. Just last night, in fact. *Wait, really?* She couldn't remember. All she knew was that Hugh had said something horrible, and she had ... *what, just left? Run off?* The next thing she remembered was meeting Forkbeard in the valley. *But how'd I get there in the first place?* There was a gap in her memory.

Oh gods ... could Hugh be right? Could Kredak Tower ... could ... could it ... Ilina whimpered, shrank down, clutched at her head.

No! If Kredak Tower was destroyed, then her father was gone and she was destitute, left without home or purpose in a world utterly changed. *That cannot be.* She stood, fists and teeth clenched. *He is mistaken.* She detached herself from the stone. *I am the rock that weathers the wind and the waves. I will remain though all else flee away. I am the Lightkeeper. I will resist all change.*

They welcomed her to the fire with smiles. Made room for her between them. Handed her a wooden board complete with cooked potato and strip of cured meat. And then carried on talking as though she wasn't even there. She sat and stared at nothing.

At last, a lull came, and Ilina spoke into it. "Has Hugh said aught concerning a mast spider?"

A SEA SOUGHT IN SONG

"Yes," answered Forkbeard quietly. "He has told me everything, but I thought it best not to relive it with you. Ilina," he said, and waited until she met his deep-sunk eyes, "words cannot express my sorrow. You have lost too much that cannot be retrieved. It is not right. Nothing in my power can change that, but know this: whether Rikard honors his agreement or no, while I live you will have a place among the Kram. This I swear on the memory of your father."

Ilina swallowed. Looked down at her lap. She felt small and powerless, like a patronized child. *This narrative has been stolen from me*, she realized. *Wrested away by he who spoke first. If I contradict him, I will be thought mad. I dare not share my mind, lest I lose all leverage.* She closed her eyes as resignation closed in. It was a bitter draught for one so drunk.

The sun and the fire were dying. The eastern sky glowed like the coals. The wind was shifting around, streaming from the peaks, whistling softly over the heath. Insects bobbed overhead, heedless of the smoke, their bodies flashing golden when they caught the light. Beyond them loomed the monolith, broken and tilted, slicing the wind like a sword. And from every side, the highlands pressed them with an emptiness as plaintive as it was remote.

Hugh gazed into the embers as though they would tell him his fate. Forkbeard studied the moons as they emerged like eyes from behind the southern mountains. Ilina stared at her cold, untouched potato. She nibbled the strip of cured meat. And then, as the fire ceased to snap and the wind drifted off, a vast silence fell. Forkbeard cleared his throat. And thus, he softly sang:

> *"Look, weary traveler,*
> *and ye shall see*
> *A glimpse of what once was,*
> *a vision of history.*
> *The ancients, they founded me*
> *in an age long ago;*
> *Now across their lost kingdoms*
> *deep forests do grow.*
> *I was a fortress—*
> *strong, prideful, and tall—*
> *Yet many a warlord's*
> *swept o'er me since my fall.*
> *Holy and blood-steeped*

AUSTIN GUNDERSON

is the ground which ye tread,
For mighty were they
who beneath me lie dead.
Naught but a whisper
rises now from their bones—
Heard faintly, perhaps,
by those who listen to stones."

Forkbeard's final word hung in the air as though reluctant to leave. A strange sadness welled up within Hugh's soul. The song's haunting lilt meant nothing to him, yet for some reason … he wished it did. A shudder spread up his spine. This whole world seemed *deeper*, somehow. Less like a fairy tale.

The old man shook out his wide-brimmed hat, pulling it down over his ears, and produced a pipe from somewhere under his cloak. He bent forward to coax a small coal into the bowl, then leaned back and took a long drag, exhaling with immense satisfaction. Hugh felt his smoker's yearning tighten. Just a drag or two, that's all it'd take to stem the ache. But Forkbeard didn't offer, and Hugh didn't ask.

Dusk had nearly bled out. From the darkness farther down the summit there came a horsey snort. Ilina was nodding where she sat, and looked none too happy about it. A doleful sigh rose from the wind. And Hugh realized with mild surprise that he'd reached a decision.

"I have seen him," he said. Across the remains of the fire, Forkbeard looked up. His eyes were points of light. "Omri, I mean," went on Hugh. "He appeared to me in a vision. He knows I'm here."

Forkbeard closed his eyes. "And here I was enjoying my pipe."

Chapter Thirteen
DECLARATION

Hugh needn't have worried about flying under the radar. When the travelers arrived at Harnaral two days later, they found the city in an uproar. A courier had ridden through the night to bring word of the fall of a certain seaport over the southern mountains. Never before in Kramish history had news from Suma induced such shock.

The travelers knew something was wrong by the time they reached Tarn Ford. The previous morning their sheep-path had plunged from the highlands into a broad river vale where the winds were idle and the shadows damp. There the path joined a stone-lined causeway hugging the bank in a gradual curve northward through fields and rust-bespeckled firs. The blight was worsening. For the umpteenth time, Ilina wondered why the stricken trees hadn't simply been burned. Did the Kram imagine their precious groves would recover as suddenly and mysteriously as they'd succumbed?

No sooner had the travelers turned their horses onto the road than they began encountering signs of civilization. Hamlets peeped at them from the valley's southern rim. Every few miles, rustic structures spilled across the road to overhang the river while watermills churned ceaselessly and flaxen-haired men in mud-caked trousers straightened and stared in suspicion. Ilina felt their eyes on her back like heavy hands.

Wagon-drivers were friendlier: doffing their caps to Ilina, who nodded curtly in return, they shouted greetings to Forkbeard as he overtook and passed them on the left. There was no oncoming traffic. *Strange.*

The road broadened to two lanes, deeply-rutted. The Tarn Valley was fertile, and the Kram had let none of it to go to waste. Stone-walled buildings—houses, inns, stables, and barns—lined up along the wayside, their heavy-timbered roofs slanted at load-bearing angles. Windmills sprouted from the high horizon, their vanes revolving swiftly in remote gusts. The ridgebeams that protruded over the road had been sculpted into flamelike shapes, each unique in some small way, and the lintels below were cased in branching patterns painted red.

The adjoining streets were empty, patrolled by careless chickens. Faces peered from windows, then vanished. They were the faces of women and children. At some point during the past few miles, the laborers had vanished from the ditches and fields. Forkbeard was muttering under his breath. Ilina's eyes darted to and fro like birds driven from their nest. And then the company rounded the final bend.

Hugh started, raising his eyes to the hilltop stronghold that loomed above them, resplendent in harsh morning light. As Ilina craned her neck, her view of the city's steeples and banners was obstructed by Forkbeard's silver shoulders bobbing before her, snowy as any summit of the south. She recalled her first glimpse of the wizard from atop the hill wall a year and a half ago, and realized with a sense of dizzy dislocation that she knew exactly what their little company must look like from above. And as she saw the sun's light flaring from high windows in successive bursts of red and gold, dread settled over her soul.

The broad column of black smoke roiling up from Harnaral's heart seemed out of place to strangers and locals alike.

The waters of the Tarn sparkled madly as the company charged across the ford. Forkbeard was in the lead and had buried his heels in his mount's ribs the moment he saw that Harnaral was burning. Ilina clung to Feather's mane and prayed she remained in the saddle. Her rides with Rikard had never seen such speed. The spray in her face was icy-sweet and the rush and splashing like music, and then with a jolt they were up the farther bank and ascending Harn Hill.

Dust curled in the sun. Switchbacks jerked them back and forth. She looked up as the world shuddered and saw a silver cloak spreading like a vast wing before her face. Then the great hill wall rose to their right and plunged them into shadow.

The ancestral seat of House Harn had stood, according to Nostolis the Younger, for five hundred and forty-five years. Founded on the site of Harn Bright-Eyes' sacrificial stand against an overwhelming force of Jaar, Harnaral had grown to encompass the entirety of its hill, had been sacked twice only to rise again twice more, and had remained the locus of Kramish power and culture following the third-century collapse of Henred's Kingdom and the Final Flight of the Kram beyond the reputedly-impassable Gnofs.

No king ruled in this place, but a mere lord: the Highlord of Kramarack. Though Harn himself had been king over all the Kramish Houses, his last

A SEA SOUGHT IN SONG

stand had extinguished the entire royal family, and so the rule of the newly-conquered highlands had passed by popular vote to Harn's cousin, who, out of reverence for the dead sovereign's memory, accepted the rule but not the title.

The headship of the High Council had remained with House Harn ever since—a fact assumed and accepted by the other Kramish lords, who contented themselves in the knowledge that no law made it thus, or else refused to begrudge the de facto hereditariness of a position now widely regarded as ceremonial. If this was how the people still wished to honor Harn, then their representatives at the Council would not dissent.

Harnaral's current iteration had stood unmolested since the end of the Third Jaar War and the final expulsion of the indigenous menace nearly three centuries past. Due in part to its repeated reconstruction prior to the advent of peace, and in part to its population density, Harn Hill had been perforated by a madcap warren of subterranean passages descending nearly to river-level.

Now a fortress deemed impregnable by experts, Harnaral boasted a massive wall fashioned from the bones of the hill itself. Over a hundred feet high and inlaid with seamless stone slabs, this great hill wall encircled a square-mile plateau of tightly-packed dwellings accessible only via the under-gate—a broad tunnel which sloped gradually up from an entrance at the base of the wall to a gatehouse in the city's central square. In order to enter the city, an enemy would have to not only break through both the upper and lower gates, but also survive the tunnel itself without getting buried alive by controlled cave-ins. A successful assault was nearly impossible with that much potential energy suspended overhead.

They heard the crowd before they saw it, even over the hoofbeats of their steeds. Ilina forced herself upright as they rounded the final bend and nearly bowled over several men standing in the roadway. She cried out as she fumbled with her reins in panicked imitation of Forkbeard, who'd skidded his mount to a halt at the edge of the throng. Men dove from her path, caroming off Feather's flanks as she yanked the horse sideways. By the time she regained control, dozens of bodies sprawled between her and her companions. Fortunately, all the bodies got up. Not so fortunately, they all started yelling and converging.

195

AUSTIN GUNDERSON

Dust was thick in the air. It caught the light like suspended submarine sediment. The broad, flat landing that fronted Harnaral's under-gate teemed with a crowd of hundreds who rippled away from the newcomers like duckweed from a pond-dropped rock. The thunder of their chorus gradually died away. Those storming up to accost Ilina seemed to deflate—perhaps because they'd seen she was a woman, perhaps because Forkbeard and Hugh were forcing their way in her direction. Hugh in particular looked prepared to inflict violence, and Forkbeard's majesty went before him like an unseen crier. His name leapt up from faceless mouths.

"Forkbeard! Thank the gods you've come!"

"You've gotta help us, Forkbeard!"

"Forkbeard's here! He'll do something!"

"They've shut the gate, the bastards! Shut it! That could be my house burning!"

"They can't do this! I live inside! I've right of passage!"

"Do something, Councilor! Don't let 'em get away with this!"

"It ain't been done before! Not in a hundred years! My granda knows!"

"Forkbeard, sir! Harl and Tam have gone for a ram! This gate ain't gonna stop us! Not for long!"

Forkbeard's head snapped to the side. He jerked the reins and his horse spun, scattering those who'd clustered round. His eyes raked the crowd. "Who said that?" he shouted. "Who's gone for a ram?"

"Harl and Tam, sir! It's that fir log they got slated for splitting. It's at Holsan's, and they got that six-horse cart. It'll get here within the hour! We're gonna show 'em!"

Forkbeard whirled again. Hugh had sidled his mount beside Ilina's, and now they turned in concert to observe their guide. His garments flashed white in the sun and his voice boomed above the yammering of the throng. "Hear me, people of the Kram!" A silence fell. Forkbeard sucked in a breath. Ilina could practically see his thoughts roil as thickly as the column of smoke blackening the sky.

The people waited, shifting. Most looked to be farm laborers, their tunics and trousers faded and worn, their hands stained brown, their boots caked with mud. Bright colors flashed here and there amid the beige, and Ilina realized there were highborn women in the crowd as well, their fashionable skirts and scarves seeming out-of-place at such a dust-buffeted rally.

Her eyes passed over a scarlet hat, its brim slanted to one side as was the current vogue, and did a double-take. No woman that: the hat belonged to no less a luminary than Perash Hommel, the chief Broanoshi nephologist. His

196

A SEA SOUGHT IN SONG

long coat—where not soiled—was white, but his expression was dark. Three novices in pale blue surcoats stood strategically, safeguarding his precious pocket of elbow-room. Ilina wondered whether he had ordered them to stand thus, of if they did so out of habit, knowing how unpleasant he'd become if forced to make unnecessary contact with other human beings.

His presence confused her. It was not in his nature to associate with rioters. And what else could this be but a riot? It was midmorning and the gate of the busiest city in Kramarack had been shut. No children were present. Harl and Tam had gone for a ram. And a field of angry faces turned now upon Forkbeard, seeking validation.

Feather, still jittery, shied sideways. Ilina tightened her grip on the reins.

"This gate has never before been shut!" shouted Forkbeard abruptly.

The crowd exploded. Boots stamped, fists waved. Toward the back, men actually began throwing dust in the air. Ilina felt a cold sweat break out over her back. *No! That's the wrong thing to say! These people are two steps from violence. Calm the storm—don't make it worse!*

"And that means one thing!" the old man bellowed as he stood in his stirrups and swiveled his steed. "Only *one thing!*"

Ilina could feel the crowd suck in a collective breath, ready itself for bedlam. An anticipatory clamor began rolling up from the back, from the dust-throwers—the ones who'd dispatched Harl and Tam. Ilina looked frantically to Hugh, but the poor man hadn't a clue what was happening. How could he? But then she saw his hand drift back to the hilt of his sword where it protruded blackly from the bedroll strapped to his saddle, and she knew he was not oblivious. *Do something, old man! Stop this chaos! If you won't, Hugh will!*

And Forkbeard's voice boomed out, cutting through the din like a thunderclap through pounding surf. *"It means there must be a good reason for it!"*

Ilina would never forget that sound. It was the shocked sigh of a hundred stillborn shouts, their pent-up propulsion released without purpose. Several men stumbled forward a half-step, overbalanced. Forkbeard had knocked the wind from this mob before it had a chance to begin blowing.

Almost immediately there arose cries of dismay, of reprimand, of clarification. Forkbeard didn't know, didn't understand, couldn't sympathize. But it was all too little, too late: the brief window for action had closed. The focus had shifted back from *what* to *why*. Ilina let out a shuddering breath of her own. The old man had coaxed these people into his hands, then dropped them in the dust. By denying the mob the sanction it craved, he'd sprinkled enough doubt to forestall conflagration.

Turning from the shouts, Forkbeard waved Ilina and Hugh forward to the gate. People grudgingly made way, their glares split between the three travelers and that iron lattice which blocked their path a short distance into the stone-walled tunnel.

The tunnel.

Ilina's head jerked up and the coldness flowing from that dark maw struck her like a wave. She'd forgotten until this very moment that she would have to pass the tunnel. Her skin crawled at the wash of cool air. The noise of the crowd faded, supplanted by a soft whistle, a hollow exhalation, a thin rasp which seemed to go on much too long.

Ilina shied back, falling behind Hugh, and the crowd swelled around her once again, its garbled insistence drowning out the chill voice of silence. *Stupid girl—you're as bad as the horse. It's just a hole in the rock. The monster's long since dead.*

High above them arched the aperture—its peak surmounted by a triple-scale graven image of Harn Bright-Eyes in the classically deific pose: alone on the hilltop, sword held aloft, surrounded by a horde of Jaar cowering in the light of his countenance. Duty in the face of certain death. It was an inspiring notion. It appealed to Ilina's pride, her blind rage, her yearning for purpose at any price.

But what if death was uncertain? What if poetic despair and obstinate resistance resulted not in victory but in defeat? Harn's sacrifice had stemmed the Jaar tide, yes. But what if there'd been just a little less distance between his small band and the main Kramish host when he'd chosen to make his stand? What if reinforcements had been mere hours away? Had that been the case, would Harn now be remembered not as a hero, but as a vainglorious fool who needlessly expended the lives of his men? How could he have known whether another day's marching wouldn't have saved everyone? How could he have been certain that hope was lost?

Ilina shuddered as Harn's stony face—resolute and radiant—passed from sight above her. She imagined the real scene had been less idealistic.

The broad entrance funneled inward to dimensions meant to accommodate three wagons abreast. It was there a portcullis with bars as big around as her leg had fallen from slots in the ceiling. Rust peppered its joints and lay scattered in flakes upon the trampled sand, testament to the grate's long disuse and the inaccessible position it likely occupied when retracted.

A SEA SOUGHT IN SONG

Beyond the bars was only darkness. No guards were visible. But why should any bother to be here at all? Even in its state of obvious disrepair, the strength of this barrier was so far beyond the power of log-toting farmers to breach that Ilina wondered why Forkbeard had bothered with dissuasion. Then she thought of the Kramish penalties incurred for vandalism and realized he'd been protecting those men from themselves.

"Sentry," barked Forkbeard into the void, "show yourself!"

Almost instantly a figure materialized, stepping into the swath of light cast from outside. He was a big man—bigger even than Hugh—and the crest on his helm indicated a high rank, though Ilina forgot which one, exactly. The faint gleam of steel and bronze offset him from his backdrop with all the otherworldly drama of a god coming down from a gale in pre-Broanoshi iconography. But to shatter this illusion all he had to do was open his mouth.

"Damn you, you fork-faced prick!" he snarled. "Why'd you have to show up on my watch? Why couldn't some other poor bastard get saddled with your wrinkled ass? You expect special treatment, same as always? You want me to open this gate for you?"

"No," said Forkbeard in a voice soft yet hard, "I want you to open it for everyone. What madness is this? You have little time left before that mob erupts in violence. And when it does, men will die. Good men, law-abiding men who want nothing more than to get back to their homes and families and conduct business and go about their lives as they always have. Men to whom this closure has not been explained. And I am one of them."

"You sayin' you gonna die, old man? Anyone coulda told you that. I'm surprised to see you still alive. It's a wonder you can sit a horse without soiling yourself."

Forkbeard sighed. "Bold words for a man behind six inches of iron, Rholesh." Ilina noticed the thumb and little finger of his right-hand twiddling behind a fold of his cloak.

Rholesh stiffened, then relaxed. "I don't have time for this. You're welcome to wait on the doorstep with the rest of the rabble, Forktongue." He turned his back, retreated toward the blackness.

"I am the Lightkeeper," said Ilina.

The officer turned, startled, recognition sparking in his eyes.

"I am the Lightkeeper!" she repeated, turning her horse to address the crowd. Terror curled in her gut, but she didn't care. She looked out at the field of faces and felt suddenly distanced from this situation, as though a simulacrum of her body performed the actions of a play scripted long ago and far away.

"I am the Lightkeeper," she cried out a third time, marveling at the clear timbre of her own voice, "and I stand here this day because my watch has been completed. The High King has returned from beyond the circle of the world. He wields the Sword of Ascension. He bears the Name of Conrad. And he comes to us from his father Henred, who yet lives! This I Declare as the Keeper of the Light!"

"Get them inside!" screamed Rholesh, his words nearly inaudible over the thunder swelling deeper and higher as more and more of the assembly assimilated Ilina's speech. The Kram surged forward as one, pressing the travelers against the gate and spooking their horses, which reared in abject terror.

Ilina, still unaccountably calm as she clung to her saddle, saw the whole spectrum of human emotion reflected in those faces raised toward hers. Some beamed with joy unlooked-for, elation strong and piercing, a torrent in a desert. It tore through them like scorching liquor, breaching the dykes of fealty and decorum, rupturing eyes and mouths and hands unused to jubilance. Still others blanched with fear or burned with hate, reeling from a threat to their normality as appalling as any from which Ilina shrank. But whether ecstatic or enraged, every face shared a common trait: all eyes were fixed on her.

The gate groaned upward and the travelers spilled through. Gauntleted hands grabbed their reins. Armored bodies closed rank behind them, linking arms across the entrance as the portcullis crashed to. The few protestors who'd made it across the threshold were wrestled to the ground by sentries and carried off, struggling. Conflicting chants broke out across the crowd— shouts of "Up Henred, down Rikard!" competing with "Long live House Harn!" and "Let us in! Let us in!" Stones clacked against iron bars and glanced off plate armor as the guards hustled the travelers up a dark corridor echoing with strife.

"Gods damn it, woman," Rholesh roared, "what were you thinking? Do you know what you've done?"

"She appears to have gotten us inside," observed Forkbeard drily. His eyes sparkled in the light of lanterns hung at intervals from the walls, too dim to have been perceived from outside. On Ilina's right, Hugh aimed a kick at the gauntleted hand of a soldier holding his reins. The poor man jerked back, nursing his wrist, then contented himself to keep the reins within arm's reach.

"You shut your trap!" spat the officer. "You *are* inside now, so you're subject to martial law. Things are different today; things have changed. You're gonna tell me everything. You're gonna come *clean*, Forktongue! I

A SEA SOUGHT IN SONG

know you're the agitator here. I know that *this*," he flung a hand toward Ilina, "is all *your* doing. You and I are gonna have a nice *long* talk, Forktongue. And then you're gonna make a confession to that crowd!"

It might have been Ilina's imagination, but Forkbeard's jaw seemed to clench. His voice remained maddeningly level. "You and I can talk as long as you like, Rholesh. I recommend a nice tea shop on Wolrum Street for that sort of thing. First, however, I shall call upon Lord Rikard."

"Like hell you will. Corporal!" he bawled, turning. "Clap this man in irons!"

"Don't do this, Rholesh." Forkbeard's warning cut across the abrupt rattle of bridle and tack, the clink and scrape of armor as more men appeared on either side with drawn blades and poised shackles. Ilina heard her own whimper echo off walls dank and pitiless.

The old man's eyes flicked to the side, but not to meet hers. She felt a danger at her right hand like a habituated void perceived suddenly anew, and she shied away involuntarily. It was Hugh, his black sword already emerging. Forkbeard's fingers were circled, the nearby lanterns dimming. Ilina's heart caught in her throat. They were going to fight. In the belly of an impenetrable fortress, hemmed in by armed men.

They would all die here.

Time seemed to slow. Ilina watched the light reflect off the metal segments of Rholesh's knuckles as they curled around his hilt. His heavy shoulder shifted, slinging open his scarlet cloak. The length of steel sliding from his scabbard hissed like a snake. The outlines of men loomed up on all sides, white heraldic sigils springing from their surcoats into the lantern's wash.

But then they faded again. The glass-cased flames were shrinking as an old man—hoary, silver-cloaked—seemed to grow. In their very midst he grew, and in the reflected light of Forkbeard's unnatural sheen there rose a visage terrible to behold, a beardless face with flashing eyes, and as the tip of Hugh's black sword cleared the edge of his bedroll Ilina saw how tightly his fingers clenched the haft, how the tendons stood from his wrist like lute-strings, how the sliver of void that was the blade formed a perfect curve with his unfurling arm. He and the sword were already one. It was all happening too fast. She had to do something, anything.

Ilina plunged her heels into Feather's ribs. The horse, already on edge, bolted up the tunnel like water through a sluice, and in the rush and crash of howling oaths and flying bodies the imminence of time flooded back in upon Ilina's mind. Limbs and weapons flashed in the silver light projected from behind, but then suddenly the Kram broke and she was through, with only empty tunnel before her. Feather's hooves beat upon the flagstones—a deafening din that drowned the sounds of protest and pursuit alike.

But Ilina wasn't about to go far. The under-way was empty of oncoming traffic, and that could only mean that the upper gate was just as closed as the one through which they'd already passed. There would be no escape without cooperation from the city guard. Grabbing the left rein with both hands, Ilina hurled her weight back, nearly driving frantic Feather straight into the wall. The horse bucked and twisted and somehow managed to keep its footing. Ilina didn't slump forward until they'd slowed to a fitful walk. Shouts and clomping footfalls echoed from behind. She wheeled her mount to face them.

"If ceremony be waived," she cried, "I may be Lady of Harnaral by sundown! Think on that, Guard of the City! Think on that, Rholesh of the Guard! There may be little love lost between your lord and Councilor Mahru, but I am the apple of Rikard's eye, the love of his life. If he learns you barred my path and assaulted my person, he will kill you himself! But I am a woman of mercy. I will overlook your zeal if you turn, and turn *now!*"

The pursuing footfalls had slowed, were faltering. She was sure of it.

"Think, guardians of the city, soldiers of Kramarack!" she shouted, recalling a similar appeal she'd once delivered before the doors of Rikard's hall, and praying her words would today prove more fruitful. "Does your blood not quench the hills? Does it not mingle in the ground, binding you fast to lord and land? Are you not the keepers of the gate? Can aught loved by Lord Rikard Harnish come to him but through you? Does he not trust you with his heart? Do you not possess the keys to his very life, and he to yours? Is not your duty grave? Is not your burden great? Will you forsake it this day? Will you take it upon yourselves to determine which eyes he sees, what words he hears, whose hands he clasps? Will you in your zeal become lord over *him?* Let us pass, therefore, and in your equity serve him best!"

Shouts rang out and were answered from up-tunnel. Ilina spun. They were close now, on both sides. *You're overdoing it, 'Lina. No one cares about equity. Get back to fear, fear, fear.*

"If you kill me, Rikard will have you executed!" Her voice—thin now and transparently afraid, which obviated the point—leapt away along unreceptive stone. "If you detain me, Rikard himself will release me and I'll have you executed! There's no way out of this but to let me and my companions go!"

A hundred yards down the tunnel, the lanterns had gone dark. Ilina squinted and saw nothing. No backlight penetrated this deep from outside; a

A SEA SOUGHT IN SONG

gradual curve had hidden the lower gate from sight. She glanced over her shoulder and perceived an advancing wall of bodies, its thousand steel facets sparking in and out of the lantern-light like a swarm of fireflies.

"Rholesh!" she shrieked, paying no heed to the panic apparent in her voice. "Come to your senses! Let us pass and incur no recrimination!"

A scream, choked off, echoed from the darkness down-tunnel—it staggered past, incomplete, a headless body that wouldn't get far. Feather whinnied and shifted. Ilina whimpered, clutching at her reins and wishing for something sharp, something deadly, something *useful*.

In her mind she saw again sinuous limbs, strangely-jointed, and a mouth black and gaping. *Fool! All your hope and striving, all your breathless fear— where have they landed you? Back in the darkness beneath rotting hills. You shall die here in this hole, unloved and far from home. None shall mourn you, none shall weep at your crypt. Your line shall die, your Light go out, the King be left adrift. This is what becomes of those who think to flaunt their fate.*

"Stand where you are!"

The voice boomed in the enclosed space, slowing the sparkling wall. Ilina spun, and spun again. Into the down-tunnel light emerged a black blade held crosswise. Close behind it was the face of the man whose neck it pressed: Rholesh of the City Guard. His helm was gone, his left arm wrenched behind his back, his face a stony mask leaking only a trickle of rage and shame. Hugh's visage loomed behind his. It was dark, and frightening, and spattered with blood.

"Your commander has superseded his lawful authority, Guard of Harnaral!" The darkness beside Hugh gave way as Forkbeard stepped forth, and his silver cloak seemed to actually *flash* as he swirled it about himself dramatically. He, too, was now afoot. "Resume your posts," he said, "and we shall settle this matter before Court and Council."

The sparkling wall didn't budge. One man, however, did step forward, hand on sword-hilt. "Captain Hammosh, are you alright?"

Rholesh opened his mouth, but Hugh twitched the sword and the captain apparently reconsidered whatever he'd been about to say.

"Listen, all of you!" said Forkbeard. "Whatever your political allegiances, whatever your preferences in leadership, I at least am known to you. I am neither enemy nor usurper. In this present crisis, all the wisdom of the assembled Council will be necessary to—"

"Shut up!" snapped the man in front of the sparkling wall, slashing the air with a hand. "Captain Hammosh, what have you to say?"

The shoulder of Hugh's coat bulged as his grip on the sword intensified. Forkbeard glanced at Hugh, raising an eyebrow, and the sword inched away from Rholesh's throat.

Rholesh swallowed. "Let them pass," he croaked. "Secure the lower gate. It is unmanned."

Hugh and Forkbeard advanced, the latter leading their three remaining horses: two with empty saddles, the third burdened by supplies. Ilina, who had hardly dared to turn her head during the exchange, fell in between them as they passed.

The Kramish wall, two ranks deep, split to make way at a curt gesture from the man in front. A blood-red arm-ring pinched the mail-sleeve above his left bicep. His ornamented helm—fashioned like a tree with boughs aflame—turned to watch them as they filed past. His eye-slits were shadowed, but Ilina thought she caught the glint of light reflected from within.

And then they were through and the wall was closing behind them. Half the soldiers ran down the tunnel. The other half stared after the little company. The man with the red arm-ring again stepped through his men and watched until the curve of the tunnel shouldered him from view.

"Now," said Forkbeard, tossing a set of reins to Hugh, "we move. *Hugh, seh hat corunle.*"

Hugh shot Forkbeard an incredulous look and then, with visible effort, lowered the sword to his side. He spun Rholesh around, buried a fist in the man's gut, then stepped back and planted a boot in his face. The Kramish guard toppled to his back and sprawled unmoving on the stones.

"Quickly now, follow me!" Forkbeard was mounted already and prodding his steed into flight. "*Resh, resh!* We have little time!"

Hugh leapt into the saddle and waved Ilina ahead of him. They took off up the tunnel, their hoofbeats immeasurably multiplied, their guide a silver glimmer at the far edge of a seemingly endless curve.

Ilina forced herself to concentrate on their dilemma. The under-way was just under a quarter-mile in length; it let out in the center of Council Square, where the gables and porticos of power overlooked a broad plaza crowded with mongers' stalls and notice-boards. Ilina estimated they'd covered at least half that distance already.

In many ways, they were in a worse position now than when they'd been threatened with shackles. With a hostile force behind and a suspicious force ahead—for it would be an incompetent gate-guard indeed that didn't immediately detain unexpected travelers without confirmation that they'd cleared the previous checkpoint—they were caught between swiftly-shutting pincers. If they had allowed themselves to be arrested, they would've at least been given a fair hearing. But now, with the blood splashed across Hugh's face and arms and …

And then Ilina could no longer ignore the horror welling up from deep within. *Why is there blood? Did he kill those other men? There were at least five of them, maybe ten … Are they all dead now? Could the old man have killed them? But how? He has no weapon but the light. Light can't draw blood, can it? And why is Hugh so angry? Back there, he looked like he wanted to kill Rholesh. But that's not … that's not like him, is it? That's not like him at all. I must have been mistaken.*

Twin flecks of obsidian glinted then in Ilina's memory: Jarlin's eyes reflecting lamplight as he delivered a warning she should've heeded. *'Fourteen of my brothers lie in ice because they opposed the will of that man. Make not their mistake. He knows not the meaning of mercy.'* Ilina shuddered.

Well, it was too late to change tack now, that much was certain. She had made her choice and announced her Declaration. What remained to be seen was whether she could live with it. *Harlith send me a clear wind. Dispel the clouds of night.*

So distracted was Ilina by her thoughts that she didn't realize Forkbeard had stopped until she and Hugh had caught up with him. She looked up sharply: why was he just standing there? Had he been injured? But no—he held up a hand to them and then gestured Hugh forward, speaking quickly in the Tongue of Secrets. Hugh raised an eyebrow, then faced the wall beside the old man, glancing over as if to calculate distance, shifting a bit farther to the side. Forkbeard spoke three syllables in a measured cadence, and then, in the breathless space unoccupied by a fourth, both men slammed their shoulders into the stone wall.

There was a muffled squeal, and a black seam appeared directly between them—a six-foot-high gap between center-hung, pivot-hinged slabs opening outward. Ilina glanced down the tunnel. Could the soldiers still hear them? Perhaps not—after all, the mob outside was no longer audible. She dismounted.

A repetition of the syllables—*"En, esh, elf!"*—and another shoulder-jarring crunch widened the gap. Ilina couldn't tell whether Forkbeard was counting up to three or down to one, but it was now clear that *esh* meant *two*. Some communicative techniques transcended language.

AUSTIN GUNDERSON

A third blow opened the passage fully. There was neither a cold breeze nor a disquieting odor—nothing but quiet darkness and old dread.

Hugh and Forkbeard slipped saddlebags off their steeds and slung them over their shoulders, slapping the horses' flanks to send them clattering up the under-way. Ilina tore her eyes from the hole in the wall just in time to see Feather vanish beyond the up-tunnel curve. Hugh was holding out her pack. Forkbeard was stepping through the aperture. Hugh was gesturing her ahead of him, his sword now cinched to his knapsack, his eyes squinting with confusion or concern.

And Ilina was shaking.

And so it was that Ilina Lightkeeper entered a second time into the warrens of Harn Hill. She did not resist the bloodstained hands gently ushering her through the hidden door, but neither did she go willingly. Like so many prior episodes of her life, this moment passed her by—or rather she passed it by, inspecting it impassively as though it lay spread behind glass in a naturalist's shop. She knew in her mind that she should feel something. Terror, or anger, or despair. The darkness swallowed as her companions manhandled the door shut behind them, and Ilina was left momentarily alone with nothing at all before her feet. Instead of straining in vain against the terror of the black, she turned her eyes inward. Upon her numbness.

She inspected it, and was disquieted by her lack of disquiet. Even mild annoyance would've counted toward normality, she knew. How was she even capable of dislocating herself like this? Shouldn't she instead be consumed by emotion? Isn't that what happened to normal people? To people like Hugh? Shouldn't she be able to *feel* things without *thinking* about feeling them? Like a butterfly posed in death she was, splayed for inspection yet vacant inside.

A cool light flashed from behind, and Ilina came suddenly face-to-face with her own shadow, projected upon a wall of rough-hewn rock only a few feet away. It was there that the cramped passage they'd entered veered left to run parallel to the under-way. The fact that only moments ago she'd been lamenting her insensitivity to a void now exposed as nonexistent was not lost on her self-inspecting mind.

And then Hugh's hand found her shoulder again, and she was moving and disturbing the silence of this passage that didn't belong, shouldn't exist. Forkbeard, glowing orb in hand, brushed past to take the lead.

A SEA SOUGHT IN SONG

"Stop."

Unsure whether she'd spoken this quiet imperative aloud, Ilina repeated herself more forcefully. Forkbeard complied and turned.

And Ilina struck the orb from his fingers.

"What is this place?" she hissed, jabbing a finger into his chest and backing him against the wall as the orb bounced away and shadows flew everywhere. "How do you know of it? And how *much* of it do you know?"

Forkbeard's palms came up, but Ilina slapped them away and stepped inside his reach. His hands fell on her shoulders, and for an instant anyone watching might've assumed the two to be father and daughter—he reaching out to calm her fit of passion, she gazing up to draw solace from his self-possession.

Ilina flinched at the thought of her own father, and at the realization that she was still observing herself from without. The stilled shadows suddenly shifted and her eyes flicked sideways. Hugh had picked up the orb and was turning it in his fingers. If he was alarmed by the altercation, he didn't show it. *Useless man.*

Forkbeard made to step away from the wall and Ilina shoved back with all her might. "I will not take another step without answers," she said between clenched teeth. "What is happening here?"

"Ilina," said the old man patiently, "why not question me without all this physicality? I will be likelier to answer. And besides, brawn is Hugh's department."

Galled by this flippancy, Ilina smacked a fist upon his chest. Her fingers tangled in the hair cascading over his robe. "Do not evade me, Forkbeard! Why are we hiding in an illegal tunnel?"

There was a pause. In the orb's harsh light, Ilina saw the old man's eyes grow dark. "Step back, Lightkeeper." The command, delivered in a bass rumble, passed straight through her body like a tremor through solid rock. She obeyed instantly and then stood perfectly still, flustered and confused. She was inside her own head again and couldn't get out. She didn't know what to think about what had just occurred. She hadn't watched it from afar.

Forkbeard smoothed his robes and combed fingers through his beard. The light leapt from his eyes once more as though nothing had happened. His voice was again warm and patient, and Ilina felt like a fool. She had tried to intimidate Forkbeard. *Forkbeard.* She glanced at Hugh, who was now prodding the orb as though he thought he might trip a power switch like the one on his own magic lamp. He seemed oblivious to the unfolding exchange.

Ilina shook her head. *Brawn is Hugh's department.* If she wished to coerce a wizard, she'd have to conjure at least enough of a credible threat to make someone like Hugh take notice. She felt her cheeks warming and couldn't remember why she'd wanted to regain a sense of emotional immanence. It certainly wasn't *useful*.

Hugh reluctantly plunked the orb into Forkbeard's proffered palm. The old man turned back to Ilina. "Now then. To which of my actions do you object?"

Ilina gaped. "To which do I object? How should I know? I don't even understand what's *happening!*"

"Then ask me a question." Forkbeard slouched back against the wall of the tunnel. An image of Rikard Harnish—propped against a pillar, red cloak swirling in air so crisp it hurt to breathe—leapt into Ilina's mind. He, too, had been prevaricating. Was affected nonchalance a male defensive mechanism?

"Why has the gate been closed?" asked Ilina.

"I do not know."

"Why did the guards try to arrest us?"

"Neither do I know that, though it is a safe bet to assume your impromptu Declaration of Return only exacerbated whatever tensions predated our arrival."

"Fine." Either the old man was being obstinate or he really didn't have any special insight. Was the mystical shtick just a big act? "Did you and Hugh give them *reason* to arrest us? Did you kill anyone back there?"

"We killed *everyone* back there. Whether that will work against us depends on what is happening in Harnaral. If Rikard Harnish has imposed martial law, then he cannot be trusted and we would have had to escape in any event. If, however, this is merely an attempted coup, then our actions will be hailed as valiant when the government puts down the insurrection."

Ilina focused on controlling her breathing, on concealing her shock. She glanced at Hugh, at the bloodstains on his hands, *such gentle hands ...*

"Before we make any decisions," Forkbeard went on, "we must determine the nature of this situation, and to do that we must enter the city. As there is no enemy without, I suspect the under-way has been shut for the express purpose of preventing the flow of information. So we will bypass it."

Still reeling from the revelation of Hugh's violence, Ilina struggled to catch up. "What, in this?" She waved her hand at the walls as Forkbeard's meaning sank in. "You mean this tunnel connects to street level? You mean there's more than one exit from the under-way? This tunnel shouldn't even exist! How do you know of it?" Her voice rose as her thoughts tumbled out freely. "And why *don't* the guards know? Did you dig it out? Is it *your* secret passage? Your personal entrance to the most secure fortress north of the Gnofs? Who gave *you* leave to poke holes in its defense? What were you planning to *do* with this breach? Was it *you* who—"

Ilina stopped, suddenly all too aware of her surroundings. Forkbeard had raised an eyebrow, his expression frighteningly fixed. Ilina glanced at Hugh, who at least seemed to be paying attention this time. Could she trust him to back her up? A mere three days ago that wouldn't have been a question, but who knew what it was that he and Forkbeard had discussed during all those long hours of riding? Who knew where Hugh's loyalties now lay? If she opposed the old man, would she find herself opposing Hugh as well? She didn't think she could handle that.

Forkbeard spoke into her silence. "Was it I who did what?"

Ilina, suddenly terrified, said nothing. *Don't say nothing! Think of something! Make something up! He can't know what you suspect!*

Forkbeard sighed heavily. "You think I called the spiderworm, don't you?"

Ilina froze, eyes wide as cormorant eggs. She dared not even breathe. Behind her eyes, she cursed the caprice of fate that had determined her sex, had made her small and powerless and stuck her in an enclosed space with two men who could break her on a whim. *It was Orlom's will*, she recited without confidence. *It was Orlom's will that you be a woman. It was his will that placed you here.*

Forkbeard looked down, and for an instant Ilina was certain of his guilt. Then he raised his head and she saw how the light swam within the caverns of his eyes. He blinked, and tears ran down his beard. His mouth worked noiselessly. "No," he finally whispered, seeming loath to speak above his breath. "Be not afraid, Lady Lightkeeper. I did not kill the Lord of Kramarack, nor order him killed, nor collude in his death. But beginning that terrible night, I undertook the work of retracing the spiderworm's path. The tunnels beneath Harn Hill are a vast maze. No more than thirty percent of them had been mapped, and half those maps were naught but cellar plans locked up in pantries by scatterbrained housewives. It took me a month before I found the hole by the riverbank through which the creature crawled. It took me two before I found this place."

Ilina swallowed. That was plausible. "Does Rikard know?" she asked.

Forkbeard looked her square in the eyes. "No. Believe it or not, Ilina, I foresaw this eventuality. Harnaral has been restless ever since Hansel's death, and it was only a matter of time before the tinder went up and someone of import needed to pass to or fro in secret. And as it so happened, that person is you. Do you regret my decision?"

Ilina felt suddenly cold. She hugged herself and shook her head.

"Alright. Now if we can refrain from accusing each other of assassination, I would like to visit Rikard Harnish and hear from *his* lips what has happened to this city. Are you with me?"

Ilina nodded. Forkbeard smiled. *With relief,* she thought, and shivered.

Hugh touched her shoulder and she jumped. But he just sighed, shook out his bedroll, and draped it over her shoulders. Then he stepped back, hitched up his pack and sword, and waited for her to follow the old man, who was plodding up the tunnel, taking the light with him.

And all of a sudden Ilina felt suffused by a warmth she had nearly forgotten—the sweet assurance of friendship, the calm confidence of support. The world adopted a brighter hue. Hugh's immense strength, no longer a threat, felt now like a shield at her right hand, his grin a guarantee of guardianship. Forkbeard's cunning, put in perspective, left her grateful their interests had aligned. Though his tactics might differ from hers, he was no fool. Were it not for his quick thinking, they might all be dead by now. She looked up at his receding silhouette and was glad. *Yes, glad.*

It was time to close the distance.

Chapter Fourteen
BRITTLE GRANDEUR

The passage stretched on and on in gentle incline. Ilina presumed they were still running parallel to the under-way, though no sound penetrated the intervening stone. The world had narrowed to a pool of bluish light cropped laterally by walls closer than her spread arms, petering out into darkness before and behind. Forkbeard walked in front, his strides strong and even, his cloak swishing against the rough-hewn rock. Hugh brought up the rear with silent steps, a hulking presence lent shape by the light's trailing edge.

Silent. Hulking. Ilina cringed. Were those really the words that described Hugh best? Had those really become his chief characteristics in her mind? She wished she could do better; it was her duty to do better. This was the man whom she'd just Declared before a public assembly.

If the three of them managed to get out of this situation alive, she would become answerable for her decisions. Those who wouldn't previously have spared her two nods would suddenly discover a compelling stake in her affairs. Even those who thought of her as a religious fraud—a discredited holdover from a bygone era, last of a line of cult leaders whose state sponsorship brought disgrace upon the Kram—would demand that she provide them with an explanation.

The reputation of the Lightkeepers might have dwindled over the years, but their influence remained as real as their responsibility. Ilina had to remind herself how much she meant to the masses. It was human nature to ignore authorities right up until the moment they did something with which one disagreed. Perceived perfection went hand-in-hand with peripherality. Only in the midst of scandal did the people's political preferences become apparent.

Ilina glared at the heels of Forkbeard's boots. The reaction of the city guard had confirmed her worst suspicions. Nothing about this job would be easy. To finally graduate from a lifetime of obscurity only to be thrust into controversy just for doing her duty was galling, to say the least. How dare the same people who'd marginalized her react to her Declaration with indignation, as though her judgements carried weight! Either her office was legitimate and her judgements worthy of trust, or she was merely a poser without any real power. Her detractors shouldn't get to have it both ways. *If you want to ignore me, ignore me! If you want to condemn me, first acknowledge my authority!*

Ilina grimaced. It was no use bemoaning human nature. What this all came down to was the fact that she should, by all accounts, be the world's foremost authority on the nature and attributes of one Hugh Conrad, and that thus far she'd proven utterly inadequate in that regard. If only she could speak his language like Forkbeard did! It was unfair to think of Hugh as silent when his every utterance was gibberish to her ears. How different he might seem if only he could describe himself in his own words. Ink on paper was simply too awkward to facilitate genuine communication, especially amid the impositions of the open road or constricted tunnel.

The time by which Ilina had assumed they would emerge aboveground had long passed when their path at last diverged from the linear. A hairpin turn to the right confronted them with a flight of high, narrow steps running up and away into the rock. After a brief and wordless pause, they began their ascent. The going was slow, due mainly to Ilina's difficulty in lifting her legs so high. It seemed strange to her that she, a huntress of seabird eggs, should be rendered so inept by verticality, but this stair was unlike the precipice of Horwell Face that proffered as many handholds as footholds, and her agility was stymied.

The stair went on and on. Ilina's face warmed from exertion and embarrassment as she clambered ungracefully from ledge to ledge. Never had she felt more like a little girl beside these towering men. And yet the more she struggled, the more she felt Hugh's calm support. He propped her up when she teetered, pushed her when she slowed, lifted her when she slumped gasping against the wall. His hands were gentle, his patient silence more eloquent than words. *Perhaps*, she thought as he waited once more for her to catch her breath, *he is capable of more communication than I thought.*

Careful, 'Lina, she chided herself. *He's a man. Don't mistake his mask for what it's meant to mimic.*

The stairway ended in a cramped room with a domed ceiling and an egress in each wall. To the right and left, arched doorways formed holes where light went to die; directly ahead, rubble choked the fourth outlet. It was for this that Forkbeard headed. The blue cast of his orb dusted runes graven overhead in concentric patterns. *A temple,* Ilina thought, but she could find little of Broanosh in its aesthetic. *This must be the city's first level.*

Forkbeard climbed halfway up the pile of stones and thrust his light into a crevice Ilina had failed to notice. The room fell into blackness.

A SEA SOUGHT IN SONG

"What will you do, Forkbeard?" asked Ilina. "What will you say if ever we reach Rikard?"

Forkbeard snorted as he dropped into the crevice. "What makes you think I will do the talking?"

Ilina gaped. The old man vanished, taking the light with him. *What does he expect of me? To justify his violence? To pacify the mob? Does he think my relationship with Rikard grants me such power?* She stood, alone and silent in the dark, and panicked.

Forkbeard reappeared. His face hardened when he saw the look on hers. "What, did you expect me to explain your Declaration *for* you? It is you who has dropped the larger stone, Lightkeeper. That mob before the gate may have been riled before our arrival, but they are well and truly frothing now. My part in the coming unrest is small by comparison to yours. This country has been primed for this hour for seven hundred years. Think on that! Your family eats and drinks and breathes the prophecies, but the common man is not so acclimated. He hears your annunciation of a foreign ruler and feels only well-founded terror. He prefers a predictable world.

"I will support you in your proclamation. I will stand beside you in defense of this man who has no conception of the chaos his coming will induce. But I will not," and here he leaned out over the lip of stone, "I will *not* do your work for you. People resent my influence enough as it is. And you are strong enough to pull this off."

With that he dropped out of sight again, leaving Ilina and Hugh to grope their way after his orb's dimming beam.

The passage into which they now squirmed was not, as Ilina had initially thought, a proper tunnel with an entrance blocked by cave-in. It was instead a string of crosscut fissures, braided like a length of rope. Ilina imagined a massive hawser strung through solid rock, then left to rot away. The effect was surprisingly consistent. The company scrambled along the precarious floor of an overhand-slanted hollow, then lowered themselves through some collapsed partition of stone into an inversely-curved space, only to clamber up a mound of talus and repeat the process. It was exhausting work, but came more naturally to Ilina than climbing a stair carved for giants.

Smaller passages branched away periodically, but Forkbeard kept them moving in as straight a line as this spiraling netherworld would allow. Grit lodged under Ilina's fingernails, sweat chilled her at every pause, and her already-tattered outfit was further flayed by the tunnel's unyielding edges.

The state of her garments reflected that of her soul. Ilina felt torn, inside and out. One moment Forkbeard was badgering her to change her mind, the next he was leaving her to her own initiative. Why? Was he just trying to assuage her doubts about his allegiance? She'd managed to avoid blurting her fear of treachery, but she knew that he knew she had entertained such a thought. How futile it was to hide from those golden eyes!

Well, even if his motive was mere self-preservation, what did it matter? Was it not a good thing that he was willing to step aside and let her lead? Two days ago she would've been grateful for such latitude, whatever its cause; now she merely trembled. Who was she to direct events? Her well-knit plans were all unraveling. Less than an hour ago, men had died because of what she'd said. Because of her Declaration.

How often she'd rehearsed that moment in her mind as a girl growing up in the cloister of Cuspid Isle! And how different had been her imagining from what had just transpired!

The numbness of shock was wearing off. It struck her then: the full weight of it. She had made her Declaration. What she had said before the under-gate ... that had been *it*. It was done now, and in the past. Like a falling star that flashed and vanished, it was a moment that would never come again. From this point on her role was to reiterate what had previously been said. All her preparation, all her longsuffering expectancy—and all that of her forebears, she thought with a soft moan—what had come of it?

Not much, in the end.

She tried to relive the event in her mind and couldn't help cringing from shame. Not in a lifetime of anticipation had she thought to deliver her Declaration in a dust-choked thoroughfare before a rabble of irate peasants who weren't even expecting her to open her mouth. Their mixed reaction had been commensurate with her delivery. The Declaration of the Return of Arlam's High King was meant to be trumpeted from the highest portico of the grandest citadel in the land, not shouted from horseback in a spontaneous attempt to quell civil unrest.

"Oh gods!" Ilina whimpered, eliciting a glance from Forkbeard. He was negotiating the boulders of an interminable incline, head bent to avoid the ceiling's low slant. Ilina reached up to brush the stone a good half-foot above her head. *Finally, I have an advantage in this terrain,* she thought with a weak grin. It soured swiftly. *But what advantage have I in leadership? None that others don't already possess in spades. Why should anyone stand behind*

A SEA SOUGHT IN SONG

me? *I can't predict the future. I'm not even confident in my ability to recall the past week!*

The horror of Hugh's irrefutable claim reared up suddenly in her mind—the blink of an image she didn't remember and would never forget, a nightmare of tumbled blocks and dust-laced air, the final wreckage of the only home she'd ever known. She would not believe it. *Could* not believe it. And as she strove to maintain control of her expression, the futility of her ambitions pressed in upon her like the surrounding ocean of stone. She was small, inept, unequal to the task at hand. Better for her to step aside. Better for everyone if her betters steered the agenda.

No, said a quiet corner of her mind. *It's not about me; it's about Hugh, about ensuring his ascension. You cannot delegate this duty. The survival of Arlam depends on his reception.* And with that she lifted her head, exploiting her stature, and took yet another step.

They were not, as Ilina had briefly suspected, heading for the Great Hall of Harn. It turned out that that particular exit from the underground and two others in its vicinity had been stoppered by teams of masons working day and night in the week following the spiderworm attack. While a moment's reflection on Ilina's part brought relief that Rikard was no longer in danger of assassination from below, the defensive measures he'd taken would force the travelers out onto street level nearly two blocks away from the government buildings abutting the central square.

Fortunately, they wouldn't have to enter the square itself. But Forkbeard's plan as he intimated it depended primarily on speed and stealth, neither of which Ilina possessed in abundance. They had to assume that word of their escape had reached the city by now, and that a manhunt was underway.

Ilina's stomach knotted as she climbed through a tumbledown aperture in a half-buried wall. They had nearly reached the end of this strange detour. Across the low-ceilinged cave there was another wall, this one with a properly latched door set into stone blocks. But the latch was rusted and hanging askew. The door squealed as Forkbeard shouldered it ajar. In the smaller room beyond, crates were piled beneath a snowfall of dust. In the corner, a ladder dangled from a trapdoor in the wood-planked ceiling. No light seeped through the chinks.

AUSTIN GUNDERSON

They could be in anyone's cellar, Ilina realized. The blue light of the orb seemed almost natural now, but the swift-shifting shadows it threw leant this milieu an apprehensive cast. All it would take would be a flick of Forkbeard's wrist—or whatever it was he did to snuff that glowstone—and the void now held at bay would come rushing back in.

Forkbeard bent his back and shoved aside one of the crates, clearing floorspace marked by a skid of dirty stone and skittering insects. Hugh, oblivious in his big boots, crunched forward. Ilina edged gingerly to the side. Small shadows were still vanishing into dark corners as Forkbeard bent down and began drawing lines in the dirt.

"This is Moraine Avenue," he said, pointing to a line. He moved his finger over a second line intersecting it. "And this is Wolrum Street. This," he said, sweeping a hand over a curving hypotenuse, "is the retaining wall that wraps behind the government district. This is the Hall of Harn," he said, drawing a rectangle before waving his finger over the space between it and the roads' right angle. "This is the central square. Here," he said, pointing to a dot in the middle of the square, "is the upper gate."

For a moment his finger hovered over that fortified egress—once the only known exit from the under-way, now a location as inaccessible as the farther moon—and then swung slowly down, down, down—past the Great Hall, past the government district, over the rooftops and alleyways of Harnaral—to come to rest just below the retaining wall. "And this is us," he said.

All three stared at the space between them and Rikard Harnish. To call it a gap of two city blocks was akin to saying the Gnof Range was only two hundred leagues across: straight-line distance was the least of a traveler's concerns.

"Now," said Forkbeard, "here is what we are going to do."

###

Hugh was relieved at the plan's blessed simplicity. No need to comprehend the delicate sociopolitical situation, buckle down for negotiation or petition, demonstrate circumspection or restraint—this was your basic, run-of-the-mill, slight-of-hand smash-and-grab. Forkbeard had to explain it twice over for Ilina, but only once for Hugh.

Hugh *liked* this plan. He was beginning to like Forkbeard, too—perhaps too much. He'd already begun to wonder whether he should let the old man

A SEA SOUGHT IN SONG

in on the real agenda, here. *That can't be a good sign. Gotta get a grip.* Needless trust always resulted in unintended consequences.

The trapdoor groaned as it rose. Dust rained down on Hugh as he threw his back into the motion, bracing his legs against the rickety ladder. Something was blocking him, stifling him, opposing his rise. The room beyond was still dark to his eyes. *Weird.* Hugh gritted his teeth and flipped the door the rest of the way open. Something gritty slid onto his face and he threw his arms up over his head, nearly toppling off the ladder. He fell forward, catching the edge of the floor with his elbows, before realizing his opponent was merely a woven rug. *Great start, genius.*

He flung the rug off his face to confront an empty room. Dim light from an imperfect doorframe dusted racks of iron implements with a colorless sheen. *Fortune must favor the stupid today. Good thing* you *showed up.*

He clamored out, knelt by the trapdoor, and extended a hand. A breath passed, and then Ilina's thin arm shot up out of blackness. Her hand clasped his. Up she came—dirty as a sergeant's mouth, light as a sigh of relief. As soon as her feet met the floor, she made a beeline for the doorway. Forkbeard came next, but Hugh didn't offer him a hand.

The next room held a staircase. At its head stood a door left ajar, from which streamed light blinding even in its dimness. Forkbeard snuffed his orb—Hugh's belated double-take failed to catch the old man's means of doing so—set his saddlebag down, and mounted the stair. Shrugging off his own pack, Hugh slid his sword out of its leather loop and over his shoulder. He hefted it in front of him, pleased with its weight and balance, and followed Forkbeard. The stone steps allowed for a noiseless approach.

Voices came from beyond the door—the murmurs and laughter of men unaware. A sharp clank was chased by a staccato outburst of what Hugh could only assume to be improper language. He glanced back at Ilina and saw her shrink reflexively against the wall. *Yeah, Sister Seemly—those ain't nice men, are they? You'd better be glad I brought this big knife.*

Forkbeard again produced his orb, holding it at arm's length and edging it just past the doorjamb. Hugh grinned to see the room beyond reproduced in convex miniature on the glassy sphere. *Ha! The thing must be some kind of prism, or maybe there are reflex mirrors inside, or …*

But the focus of Hugh's attention alighted only briefly on technological novelty before shifting to tactical threat appraisal. He considered the five men who, armed to the teeth, were ransacking the premises.

Two versus five was no cakewalk, not even with the element of surprise on their side. They would have to divvy up this assault. Hugh pointed at himself, then at the three men on the left, and then at Forkbeard and the remaining two, who stood toward the farther door. Hugh had no idea how the wizard was able to fell opponents with beams of light from his hands, but who was he to question a proven asset? There would be time for debriefings later. Right now, they needed to reach this Rikard fellow.

Forkbeard stowed his orb and leaned past Hugh to whisper something to Ilina, who looked like a woman trying desperately to hide her fear. She was to stay here while they cleared the room. The work wouldn't be pretty—they had to be quick and, above all, prevent anyone from getting behind them or hemming them in. If that happened, or if anyone managed to grab the girl … well, Hugh didn't know what he'd do. But there was no chance for a better plan.

Forkbeard turned again to face the door and Hugh raised three fingers. Then two. Then one.

And as one they burst into the light.

So focused was Hugh on the man before him that the first thing he did upon clearing the door was to crack his shin on an iron pulley-block projecting beyond a low shelf. He grunted and staggered forward, dropping his sword, bending at the waist, and it was this more than anything that saved his life. His opponent's blade clove dust-choked air that only an instant before had been occupied by Hugh's head. Hugh cursed and committed to his motion—straight through a pile of metal wheels and into the other man's legs.

They both went sprawling, but then Hugh was up first and his hands found the iron block on the shelf and he swung it up and around and into the other man's head as he rose. The impact jarred Hugh's arms. And then there was nothing for it but to scrabble around after his fallen sword in the strobing light emitted by Forkbeard from behind. The others would be on top of him in seconds. A shriek from Ilina sliced through their shouts.

"Ut! Oam tel! Yisleh oam lishet fimmil ut mel yir!"

Dammit, woman! Didn't the old man tell you to stay back? At least her outburst seemed to have stalled their opponents. The man who staggered to his feet in front of Hugh paused, looking up and lowering his blade in the same instant that Hugh's fingers closed around the hilt of his own sword.

Hugh rose, flinging an iron wheel into the other man's face and sweeping black steel at him from the side. The blade bit into the man's mail surcoat and lodged there, and then Hugh was driving forward, feet flying through fallen implements, forcing the soldier back, back and down, down into the floor. Hugh wrenched the sword out and raised it again.

A SEA SOUGHT IN SONG

And then a bolt of pain smacked into his head and he hit the floor himself, hard. The room spun. His ears rang. *What just happened?*

He looked up just in time for his reflexes to interpose his sword between his head and the blade that would've split it. The new soldier rained down blows and Hugh abandoned instinct in order to roll straight into his legs, felling him, bringing the two of them face-to-face. Hugh heard more than felt a squish as an elbow landed in his eye.

He made a grab for the other man's sword while trying to hang onto his own and ended up with control of neither. The man was driving his right fist into Hugh's side, pummeling him without pause. So Hugh took the man's left index finger and snapped it back at the knuckle. The crack was audible. And, in that brief window of ungovernable pain, Hugh broke the soldier's hold, threw him off, and rose to snatch his sword.

And then arms were grabbing him, holding him back. Two, then four. Arms from behind, entangling him like the tendrils of some thicket. He roared and surged forward, then felt a numbness spread over his back, his shoulders. Sluggishness crept up like a cold sweat.

Hugh's eyes seemed to clear, and he saw that his opponent was likewise restrained by his comrades. Hugh glared forward, breathing heavily, but then relaxed and lowered his head. Ilina and Forkbeard held on for a moment longer, gripping his arms as though he dangled from a cliff, then hesitantly let go. Forkbeard's left hand lifted from Hugh's back. The numbness dissipated.

Hugh's opponent was cradling his left hand and spitting venom with his eyes. *Yeah, well, better luck next time, pal.* Hugh turned to Forkbeard. "Alright Grandpa, just what the hell is going on?"

"These men are loyal to Rikard," he said. "There has been a coup attempt, apparently."

One of the soldiers, a shorter man with a silver-streaked beard, stepped in front of Broken Finger to rattle off some words that ran together and sounded hostile.

"Kelah here says that Rikard is in danger," translated Forkbeard. "He says that this team has been tasked with getting him out of the city. He claims that we have impeded their mission and imperiled the sovereignty of Kramarack. He also addresses you, specifically, in language I am loath to repeat. It involves your sword and a certain orifice."

Hugh chuckled. "A sign of respect, compadre—that's all that is. So, they're trying to sneak Rikard out the back way, is that it?"

"Yes." Forkbeard frowned.

"Didn't know he knew about this tunnel, did you?" asked Hugh cheerily.

"No." The frown deepened.

Hugh paused for effect, glancing at each of the others in turn. They were all looking to him, he realized—the Kramish soldiers with fear, Ilina with concern, Forkbeard with curiosity. For some reason he couldn't identify, he was now in a position of influence. Perhaps it'd been the fight. That'd certainly invigorated *him*: he felt emboldened, energized even after the wizard's numbing touch.

He'd have to have a talk with Forkbeard about that later, he reminded himself, and let him know exactly what would happen if the old man ever again used magic on him without permission. Hugh would've been worried about whether he was still under some kind of spell, but the sensation was already gone, and events weren't allowing him time to obsess over it.

"Well, what're we waiting for?" asked Hugh. "I'm tired of running and hiding. Let's go find Rikard and turn him around."

"He says he wants to stay and fight," translated Forkbeard with a gleam in his eye. He rounded on the soldiers, challenging them to suggest otherwise, demanding their assistance, but Ilina was no longer paying him any heed.

Instead she was gazing at Hugh, drinking in the sight of him, committing this moment to memory. This moment when he first accepted responsibility, assumed command, and justified her Declaration.

It's real. He's real. This was really happening, and not just inside her head. Her hope was becoming flesh.

That Hugh's ear had been bent by a warmonger seemed suddenly trivial. That he didn't comprehend the stakes no longer mattered. Ilina's trepidation fell away. Everything would now change, and she didn't have to be afraid. Hugh himself appeared unaware—as though, to him, destiny was no more than instinct. And that was as it should be.

The soldiers were arguing, of course. Their protestations pressed in upon Ilina's reverie. They had a job to do, a duty to uphold, and neither rabble nor royalty newly arrived had any standing to give orders. *Royalty.* Ilina hid a smile. Their spokesman had actually used the word.

"Peace," she said, raising a palm.

"We don't answer to you, Lightkeeper," growled Kelah. His eyes were locked with those of Forkbeard.

A SEA SOUGHT IN SONG

"No," she said, "you answer to Rikard Harnish, Highlord of Kramarack. Or used to. For one greater than Rikard is here."

He spun on her, then stopped. His eyes flared.

"Yes, soldier," she said, unable to contain her grin any longer. "Our High King has returned."

The sun in their eyes was thickly orange, tinged by swirling smoke. It was hard to tell as they jogged whether the fire at the city's heart had yet gone out. Their guides rounded an alleyway's entrance and the company plunged into shadow. A cluster of men blocked their path and Hugh dodged, reaching back to grab Ilina's arm and yank her aside. Her careless grin unnerved him. Shouts fell behind them as they pelted through the gloom and burst back into brightness.

Chaos was everywhere. Some streets had been deserted, others appropriated as outposts of unrest. Flakes of ash wafted through lateral shafts of light. Smoke stung their eyes. Ahead, a crowd congealed. The company knifed in, elbowing their way viciously through the throng. People cursed and shoved back, and Hugh tried to shield Ilina with his body. Now that she'd finally relaxed, he was getting anxious. The longer they stayed out in the open like this, the more likely they were to get cornered and crushed by whatever forces were taking control.

"How far?" he shouted ahead at Forkbeard.

The old man didn't answer. Hugh and Ilina broke through the crowd to find him facing a squad of soldiers across a swiftly-emptying space. Red bands encircled their upper arms—an insignia so distinct that even Hugh could identify it. Kelah and his four fellows stood shoulder-to-shoulder, blades drawn. Hugh saw Broken Finger holding his sword awkwardly in his left hand and felt a twinge of guilt, which was then swept away by a flood of tactical appraisals.

That he'd thrown the girl behind him without conscious thought wasn't a surprise, but, upon reflection, the stance into which he'd fallen made little sense. Why was his sword up beside his ear? Shouldn't it be held out in front of him? Hugh shook his head, suddenly distracted, unsure.

The rebels charged.

Hugh saw red. His sword whirled into a black arc. His body moved of its own accord, trailing the blade. A tap on Broken Finger's shoulder, a sliding sidestep, a forward lunge, a spin, and Hugh went clean through both lines of battle like a wind through a copse. He was hacking now, and slicing, and sweeping—not wildly but artfully, and he laughed as red blood spiraled through golden air. This was a dance whose steps he knew. His sword was a scythe in his hand, and this harvest white for reaping. His soul rejoiced that the labor fell to him.

Hugh stood panting in the street. Blood was pooling between the cobblestones under his feet. Armored bodies sprawled about him.

He looked up—panicked, confused.

Six men and one woman stood in a row ten paces away. They gaped at him. He squinted, identifying each in turn. Yes, those were his companions. Ilina, and Forkbeard, and Broken Finger and the rest. But why were their mouths hanging open? What had happened?

"What's wrong?" he asked.

Forkbeard shook his head as if waking from sleep. "Nothing. I did not know you were that good with a sword, is all."

Hugh glanced from Ilina's white face to the bodies by his feet. There were eight of them. His hands—moments before so sure, so precise—were shaking. "Neither did I," he whispered.

The Beached Wolrum, a disreputable yet popular watering-hole that fronted Telaktai Street in Harnaral's western commercial district, would've presented its visitors with an imposing aspect had it not been situated between two enormous warehouses. As it was, the three-story former-theatre possessed just enough relative charm to pass itself off as a respite from the meat-packing bedlam that typically surrounded it. But where grimy workmen would on any other evening have been jostling past its thickly-lacquered doors or leaning on its balustrades, guardsmen with helms on their heads and blades in their hands now patrolled in grim suspicion.

The checkpoint officer nodded, his soldiers shouldering aside a heavy crate, and Ilina, Hugh, and Forkbeard passed through their third barricade en route from the lower terraces to the new—and hopefully temporary—seat of the beleaguered Kramish highlord.

Having barely escaped a palace coup early that morning, Rikard Harnish had been forced to retreat with loss across the central district of Harnaral to reestablish himself in this hastily-fortified inn. All afternoon, those who remained loyal to the will of the Council had been streaming into the Beached Wolrum from all directions, in hopes of breaking the rebels' grip on the central government district and retaking the only exit from the city that didn't require a leap into space. But the conflict had stalled, both sides seemingly content to sit and wait the other out.

At this point conventional wisdom would've favored the rebels, what with their monopoly on the means of travel, but, for Rikard, time was proving advantageous. The citizens of Harnaral, given opportunity, were siding with tradition—flocking in ever-increasing numbers to the Harnish banner that flapped defiantly from the Beached Wolrum's peaked facade. By nightfall, it was hoped, the momentum would shift.

Ilina, glancing up at the topmost window and at the lookout leaning against its scalloped trim, knew such hope was feeble. If Rikard had expected victory, he wouldn't have sent men to scrounge for a bolt-hole. She feared what she would find when finally brought before him.

A thought struck her, and she gave it voice. "You there," she shouted at a passing sentry, "what started this rebellion?"

"The hell should I know?" the man snapped. "Bastards don't care for due process, I suppose."

Oh, we are in trouble, thought Ilina as the company hurried inside. *Words alone can defeat men who know not why their enemy fights.*

"We can't assume that, Nalhe! The world has changed! We made assumptions this morning and look where that got us!"

The cavernous interior of the common room—once an auditorium—may have slurred and multiplied the words, but there was no doubt whence they came. The man in the red cloak stalked a stage once home to prominent actors and then to two-bit lutists, and Ilina wondered whether the planks now struck by those proud boots hadn't reverted to their original function. *Is this naught but a performance?*

A stooped man in a judge's red-and-black followed the speaker's movements from the floor like a spectator at a play. No one else was present. The company approached unnoticed; Forkbeard had cowed with a glance the guard who'd demanded they wait to be announced.

"We can't just *sit* here!" shouted Rikard Harnish as he pivoted and flung his cloak out of his way. "They may not be coming up the wall this very moment, but what about tonight, or the next night, or the next, when our eyes grow weary and our minds begin to slow? And what happens when word starts filtering back? What happens when it achieves saturation? What do I say to the man who looks me in the eye and asks 'Will Kramarack survive?' What do I *say* to that man?"

"You tell him you will fight," boomed Forkbeard, striding down the center aisle past rows of booths and tables, "and that he must join you, if he wants to live."

Rikard jerked around, nearly tripping on his own cloak. "Ilina!" he gasped, then leapt off the stage and rushed past the old man to where she was emerging from the dimness under the mezzanine. He swept her up in his arms and swung her around, grinning stupidly. "Harlith be praised! I thought I'd never see you again."

Ilina, her hands planted on his chest to maintain breathing room, deliberately calmed herself. *You're going to marry him, 'Lina. You're going to* marry *him. Get a grip. This is nothing.*

Craning her neck as Rikard wound down, she saw that Hugh was still hanging back in the shadows. He looked none too happy. *What, is he afraid of a similar reception? He must think our customs strange indeed to entertain such anxiety.*

"What happened, Ilina?" asked Rikard, leaning back to look at her without letting go. "How did you escape? Where have you been?"

"I ... we ... we were delayed," she stumbled. That part of her memory was still muddled. She didn't want to think about it. Why couldn't she *think* about it? Tension redoubled its grip on her neck and shoulders.

"Time enough for that later," interjected Forkbeard from behind. "There is much to tell, and this is neither the time nor place." He shot Ilina a troubled look, then turned to bear down on Rikard, brows knotting like storm clouds pressed against the mountains. "What has happened here, Rikard? What has become of your city?"

Rikard released Ilina. She dropped to her toes and immediately backed up two steps. Hugh had yet to approach, she saw.

"*My* city? If only I could say it was mine! When one piece of news can tear it apart, I wonder but that the end hasn't already come!"

"Speak plainly, man! What news?" Forkbeard stepped forward, and Rikard, backing up, bumped into a waist-high wooden booth.

"Wha ... I thought you knew! You told me just a moment ago that I should fight!"

"You asked about survival. That question only *has* one answer. Now tell me why you asked it."

Their faces were only inches apart now. "S-s-suma," Rikard sputtered. "Word arrived at dawn! The city of Suma has fallen!"

A SEA SOUGHT IN SONG

Forkbeard bowed his head. Ilina took an involuntary step back. She clutched at the edge of a booth.

"Three years ago!" roared the highlord.

Now it was Forkbeard's turn to stagger back, and not from the force of the other man's voice. Ilina clutched the railing like it was the last solid thing in the room. Suma was no more than three months away by land. If word of such a catastrophe had taken three years to reach them, then that could only mean their news had been censored. Was currently being censored. It meant the Habridi traders were not to be trusted. It meant …

Oh gods, it means the world we know is made of lies. How long have we been kept in the dark? And about what? And Suma … oh, poor Ilith … my correspondence … Ilina felt sick. She'd received a letter from a Suman contact just last spring. It had mentioned none of this.

Rikard's laughter was hollow. It echoed in that hard-walled space. "Do you think me weak, old man, that just any old bad news could incite rebellion against me? Do you know what this means? Can you fathom its implications? I've been doing nothing else all day!"

He swung around to stomp back toward the judge—Nalhe, Ilina presumed—who'd been watching this reunion with dispassionate impatience. *How can anyone remain calm at a time like this? Are* you *part of the conspiracy, you weaselly little clerk?* For a conspiracy was assuredly afoot—broader and more insidious than even Ilina could have foreseen in the darkness of her dreams. *It has come upon you at last, girl. Had you really been so lulled by the vain assurances of the unlearned? Brace yourself now, and accept your fate.*

It was at this moment that Hugh stepped into the light.

Ilina straightened. Now was her time. But Forkbeard was slumped opposite her, mouthing strange words to himself. That simply wouldn't do. She offered him her arm and he, surprisingly, took it and stood. They shared a look, then turned as one to face Rikard, who'd reached the stage. Hugh was descending the aisle behind them, the black sword still naked in his hand. Ilina took a deep breath.

"Hear me, Rikard Harnish, Highlord of Kramarack!" she cried. "I am the Lightkeeper! I stand here this day because my watch has been completed. The High King has returned from beyond the circle of the world. He wields the Sword of Ascension. He bears the Name of Conrad. And he comes to us from his father Henred, who yet lives! This I Declare as the Keeper of the Light!"

AUSTIN GUNDERSON

Rikard went very still. Then he slowly turned. Hugh stood now at Ilina's left hand, but the Lightkeeper kept her stare fixed on her betrothed. That part of her mind not occupied with maintaining an appropriately authoritative bearing was morbidly fascinated with what this pronouncement would do to their relationship.

It had been her secret terror since the day she knelt and offered Hugh his sword, but now that the moment of truth had finally come she found herself at peace. The Declaration itself was inevitable, like so much of life. Like change itself. She thought of all the change that'd swept over her in the past year and wondered at her own calm. *This is why I lack feeling*, she thought. *So that I may stand firm here, now, in this moment. It is a mercy to aid my life's work.*

The highlord was advancing, his face twisted by displeasure. He walked right up to Hugh. Stared him in the eyes.

Ilina softened her tone. "Rikard," she murmured, "make no delay. Bow to your rightful king."

The highlord glared at the Lightkeeper. She could see what a great battle raged behind his eyes. Fears and doubts and suspicions locked in swirling chaos. *Oh, you must humble yourself, proud lord! Arlam has no time for your brittle grandeur.*

"Come," she said, taking his hand, pretending not to notice his flinch. "We'll do it together, you and I. Councilor Mahru, join us."

Forkbeard took Rikard's other hand—now limp—and, with Ilina, turned to face Hugh Conrad. Blood had dried like Jaar war paint on Hugh's face, and Ilina was pleased to note how it transformed his confusion into ferocity. *It's the little things.* She tugged down on Rikard's hand as she curtseyed, and saw his forehead dip. *The little things, indeed.*

Hugh stuck out a hand—thumb up, palm turned on edge.

And Ilina laughed.

Chapter Fifteen
JUST PLAY GOD

"What the hell?" chuckled Hugh.

Redness bloomed on his bloodied cheek as, against the back wall, a sconce lamp flared to life. The skylights were failing with the onset of night, and servants had filed in to prep the common room for continued use. Points of light, warm and bright, multiplied in an arc—their collective glow shifting both shadows and mood. Despite Hugh's genial tone, the glint reflected by his eye as he turned to Forkbeard wasn't particularly friendly. His extended hand remained unshaken.

"This is Rikard Harnish, Lord of all the Kram," hissed Forkbeard out the side of his mouth. His gaze remained downcast.

"That's what I thought," whispered Hugh. "Why's he bowing at me?"

"He is acknowledging your authority. Now be silent and accept his homage."

"*What?*" Hugh spun back to Rikard, and the contact of their eyes as the other man raised his head was like a spark igniting kerosene. Hugh rocked back from the wordless heat of Rikard's hatred, then felt his own anger kindle. "No, I don't want this!" he spluttered. "What've you said? What've you told him about me? Take it back!" He glanced from Forkbeard to Ilina, whose eyes were wide. "Take it back, please."

Forkbeard was unmoved. "There is nothing to recant. The sooner he accepts you for who you are, the better."

"Well, I don't know *who* you think I am, but I didn't ask for *this!* What're you trying to do, get me killed?" Hugh's mind whirled. Ilina must've name-dropped his father. *Why? Why would she do that?* She had that weird look about her again: that creepy eager reverence. Her hand squeezed Rikard's like a clamp, but her eyes were all for Hugh. She was looking to him, waiting on him. And, as the final lamp was lit in some far corner, enlightenment finally dawned.

She thinks I've come here to take my father's place. She thinks I want to be king. And Rikard thinks I'm gonna usurp his throne!

Shit shit shit. I cannot let this happen. Hugh glanced around, looking for some way out. He noticed his stiffly-outstretched hand, curled now into a fist. *Oh, you idiot—these people don't know how to shake hands! Quick, show him you're just a normal guy.*

AUSTIN GUNDERSON

With a weak grin Hugh set aside his sword, stepped forward, grabbed Rikard by the shoulders, and smacked their foreheads together.

It didn't have the intended effect.

Rikard went rigid, his face flushing as crimson as his cloak. Ilina's face went white. Forkbeard groaned. Hugh, confused and flustered, unhanded the highlord. *Damn this land of eggshell carpeting! What'd I do now?* He stepped back to survey the damage.

Ilina released Rikard's hand, and it was as though an enchantment had been broken. Rikard turned on her, speaking low and fast, his voice turgid with resentment. The girl said nothing—just kept shaking her head, backing away. She looked as though she wanted to melt right through the floor, as though Hugh had shamed her personally, as though he'd shamed her whole family for all time. Forkbeard cut into Rikard's tirade, and then suddenly the two of *them* were at loggerheads. Their voices rose by increment until the Lord of the Kram was giving full vent to his outrage, gesticulating like some ground controller on the tarmac. Ilina seemed to have shrunk. She was retreating unnoticed.

Oh no you don't, princess! Time to get a second opinion.

Hugh dodged behind Forkbeard and grabbed Ilina's arm en route down the aisle. So despondent was she that she didn't even protest—nor did the others seem to notice—as he towed her up to the old man in the red-and-black robes who stood below the stage and clutched a sheaf of papers in one hand. These Hugh snatched away before patting down the man's pockets for a writing implement.

The man, face impassive, held up a pen. Hugh blinked. Then he took it, sat on the rim of the stage, and started scratching on an unused portion of a page. Ilina stood by, staring at nothing.

"What did you say about me?" wrote Hugh. He jabbed Ilina with the paper until she glanced up.

She took the pen. *"That thou art the rightful High King of Arlam."*

Wonderful. Just wonderful. "And he believes you?"

"I am the Lightkeeper. The announcement of thine advent is the purpose of my life."

She wrote it nonchalantly, as though merely stating the obvious. But to Hugh it was as though she'd slapped his soul. And, as he gazed with shock into her guileless eyes, the pieces of the puzzle that was the past two weeks began sliding together, each connection more jarring than the last. *So this is why her ancestors erected a skyscraper in the middle of nowhere. This is why she made it her home despite its lack of function. It's why she learned English*

228

A SEA SOUGHT IN SONG

when no one else would. It's why she decided to trust me. And it's why she accompanied me here.

But that's insane, protested Hugh's mind. *Who does that for someone they've never seen? Who orders their entire life around ancient history? As far as anyone here knows, my father's been gone for seven hundred years! That a tower was built is comprehensible, but why in blazes was it manned this long? Why would any girl throw away her life for such an improbable cause? Why, Ilina, why?*

They were questions too painful to express. Hugh's mouth hung agape; his pen sank away, unused. He stared at her in sudden sorrow. At the frightened fervency of her slowly kneading fingers. At the struggle in her eyes that had nothing to do with his identity, and everything to do with the inadequacy of her response to it. And then the answer came to him.

Holy hell, he thought. *I'm a religious figure.*

And with this final piece, the puzzle lay complete before his feet. Hugh was a promised messiah. He'd arrived from the wildlands into which his father had departed. In fact, Ilina had probably been expecting his father this whole time. So why settle for Hugh the son?

Because of the sword.

The sword had belonged to his father the king. It was only after finding it in the wreckage of that Eskimo boat that the girl had begun to get creepy. It must have been a sign to her. Descriptions of its appearance would have been relayed across centuries to accumulate in that maritime library now lying dead and buried on the far side of the sea. And even if she hadn't recognized the weapon on sight, it certainly corresponded with the return-to-sender hilt-extension she'd had in her possession. *Either way, buddy, she's your most devout priestess, and you're the answer to all her prayers.*

Hugh shook his head, massaged his brow, tried in vain to order his thoughts. *No, not a priestess—more like a shrine virgin. Oh God. Shit shit shit! Damn you, Father—what've you dumped in my lap? I thought* you *were the religious one! What happened to* your *devotion? Did you just play God to these people like that wizard in Oz? Did you hype them up for an empty hope? How am I supposed to* deal *with this?*

He looked at Ilina's bittersweet beauty, at the curve of her neck and the tightness of her lips and the strain within her eyes, and knew he could never feign deity to her. She was a real person—living, breathing, dreaming, hurting—not some pawn in a quest for power. *Maybe I'd lie to a horde of savages like the ones who attacked me up north ... but no. Not now. Not to you. Not for anything in this world.*

229

But how could he tell her the truth when it'd invalidate her life's pursuit?

A new harmonic had entered Rikard's tone. Hugh looked up to see the back of the room filling with soldiers. Forkbeard's posture was subdued, placatory. *Damn, this is serious.* Hugh slapped his paper flat on the stage, defiantly turning his back on the storm. *"What did I do to offend Rikard?"* he wrote.

Ilina stood with eyes shut, listening as the highlord's verbal onslaught overwhelmed Forkbeard's defense, her face blanching an even paler shade of resignation. Hugh snapped his fingers to recall her attention. She bent to respond.

"The fault is mine. In greeting thee the night of thy arrival, I ..." she scribbled out a word, glanced over a shoulder, *"I employed a gesture better suited to an intimate context. I am ..."* another pause as her shoulders constricted, *"not well-versed in social cues, it appears. I am out of practice. I mislead thee in what small insight I thought to impart concerning even our most elemental customs. I am sorry."* She turned away.

Hugh was dumbstruck. *Better suited to an intimate context ...?* His eyes widened. *Does that ... does that mean what I think it means?* A grin crept onto his face. No, it couldn't mean that. No way. *In your dreams, pal.* It was too easy to be true. *You'd better get a grip before you embarrass the girl even more.*

Irrationally, Hugh's grin widened.

But wait ... If a head-butt was more intimate than a handshake, then what had Hugh communicated just now? His grin evaporated as he turned to meet the highlord's baleful visage, blocked no longer by Forkbeard's rigid form. A double column of Kramish guards was advancing down the aisle, and the thump of their boots upon the boards was like the noise of cavalry. Forkbeard glanced back helplessly as they shouldered him aside.

Oh God, realized Hugh, *Rikard thinks I wanna make him my bitch. I humiliated him in front of his girlfriend. I took a delicate political situation and made it personal. I couldn't have screwed this up worse if I'd tried.*

The thumping thunder rose. Ilina stood by, shifting in little half-turns, her nails digging into her palms. Hugh was sweating. *What do I say? If I pretend I knew what I was doing, then he's honor-bound to oppose me. But if I claim ignorance of the gesture's meaning, I implicate Ilina—and who knows how that'll come back to bite her. There's no way out of this. Think, dammit, think!*

A SEA SOUGHT IN SONG

Nothing came to him but the soldiers. They swept up and curled round like a glittering wave poised to break. Their leader reached out to take Hugh's arm.

"Teh oamet lo has hauk," cried Ilina. *"Ha whem ha tan haumhu ut!"*

In the drawn-breath pause created by her cry, Hugh dropped paper and pen, sidestepped the grasping guard, and, drawing the black rod from his coat, dodged out of the pocket. He leveled the rod at the aisle and waited half a second for a soldier to pass from in front of the sword, which leaned against the wooden partition halfway to the doors. Then Hugh jammed his thumb against the rod's emerald pommel.

The black blade flipped straight through the partition and the intervening booths, shattering slats and spraying splinters. Hugh caught it upon the tip of his rod and spun, sweeping it back and around. The surrounding Kram flung themselves to the ground. Even the old man in red-and-black robes hit the deck. Only Ilina was left standing.

"Forkbeard!" shouted Hugh. "Tell Rikard I only meant to express my gratitude for his welcome. Tell him that if he stands down now, his welcome is what I'll remember."

Forkbeard rattled off something to Rikard, who crouched, gape-mouthed, behind an upended table. Rikard's face hardened. He raised his hand.

High overhead a skylight exploded. Shards of glass rained down as a burning arrow buried itself in the surface of the stage only a few feet away from Hugh, who turned to stare at it, uncomprehending.

A silence fell.

It was broken by the clap of the Beached Wolrum's front doors slamming back against their posts. An officer stumbled through, backlit by red. Screams and shouts crowded behind. *"Tehr rhim!"* he cried. *"Tehl gruth yiret!"*

Chaos erupted. Rikard rose, flinging his table aside. He jabbed a finger at Hugh, unloaded a mouthful of unintelligible rage, then flipped his cape in the air and stormed out the front doors. All but three of the soldiers leapt up to follow him. Of those left behind, one rushed to stomp out the flaming arrow, one approached Ilina, and the third glowered at everyone from a safe distance, hand on hilt.

Forkbeard tottered up, much diminished in Hugh's eyes. Whether or not his association with Hugh had become a political albatross, the wizard clearly wasn't the one in charge around here ... at least not anymore. "What's happening?" Hugh asked.

"The rebels are attacking," grimaced the old man. "Either someone was sleeping on watch, or Rikard can no longer trust his own men."

"Yeah, that's a bummer. I think it makes him irritable. So what's this rebellion about, anyway?"

Forkbeard shook his head. "My apologies; I keep forgetting you cannot overhear us. Kramarack has just learned that its nearest neighbor was sacked by the Tunnoltan Imperium."

"Omri," growled Hugh.

During their conversations on the road from the sea, Forkbeard had recounted to him, by way of rumor and conjecture, the Imperium's campaign of conquest that spanned the past several decades—how its every assault had met with overwhelming success, how no nation had yet arisen to stem its northward tide, and how its advance now seemed inevitable. "Then war *is* coming," Hugh said. "I take it these rebels don't think Rikard's up to the task of national defense?"

"That, and more," said Forkbeard. "The seaport of Suma fell three whole years ago, and yet we did not hear of it until today. And it is only a three months' journey away."

Hugh fell silent as the news sank in. Was it even possible for something like that to be covered up for so long? Were these people really so isolated from the rest of their world that they wouldn't notice a hostile power defeating a close ally? Or was it more likely this news itself was the deception—a sensational rumor concocted to sow strife? If so, it seemed to be working. But either way, the enemy they faced was subtle to a degree that frightened Hugh, though he'd admit no such thing in front of *these* people.

Regardless, civil war wouldn't help matters. But how could such an escalation be defused? *Probably by killing somebody. There's always a linchpin.* Hugh wondered who'd brought the news in the first place. Where was the messenger now?

Ilina, having waved away the concerned soldier, stooped abruptly to retrieve the writing-paper Hugh had dropped. She turned aside and started scratching away. The solder and his two companions had withdrawn toward the doors to assume a defensive posture. There they shifted and swayed like pensive penguins, their swords staying sheathed seemingly by sheer willpower. Mingled shouts drifted down through the shattered skylight.

Are the rebels right about Rikard? wondered Hugh. Perhaps a change in Kramish leadership would be just what the doctor ordered for the sake of the all-important mission. After all, it appeared this current administration had no intention of offering Hugh aid or comfort. *Yeah, but who's in the running*

A SEA SOUGHT IN SONG

to replace Rikard Redcloak the Regal? He *at least respects Ilina. Those goons at the gate would've had us all killed.*

The sounds outside grew louder. And then suddenly Hugh felt something again in the pit of his stomach: a stirring of that inexplicable premonition which had returned to him again and again since the night this all began, when he'd stood frozen in the darkness beyond his father's door. It was the terror of an unknown thing. A sense that something was about to change. *It's getting stronger every time,* he thought, and shuddered. Ilina looked up. Their eyes met.

"No matter what betide," read the paper that she held, *"I beg thee to spare Rikard's life."*

"What?" blurted Hugh. "How am I in a position to do *that?* Did you ask the same thing of *him?"*

"She did," said Forkbeard. "She has risked much for you, my lord."

Hugh, startled to receive such an unambiguous answer, stared at the girl in wonder. *Yes, I suppose she has. Though why she's done so is beyond me. I'm no god. Hell, I'm not even a king, no matter what I keep being told. I've only got one follower—maybe two. But I can't keep pretending I don't value her devotion.*

I should do something, he realized. *Show her a sign. Some sort of approval, some gesture of thanks.*

Hugh smiled. He knew exactly what he'd do.

As he walked to Ilina, he allowed himself to contemplate her beauty. In his experience, she was a rarity—a delicate damsel who stood up to power and faced down danger despite a timidity she kept well-hidden. She was crazy, sure, but that kinda went with the territory. His sojourn in this land had improved dramatically the instant he'd laid eyes on her. She really *did* mean something to him, and he wanted her to know it.

So he stepped right up to her. Held her gaze tight. Laid gentle hands upon her shoulders.

And lightly tapped her forehead with his own.

Ilina's eyes widened. Hugh felt her tremble through his palms. *Yes,* he replied in thought, *I read what you wrote. You can say whatever you like about what you meant at our first meeting, but know now that I* mean *this ...* whatever *this means.*

A gap appeared between her lips, but whether the shape of it connoted panic or delight Hugh could not determine. And neither was he given time to discover the truth, for at that moment the doors burst open.

"Take heed!" cried Forkbeard. A crash punched Hugh's ears and he spun, flinging Ilina behind him.

Men poured through the front doors—some staggering backward, others bludgeoning them aside. Red was everywhere: on helms and surcoats and armbands, on faces, tables and walls. Kram grappled with Kram in Rikard's audience chamber. For an instant the defenders seemed to rally—overturning furniture and congealing behind it into a line of battle—but then the intruders knifed through and resistance buckled again.

And the three travelers stood alone before the flood.

Up came Hugh's black sword. Since the night he'd drawn it from the stomach of his friend, Hugh had resisted the blade's allure. It seemed to him indecent to delight in a weapon so stained. Besides, he was no swordsman; what little fencing he'd done in the past was nothing if not injurious to his ability to wield something so huge. There was no finesse to its heft, no margin for error, no chance of recovery once he'd committed to a stroke. A blow that didn't fall true would leave him naked. The sword was a necessary encumbrance—a burden he'd vowed to bear, nothing more. That it seemed to afford him respect wherever he went was a happy side effect.

Or so he told himself.

But it fit him. And this was a strange thing, for it hadn't seemed to at first. The balance of the blade when drawn forth from Miles had felt *off* to Hugh—as though whoever forged it had been either unusually strong or enamored of windmilling in a fight. Even the shape of its extended hilt had chafed inside his fist. But now ... now his fingers seemed to sink into the metal as they closed, and the blade—fashioned of the same substance—fairly leapt at the prospect of blood. Hugh Conrad was tired of walking on eggshells.

Time to make a big ol' omelet.

The first rebel was bearing down on him, backlit, blade low and drawn back for a gut-thrust. The man was young and flaxen-haired, his leather armor dark, his eyes unseen beneath his helm. And thus there wasn't light to leave them when the tip of Hugh's black sword caught the cartilage of his throat.

The second man was not ready. Hugh reached behind himself to shove Ilina lightly aside, then sidestepped the first man as he passed between the two of them to crumple against the stage. A sweep below knee-level and the second man went flailing after.

And then Hugh was in their midst, advancing up the aisle, sword no less deadly at close quarters, his enemies as ungainly in response as a group of

A SEA SOUGHT IN SONG

inanimate mannequins. That they should rightly be the blademasters and he the awkward novice did not occur to his mind. Such dour logic had been superseded by a vision—an *awareness*—exhilarating in its clarity. For now Hugh knew without doubt the disposition of his danger and the paths of his opponents' blades. He could *see* them like faint fissures in the air, afterimage of sparklers spun by twilit celebrants as the bride and groom withdrew. To parry now was easy, to skirt and strike euphoric.

This was no battle, but a dance. And Hugh danced with his sword as bodies fell before him. He let it take the lead.

And then suddenly he was alone before the open doors. Red light and jarring sounds beat upon his face. Hugh blinked, turned. The aisle was choked with corpses. At its foot like a graven image stood an old man with folded hands and forked beard. Hugh heard retching and saw Ilina straighten from behind a table by the stage. She leaned against it for support, wiping her mouth.

Hugh lowered his eyes to his white-knuckled sword hand. With effort, he opened his fingers. The black rod fell to the floor, its coupled blade bouncing free with a clang. *So many broken eggs. So very many. Too many. Once cracked, they cannot again be made whole.*

Why me, Father? Why must it be me who puts your world to rights? Wasn't one planet enough for you to screw up? Shouldn't Earth's salvation have been sufficient duty for me and mine? I'm so tired of bearing this burden. Of being the bringer of death.

Hugh raised his head to see men running, rage writ upon their faces in the bloom of burning buildings. He couldn't comprehend such anger, but, no matter what arcane grievance they might've presented in defense had he sat them down and asked, he knew it could have but one root. *When my father deserts you, it creates a void. Right now, you don't like the guy who's filled it. Believe me, I understand.*

Hugh bent slightly at the knees, brought his hands up. *No more death. I'm done for the night.* If his current luck held, he could take on the entire Kramish army single-handed. For soldiers who presumably practiced hand-to-hand combat day in and day out, they'd proven surprisingly inept. *No need to destroy a man I can simply lay out flat.* He flexed his fingers.

A high scream and low shout came from behind as rebel soldiers rushed him, but he paid the noise no heed: his opponents were closing so fast he had little space to think. Already this bunch seemed better prepared than the last. There were at least ten of them, and their swords were in their hands, and they fanned out as they drew near.

AUSTIN GUNDERSON

Hugh dodged the first blow by stepping into the second—a steel slap that glanced off his shoulder like a ricocheting bullet. The sting of it left him stunned for just a second, but that was time enough for a knobbed pommel to sink into his throat. The world tipped up behind him. The threshold of the Beached Wolrum drove all breath from his lungs.

He struggled to rise as a blade flashed red above him. And then bolts of white light striated his vision and heavy thumps were followed by swiftly-fading footfalls.

"Fool!" cried a horse voice. "Pick up your sword!"

Hugh sat up, rasping his assent as he gulped down air. He clawed for the blade. Shadows swept past and then Ilina's arms were around him, gripping him, pulling him to his feet as Forkbeard stood guard—a tall black shape cut from spreading flame.

For the fire raged unimpeded now, and its roaring overwhelmed even the shouts of skirmishers and the clash of their steel. The rooftops across the street were going up one by one. Hugh winced as Ilina squeezed his bruised shoulder. He pulled away to retrieve the rod and sword.

"What happened to Rikard?" he shouted at the wizard.

"I cannot tell," said Forkbeard. "It appears he was drawn off. Let us hope it was not into a trap."

At that moment a group of men farther down the street flopped as one to the cobblestones. It was not a coordinated maneuver; some continued to flail in prostration. From around the corner opposite them appeared a squad of soldiers who fell quickly into line—leaning back to support the weight of heavy winch-crossbows like the one Ilina had hefted to greet Hugh. As they stood thus poised, a second line of archers ducked through their rank to kneel in the street and crank their drawstrings taut. Men looked up from their scavenging to scatter toward alleyways and recessed entries. Behind the double-line of bowmen came a clanking column of Kramish knights.

And at their head strode a man whose crimson cloak fell now in ribbons.

"Rikard!" breathed Ilina.

The archers filtered back into the main body of loyalist troops as the swordsmen began their push down the street and the remaining rebels vanished into the smoke-wreathed woodwork. Rikard Harnish swept up. He exchanged terse words with Forkbeard, embraced an obviously-reluctant Ilina, and shot a disgusted glance at Hugh, who glared right back. *Like you could've done any better under the circumstances, you peacock. Just what've you been up to this whole time?*

A SEA SOUGHT IN SONG

"This way, Hugh," said Forkbeard. "We are to accompany Rikard until the fire has been contained."

"Oh we are, are we?" Already Hugh could see men with sloshing buckets running from a cross-street well, but the futility of their task was obvious. His gaze bounced from wooden walls to wooden doors to wooden beams to wooden roofs. Three-story columns of flame were dancing on the steeples, and Rikard's plan hinged on *buckets?* Short of a thunderstorm, this inferno would keep spreading until the entire city was ablaze.

Either the rebels were madmen, or they'd expected Rikard to stay and squelch the flames instead of charging out like John Paul Jones. *Probably trying to impress Ilina*, Hugh thought, and grinned. *Yeah, that's it—I've scared the living shit out of Redcloak here. I grabbed his girl! And he just* had *to save face by killing somebody.*

But now the threat posed to one man by a romantic rival had, because of that one man's panic, morphed into a very real danger menacing an entire city. *How are they gonna stop this fire? With what will they block its path?*

They'd need a firebreak. The adjacent buildings would have to come down.

But they won't be able to bring 'em down fast enough!

And suddenly Hugh knew what he had to do. He leapt away toward the flames.

Forkbeard was trailing after Rikard as the highlord marched off down the street. Ilina was turning to go. She glanced back to see if Hugh needed further assistance; his arm was obviously injured, whether or not he wanted her to know.

But Hugh was not there. He was running the other way, black sword in hand.

Ilina screamed his name.

Heat assailed Hugh like a physical impediment. He pressed into it as though he could break through. The roar of the fire was all around him now, and the very light was alive with menace, and ash swirled like burning snow. The storefront to his left bulged outward—its windows exploding, its gasses escaping. He dove into a forward roll as shards and splinters shot overhead.

Back on his feet, he looked up. Two more buildings to go. Three, to be safe. And then he was there, rounding the corner of a shop thus far unscathed. The fire was behind, the darkness ahead.

He dropped the sword.

Its clattering was inaudible under the voice of the flames, but somehow Hugh knew where it lay without sparing a backward glance. He could *feel* it somehow, like an itch in his brain, a phantom limb. The rod in his hand itched sympathetically. It yearned to reunite with its other half.

Be patient, thought Hugh. First, he needed to reach the end of this alley.

As he skidded into a small rear courtyard overhung with cargo lifts, planters, and jutting beams—dark against the light of moons and flame— Hugh sensed a shadowing presence. He spun behind the corner of the building, pressing the emerald of his rod, and the black sword left the street a hundred feet away to rush him through cracking stones and splitting beams, colliding with its consort at the very instant a slight female figure stumbled into the courtyard and reeled away from a wall suddenly severed from its footing.

Dry mortar sprayed from the lengthwise seam Hugh had sliced, but the wall's load-bearing posts, caught at unawares, remained upright. He lunged forward to snatch Ilina back from the falling slats and tiles. His arm circled her waist for but a breath before she swatted him away.

"Whemhaut seh, seh taek?" she railed. *"Tehl mel laroh oamolkait run!"*

"Glad to hear it, sister. Just keep that mouth of yours away from this wood, or I'll have to start all over again." He tossed the sword back into the alley beside the nearest cornerpost and took off around the rear of the building, dodging the crates and carts which hunkered in the dark. He could hear Ilina keeping pace behind him, still irate. *Wonder if I'd still like her if I knew what she was saying.*

Hugh smiled. He was sure he would.

When they reached the far corner, he summoned the sword to follow them through the building's back wall. This time it was just too much: the rear cornerpost they'd left behind slipped sideways off its stump and struck the pavement. The whole building slouched. Windows shattered from their frames, boards and beams snapped and splintered, mortar exploded outward, and shingles cascaded from the roof.

But Hugh wasn't finished. He took off toward the street through a narrow slot between this shop and the next, glad he'd chosen a building as far from the flames as he had. Already he felt heat radiating from the shop at his right hand, which just one minute before had stood untouched. The inferno was in there now, eating its guts. And only now did it occur to him that he should've begun his demolition on this nearer side.

Hugh burst onto the street, nearly colliding with a man parting several gallons of water from its pail. Ducking the stream, Hugh rolled and spun past the pail-bearer before the man's lips could even open. The rod departed Hugh's left hand as his right shot up to snatch it and point, quivering, at the front-left cornerpost of the building now next-in-line to be consumed.

And then Hugh stood, waiting, trying to ignore the fireman's belated alarm, as Ilina took what seemed like forever to follow him through the gap.

At last the girl emerged, gasping for breath, arms arched overhead in apprehension. Her blue dress, stained and shredded from their subterranean trek, swirled in strips about her legs, and her knees flashed through rents in her white leggings. Her hair was wild and steamed behind, its auburn intensified by the glow of the flames. Her face, sooty and flushed, was something fierce and scared and beautiful. Hugh reached out to catch her and pull her close before she could protest, and then he pressed the emerald of his rod.

The shop began sliding away from them almost before the sword had returned to his hand. It collapsed so fast that for an instant Hugh thought he and Ilina were the ones in motion. But then the edge of its roof had struck that of its burning neighbor and smoke was everywhere as the whole structure imploded, all three of its stories toppling into the courtyard behind. Dust and ash billowed outward. Hugh leapt back, bearing Ilina through the air, and his shoulders struck the cobbles as debris fell about them. He rolled over to shield her body.

And suddenly she was so close, so *present*. Her eyes, liquid in red light, were more alive than any flame. The tip of her nose brushed his own. Her chest rose and fell beneath his, and he felt an excitement, an exhilaration unlooked-for, radiating from her like heat.

A shout from behind broke the spell.

It was Rikard, of course. He was running back down the street toward them. As Hugh rose, pulling Ilina to her feet, he mentally replaced the unintelligible invective pouring from the highlord: *It's just not fair! How come you get to hold the girl? You don't even have a big billowy cloak!*

"Forkbeard!" Hugh shouted. The old man appeared from among Rikard's men, who were scattering to aid the pail-bearers. "I'm making a firebreak," said Hugh. "Tell Rikard to focus on dousing the buildings I knock down. It's pointless to waste water on *that*." He flung an arm at the inferno, which, as though on cue, coughed up a gout of flame.

AUSTIN GUNDERSON

Forkbeard turned to relay Hugh's words, but Rikard shoved past the wizard to bawl directly in Hugh's face. The highlord stretched forth his hands—Hugh assumed to grab him by the collar—but the man's motion was abysmally slow. Hugh sidestepped and swatted his wrists away.

Rikard, livid, tried again. But Hugh just received the grasping arm, directed it forward as he turned and, shifting his weight, launched Redcloak the Regal into the air. The highlord struck the street with a solid thud and lay there, gasping. Men stared in shock.

"Tell them, Forkbeard!" Hugh shouted. He was already running back toward the building he'd brought down. Precious seconds had been squandered. It was time to circumscribe this fire.

Ilina stood still to see the turning of the tide. Its swiftness took her breath. In a single moment, Hugh transformed from a stranger in a hostile crowd to the crowd's de facto leader. Kramish soldiers pelted after him into the night, leaving Rikard to clamber to his feet by himself. They knew their highlord could do nothing more than he already had. But Hugh ... Hugh could topple a three-story building in the time it took to run a lap. Ilina hadn't even needed to articulate a defense for such destruction; the soldiers had understood what Hugh was doing almost instantly. And they wanted to be part of it.

The same could not be said of Rikard. It was with a cold fury that he rose, and with an eerie calmness that he turned to face Ilina. Some of his men approached belatedly, but it was only to ask his permission to help the stranger.

Rikard shook his head. "Defensive. Perimeter." His voice was deceptively low.

The men actually hesitated. Some even looked to Ilina. She stepped back, astonished. *They seek my approval? Why? Does the will of their lord mean so little to them?*

Blushing, she rationalized furiously. *Mere fear and confusion could not do this. It is the hand of Orlom on their minds. It is the hour of Hugh's Ascension, when his majesty is revealed in the hearts of his subjects. My Declaration was premature. This is the real thing. It's really happening, right here and now.*

A SEA SOUGHT IN SONG

"Do not fear," she said aloud. "Your offer, though noble, is unnecessary. The High King has this well in hand." She would have run after him herself, but she hadn't managed to do anything besides slow him down the last time.

"King?" repeated a soldier with dark beard and bloodied shirt. The others looked up in shock. All were staring at her now. They hadn't heard. Already they valued Hugh's will above their own highlord's, and yet they hadn't even heard. It was becoming apparent that nothing inhibited the spread of rumor quite like civil war.

Rikard interjected. "*Move*, you slack-jaws! The perimeter, *now!* You want the rebels to just *walk* back through here?"

They moved, melting away in either direction, unshouldering their weapons. But it was with an uncertainty—hint of a hope too dear not to fear—that lightened Ilina's heart. Somewhere off to the left, a shuddering crash punctuated the fire's roar. Another building down. She turned to face the storm.

Yet not a ripple disturbed Rikard's face. He stared at her flatly. A minute passed as the flames leapt up.

And suddenly the compulsion smote Ilina to be the first to speak. To abase herself, to apologize, to plead for mercy instead of judgement. She knew what her Declaration had done, was doing to him, this man who had offered her nothing but support until such would have ensured his own humiliation. She knew what manner of pain continued support would cost him now. She longed to offer up her hand, to take his side against all comers. Her promise of marriage was double-stranded, after all—first to her father and now to this man—and she felt as though this stand she was taking was a betrayal of the words she had sworn: *I shall honor you, wait for you, and seek your good above my own.* How could she now keep that pledge?

She remembered the day she had made it.

It had been three days after the slaying of Rikard's father, on the morning of her departure from Harnaral. It was the first time she had seen the sun since it left the high windows of the Great Hall of Harn to congeal on Forkbeard's fingers. Once the chaos and madness of the attack had subsided, and the solicitous physicians had withdrawn, and the people asking if she was quite *sure* she was alright and wouldn't she like to cry on their shoulders had looked into her dry eyes and slunk away, disturbed, she'd closed and locked the door behind them. And attempted to forget.

But the memory of what she had seen simply refused to fade. So she sat upon her bed, shaking uncontrollably, starting at the smallest sounds. The dumbwaiter in the corner, whence rose plates of food she set aside to attract flies, gaped in silent witness to the immediacy of the underworld. She shut its little door and shoved her bed inch by inch as far from it as she could. When she tried to sleep, she would see again that hagfish maw and hear the skittering of strangely-jointed limbs and would claw her way out of her sheets to crouch gasping in the dark. Sometimes there would be pounding on the door and voices demanding to know why they had heard screams. And Ilina would hear her own voice reply cooly that it must have been a nightmare, that she was perfectly fine, that everyone should go back to sleep and rein in their ceaseless fretting. And the voices would recede. And she would sit quaking well past the gray of dawn, waiting for the floorboards to erupt.

Rhinya did not come to her, now that she was actually in need. No one seemed to know where the servant girl had gone. But Ilina was sure she knew. She whimpered, biting her blankets to stifle the sound. *You may steal my life but not my soul I need no lost god's aid! You may steal my life but not my soul I need no lost god's aid!* These words, shouted so brashly in the face of death, ran circles through her head as though repetition would make them true, but it was not long before Ilina's humanist manifesto had devolved into pitiful prayer. *Harlith send me a true wind, blow me to the right. Harlith send me a clear wind, dispel the clouds of night. Harlith send me a sweet wind, my soul to set alight. Harlith send me a strong wind, revive me with thy might.*

On the morning that followed the third sleepless night, Ilina determined to leave. As she emerged slowly from her room, squinting red-rimmed eyes, her traveling-bag in hand, she was presented with a city very different from the one she had last seen. The ubiquitous bustle had not abated, but it proceeded now in an eerie near-silence, as though each shopper were a thief and every worker a night watchman. People hurried this way and that as she stepped out into the street—their shoulders hunched, their eyes downcast. None looked up in recognition, none called out her name. Ilina walked the busy streets as though alone. The gable-top banners streamed like shrouds. The lintels and ridgebeams, flushing scarlet in the dawn, might have been smeared with blood. Harnaral, splendor of the Hidden Kingdom, jewel in the Crown of the World, was haunted.

Nonetheless, word of her movements must have been conveyed to Rikard, for he met her at the gatehouse. "Ilina, Ilina!" he cried, running— actually *running*—across the square from the direction of the armory. He wasn't even wearing his cloak.

So she stood and waited. She had to: her horse was being brought up from the stables.

A SEA SOUGHT IN SONG

"Ilina," he said again as he skidded up. Then he seemed to forget what he had to say. His arm lifted toward her and fell back.

"Speak," she said at last. She could see her horse approaching from over his shoulder, along with the servant who would accompany her to Land's End. She had given short notice of departure.

A pained look spread over Rikard's face. "I thought ... did ... do you have an answer?"

"An answer? For what?"

A beat. Confusion replaced pain in Rikard's eyes, and was in turn driven out by annoyance. "You didn't get it, then." He scowled, glancing away. "Damn you, Forkbeard," he muttered, "I *said* it wouldn't work! I mean, under the *plate?* Really?"

Ilina sighed. "My soul weeps for you in your loss, Rikard, but I really must be going." *For the place of your abode afflicts my fragile soul. And I have no comfort to offer you, you who appear to require no cheer. And I no longer know what to think of your aloof advances. And while your fallen father may need attendants at his funeral, my ailing father needs me home. And I am weary, and sick at heart.*

"Wait, wait!" His eyes lit up again. "This is better, actually. What I would have done had things been different. Ilina," he said, locking his eyes with hers and sinking to his knees, "I must ask much of you, for I would give you much of me. And I must offer you myself, for you have presented to me such a hope of joy as I dared not imagine before we met ... Ilina," he said, stumbling to the end of the formal recitation, "you I love with all my heart and admire with all my mind. I would see our destinies twine. Will you marry me?"

The world stopped.

But not long enough. *Too quick, too quick! I have no time! What shall I make of this? What answer shall I give? A fortnight ago I would have daydreamed of this moment—what now impedes my tongue?*

She looked into his eyes and saw sincerity. Or what seemed like sincerity. She looked into her own soul and saw pain and fear and prevarication. *What better cure for all this fear than to wed this man who is so sure? What better reward for all this trouble than to return to Father with a pledge of troth? And what does it matter whether I wish it or no? Orlom be the judge.*

"I will," she said.

Rikard's face, which had begun to look strained, burst into a smile of such radiance it lifted even Ilina's lips.

She turned toward her horse.

"Wait," said Rikard, "we should sign a Petition of Troth!" Ilina glanced over a shoulder. "I mean, don't you think?" he finished lamely. His eyes were now desperate. And deeply shadowed, she belatedly observed.

"I must go," she reiterated, suddenly overcome with a desire to escape this tomb of a town and contemplate the ramifications of what she'd just declared. "But fear not, Rikard Harnish," she said, and her voice softened at the thought of the light her declaration had loosed upon his face. "I leave you now only to return. My word is sure. I shall honor you, wait for you, and seek your good above my own. I am a Lightkeeper."

And as she spoke those words, standing in the midmorning shade cast by the gatehouse of Harnaral so many months ago, her ancestral status had seemed the foundation of integrity. But now, as she stood in a city aflame, her duty to that selfsame Light threatened to nullify her pledge.

To endorse Hugh's claim was to erode Rikard's already-unstable authority. But to rescind her Declaration would be to betray her very nature. No oath was necessary to become a Lightkeeper; Orlom himself had decreed it at her birth. She had no choice in the matter, no recourse, no option to transfer her shift to someone free from conflicting interests. Moreover, were she to abandon this duty for the sake of Rikard's pride and her own self-satisfaction, she would effectively discard all basis for his vanishing faith in her word. He might not see it that way immediately, but it would be true nonetheless. She could not allow that. Not though all Heaven and Arlam begged it of her.

Some betrayals were simply worse than others.

I am the rock that weathers the wind and the waves. I shall resist all change. The sea itself must step aside to leave me in my place.

And what of Hugh, he for whom you've risked so much? Will he leave you in your place?

She shivered despite the heat.

"Where did you find him?" The question came so quietly that for a moment Ilina was unsure whether it had been posed by her own mind. But while her gaze had turned inward, Rikard's had yet to waver. His eyes glowed like coals that kept their burning hidden and combusted what they touched. It would not do to leave him in the dark.

"On my doorstep," she answered. "His ship had foundered in storm. He and one other alone were borne up to my tower."

"One other? Another like him?"

A SEA SOUGHT IN SONG

"A Jaar sailor. Hugh commandeered one of their craft." Ilina frowned. What *had* become of Jarlin? Vanished, like so many others. She thought of Rhinya and stiffened against the gust of dread that smote her.

Rikard scowled. "From Tejilim? Then he set out from *my* shores?"

"What?" Ilina shook her head to clear it. "No. Hugh came out of Utter North."

The highlord did not speak, but Ilina could tell he had been shaken. The cobbles trembled from a distant concussion.

Rikard, his anger spent, was thinking. Ilina could tell. Ever since his father's death, the young highlord had been forced to deliberate deeply. When he'd visited Cuspid Isle last year, she couldn't help but notice the change. The pressures of rule, the opposition of the Council, the fear of foreign malice—all had taken their toll. Though his hair had been as jaunty and his eyes as piercing as ever, his chin had not risen so high.

She remembered being unsure what to think of his newly subdued demeanor. She remembered being far more concerned with the antiliga root she'd caught him chewing in her hothouse. That too had been a signal of his stress, but at the time she'd been too irate at the threat of blight posed by Rikard's new habit to imagine what could've impelled him to get hooked in the first place. *I wasn't particularly supportive*, she realized. *But that made two of us.* Now, in retrospect, she doubted he would've ever been willing to countenance her Declaration had his self-assurance not been upended by that monster from the pit. And that, at least, was a change of which she approved.

"And you're sure about him?" asked Rikard. "You really believe he is Henred's heir?"

Ilina shot him a *what-do-you-think* look. *No, I just like the idea of my name being a synonym for 'dupe' eight generations hence.* She rolled her eyes.

"What proof do you have that he is the one?" pressed Rikard, his anger staging a resurgence. "How can you be sure he isn't an imposter like all the others?"

This was no time to build a comprehensive case. So she lead with the strongest evidence she had. "You saw his sword?"

Rikard could hold his own when it came to exasperated looks. Ilina supposed she deserved this one. Undeterred, she forged ahead. "The hilt extension? That's not his. It's mine. It's an heirloom of my house passed down from Kredak Lightbringer himself, last known confidant of High King Henred. Tradition has it the king entrusted his scepter to Kredak on the day he departed these shores for Utter North. It's been waiting all this time to reunite with Henred's sword."

Rikard's eyes couldn't help widening. Not everyone in Kramarack would have known what this implied, but Rikard had made it his business to understand the dealings of her house since before their courtship began. "You mean …"

"Yes. Hugh wields the Sword of Ascension. Verily I tell you, the High King has come again."

Chapter Sixteen
SKY FULL OF FIRE

22 November, 1951

"What must I do?"

Henry looked up from his wallowing. The sound of Hugh's voice in that chamber of desolation seemed obscene, and no more so to father than to son. Brusque when it should've been gentle, sharp when it should've been soft, direct when it should've been decorous, Hugh's tone sliced through the old man's sobbing like daylight through a dream.

Hugh was beyond dreaming. For twenty-four years he'd imagined his father was still alive—still holed up at the ends of the earth squinting at pottery fragments or something—and then this fancy had come true. His father had indeed returned—first as a tinny voice over a phone, then as the resident of the family estate as though no time had elapsed at all. And for a time, it had seemed too good to be true. But if Hugh had nursed doubts regarding the reality of the situation, those had died with Miles. He'd never imagined watching his former squad-mate, now a malnourished ninety-year-old, show up in a secret bunker to rip the guts out of an innocent woman. He'd never thought to see his father kill his friend in self-defense. Those weren't images his mind could have concocted.

Though this madness seemed surreal, it was anything but a dream.

Hugh lowered his arm and Miles sank back, lifeless, to the floor. The black sword slipped from his stomach, its tip popping up from the lips of the wound, flinging blood across Hugh's knees. Hugh flinched, then lurched upright. Suddenly it was all too much. He looked at that implement of death—still gripped by the hilt in his fist—and released it with an unthinking cry. It thumped to the carpet beside the corpse. The carpet was red. And wet.

Henry's renewed sobs were deep, wracking. His shoulders heaved as he slumped between the slain. Light from the kitchen bathed the bodies, the blood, the overturned furniture in a spectral half-sheen. Hugh cleared his throat.

"What must I do?"

His own voice sounded dead in his ears. He was past rage, beyond blame. *I am man no longer, but a pestilence made flesh. Lead me to my slaughter.*

AUSTIN GUNDERSON

Henry sucked in a breath, and silence fell. Then the blind man stood.
"Take the sword."

Hugh picked it up again.

"You must go to Arlam, Son. There is another there."

Rage flared again in Hugh's chest, then died like fire in vacuum. Nothing could find purchase in his evacuated heart. "Who?"

"Daniel Forsythe. I sent him a week after Miles."

Dear old Dan. Even now Hugh could see his spare face, could hear his gentle laughter. Daniel Forsythe had been like a father to Hugh for a time, or had tried. *A father. Hard to tell what that even means anymore.* Hugh glared at his birth father. *It's certainly more than* you *can say, you royal faker.* "And when did you send *Miles?*"

"Two weeks ago."

Expressionless, Hugh turned and bolted from the room. The math was unthinkable. If it'd taken Miles only two weeks to age decades, then Daniel, twenty years his elder on Earth, might already be dead from natural causes. *Let alone violence.*

There was no time to spare. No time for backup, for outfitting, for preparation of any kind. For all Hugh knew, each passing minute might equal a month on the other side. He felt his wrath rear up again. *Damn your incompetence, old man. Damn your secrets and mysteries and mystical bullshit. What is this, some sick time-trial? You can't even put me on notice? It's not enough for you that I clean out your toilet—now I gotta follow you around in case you shit your pants?*

He blundered into the kitchen, cracking his shin against a table's edge and tripping straight into the far wall. *Why's it so dark? It shouldn't be this dark.* He groped for the garden door, wrenched it open to a squeal. Fell into starlight. The clouds had retreated and a gray luster dusted the fields and stone wall. The honeysuckle vines lay twisted like barbed wire, their low ramparts overrun. Away down the hillside, nothing stirred. *There's nothing left to stir that hasn't already attacked.*

The air was chill and stagnant as Hugh skirted the southeast corner. His boots crunched the gravel driveway as though it were made of brittle ice. The front of the house was dark beneath the trees, its porch light burnt out or something. But off to the side crouched a confluence of silver curves. *There.* At least his car was in one piece.

Hugh popped the trunk and fished for his flashlight. Found it and toggled the switch: nothing. He swore and swung into the driver's seat. Wrenched at the ignition and was rewarded with silence. *Does nothing in this damned*

A SEA SOUGHT IN SONG

place work anymore? Whatever the Thing-That'd-Been-Miles had done with its fingers had affected more than just the fire.

Hugh twisted to lunge over his seat-back, snatching up his coat, rifle, and some extra batteries off the floor. He stuffed them all into an emergency knapsack, then slammed the door and pelted back into the house.

"Father!" he shouted in the dark. "Father, which mirror did Dan use?"

"The ivory one." Henry was close enough to touch.

Hugh jumped. "Christ!" he exclaimed.

"Do not use that name in vain!" hissed Henry, shoving the sword's scabbard into Hugh's hands. Hugh bristled, his detachment slipping, as the old man sermonized. "You know as little of Christ as you do of the mirrors. Do you know where the golden one leads? It leads," he continued without pause, "to a mile-high drop straight into the heart of the Enemy's fastness. You would feel a stiff breeze and then die instantly."

Hugh blinked. "And how do you know *that?*" *And how many of your guinea pigs had to die before you'd mapped out all the booby-traps?*

"Miles wasn't the first I sent, Hugh. You have entered a conflict you do not yet understand. This is no time for assumption. Your success in Arlam will depend on how carefully you listen to me now."

Hugh felt his face go up like a torch as his stoniness collapsed. *Ah, of course. I must listen while you talk. I must do all the work while you hand down directives. All will be well just so long as I comply. It was you who created this mess, and you who must maintain control no matter how badly you've screwed up. Mine is not to wonder why, but to simply do and die. Just like Miles.*

Just like Mother.

Henry was still talking. "Fortunately, I have a means to communicate, but the time slippage necessitates written messages only, and a delay on your end of at least a factor of ten. Although if Miles' apparent age is any indication, it's possible the temporal ratio may not be constant. And if one accounts for Andrew's report, we may have to contend with a nonlinear timestream derivation. That could complicate matters. In any event, strict coordination must be observed. If there's one thing to be learned from all this, it's that I need to be more directly involved in field operations."

Hugh gaped at his father. *You want to be more directly ... Did I actually ask you for advice just now? What was I thinking?*

No more.

He leaned close and spoke loudly. "How do I find Dan once I'm through?"

AUSTIN GUNDERSON

The old man was suddenly silent. So, his son shouted louder. *"How do I find him?"*

Henry seemed to wake from his reverie, but when he opened his mouth the words which emerged were as thick as those of a sleep-talker. "If he yet lives, you will find him in the south. It is no easy journey. Once you cross the White Sea to Kramarack, scale the Roof of the World, and swim the Sea of Sand, your ordeal has only begun. But you must delay a moment longer. There are things you need to hear, truths you cannot misunderstand …"

Hugh's words were shards of ice. "I'm leaving now," he said, "before you can waste any more of Dan's life. Goodbye." He turned to go.

Henry's arm snaked out to snag a fistful of his son's shirt-front and wrench him back around. It nearly worked, too: the old man's strength was incredible, even in grief. But Hugh was ready this time. The instant he felt the pressure he twisted into it and lunged backward, slamming his father against the wall. Henry's fist snapped open.

"No!" Hugh snarled. "I'm done listening to your con act! I let you alone for three months and you throw everyone I love down some kind of trans-dimensional shithole. You want me to clean this up? I do it *my* way." He stormed back out the door.

The door took too long to crash shut. "Hugh, wait!" Henry's cry was piteous, even in the ears of his son. "You don't understand! I can help you! You don't stand a chance on your own. Come back! Please …" and now he really *was* weeping, "please come back! I can't lose you, too. I can't! I lo–" And then his words were lost as the wind rose and the shadowed grasses seethed.

Hugh started to run. South. Toward a hidden bunker with an ivory mirror. Past the borders of his world.

###

29 Halanen, 781

Flames like wings swirled in Hugh's wake, their pinions licking the stars. The air that blasted his face was a joy and shock after the furnace from which he emerged. A wave of heat scorched his back as behind him the warehouse crumpled. He hit the ground running, whipped the sword around his head, and released the rod's emerald swatch. The blade buried itself in the cornerpost of a shopfront, its impact inaudible under the inferno's scream. Hugh rushed past to drag it, wireless, straight through bricks and beams.

A SEA SOUGHT IN SONG

As the shop collapsed behind him—at least he thought it'd been a shop, though fire was the great leveler, the great disrespecter of persons, and the structures it touched swiftly lost distinction—Hugh noticed that he was alone. The soldiers who'd rallied to him had fallen behind once more. He thought it strange that this kept happening. Weren't they supposed to be the warrior elite? Hadn't they known these streets all their lives? *That's probably the problem*, he thought. *They're overcome by grief at the destruction of their stomping grounds. They're slow 'cause they're still in shock. I need to make allowance for the effects of nostalgia.*

Hugh rolled his eyes. *Nostalgia never saved anyone. They'd better get a move on if they wanna rescue the rest of this place.*

Just then they appeared. Three of them, grime-faced and gasping, rounding the corner like tight ends trying to keep pace with a breakout rusher. Across the alleyway a shed went tumbling, and they cringed away from the explosion of flame. Hugh stood still, unfazed. He had seen the air make room.

"Hey!" he shouted, and the soldiers saw him. "You people can't help me! You can't knock down anything farther away than your arm, but I can! Go back! Start throwing water on the rubble!" Just because their sluggishness worried him didn't mean he *wanted* them here.

But of course they didn't have a clue what he'd said, so here they came, striking a defensive posture around him as even more soldiers pelted up. *Ugh. Why'd you have to get all evangelistic on me, girl? Why couldn't you just let these people draw their own conclusions? Now there's nowhere they won't hound me.*

He shook his head. Annoyance could wait; his work here wasn't finished. Three-story flames still threatened a residential block up the hill to his left. It was the last remaining gap in Hugh's impromptu cordon. He dodged out of the soldiers' pocket and sprinted up a side-street between blackness and bright burning.

And there, in the half-light of the smoke-choked street, stood a man with a red arm-ring. Behind him a wall of rebels was materializing from the pall. His raised arm halted them.

Hugh slowed, and the two leaders converged alone.

They had met before. The warrior's arm-ring and masked helm—fashioned like a tree with boughs aflame—caught the light as he circled to face the left, face the flames, and Hugh recognized the glinting ornaments from that morning's altercation in the under-way. His grip tightened on his sword. There was something unnerving about this man. Hugh felt the tugging of the blade, and forcibly restrained it. He would *not* rush forward blindly.

The warrior unslung a double-bladed axe. *"Tehlet rinulai!"* he cried, spreading his arms wide.

"He asks you to join them," said a voice at Hugh's shoulder.

Hugh jumped and spun, too startled even to curse. His sword swept through empty air, but then Forkbeard straightened from his swift crouch and placed a hand on Hugh's left arm.

"What the hell!" shouted Hugh. His body shook with congested adrenalin; it needed an outlet *now*. He whipped back to face Arm-Ring, who'd continued to close the gap. The rebels were circling behind their leader, along the untouched shopfronts on the right, as the smoke behind them disgorged row upon row of armed men. Too late Hugh realized he was being backed against the flames.

Idiot! It doesn't take a fencing master to understand basic maneuvering! He felt his surety shriveling like so much paper in this blaze. It appeared he'd sprinted smack into the main body of rebel troops. It was two against an army. He'd been dealt a dead man's odds.

Shouts from behind heralded his bodyguards' approach. Hugh half-expected the sounds to fade again as soon as those men caught sight of the shield-wall ahead, but then the soldiers skidded up on either hand and would have stepped in front of Hugh had he not spread his arms to shove them back. His heart warmed even as he snarled and flung high his sword. *These* are *real soldiers. Men like I used to know. I can* stand *with these men. I can* trust *them, even if they're slow.*

But can they say the same of me?

Hugh grinned madly. "Gird up your beards, wizard—we're holding 'em here."

Blue light flashed amid the red, and Hugh turned his head. A smile had crept into Forkbeard's eyes. It emerged slowly, like a thing from the forest. A thing that was not a deer.

Hugh hurled his sword. End-over-end it sailed, a tongue of night leaping against a sky full of fire, and then a single cry rose as it plunged into the mass of bodies congealing in the street. And just like that, Ilina's messiah stood defenseless. Arm-Ring charged.

He was faster than Hugh had expected. By the time Hugh made contact with his rod's emerald swatch, Arm-Ring had already halved the intervening distance. But the blade was faster still: it zipped past the man's shoulder to clang against Hugh's pommel. Arm-Ring threw his feet forward and his shoulders back. Hugh foresaw the slide and upward strike an instant before

A SEA SOUGHT IN SONG

they happened, and he bore down upon his sword with all his might to drive his opponent's axehaft to the ground.

Too late he saw the knife.

As Arm-Ring swung the axe up with his right hand, he used his left to casually slide a dagger into the meat of Hugh's unprotected forearm. Hugh's hand sprang open just as blade met haft. The battle-axe buckled and the sword spun away, its hilt separating in flight. The man with the red arm-ring flashed past in a cloud of dust and smoke as Hugh staggered aside, empty-handed, bleeding and blinking as though awakened from a dream.

The rebels surged forward. Hugh's loyalist companions hurled themselves into the fray. And then Arm-Ring was up and incoming. Hugh snap-kicked the man's knife away before he even realized what was happening, and then they'd locked arms and were grappling in the street as countless blades flashed red around them. Hugh's blood and sweat spattered the burning-tree mask. Arm-Ring's eyes leapt from their slits as though they themselves were what had set his helmet's embossed blaze.

Hugh snarled in rage. This man was no noble-minded revolutionary; he was a menace, pure and simple. *Time to go to hell, you pyromaniac; you'll be happy there.* Kneeing Arm-Ring in the groin, Hugh slammed his own bare forehead onto the other man's abruptly-bowed helm. "How's *that* for intimate?" he gritted. The rebel toppled backwards.

And kicked Hugh's feet out from under him.

Hugh hit the ground hard and immediately had a mask in his face. He scrapped and strove with Arm-Ring as combatants tripped over them and bodies fell beside them. Blue light flashed, arcing overhead as Forkbeard whirled in the corner of Hugh's eye. The crush of foes was relentless. Men lay in the street, hacked and trampled, their mouths gaping silently as the nightmare roared. Burning chunks rained down.

"He says Rikard has betrayed us," shouted Forkbeard. For the wizard was standing nearly astride them now, Hugh realized—spinning and spinning, arms extended, to blast clean their small circle of space.

"What?" yelled Hugh as he wrenched at Arm-Ring's grip.

"He says Rikard is in league with Omri! He says he has witnesses to prove it!"

Belatedly, Hugh picked out the sound of Arm-Ring's screaming from the general tumult. It was a sound that'd been going on for a while now, he realized. *Stupid mask. Not even Batman covers his mouth. If you wanna be heard, you gotta be seen.*

Rearing back, Hugh tore his left arm free, punched the rebel in the throat, and then ripped off the unhelpful helm.

The face beneath was wild and fierce—framed by lank blond hair, split by a crooked nose, vented by a mouth stretched in proclamatory rage. Hugh punched it again for good measure.

Arm-Ring spit blood and kept on screaming.

"He says the nation is in peril," shouted Forkbeard from above. "He says Rikard must be stopped! He says he did not kill two good horses to get here only to be silenced by those too blind to look beyond the reputation of one man!"

Hugh's fist froze mid-swing. "Wait. *He's* the messenger? The one who started all this?"

Though the rebels had by now drawn back into an uneasy ring, Forkbeard couldn't afford to relax his defensive posture. The wizard had to echo Hugh's question several times before Arm-Ring realized that it was he who was being addressed.

"He says we have all been deceived," translated Forkbeard. "He says the Habridi traders confessed everything. He says he was there in Blushu, that he heard it with his own ears."

"Heard *what?*"

"That Rikard Harnish knew of Suma's fall for three years and said nothing."

The cloth was grimy, and wet, and it clove to Ilina's lips, drawn between them as she gasped. The taste of it was acrid, as were the scents of soot and sounds of slaughter, of oblivion unleashed.

All around her steel helms, bright with deathly light, bobbed and jerked in frantic concord. Her dress was so torn now that it barely impeded her legs, yet still she panted as she strove to keep pace. Rikard was just ahead, his tattered cloak whipping between back-slung shields like a train of flames, and before him went the vanguard, their swords all alight, and to either side rose ramparts of smoke.

Ilina reached behind her head to tie the handkerchief over her mouth. An uneven flagstone caught her toe and the stony street pitched up, but the soldier beside her grabbed her arm before she could go down. She stumbled, found her footing again. The man let go.

A SEA SOUGHT IN SONG

Shouting. Ilina jerked her head up. Someone was shouting ahead. All around her the men were shifting, slowing, unslinging their shields, pulling their weapons free. Rikard's red rippled in a chink, but then the ranks slid shut and all Ilina could see was a wall of plate and mail. One faint voice surmounted the din. Thunder from a hundred throats leapt up in response. Ilina went up on her toes, then jumped in place. She glimpsed an open space maybe ten ranks ahead, and what seemed like more soldiers beyond that.

Oh Harlith it's the rebels.

Heat buffeted her in this shiftless air, and the gale god felt as far away from her now as ever he had, but this time it was not his own negligence at fault. No, this was a supplanting. So much fire. The entire northern warehouse district had gone up like a torch. *My god, let not Wishtu have his way! Peer now between these flames to bear us up from death.* But that was no good—wind only *aided* the Lord of Heat. *She* knew that. *Oh god, then if that be the case ... absent yourself. No, wait!*

Ilina didn't know *what* to pray anymore. She couldn't even decide to whom she was *speaking* half the time. If Hugh was Harlith in human form, then how could he possibly hear her? He couldn't even speak her *language!* And, even if he could, he was now far out of earshot behind a curtain of flame.

More shouting, and then fear. It ripped through the assemblage like a breeze, and for an instant Ilina thought her ill-bidden request had been fulfilled. Steel armor clacked together around her and suddenly she couldn't move. Yet they were moving forward, all of them—a human wall. Ilina shuffled her feet, trying frantically to stay off the toes of the soldier behind. "Shields!" roared someone to the left, but the nearby soldiers left theirs on their backs. *Too far from the front*, grasped Ilina. *We're out of harm's way here.* But that was wishful thinking and she knew it.

More shouting, of which she discerned but a single word: "Loose!" Screams now, and curses, the impact of which she felt as strongly as if they'd been directed at her, as if they couldn't *be* directed at all but cut down everything within their reach like ancient Jaar berserkers. *"Loose!"*

The collective jolt this time was quicker, harder, and then they were jogging, and then they were running. The soldier at Ilina's back nearly knocked her over, then scooped her up bodily to get her out from underfoot. She clutched at his encircling arm and drew up her dangling feet, too terrified to struggle or glance back. Her teeth clipped her tongue in the shaking. Tight she shut her mouth against the pain and fear, against the disclosure of her frailty. She was high enough now that she could see ahead, and what she now beheld would remain with her forever.

The front ranks met in a frenzy of force. The rebels appeared to have been caught flat-footed, and Rikard's soldiers pressed the advantage of their momentum, driving the enemy back up the street. This momentum found its root in the rear; the ranks compressed—men behind propelling those in front—and suddenly Ilina was very near the fighting, indeed. Pain replaced rage as the paramount sensation. Men who had been fellows at dawn hacked madly at each other in the fire-brightened dark, shoving and thrusting until even the dead remained upright.

But it was not this sight that would lodge most deeply within Ilina's mind. For over the river of shivering helms, over the flashing blades that rose and fell like spouts of whitewater spume, over the heave and wrack of battle and maybe a block away up the street, there rose the figure of a man. Into the air he leapt, and there he hung, and if the battle had not raged below him unabated she would have assumed that time had ceased. The sword in his hand did not flash.

And then he fell back and was gone.

Ilina cried out, unaware of what spilled from her lips. A word. A name. Hugh.

It was his name she was crying. That figure had been Hugh. The rebels had him surrounded.

The world was exhausted. Time unfolded tentatively, oozing like footage from an overcranked film camera. Fractures filled the air—spiderwebbing in all directions, protruding from the leading edge of every blade and limb. The sky was coming apart at the seams. Hugh dodged and wove through the matrix, dragging his sword through unresisting bodies.

From his left hand dangled, unmasked and unconscious, that messenger whose coming had struck a fatal spark in this damned tinder-box of a city. Arm-Ring's limp bulk felt unnaturally heavy, as though it were some waterlogged sack dredged from the bottom of a pond. *Guess adrenalin can only do so much*, thought Hugh as he spun and sliced his blade across yet another neck, slowly bowling over a man opposite him with the weaponized body of his erstwhile opponent.

The rebels had been spooked: a large body of Harnish troops had materialized down the street, ending Forkbeard's stalemate. The hostile

A SEA SOUGHT IN SONG

circle had caved in on them faster than the old wizard could light it up, and then the world had slowed. Somewhere, an aural floor had collapsed and sent the cacophony of battle tumbling into a lower register. Hugh had leapt to his feet, hauling Arm-Ring upright, and had nearly dislocated his shoulder when the other man simply wouldn't ascend at an equivalent speed. It was as though their bodies labored under different rules of physics.

Hugh gritted his teeth and flung away the sword. It spun off into the crowd, cleaving flesh and armor alike, whirling as blue light strobed from Forkbeard's fingers. None moved to avoid it. The rebels inched through the air like trees nudged by a breeze, and like trees they were hewn down.

I can do better than this, thought Hugh. *It's time to lighten my load.* He grabbed Arm-Ring's wrists with both hands, crouched, and started sidestepping in a circuit until the messenger stretched out nearly parallel to the ground. Hugh felt the blood go to his head. Throbbing, pressing, flooding. He was not uninjured, and he watched, sickened, as his forearm spurted scarlet. It was all he could do to maintain his grip on Arm-Ring's wrists, especially without dropping the magic rod, yet the other man might've been moving through water for all the momentum he amassed.

And then Arm-Ring awakened. Hugh watched his eyelids split, saw the panic start to bloom. It would've been comical had Hugh not hated the man.

With a cry Hugh let go and Arm-Ring receded through the air, colliding with his fellow rebels gradually, though not gently. Hugh hit the swatch on his hilt and then the sword was there—a rabid retriever overeager to please. Now unencumbered, Hugh hacked and slashed his way beside the airborne Arm-Ring—outpacing him, cluttering the blood-spangled air with human debris.

The fire roared and Hugh looked up. Saw a confluence of fissures converging in the smoke ahead. Like steps they slid together, one after another, each stemming from an impotent weapon in the vast melee. And suddenly, without conscious thought, Hugh knew he could ascend them if he wished.

So he did.

Hugh sprang into the air. His left foot launched off a man's hip, his right off a man's shoulder, and then …

And then he took a third step. And a fourth. And the street receded below him as Hugh Conrad leapt up an intangible lattice. A wind seemed to enwrap him, to steady him, to direct his steps. The air-fissures shifted like boughs in a breeze. Hugh crouched atop their tips and looked down upon men's heads—men reacting too slowly to even realize he was there.

But Hugh was aware—oh yes *he* was aware!—and he felt it then: the power, the joy. The freedom. An ecstasy surged through his mind, his body, his whole being. *What's this? Am I nuts? Am I Superman? Am I really walking on air? How is this possible? Is there nothing I can't do?*

And then the air-fissures rippled away to the winds, the lattice of immanency collapsed, and Hugh fell back as real blades converged from every side. But as he fell he spun, sword extended, and like a rotor he carved a swath. He landed in a crouch as men recoiled slowly.

Is this what you meant, Father, when you said that nothing here would harm me? Am I invincible in this place?

It certainly seemed that way. Hugh laid about himself with abandon now, confident in his power, and blood fountained like sheets of flame.

Arm-Ring finally struck the street. The look on his face was priceless.

And the rebels began to flee.

Ilina squirmed in the soldier's grip. Something was happening. Something was happening where she'd last spotted Hugh and she couldn't make out what it was. The enemy crowd was moving—moving *toward* them, away from Hugh—and the sounds of combat had changed. The cries from up the street had risen in pitch. Dust and smoke were swirling strangely there, and chaos was rippling outward through the rebel ranks.

And then their line of battle simply dissolved. The front-rank rebels wavered, feeling their support withdraw from behind, and that hesitation was all Rikard's loyalists needed. With a shout they stormed forward, stumbling over corpses now free to fall, fracturing their own shield-wall. Bedlam churned before them.

What is happening? I need to see! But this confounded chaperone-soldier wasn't letting Ilina move. She squirmed again, eliciting only a tightening of his grasp. *Harlith bowl you over!* she cursed silently, pushing herself up against his encircling arms, then grabbing his shoulders as he turned away from the fighting. She pinched his hips with her knees, scrabbling frantically for a foothold, squirming up and out of his arms with a technique she'd learned whilst traversing the caverns laid bare beneath Horwell Face whenever the sea withdrew.

She felt the soldier sway beneath her as she clambered up his chest, and heard him swearing, but spared no further thought for the travails of her

A SEA SOUGHT IN SONG

mount. *Our shield-wall is collapsing!* she thought. *If they manage to re-form, they could crack us like an egg. They have the numbers.*

"Stand firm!" roared a voice—*Rikard's!* thought Ilina—and then she saw him shoving his way forward to peer through the front line of shields, which coalesced around him as if by magnetism. There was a lull in which the only sound was rebel screaming and the thunder of flame. But the tableau was lurching away.

"Put me down!" she yelled at her soldier, beating on his helm.

An oath came from below. "You want down, milady? Then get off my face!"

Ilina started, glancing down at a heather-red visage. "I know you!" she blurted.

The man grimaced. "Brigord," he mumbled. "Name's Brigord."

An image flashed in Ilina's mind: a gloved hand on her wrist before the Doors of Harn, stark heraldry, white on red, and eyes that glinted through bronze-entwined slits. *Eyes that looked away, that couldn't hold my gaze.* Though this soldier's helmet was comprised of unornamented steel, the eyes that glared from under it were the very same.

"Brigord!" she said. "Of course. The decorous doorman. Stop here, Brigord, and hold me up. I want to see."

"Hell's charred hands! Do you want up or down?" The man looked like he wanted to throw her away entirely, but Ilina noted with approval that he'd stopped moving.

"Up," she said.

He complied, hoisting her onto one shoulder. Ilina's legs dangled and, without thinking, she wrapped an arm about his neck to steady herself. Brigord dodged a sprinting squad of reinforcements, stumbled to the street's intact side, and leaned against a doorframe, muttering darkly.

By now the Harnish line had completely re-formed. It curved away from the unburned block on Ilina's right, leaving only a narrow gap on the left between blades and blaze. *How blistering it must be for the soldiers of that flank*, thought Ilina, but the observation flew from her mind as she saw what was unfolding ahead.

A torrent of rebels rolled down the street and broke against Rikard. No charge this: they were fleeing the wrong way, flinging aside their swords, throwing themselves against the shield-wall, fighting to get through and getting carved up like so many sides of beef on a butcher's slab. The less trusting among them made for the gap by the flames, but there the loyalists had formed a gauntlet, and those rebels who didn't get hacked to death were tripped and shoved into burning shopfronts. A bare handful made it past, and these blazed like torches until they fell.

All of this was peripheral. For behind the heedless runners, a mere hundred yards up the street, in the heart of the rebel horde, a figure was walking in the air. Smoke whorled about him as he stalked and swayed perhaps four feet above the crowd, and below him strong men fled in terror. From his outflung hand flashed a black shadow, and to his hand the shadow returned, trailing blood. He drove the rebels before him like a flock of sheep upon the hills.

But then the figure seemed to stumble. He crouched, teetering, flung his arms out for balance, and finally dropped to the ground, just missing the last of his sheep. The rebels had been routed. Those not dead in the street had either fallen to their knees with upraised hands or had run the opposite way at the outset to avoid getting caught between the anvil of Rikard's wall and the hammer of Hugh's sword.

For the air-walker was indeed Hugh Conrad, Ilina saw—Hugh the Awaited One, High King of all Arlam, he whom she had Declared. Pride flared warmly in her chest. *You see now? Rikard, do you see? Will you not concede? Will you not stand with me?*

Hugh strode toward the bristling wall, lit in chiaroscuro by the fire on his right. Arm-Ring stumbled alongside, head bent askew to accommodate Hugh's grip on the nape of his mail-coat. Forkbeard brought up the rear, his silver robes streaked with red.

Surrendered rebels cringed upon the cobbles or burrowed under corpses as the great men passed. Hugh stepped on some of them, grinding their limbs underfoot, sneering at their muted cries. A boiling rage had seized him. It took an immense exertion of will for him to keep his sword-arm swinging stiffly at his side. *These people are* helpless! *They can't even stop themselves from burning their own city to the ground! Do they need me to do* everything?

Ahead of him, the shield-wall stayed shut.

"Rikard!" he bellowed, forgetting he spoke a strange tongue. "Your people aren't rioting because you didn't know what happened—they're afraid that you *did* know! I have the man who started this mess, and if you wanna save your city you must answer his claims! Come out!" Forkbeard's translation followed like an echo.

A SEA SOUGHT IN SONG

Hugh flung Arm-Ring forward. The man skidded, but kept his feet. Whipping a venomous glare back at Hugh, he stood, squared his shoulders, and proceeded to hold forth.

But before he could utter more than a few words, a fissure split the air, creasing the flames beyond as though they were but streaks of paint upon a folded sheet. From behind the shield-wall the fissure arced to end at Arm-Ring's brow. Arm-Ring himself didn't notice. In fact he seemed quite languid, and his speech dragged as though it bore immense weight. Hugh started, then saw that even the flames themselves barely shook.

Still Hugh hesitated. *What the hell is going on?* He didn't understand what was happening to him—why he saw seams in space, why they were able to hold his weight, or why the rest of the world had seemingly ground to a halt. Maybe this was normal. Maybe it wasn't because of the sword. He didn't think so, but maybe it wasn't.

Perhaps there were procedures, techniques for harnessing this magic. Perhaps he was not the first to wield it. But how was he supposed to find out? Who would be safe to ask? These people were looking to him as some kind of messiah. Would they riot again if he revealed his own ignorance?

He glanced back at Forkbeard. The wizard was an enigma. While he claimed to support Hugh, his deference to Rikard was hard to miss. Was it because he didn't think Hugh quite up for the job of king, or was he just trying to play both ends against the middle? Either way, Hugh was certain the old man was keeping his cards close to his chest. Nobody who could fight by shooting light out of his fingers could *only* fight by shooting light out of his fingers. There was more there than met the eye.

And what of Ilina? If anyone in this looney-bin world could be legitimately called his friend, it would have to be her. No matter what delusions about his nature she was under, it had been she who'd taken him in and shown him kindness before even suspecting he was some kind of inter-dimensional sovereign. Nothing could take that from her—not her irrational traditions or inane political aspirations. No matter how solicitous she became, Hugh would always remember her as that scared girl who let him in out of the cold at the point of a crossbow. Maybe he could confide in her. Maybe she was even *expecting* him to. He squinted at this new thought.

And that's when he noticed the arrow. It was already halfway to Arm-Ring's forehead, sliding along its anticipatory groove.

Hugh moved without thinking, and, to his horror, found his body unable to respond. Instead of exploding forward it merely unfurled, as languid as a careless stretch. Either fatigue had finally brought him down or his mind was spinning faster than ever it had in his life and all else was unhurried by comparison. Arm-Ring was only ten feet away, but that distance seemed suddenly insurmountable as Hugh strained his leaden limbs into a sprinter's extension and the arrow oozed steadily along a perfect path.

Arm-Ring's death was fifty feet away. Forty. Thirty. Hugh screamed, forcing his legs to pump against an atmosphere that felt like mud. His foot hit the ground and he leaned hard right to pivot in front of the oblivious target. His sword-arm swept gradually back. The arrow was ten feet away.

Hugh bellowed and with all his might threw his entire body into a double-handed lunge. His blade arced down with a jolt, intercepting the arrow just behind its point only two feet out from Arm-Ring's face. The arrowhead spun, glancing off Arm-Ring's scalp. The shaft shattered across the bridge of his nose. Hugh went tumbling past, his body abruptly on par with his mind.

He stumbled to a stop, then looked up. The fires licked at normal rates. Arm-Ring was reeling and batting the air. But the host of Kram was silent. They stood with mouths agape.

Damn, that was close. This'll take some getting used to.

Behind him, Forkbeard was shouting. Hugh thought he knew what the wizard was saying, but didn't wait for him to offer a translation. "Who fired that arrow?" Hugh roared, stepping in front of Arm-Ring. "Come out! Show yourself! Rikard, where are you? Control your men!"

"Hey, watch it, Lady! What's wrong with you?"

With a start Ilina realized her fingers were digging into Brigord's neck and cheek. It was an empty awareness, as immaterial in that moment as the knowledge that her appearance—disheveled, nearly indecent—likely had onlookers convinced she was some random floozy attempting to capitalize on societal breakdown. Her whole body had gone stiff, and so it was only with effort that Brigord pried her hands from his face.

But by that time Ilina's mind had recovered sufficient faculty. She pushed off Brigord's chest and dropped to the street, ignoring his bewilderment. The import of what she had seen was breaking over her like a wave.

Rikard nocked another arrow to his bow. The soldiers around him had turned, were looking at him with a confusion similar to that which Brigord had just directed at her. The man from whom Rikard had snatched the

A SEA SOUGHT IN SONG

weapon stood with brows drawn and hands half-raised, as though he couldn't decide what to do. A pocket had opened around them. Rikard raised the bow.

And Ilina, sprinting up behind, struck it from his hands.

"How dare you?" she screamed as the bow and arrow clattered on the stones. "Do you realize what you're doing? Do you even *know* what's happening? What's at stake? Oh gods ..." she whimpered as he rounded on her, eyes burning, "... you *do* know. You knew all this time."

And now it was Rikard's turn to be bewildered. "Ilina?" he blurted, his expression twisting oddly. "What in Harlith's name ... What are you doing here? Corporal!" he barked to the erstwhile bowman. "Escort the Lady Lightkeeper from the field."

The corporal didn't move.

Rikard glared at the man, and the man looked away.

Behind them, the ranks were parting. A gap had opened in the shield-wall, and through it advanced Hugh. Rikard faced him wordlessly.

"Lintelosh fi yir, Rhonorhimin," said Hugh in a voice of iron. *"Laroh sehret hamoshel om arak larohlem. Lo kalthomet seht oamolmai umaresh."*

Above the fire's thunder resounded Forkbeard's echo: "It is the end of the road, Highlord. From your hands the land has passed. To justice now submit."

A simmering moment passed. Then Rikard bowed his head and spread his hands.

Hugh nodded in acknowledgement. He gestured to soldiers on either side, and they hesitantly moved to take their highlord into custody. Rikard didn't resist. Hugh, wholly ignorant of Kramish custom, had no idea whether there was precedent for what was happening. Ilina's stricken face told him no, there wasn't.

But that doesn't matter. For now, it was enough that his orders were being obeyed. They'd sort out the details later. *Better to beg forgiveness than permission. Better still not to beg at all.*

And best to be begged by others.

Hugh Conrad, the alien from Utter North, was now in a position to be begged. He had burst like a freak storm above the stage of Arlam, and only the blind could've failed to notice. By effectively deposing Rikard, he'd declared himself a player in a game he didn't fully understand. No longer was this the covert operation he'd envisioned. The south lay open to him, yes, but at what cost?

Mission creep. Damn. The more things change, the more they stay the same.

He looked at Ilina, at her tattered beauty, the agony in her violet eyes.

Well, guess I'll just do what I always do. Improvise.

"Now," he said, turning to face the flames as Rikard was led away, "let's put out this fire."

Epilogue
SHADOWS

30 Halanen, 781

"Tell me what you are thinking."

It was Rikard who had broken the silence.

"You never would before, you know." A cold laugh. "Perhaps you will now. Perhaps everything will be different." The laughter trailed off.

A silence crouched between them. Time passed. Shadows slid along the floor.

Rikard cleared his throat. "Remember what you–" His voice broke.

Ilina looked up. The world of sliding shadows lurched down and away, replaced by color and light and a face she had once known, or thought to know. Now contorted, it overhung his knees as he leaned forward, swallowing, straining against a weight intangible. The chain from his ankle-shackle seemed to shrink behind the leg of his chair—a cord of shame at odds with the rich fabrics and patterns of their opulent surroundings.

Shafts glittering with dust streamed from western gables, freezing in radiance swaths of tapestry or hanging wall, letting the rest seethe with mystery. The ubiquitous reds blushed deep with telcot milk dye, and the air hung heavy with springtime incense. Exquisite, unyielding. *A prison fit for a lord. How very Kramish.*

"Remember what you said to me," he continued in a whisper, "that day out on the hill wall? The day my father died?"

Ilina did not speak. Rikard raised his head and met her eyes, but she did not even blink.

"You said a great change was coming." Each word trembled, as though it'd been torn alive from his throat. "You spoke of a current that would sweep the whole world over a cliff."

Ilina sat very still. She wasn't at all sure she wanted to hear what came next, but she couldn't bear to turn away. These were words that should have been spoken long ago. Before it'd come to shackles. Before it'd come to death. She owed it to herself to hear them out.

"You were right," he hissed. "Gods damn it, but you were right. And I stood there like a blind man and thought to comfort you. You! You who had gazed into the eye of Oblivion. I was a fool. But I didn't know it till I was forced to assume my father's place. Do you know what I found among his things the *day* after his funeral?"

Ilina shot a glance to where a guard in full armor melded with the shadows of the far wall. "Surely now isn't the time," she murmured. There were no confidences here. Anything he shared with her could return to haunt him before the adjudicating Council.

The highlord laughed. "What does it matter?" he shouted, throwing up his hands and startling a reaction from her at last. "By now they'll have found my records and learned everything I know. The tiger is in the pen. I might as well speak plainly—*gods*, what a change! There's no stopping it now."

Ilina leaned forward, a chill slipping down her spine. "No stopping what?"

Rikard's eyes seemed as feral as those of his idiom's heath tiger. "War!" he snarled, his knuckles whitening on his knees. "Don't you see? This—*this*—this is the edge of your cliff, Ilina. Here. Now. We are being goaded, the whole nation of us. I thought I could hide it, thought I could shelter you all, but now the jig is up. And now ... now I'll be seen as a fifth column. Now all I've done—all my father did—it'll all be ... *treachery* and ... and *fattening* ... for the slau– *ah!*"

His face twisted with horror. His chain rattled as he slid forward off his chair, and his knees struck the heather-red rug with a thud. Ilina was peripherally aware of the guard starting forward, hand on hilt, but her own eyes were flared and fixed on those of Rikard Harnish, who was coming apart at her feet.

"What have I done?" he cried over and over, his body wracked by sobs, his hands grasping vainly at his face as though it was within the power of his own mind to reverse time. "I have doomed us all—*me! I* did it! It's because of *me* that war will come. Because I was *sloppy!* Oh gods ... I've played right into his hands ... he knew this would happen ... foresaw it ... played us this whole time ... this whole *time* ..." Rikard was weeping uncontrollably now, his hands like claws tearing his flaxen hair.

Ilina realized her mouth was hanging open. Snapped it shut. Glanced at the guard, who'd retreated to his shadow. The man didn't even meet her eyes. Whatever would transpire, *that* one would be of no help.

Fine. It falls to me, then. The care of this man is mine by right, anyway. She cocked her head at the thought. *What a strange feeling. Am I fit for such a role? I do not know. There is much I do not know, it seems.*

A SEA SOUGHT IN SONG

"Rikard," she said, slipping off her own seat to kneel at his level. "Hush now, be calm." She laid a hand upon his shoulder and felt his terrible shudders. A clawlike hand closed over hers, holding it fast. Cold sweat broke out across her body, but Rikard's focus remained inward, his rage self-contained. Still, he grasped her hand as though it were a lifeline.

"Rikard," she whispered, "you must tell me what you fear. You cannot go on like this. You must have courage now, and reveal all."

The highlord didn't look up, but his body tensed. "You of all people," he rasped, "should know what it is I fear. It's not the truth but *lies* that require courage. Oh, blessed Harlith forgive me! I thought I was strong, but I'm not … I'm not." Fresh sobs took him. His body slumped against hers and she wrapped her arms around his shaking shoulders. *Gods give me the strength he lacks.*

"Try to imagine what it was like," he said, regaining some control. "Try to put yourself in my place, Ilina. To discover that you're bordered by an imaginary nation. That every interaction of the past year—every trade, every letter, every messenger—was nothing but a prop in the most elaborate play ever staged. Think of the effort required to pull it off. Just think of the power. *Think* of it! Let it stagger you."

"I've been doing naught else," she said quietly.

"It was the monks of Cloudfall who made it possible," he went on, words tumbling now as though through a broken dike, "and the Habridas who carried it out. Indeed, a strange fortune has guarded the great play since its inception. Remember the blizzard that delayed the spring caravan of '78 for over three months? It never happened. The southern Gnofs were nearly snowless that year. But that was the last caravan to leave Suma before its fall. It left less than a week before the Tunnoltans arrived. A refugee caught up to it in the foothills, and the traders took that man with them to Cloudfall Abbey, but that's as far as any of them went. When the abbot heard about Suma, he quarantined the caravan and sent for my father. And my father swore them all to secrecy on pain of terrible death."

Ilina blanched, pulling back from her embrace. "Then … then it was the *Kram* who hid it this whole time? It was … *you?*"

"My father," said Rikard more coldly, "saw the world through ancient eyes. To him, the Law of the Land was a sacred seal of safety. He *knew* what we'd do if word of Suma's fall got through. And *he* would do *whatever* it took to keep us from that course. In his eyes, he was saving us from ourselves."

AUSTIN GUNDERSON

Ilina saw again in her mind the bramble-choked inscription. "Let he who makes war on his neighbor gain doubly the fate he would pay," she recited, voice dead.

Rikard forged ahead. "My father thought he could detect a hidden hand at work in each tale of defeat that arrived from the south. Where others saw superior Tunnoltan tactics or overwhelming force, he saw a supernatural advantage—a hijacking of King Henred's decree. He did not believe Omri had *ever* attacked first. He thought the monster was provoking each opponent, goading them into drawing first blood. And he was convinced that if Kramarack acted preemptively, we would fall as swiftly as the others. And then there would be none left. So he lied to keep the peace."

"But how?" Now it was Ilina's voice that broke. Rikard's tumbling words faded in her mind like evening rain, replaced by shrieks of mistrust. She thought of her illusory correspondence. "I spoke with Ilith just last year, Rikard. How did you do it? *How?*" Part of her was aware she was shaking him, and the rest of her didn't care. This man, to whom she had pledged her loyalty, had contrived to simulate … well, *everything.* An entire world. If he could do that, what *couldn't* he do?

"The monks," sobbed Rikard. "The monks of Cloudfall Pass! While the caravan was delayed they copied every last letter borne from the fallen city. Then they sent them on. The replies from home went straight back to the abbey. The monks used the letters they'd copied the first time as templates for forged replies. They're very good at transcribing manuscripts, you know."

Ilina released Rikard as though he'd sprouted horns. She sat back hard against her chair, mind reeling. *Betrayed … we are all of us betrayed. We trusted the Habridas, and they played us for fools. The Pact of Homel is worthless. For if they lied to us, perhaps they revealed the truth to others. Perhaps the Hidden Kingdom lies exposed to the South at last.*

So many of the things the Kram took for granted had been entrusted to itinerant traders. This Ilina had known in abstraction, the way a sheltered princess knows her safety depends on the brutality of bloodstained men on distant fields. But the extent of the dependance had not fully struck her until this moment. *Absence speaks louder than presence. Why can't we comprehend what we have before it's taken away?*

That the Habridas would abandon their oath was intolerable. That they should do so at the highlord's direction, however … that was unthinkable. Ilina stood abruptly. She backed away from Rikard—her hands clutching her arms, forming a subconscious shield against the gaps now yawning in her picture of the world. An unseen rock had been removed, and she stumbled on unsteady ground. Lost in her own backyard.

"We know nothing," she breathed, and her eyes drifted from Rikard's blotchy face to the swaths of shadow striating the room. "If we can be deceived on such a scale, the rumors themselves may be a bluff. Perhaps liberty yet lives beyond the Sea of Sand. Perhaps …"

But no. Memory reared up in her mind, and she tasted again the dread certainty of her nocturnal visions. No bluff this, no elaborate pageant. The Enemy had no need to feign strength. The show had simply ended, the curtain been withdrawn. What spread before them now was reality in all its starkness.

Rikard's words came back to her: *'My father did not believe Omri had ever attacked first.'* It was the fantasy of a child. But in service to this suspicion, Highlord Hansel had prevented what would've surely been a war. And Ilina knew that no war against Omri could possibly succeed.

But now that the Awaited One has arrived …

She shook her head, banishing the thought. Despite her enthusiasm for Hugh, she knew better than that. She had seen too much.

Could it be that Highlord Hansel had seen what she herself had seen? Could it be that his deception had granted them all a stay of execution? Could it be that, in the end, broken trust was a small price to pay for survival?

And what of Hansel's son? He had been so afraid. Ilina recalled the dark mood that'd shadowed Rikard during his last visit, and pieces of his puzzle began falling into place. His inherited boots had not been small in the wake of his father's murder, but now she tried to slip them on—to imagine what she might've done had the secrets been handed to her. She tried to imagine herself publishing the facts, knowing full well what would then transpire. Tried to imagine how it wouldn't have been her fault.

She couldn't make it work.

I would've done the same, she admitted. *The Enemy is too powerful to contest. To delay his triumph, there's nothing I wouldn't conceal—no, not even this.* Could it be that she and Rikard were seeking the same thing?

She looked at him again and he stared back, remorse and defiance flickering over his face. She imagined what it was that *he* saw. A woman, surely—but cold, unflinching, robed in sea-storm blue. With her girdle of silver scales and the starry brooch gleaming from the maroon of her borrowed cloak, she doubtless cut a formidable figure. She was the Lightkeeper, after all, though she couldn't quite remember the condition of her Light.

AUSTIN GUNDERSON

Yes, Rikard, you see all of that, she mused. *But it's not why you stare, nor why you spoke. What holds your gaze is the only other person in all this world who might understand what you have done, what you have become. You see your only hope of absolution.*

Ilina uncrossed her arms and sank to her haunches. She looked Rikard straight in the eyes.

"Why didn't you tell me?" she asked.

* * *

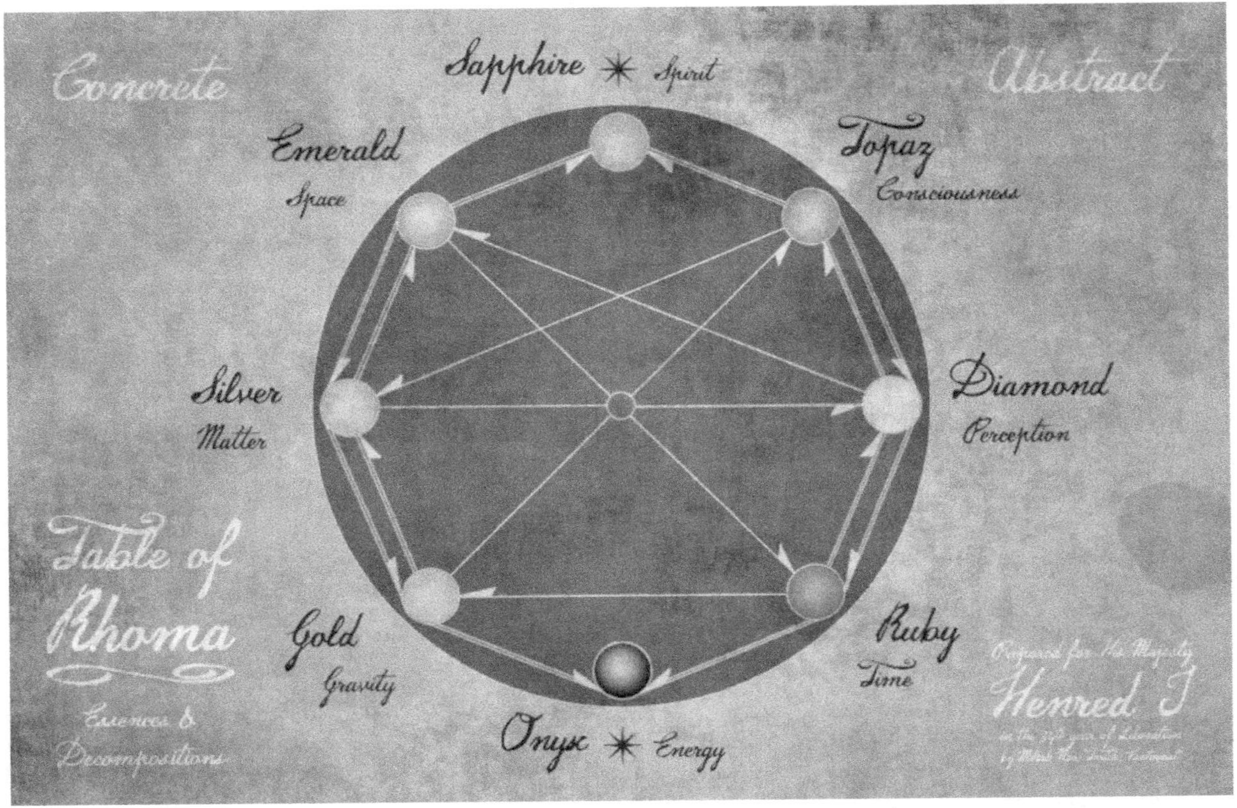

Concrete
Abstract
Sapphire ✶ Spirit
Emerald
Space
Topaz
Consciousness
Silver
Matter
Diamond
Perception
Gold
Gravity
Ruby
Time
Onyx ✶ Energy
Table of
Rhoma
Essences &
Decompositions
Prepared for His Majesty
Henred I

About the Author
AUSTIN GUNDERSON

Austin Gunderson is the author of "The Heir and the Herald" tetralogy. It was a math curriculum that sparked Austin's love for storytelling. He was in fourth grade and was supposed to be studying long division, but the mining colony of gnomes whose procurement and distribution of jewels formed the backdrop to the day's lesson had seized his imagination. Who were these people, what drove them to delve as they did, and which threats confronted their quaint kingdom?

It would be years before Austin began constructing his own fantasy world. He grew up in Washington State where the shining summers were for waging war in the woods and the somber winters were for reading. At the age of twelve he devoured The Lord of the Rings. As soon as he turned the last page he began it again, in awe of a secondary world so vast and deep it overspilled his memory. And then he began dreaming his own dream.

Now Austin is privileged to make his living from what he loves. By day he edits video; by night he writes high fantasy. He lives with his wife and three daughters in the shadow of North America's steepest mountain range. If he has anything to say about it, he'll be telling stories for the rest of his life.

THANK YOU
FOR READING!

If you enjoyed this book, we would appreciate your customer review on your book seller's website or on Goodreads.

Also, we would like for you to know that you can find more great books like this one at
www.CreativeTexts.com

www.ingramcontent.com/pod-product-compliance
Lightning Source LLC
Chambersburg PA
CBHW051533020726
47506CB00009B/1009